For my students.

REBECCA MCQUEEN

Red Flags

kindle direct publishing

Contents

Preface

1920s Berlin, called The Golden Twenties, was a phoenix from the ashes of the Great War.

Before the Great War, western cultures were obsessed with a desire for innocence in a rapidly changing and vastly cold and uncaring world. The Great War destroyed that innocence, real or not. 20 million people died in the Great War, and the few who came back would carry emotional wounds for the rest of their life. Though the war was long over, "shell-shocked" veterans relived images of their friends choking on mustard gas, being charred by grenades and bombs, watching their bodies swell, devoured by rats in the stinking, muddy trenches of France and Belgium. For this reason, those lucky (or unlucky) enough to survive the mass casualties of The Great War were called The Lost Generation.

German soldiers returned home not to the powerful German Empire they'd left, which had united Prussia, Germany, and part of Czechoslovakia under Kaiser Wilhelm I, but to the reduced and weaker Weimar Republic. Right around the time the Russians were gunning down Tsar Nikolai and the Romanovs in the name of liberty, the Germans found themselves living in a democracy, with a president, a chancellor, a constitution, and everything.

The relaxed moral attitudes of the Weimar Republic, breathing free after a century of an authoritarian monarchy, caused hundreds of cabarets to spring up in Berlin. Desirous to be like Gay Paris or jazzy, teeming New York, Berlin became a mecca of artistic expression, flamboyance, and celebration. Homosexuality, transgenderism, and polyamory were widely accepted in Berliner cabarets. Artists from around the world flocked to Berlin to find a more open way of life, including Americans seeking freedom from Prohibition (literally and figuratively).

While the party raged behind the red doors and velvet curtains of the cabarets, outside Germany was hungry. In addition to the country being emotionally and physically flattened by the Great War, afterwards they were embittered by the Treaty of Versailles, where European Allies forced Germany to give up territories while also imposing a steep reparations tax to be paid to countries damaged in the war. The worst part of the treaty was Article 231, also known as the "War Guilt Clause", which required Germany to accept all the blame for starting the war. This was particularly insulting because the Great War was started by the assassination of an Austro-Hungarian archduke by a Bosnian Serb.

It was a time for change, a time to look back on how their country sank so low, and a time to look forward to what it could be.

And out of this stew of new values, disillusionment with the powers that be, and social unrest, a Führer was born.

1

1930: The Cabaret

Hildegard was hungry, and hunger pains gave her a headache, which caused her to be irritable and sullen: a fine welcome into her teenage years. It was 1930, two years after what her mother called "The Crash." Hildegard had never known a time when food was secure and plentiful, but at times things were better. Now, however, her life had taken a dip for the worse.

Her mother, Wilhelmina Appelbaum, was known to everyone but Hildegard as Minni Von Bismark, her stage name. During Hildegard's 12 years on this green albeit singed earth, Minni Von Bismark had been a small-time opera singer, a big-time cabaret entertainer, Bauhaus model, and even a movie starlet. With a round, innocent face, wide blue eyes, and golden hair characteristic of Aryan Europeans, Wilhelmina sported pencil-thin eyebrows, thick kohl-lined eyes, and stylish pin curls that enabled her to attractively tiptoe on the tightrope between angelic and vamp.

Lately, she was more small-time performer and occasional prostitute than aspiring ingénue. Hildegard was usually taken care of in the evenings by a rotund and sanguine housekeeper named Cunegunde, but now Wilhelmina was obliged to cart her progeny to the cabarets, where free daycare was offered by the women and men powdering and corseting themselves backstage. Which was fine with Hildegard. She loved the sparkles and smells and cackles of the cabaret, named Babbel, and loved even more watching her mother's entrance onto the stage and the faces of the people who paid, in Hildegard's mind, for a two-hour love spell.

Hildegard would watch, enraptured, as her wisp of a mother moved sumptuously across the stage and onto the floor, singing with her clear lark's call and somehow managing to have an eye-to-eye moment with every table. It was like she made them feel special for one everlasting second, made them feel seen, desired, human but divine… it was like she welcomed them in for one moment into the starry gates of heaven. This moment, Hildegard was convinced, was what kept people coming back every weekend and most Thursdays.

But after The Crash, fewer and fewer people began to frequent the cabaret, and sometimes people were too drunk, and sometimes men were too bold and grabby, and somehow it spoiled the magic and made it cheap. What also gave Hildegard a twisting sensation in the pit of her stomach was when, with increasing frequency, Hildegard would have to wait at the cabaret after the show for half an hour. Sometimes a friend of Wilhemina's, Vam Der Blegsam, would walk Hildegard home at a snail's pace, and Hildegard would have to sit quietly outside the apartment door for an hour or two, and then a man, face still slick with sweat, would emerge. Sometimes they would apologize, sometimes they would ruffle her hair (which she hated), sometimes they would offer her a bonbon or a Deutsche mark or one time a cigarette. And Wilhelmina would explain she had to work doubly hard because she was both mommy and daddy.

As to what happened to Hildegard's actual father, Wilhelmina would always be frank. "Your father and I were childhood sweethearts in Cologne. When the Great War started, he signed up right away. So many signed up in 1914, only to be blown to bits and crushed under tanks. Your father wanted to marry me before he left, but I did not want to become a widow, as so many were quickly becoming. So he was very careful, and very lucky, and in 1917 he came back on leave and we got married and I had you in 1918. But then that winter, he got very sick with pneumonia, and he died." Her voice softened with bitterness. "And I became a widow anyway."

Hildegard once heard a different version of that story, told to her by a drag queen called Empress Varvara Alexia Zlovitzskia, but whose real name was Franz Muller: "Your father never died of pneumonia. He got back from the war and wanted your mother to play house, and she got sick of it and left. Half the women in Berlin are war wives who got more than they bargained for and came to the city for a taste of freedom." But Hildegard took this revelation with a grain of salt, as Wilhelmina called the Empress "an old bitch with back rolls."

On this particular September evening in 1930, when Oktoberfest was at its lurid zenith, Wilhelmina was trying to save up enough for Hildegard's birthday cake. Food was at an all-time low. Adding to Hildegard's hunger-induced headache was the uneasy feeling she got whenever the men in brown suits came to the cabaret, which was more and more often. They wore scary-looking badges that looked like big black spiders. There was a man who came with them, dressed in a formal gray suit, with a big bushy mustache and stern eyes, and he only watched Wilhelmina. He never hooted or hollered. He never made a sound.

Disappointed that there would be no cake, or even maybe dinner, for Hildegard, Wilhelmina got uncharacteristically drunk. Her belly full of liquor and not much else, Wilhemina got up on stage and stood with a blazing energy, fists balled. Her voice was so powerful and moving that at the climactic finale of the song, everyone in the cabaret stood up and began applauding and cheering. Even the man in the gray

3

suit with the mustache stood up, his eyes trained on the enchantress as she swooped into a bow and wobbled offstage.

Wilhelmina passed out shortly after the final act. Hildegard brought her some water, but Wilhemina could utter nothing except "sorry, baby, sorry... Mommy's very tired, just let me rest for five minutes, sorry, baby..."

"Looks like Minni's mini won't be available tonight," Empress Varvara chuckled. "She's out cold."

"Enough, you ass," Vam spat back. "It's Hildegard's birthday, don't make it worse. Hilde, I would take you home, but I've got somewhere I have to be..."

"And where I'm going, little girls aren't invited," Empress Varvara said curtly, but seemed to reconsider. "Sorry, kid. Happy birthday," the Empress extended a few paper Deutschmarks as a conciliatory gesture.

"Sorry, baby..." Wilhelmina murmured.

"I will take them home," came a voice from the darkness. The man in the gray suit stepped forward into the backstage room.

Vam pursed her lips. "I don't know if that's a good idea..."

"Why not? She goes home with strange men all the time. What's the difference if she's unconscious this time? Maybe she'll enjoy it more. You have a car, mystery man?"

Choosing to ignore Empress Varvara, the man in the gray suit gingerly picked up Wilhelmina in his stout arms, turned his clear eyes onto Hildegard, and jutted his chin toward the door.

He did, in fact, have a car, with a driver to boot. Hildegard's nerves were at full attention, her hair standing up on her arms, but she pretended to look out the window at the city's golden light drifting by. She gave her address to the driver and watched carefully in case a wrong turn was made.

The man in the gray suit said nothing, only looked ahead.

Then he said, "Gregori, pull over."

"We're not there yet," Hildegard said nervously.

"I know," the man said, and Gregori opened the door. Gregori jumped back like a spooked cat as Wilhelmina stuck her golden head across the man's lap and vomited onto the street. The man carefully pulled Wilhelmina out of the car and postured her on his arm so she could walk. He walked her into a diner and sat her down on a plush leather booth.

"Too much Oktoberfest for this angel, eh?" The waitress, a woman who resembled a dumpling, winked at the man.

"We'll have two coffees, an apfelschorle, a bowl of goulash and spaetzle, and a slice of cake."

"Chocolate or honey almond?"

"Both."

Hildegard's eyes did not leave the man as he received his coffee and set the other in front of her mother. "I am Otto," he said.

"I'm Hildegard."

"And I'm Wilhelmina," her mother said, slumping over with her hand on her forehead, weakly taking the coffee. "Thank you for this."

They sat in silence, Hildegard sipping her fizzy apple drink through a straw and relishing its effervescence, until the goulash arrived. Wilhelmina pushed it away at the memory of what she left on the street, but Otto quietly urged "you must eat it," and Wilhelmina obediently took a bite, nodding thanks to Otto.

The dumpling waitress brought out the two slices of cake, and Otto asked, "Which one would you prefer, Hildegard?"

"Chocolate."

"Please wrap up the other cake in paper."

As the waitress left, Wilhelmina stared at Otto through her kohl-smudged eyelids. Her dark lipstick, normally perfectly lined in a sharp Cupid's bow, was smeared. "I know you. You've been coming

5

to Babbel for a while."

Otto nodded.

"Was this your plan? Wait until I was hungry enough and ask me out on a date? Some date."

Otto said nothing. He drank his coffee.

"So what do you do, Herr Otto?"

"I own a steel factory in Bavaria. I come to Berlin for business."

"A factory man. And do you do business with those brown-suited boys at Babbel?"

"Sometimes."

They went back to sitting in silence until the waitress brought back the second slice of cake, wrapped in paper. Otto presented it to Wilhelmina.

"So, Otto, you think you can just buy my love?" Wilhelmina scoffed.

"I'm not asking to buy your love," Otto replied. "I'm asking to earn it."

2

1931: Coming Home

Six months later, Otto Richter and Wilhelmina Appelbaum were married.

Wilhelmina saw the writing on the wall: more and more brown suits were starting to show up at Babbel, getting louder and rowdier and more bold, but also attitudes were starting to change towards Kabarett in general. Nightclubs were eschewed by an increasingly conservative middle class. After all, where did Kabarett come from but France, the infamous Moulin Rouge? And wasn't France the country that just tightened its fist on the borderlands when reparations couldn't be paid? Better to find a new form of artistic expression, something that didn't borrow from Allied countries, something uniquely German.

Added to that, there was nothing to eat in the city. People queued up in the streets for unemployment. To this, Wilhelmina threw up her hands. Performing in the city was lovely and culturally stimulating, but man cannot live on cultural stimulation alone. And Otto, in addition to the lucrative factory, owned a picturesque piece of property in Southern Bavaria that looked right out of a postcard. Rolling green hills, turquoise lakes, and mountains like fingers that caressed the heavens. Plus, a more normal childhood for Hildegard, like the pre-war idyllic childhood in Cologne that Wilhelmina enjoyed, might be better for her growth as a person. Stability.

Also, Otto was a good man. And how many good men were even still alive these days?

As for Hildegard, she demurred. She and her mother had made it this far, and yes it was a hungry existence, but people were hungry everywhere. At least she wasn't bored in the city.

The wedding was short and sweet. Vam was in attendance as a witness, as well as the Babbel owner, Herr Meyerowitz. Wilhelmina wore a smart wool suit of periwinkle that brought out her eyes and made her look like Gabriel come down from heaven. There was no kohl on her eyes today, no dark cupid's bow. In fact, there would be no more of this vampy look from Wilhelmina. It made her look younger, lighter, less tired. As they took a sleeper train down to Bavaria, Wilhelmina remarked that the fresh country air made her feel lighter and more energized.

"Many people came to my village since the 1850s to take the air," Otto said. "It was a mountain resort town. And... after the war..." He stopped.

"You don't have to talk about it if you don't want to," Wilhelmina said, wrapping herself around his arm and laying a head on his shoulder.

And he didn't.

In fact, Otto never talked. This annoyed Hildegard, who was used to the babble and chatter of backstage cabarets and nightclubs.

"You aren't going to replace my father, you know," Hildegard petulantly told Otto after the wedding.

"I'm not trying to," Otto responded simply.

Himmelberg, or "The Mount of Heaven," was aptly named. Snugly nestled in the crevice of Mount Siegfried, it was large enough for the children in smaller villages nearby to attend school, but small enough that everybody knew your name and, to Hildegard's dismay, your business.

Himmelberg boasted a small ski resort. It was really more of a large inn, where guests could board a sleigh and be taken to the top of a wide, sloping meadow covered with snow and ski down. Der Schneehirsch (The Snow Stag) was not as chic as later German ski lodges, but the inhabitants of Himmelberg were convinced it would turn their town into the next Mont Blanc.

When the new Mrs. and Miss Richter arrived, the town's mayor, Herr Auguste Fischer, was there to welcome them at the train station. With him was his wife, Frau Pauline Fischer, and their daughters, Irena and Ygritte.

"Welcome home, Otto!" Herr Fischer beamed, clapping Otto on the back.

"Thank you," Otto said, and he left to direct the valets on where to send Hildegard and Wilhelmina's scant luggage.

"We're all so excited to meet you, Frau Richter," the mayor bubbled, kissing Wilhemina on the hand. "We can't believe it. We simply cannot believe it. We couldn't believe our ears when we heard Otto Richter put an end to his bachelorhood."

"Believe it," Wilhelmina said, then she flashed her most winning smile. Hildegard observed that, though she had quite literally chucked her kohl and rouge out the train window, Wilhelmina was still enchanting the room, but this time with only one table. "Please call me Wilhelmina, Herr Fischer."

"What a lucky man to entrap such a charming bride. And to come home with such a winning family! What a prize! Who might this young angel be?"

"This is my daughter, Hildegard."

"Charmed to make your acquaintance," Hildegard said, sweeping a bow like her mother used to do at the end of an act. If Wilhelmina

9

wanted to play royalty, Hildegard would be a willing supporting actress.

Irena and Ygritte exchanged glances and burst into snickers. Hildegard turned her eyes on them slowly, a trait she had picked up from Otto and had been practicing.

"Have I done something funny?"

"You bow like a sultan at a carnival," Ygritte smirked.

"Maybe like Scheherazade at the palace," Hildegard retorted.

"Who's *that?*"

Hildegard opened her mouth to make a comment on these country bumpkins' illiteracy, but a squeeze on the shoulder from Wilhemina made Hildegard swallow her words and force a smile instead. "It's a wonderful story about a noble maiden who makes a sultan fall in love with her. Why don't you two come over some time and I can tell you all about it?"

"Ha ha! Kids!" Herr Fischer nervously shoved his daughters aside. "What fun. Now, Frau Richter, I know you and Hildegard may be tired after a long journey, but the whole town is so excited to meet you—big news travels fast in a small town, heheh, you know—that we would love to host you and have a big town dinner at the biergarten. What do you say?"

"I say I'll have to check with my husband, but that sounds lovely!" Wilhelmina smiled.

"Perfect! I'm going to go right now to let everyone know. You check with Otto, but we know how it is… the husband cannot say no to his wife, not really, eh? Heh heh!" And with that, the Fischers bustled away.

Wilhelmina sighed in relief. "Nice save, Hilde."

Hildegard emitted a preteenly groan of angst. "They're not *all* going to be like that, I hope?"

"You know what they say, you catch more flies with honey than with vinegar. They may not be used to the modern tastes of Berlin. But they're still Germans, like us, through and through. You'll make friends here if you keep that in mind."

"I guess," Hildegard brooded.

At home, with their measly luggage and bags of new clothes, Hildegard stared at her new digs. Otto's house was large, the size of a gasthaus, but not as grandiose as some of the villas Hildegard had passed by in Berlin.

Her room had a view of Otto's property, a meadow which swept back into the stretching peaks of the Alps. From here, she could see a barn and hear the cows meandering through the pastures, their gigantic bells clanging as they crossed the country roads. She could even see a road that led away from the town, out into the wilderness, away from here.

She turned at a knock on the door. Otto cleared his throat and came in carrying two parcels wrapped in paper.

"These are for you." He handed the parcels to her.

Hildegard unwrapped the larger parcel first. It was a doll with yellow yarn hair and a blue dirndl, the traditional dress of Germany. Her eyes were lapis lazuli and two red dots were splotched below them to show rosy cherub's cheeks.

"Are you too old for dolls?" Otto asked, shifting on his feet.

"I... don't think I've ever had one," Hildegard said uncertainly.

"Okay, maybe no doll. Open the other one," Otto directed.

Hildegard obliged, unwrapping the rectangular, heavy object that could only be a book. It was a copy of *Faust*, by Johann Goethe.

"He wrote it not far from here," Otto said. "He's German."

"Thank you," Hildegard said.

"Okay," Otto said, turning and closing the door behind him.

Hildegard put the book and the doll on the shelf above her bed, next

11

to the empty bottle of Egyptian perfume her mother had given her. Then she lay down on the bed and stared at the ceiling.

The biergarten was connected to the rathaus, the town hall. It stretched forth into the town square, attractively lit overhead with cafe lights. In between the rathaus were two gasthauses, Zum Hirschen and Zur Rentier.

Zum Hirschen (marked by a wooden stag sign above the door) was run by Frau von Braun, a red-faced woman with arms like an ox. She had dark golden hair, almost coppery, that she kept in the traditional braided bun. At Zum Hirschen, Frau von Braun would serve tender veal steak with rich hunter's gravy and buttery, wriggly noodles piled in a gigantic blue and white bowl that had been in her family since the 1750s. Also, a bowl of stewed red cabbage. The *pies de resistance* was Frau von Braun's "Braunbrauen", a malty, caramel-colored märzen that was reminiscent of Oktoberfest all year long. Frau von Braun liked to brag that Paulaner stole the recipe from her great-great-great- (and so on)-grandfather, who was a Munich monk.

Zur Rentier (marked by a wooden reindeer sign above the door) was run by Herr Weissman, a man with a cherry for a nose with dark hair slicked down in a style that had not changed since before the Great War. At Zur Rentier, Herr Weissman would serve pork schnitzel ("But we can do any schnitzel! If it walks, I can schnitzel it. What do you like? Pork? Chicken? Reindeer? Just not veal, anything but veal") hammered down so thin, it was almost as slender as a cabbage leaf, delicately breaded, and topped with a slice of lemon. On the side came gigantic steaming, spongey knödel that were as big as your fist. Also, a bowl of stewed red cabbage. And to wet his guest's whistle, he would bring a foamy glass of "Weissman's Weissbier", a wheat beer the color of tupelo honey. "Like liquid sunshine!" he would beam. "God himself could not brew a more heavenly beer! Well, maybe not God, but certainly St. Peter!"

The two innkeepers lived in a perpetual state of competition. Frau von Braun argued her inn was older; her family had been here since the middle ages.

"And how exactly is your family supposed to have been here since the middle ages when your great-great-grandfather was a monk from Munich, eh, Frau von Braun?" Herr Weissman crossed his arms. "Are you supposed to remember because you've been here this whole time, you old dinosaur?"

"I'm younger than you, Rip Van Winkle," Frau von Braun put her hammy fists on her even wider hips. "I remember when your family moved here from Ravensberg."

"Nein, nein, nein, you misremember! We moved *back* from Ravensberg. My father fought in the Prussian War, and we moved there to help my mother's nerves, God rest her soul. The Weissmans have been in Himmelberg since before it was a collection of shepherds and barns!"

"Oh, go slick your hair and brew your pissbier, Arschgeige."

Tonight, because neither innkeeper could stand to see the other host the newcomers (or lose any business), both Frau von Braun and Herr Weissman were serving the town. Long wooden tables stretched out, and they buzzed in between, keeping well out of each other's way.

"Hey, Lars, you need a topper? You could use some meat on your bones, you're still growing. Bah, what are you doing with that rubbery schnitzel? Take another helping of spaetzle. God bless your mother, how many pairs of pants do you go through a month?"

"Frau Zimmermann, how about another knödel? Nein, nein, nein, nein! I insist. It's much better than that dry spaetzle, like eating dried earthworms. You come and see me when the baby is due; I just slaughtered my heifer, God rest her soul."

Hildegard sat at a short table for the young people. Here were seated

13

her soon-to-be schoolmates, and she wished her mother were sitting with her.

"Hildegard, eat, baby! You've barely touched your rehbraten. Do you want some more gravy? Ach, what's this? Herr Weissman has given you a little beer? Nein, get rid of that piss," Frau von Braun tossed it over her shoulder, "Let me get you some of my Braunbrauen, it's the toast of the town! I bet you had a lot of Paulaner in Berlin, right? Well... did you know... they actually *stole* the recipe from my family! Yes, it's true, believe it or not! You see, my great-great-great-great—"

"Don't throw out my beer unless you're going to pay for it, you old relic!"

"Bean-counter, mind your own business!" Frau von Braun stormed off.

"I'm pretty sure they used to be lovers," a boy said, leaning forward in a conspiratorial tone. "It was before we were born, obviously, but I think he spurned her."

"No, *she* spurned *him!*" a girl said. "He proposed to her, but she thought she was going to marry Herr Fischer."

"Why don't they just bury the hatchet?" Hildegard asked. "Why keep the grudge?"

"Eh, I think it gives them something to do," the boy shrugged, then extended his hand. "Felix Baumann."

Hildegard shook it. "I'm Hilde,"

"And I'm Johanna," the girl said. Her hair was white like early corn.

"So, Berlin. We've heard your mother was a Bauhaus model," Felix said.

How did they find out? What else *have they heard about us?* "Oh, she just passed through when they needed her," Hildegard tried to sound flippant, nonchalantly stabbing a noodle.

"That's excellent, really excellent. I'm an artist, too." He pulled out a sketch pad, flipping it open. Hildegard flipped through delicate pencil drawings, renderings of landscapes, birds, a fox creeping through the snow with an extended paw.

"These are wonderful! You're really talented!" Hildegard exclaimed.

"Yeah, thanks. I want to study in Berlin someday, but I also want to go to Paris, that's where all the great impressionists studied."

"Why go to Paris? It's full of frogs," a red-faced boy said. Felix rolled his eyes.

"I'm not saying I want to *be* French, Karl. I'm saying I want to be the best. Germany has the cornerstone of modern art, but I want to study the past so I can be ahead of the future."

"So you actually brought your sketchbook to dinner?" Johanna asked drily. "For what purpose?"

"Because inspiration can come from anywhere," Felix blushed, flipping his sketchbook shut and carefully placing it below his napkin.

"I think it's really good, Felix," Hildegard repeated. It was nice to have a kindred spirit here, a fellow artist. It would be like having a little shred of Berlin—the good parts, anyway.

"So, Hilde, what's the best part about Berlin?" Johanna asked.

"Um…" Hildegard thought, sipping her beer. What could she say that didn't betray her mother's recent profession? Wilhelmina had cautioned Hildegard that some people would not understand Kabarett and might misjudge them and Otto. "Play your cards close to your chest until you're sure you can trust the person you're talking to," Wilhelmina said.

"In Berlin, there's always something going on. All kinds of people were on every street corner. You can walk down one street and see stylish ladies with felt hats sipping coffee, and on the next street there's a contortionist or a statue… but when you look closer, it's a man standing perfectly still… and he can do that for an hour!"

"Psh, I could do that," Karl said. "Watch." He stood on the bench of the table, stoically holding his napkin like a scroll.

"Who are you supposed to be?" Johanna asked.

"I'm Julius Caesar, isn't it obvious?"

Felix tried to slap Karl between the legs, and Karl dodged and gave Felix the middle finger. "How about this one?" He squatted forward with his fist on his chin.

"That's The Thinker!" Hildegard exclaimed.

"No, it's The Sphincter!" Karl said, ripping an enormous fart in Felix's face. Felix pushed Karl off the bench and all the kids collapsed in fits of raucous laughter.

At the other end of the town square, Wilhelmina and Otto sat with Herr Fischer and other notables of Himmelberg. Hearing the children's laughter, Wilhelmina smiled, relieved. "It sounds like the kids are getting along."

"Yes, Hildegard will be the star of the show at school," Frau König, the headmistress of the school, smiled. "It can be tough to be the new girl, but the students are excited to have someone from glamorous Berlin!"

"Yes, but I hope the fame doesn't go to her head," Wilhelmina sighed. "Hildegard has a thirst for knowledge and a creative spirit, but I want her to get a traditional education and have a stable set of friends."

"I assure you, Hildegard will feel right at home and will receive a top education in my class," Herr Pfeiffer said emphatically. "I studied at Ludwig Maximilian in Munich, and I place an emphasis on the classics. I also want to educate my pupils in the sciences, because I believe Germany will be at the forefront of quantum physics. In fact, my schoolmate was Max Planck—"

Frau Zimmermann rolled her eyes, and her husband subtly kicked her under the table.

"Well, you can count on us, Frau Richter," Father Schafer, the town's parishioner, smiled. "I believe the community of Himmelberg ascribes to the old saying, 'it takes a village to raise a child.' And if we are not supporting our brothers and sisters in Christ as a community, as iron sharpens iron, are we really living by His Word?"

"Amen," echoed Frau Zimmerman. "And, theological ramifications aside, we're proud of our community. We may not have the bells and whistles of Berlin, but we're a German community through and through."

"That's perfectly fine with me," Wilhelmina smiled. "We're looking forward to a life without bells and whistles."

"Speaking of Berlin, what's happening in the capitol, Otto?" Herr Zimmermann asked, taking a large bite of venison.

"Nobody's satisfied with Chancellor Brüning's economic plan," Otto said, cutting into his schnitzel. "All four parties of the Reichstag parliament opposed President Hindenburg's bill to reform finances, but he went ahead and pushed it into law anyway."

"What's the point of the Weimar Republic if Hindenburg still insists on acting like a king?" Herr König said angrily.

"The Roman Empire was a republic before Caesar," Frau Schumacher reminded him.

"Yeah, and look what happened to Caesar," he murmured.

"And we could've handled that in the elections," Otto continued, sipping his beer, "But Brüning asked Hindenburg to dissolve parliament and hold new elections for new parties."

"What a bastard," Frau von Braun said, tossing Otto's Weissbier over her shoulder and refilling his glass with Braunbrauen.

"And we could've beaten him again, but there are just so many new political parties voting every which way. 30 new political parties. We have a majority here in the south with the Centre Party, but we only have 12% of the popular vote."

"How can we get anywhere with this!" Herr König exclaimed.

"I wish we could have a more direct form of government," Frau Schumacher pondered. "I'm not saying I want a full-on Kaiser, but it would be nice to have a real leader in charge, instead of Hindenburg, who seems to be under Brüning's thumb."

"That's what the NSDAP thinks," Otto nodded.

"The Nazis?" Herr Zimmermann asked. "Aren't they led by that kook who tried to stage a revolution back in '23? Himmler?"

"Hitler," Wilhelmina corrected. "We used to see posters of him and his little mustache all over the place in Berlin."

"I think Brüning has a point," Frau Zimmermann said. "I'm sick of paying off reparations to these slovenly countries who can't get off their asses. The sooner we're done with the Allied countries, the better."

"Why don't we just stop paying the reparations?" Frau Schumacher asked. "I wish we could build a big wall between Germany and France, and say 'up yours, you rebuild your own bloody infrastructure.'"

"A wall going through Germany," Frau Zimmermann laughed, "There's an idea."

"I didn't say *through*, I said *between*, Klara," Frau Schumacher glared.

"One thing's for sure," Herr Zimmerman said, "something's got to happen."

"Indeed," Otto nodded sagely.

Frau von Braun and Herr Weissman cleaned up as the party neared its end. Otto, Wilhelmina, and Hildegard headed home, Wilhelmina's sensible new shoes clicking against the cobblestone streets.

"Isn't it nice to have your own room? Now that Otto is your father, we have lots of space," Wilhelmina said breezily, opening the curtains of Hildegard's room.

"He's not my father," Hildegard said in the doorway.

"You're right, he's your stepfather. Your father's soul is in heaven, God bless him. And look at this spectacular view! I'm sure right now your father is bragging to the angels that you have a better view of

18

heaven than they. What a postcard!"

"Why can't I sleep with you? Why do I have to be alone?" Hildehard sat down grumpily on the bed, eyeing the old-fashioned quilt with disdain.

"Hildegard, in six months you're going to be fourteen. You're on your way to becoming a young woman. And young women deserve their own bedrooms with their own space."

Right now, Hildegard wished she had a few more hallways of space between her room and her parents'. She pressed her ears between her pillow and rolled over, groaning in disgust. It was odd... she was no innocent; she knew what went on behind the door at the apartment in Berlin. She knew plenty about what adults do from the talk backstage at Babbel... and some of what most folks didn't do, but paid the Kabarett performers to do because they were too scared to try it in their normal lives. It hadn't bothered her.

But here, it was so different. It bothered her *because* it was normal. Her mother was married, and that's what married women do. No magic here, just normal everyday birds and bees. That's how married couples got babies. Hildegard felt her stomach sink at the thought of having to share her mother with yet another human being.

Wilhelmina suspected as much as the months went on.

"You've been giving me an attitude lately, Miss Teenager," she said, not looking up as she milked their cow, Valkyrie. "What's up with you?"

"Nothing," Hildegard said to the ground sulkily.

"Something wrong at school?"

"School's fine."

"Something wrong with me?"

Hildegard swallowed, unsure of how to start. "You... you and Otto are married now."

"Last time I checked, yes."

19

"And you do… married people things."

"Spoken like a nun from the abbey! My, what a little prude you've become! You used to curse like a sailor from all the talk you picked up at Babbel. I'm glad to see that school is a good influence on you, little heathen."

"Mutti… are you and Otto going to have another baby?"

Wilhelmina paused, then she turned back to milking. "No."

"Oh," Hildegard had to admit this was not the answer she had been expecting. "Why not?"

Wilhelmina took a moment, sighed, and turned back around with the frank look on her face she reserved for "shooting straight sessions."

"This stays between us?"

"Sure."

"Otto cannot have children. It's partially why he remained unmarried for so long. He didn't want to burden a young woman with childlessness. But I told him that was fine with me, I already have a child." She rested her elbows on the tops of her thighs. "We don't always get what we want, Hilde. But if you've been dragged through the dredges and the ditches of life—which I pray to God you won't experience much of, but eventually life will deal you a nasty deck—you learn to be thankful for what you have."

"I understand."

"No, you don't. Not yet. But you will soon," Wilhelmina's eyes were sad, as if observing her daughter growing up too fast, getting too old, right before her eyes.

"So… I guess you're stuck with just me?" Hildegard smiled.

"Hilde, I don't know if this house can take any more Appelbaum women," Wilhelmina chuckled, turning back to her milking.

"Mutti, let me do that for you."

"Do you know how? Here, sit down on the stool. Now don't yank on it, she's just a lady, poor thing, not a dominatrix. Gently pull from top down to the bottom with your two fingers. Like a tube of toothpaste. Perfect."

Hildegard watched the squirt of milk shoot into the bucket. It was oddly satisfying, like snipping a braid with a pair of scissors. It would become her favorite chore, because she could let her mind wander off into the void while still doing something useful. If her mother could find happiness here, so could she.

Hildegard had struggled to catch up to the curriculum of the Himmelberg school. Frau König offered to help Hildegard fill in the gaps of her knowledge after school and on the weekends, but Hildegard declined. It was an injury to her pride, and she felt shy opening up to strangers about all that she discovered she did not know.

"Alright, let's make a deal," Frau König said. "You can catch up on your own, but if your grades drop to a D, you let someone step in and tutor you. It doesn't have to be me; it could be Herr Pfeiffer, or even a fellow student. Deal?"

"Deal," Hildegard smiled a little.

Today Herr Pfeiffer was starting a new unit on Faust. "One of Germany's greatest contributions to the world canon of literature!" he exclaimed. "A tale of ultimate power! Of love! And of trying to best the devil himself, oooh!" Herr Pfeiffer wiggled his fingers dramatically.

Hildegard was excited to begin this unit, because she had been reading the book Otto had given her months ago. Finally! An area where she wasn't behind!

She was feeling so good about the unit and how it might affect her dismal grades, it carried her all the way into Science.

"And who can tell us about the theory of relativity?" Herr Pfeiffer asked. Hildegard raised her hand, tentative. Herr Pfeiffer nodded, encouragingly.

"I don't know if I'm going to get the answer right," Hildegard said uncertainly.

"Go on, Hildegard, the only wrong answer here is 'I don't care,'" he smiled. "Why don't you tell us whatever you remember about the topic?"

"Well... I think the theory of relativity is that time and space are connected. One depends on the other. If you want to move across the same amount of space in a shorter amount of time, more energy is needed. And... something about traveling through space and time. E equals m and c, and E equals energy and m equals mass."

"E equals mc squared," Felix jumped in.

"Excellent, Felix. And wonderful job, Hildegard. That's an excellent introduction to our lesson today."

"Oh! And Albert Einstein invented the theory," Hildegard smiled.

"Isn't Einstein a Jew?" Irena wrinkled her nose.

Hildegard turned to look back at her. "I don't know what a Jew is; I only remember that Einstein invented the theory."

"Jew or not, Einstein won the Nobel Prize in Physics for Germany," Herr Pfeiffer pointed out. "And, as an interesting side note, children, his theory of special relativity was first accepted by physicist Max Planck, who was one of my schoolmates. So, who knows? Maybe you're sitting next to a future Nobel Prize winner in this very classroom."

"Not if they're a Jew," Irena said under her breath.

"Let's open up our textbooks to Chapter 13, on page 267. Irena, would you like to read the first column, since you're so chatty today?"

"Yes, Herr Pfeiffer," Irena said.

After school, Hildegard, Johanna, and Felix walked down the lane from the schoolhouse.

"What's a Jew?" Hildegard said.

"I think it's like a gypsy," Johanna said. "My father says they're like swindlers or con men or something."

"A Jew is someone who believes in a different religion, dummkopf," Felix rolled his eyes. "Don't you remember when Father Schafer taught about this in Sunday school?"

"No, but there's something about Jews that's related to gypsies," Johanna persisted. "My father says a lot of them used to live in Russia, and then the old tsar—remember, the one who got shot up in the Russian Revolution—he kicked them all out, and they all came over here. So they don't have any property of their own, which is why they try to swindle it out of Europeans."

"Yuck," Hildegard said, but her stomach twisted. She and her mother had come to Himmelberg with nothing of their own and had latched onto Otto and his property. Is that what the villagers thought of *her*?

"Don't let Irena bother you, Hilde," Johanna said. "It's pretty obvious to everyone that she's jealous of you. She's used to being the class leader, and you showed everyone how clever you are. She's intimidated."

"I don't think I'm particularly clever," Hildegard said, although the compliment made her smile. "You're leagues ahead of me in mathematics."

"We'll help you catch up, don't worry," Felix put a hand on her shoulder. "If you can grasp the theory of relativity, you can do algebra equations with your eyes closed!"

"Ha ha," Hildegard said.

"See you tomorrow," Felix waved as the path diverged.

"Tschüss!" Johanna said as Hildegard headed toward the Richters' house.

Hildegard walked slowly but was aware of footsteps behind her. She inclined her head deftly to look and saw it was another schoolmate, Henri.

"Oh, hi, Henri. You scared me!"

"Were you really scared, little mouse?" Henri laughed.

"Yep," Hildegard said awkwardly, continuing on.

"Hold on, Mausi! Wait up!" Henri jogged up beside her. "You were really clever today, did you know that?"

"Thanks, Henri, but I only got one answer right."

"I'm sure you know loads more. I'm sure you learned all *kinds* of things in Berlin," Henri said pointedly.

"I guess," Hildegard said, wary. She was nearly to the Richter barn.

"I know some things too."

"Oh, really?"

"Yes. I heard some things about your family. About your mother."

Hildegard said nothing but quickened her pace.

"Do you want to know what I heard?"

"Not particularly."

"You know what I heard about your mother?" Henri repeated. "I heard your mother was a whore before she came to Himmelberg."

Hildegard stopped. She clenched her fists. "You heard wrong."

"I heard the reason why your mother can't get pregnant is she had too many abortions in Berlin," Henri continued, following her around the barn as Hildegard turned to walk away.

"Henri, drop it," Hildegard said. "I'm warning you."

"Were you a war baby, or a whore baby?" Henri laughed, and right as Hildegard spun around with her fist raised to strike, her arm was caught. She looked up, and to her surprise found Otto staring down at her.

"Enough, Hildegard," he said. "Go home."

"But—"

"Do as I said."

Hildegard dropped her arm and, hastily wiping hot tears of anger from her eyes, turned and ran away. She charged blindly back to the house, where she sat with her arms around her knees, wishing she had never come to this stupid small-minded town, wishing her mother would have never married Otto, wishing they could still be in Cologne and with her real father, wishing her real father were still alive.

"Hilde?" came her mother's voice, and a soothing hand was rubbing her back. "What's wrong?"

"Why did you bring us here," Hildegard struggled to keep her voice even. "We... I don't fit in here."

"Oh, Hilde," Wilhelmina pulled her into a hug. "I'll tell you a secret. Nobody fits in anywhere. If we had stayed in Berlin, there would still be some dummkopf who felt he could take liberties, or some nosy neighbor. And, if you remember, kiddo, things weren't exactly on a high note in my career. As you would've gotten older, the men at the cabaret would've started asking for you instead of for me, or, God forbid, would've followed you home. And that wasn't something I was ever going to let happen." She sighed. "Humans are... cruel. It takes effort to be kind. It takes effort to extend grace."

Someone cleared their throat. It was Otto. They had not heard him enter, but now he was standing in the room with a tight hand clutching Henri's shoulder, and Henri looked as if he had been beaten six different ways to Tuesday. He had a bloody nose, red marks on his elbows, his left knee was skinned, and he had the beginnings of a whopper of a black eye.

"Henri had a little fall," Otto said. "He was on his way to come apologize to you, and he tripped down the mountain. I saw the whole thing. Thank God I was there, or he would have been *really* hurt." He turned Henri to look up at him, practically hoisting the kid up by the neck of his shirt. "You really should be more careful, Henri."

"Y-yes sir," Henri said in a decibel above a dog whistle.

"Now that you're safe and sound, do you have something to say to Hilde?"

"S-s-sorry."

"Goodness!" Wilhelmina's eyebrows rose. "Sorry for what?"

Terrified, Henri looked from Wilhelmina to Otto, from Otto to Wilhelmina.

After an excruciating silence, Otto said: "Oh, just schoolyard trouble. Right, Hilde?"

"Right," Hilde said quickly.

"Now run home to your parents," Otto said. "And let's not have any more clumsiness, eh?"

"Y-yes, Herr Richter." The minute Otto released Henri, there was nothing left but a cloud of dust down the road.

Otto said, "I'm going to go smoke my pipe."

The next morning, when Otto unfolded his newspaper, a little pressed edelweiss fell out from between the pages and into his lap. He looked up and saw Hildegard watching him from the door. She hastily ducked her head out and went to her room. Otto slipped the edelweiss into the pocket near his lapel.

And that was the last time anyone said any foul word about Wilhelmina ever again.

3

1933: Christmas

Himmelberg had, over the summer of 1931, installed a movie theater in an old decrepit auditorium. The theater, Herr Weissman noted with grim satisfaction, was on the Zur Rentier side of the stadtplatz.

"A ski resort *and* a movie theater! What more could you ask for, heh heh!" Mayor Fischer declared.

Hildegard couldn't get enough of it. Yes, the seats were a little moldy, and yes, it was cold at night because the roof needed to be thatched, but she was absolutely enamored with the silver screen. The movie that had made her fall in love was Charlie Chaplin's 1921 *The Kid,* although she (as well as the other kids) were suckers for Boris Karloff's *Frankenstein.*

Karl, so exultant that he shared part of the name of the starring actor, was determined to make his Frankenstein impression his signature quirk. After two years, his fellow classmates, and sometimes even his teachers, started calling him Karloff.

"Graaaaaaggghhh!" he would moan, clomping around the school-yard with his arms extended, making the girls shriek and giggle when he swiveled towards them.

"Are you doing an impersonation, or are you just being your regular idiotic self?" laughed Johanna, jumping out of his way as he made a grab for her.

"I'm Frankenstein, and you'd better watch out, Fraulein Johanna!" Karl grimaced.

"Actually, you're not Frankenstein. Frankenstein was the name of the scientist," Felix said, not looking up from his sketchbook.

"You're right, I'm not Frankenstein. I'm Frankenstinker!" Karl ran up to Felix and farted in his face.

"Ugh! You're 15 years old, Karl, aren't you ever going to grow out of that?" Felix got up with the rest of the kids and moved well out of the way of the stink cloud.

"Nope!"

One day, Herr Weber, the caretaker of the theater, started showing news reels as well as movies. "They've begun sending them to us by postmail! Can you imagine what this will do for the theater! No more radio or newspaper, you can get all your news by watching it! This will launch us into the twentieth century!"

Hildegard had heard the name Hitler bounced around at the dinner tables, gasthauses, and a little at school. She might have even heard a snippet of his voice on the radio. But seeing Hitler at the theater in black and white, twenty-feet-glory had a different effect.

"For fourteen long years, these parties have raped German freedom, beaten German men with clubs," he rasped. He seemed to make eye contact with everyone in the crowd, the same way that her mother would have "a moment" with every table at Babbel. "Before two or three months pass, this terror will be removed... *if* you vote for National Socialists."

Hildegard was in the dressing room of the trachten store while Gerda and Wilhelmina stood by, listening to the news on the radio.

"I don't get it," Gerda said. Gerda Roth had auburn hair and worked in the trachten store selling traditional German clothes and ski suits to unprepared tourists. "I thought the Communists were socialists? Aren't the Nazis against the Communists?"

"Otto says that the party has changed a lot from its beginnings after the Great War," Wilhelmina said. "It's a labor party for working class Germans, but I don't think anyone in the NSDAP believes in no possessions or wealth, like those woo-woo Russians."

"So it's Socialist in that it's a party for the social groups of common German people," Gerda said.

"Exactly."

"Well, at least *someone* is doing something about this government," Gerda said. "Hildegard, is it alright if I come in? Or do you want your mother to?"

"I don't care," Hildegard whimpered from the dressing room.

"We'll both come in," Wilhelmina said, and in a moment all three women were crammed into the dressing room, admiring a red-faced Hildegard in her first brasier.

"Oh, don't look so embarrassed, Hilde," Gerda adjusted the straps on the shoulders. "Remember that half the people in this village are wearing brasiers. Except for Frau Neumann, and everybody wishes she would. That's why you have to wear it, Hilde, otherwise your udders will sink so low, they'll practically drag on the ground."

"I hate to break it to you, Gerda, but that usually happens anyway," Wilhelmina straightened her daughter's shoulders. "If you remember to use good posture and stand up straight, it makes them look bigger. Trust me."

"It won't make much of a difference," Hildegard said miserably.

"Oh, don't worry, Mausi. It's the Appelbaum way. They look small now, but in a few years—boom! You won't be able to shove them in."

"And the boys won't be able to stop looking at you," Gerda winked.

"And you should enjoy it, because Appelbaum women grow big quickly," Wilhelmina shrugged. "Big hips for big babies..." she drifted off, aware of Gerda's presence. "And, speaking of which, Gerda, I think I'll need a new skirt. I've let out about all this one can take."

"We just got some new items in on Tuesday," Gerda said. "I think you'll love them."

Wilhelmina smiled sadly at her daughter, who was springing up in front of her eyes, who looked so much like her. Not a trace of her father in her. It was like her father never even existed.

Meanwhile, her own body was starting to show signs of age. The bags under her eyes which used to only appear after several nights at the Kabarett without sleep had grown more or less permanent. Her chin, once sharp and elfin, had become chipmunk-like. She had become plumper, and she was growing to resemble her own mother. Her mother had a round, jovial face, accented by two rosy apple cheeks and a warm smile. Her mother had lost a tooth when she was a young woman, which inclined her to smile with her mouth closed and keep her quips short and choppy in the company of people she did not know well. It made her seem reserved; so, too, was Wilhelmina growing reserved in the town of Himmelberg. It wasn't that she felt shy; she just felt comfortable enough in her own skin to avoid making retorts and cracks in self-defense, like she had to for self-preservation backstage in Berlin. Maybe she was just becoming wiser, which allowed her the strength to withhold her words. Perhaps it was Otto influencing her.

"So, Miss Mausi," Wilhelmina said, trying to sound casual, "*Are* there boys who can't stop looking at you?"

"Some of them treat me differently than when I first got here," Hildegard admitted.

"Are there any of them you particularly like? Like Felix, maybe?"

"Felix is more like a brother to me," Hildegard said, wrinkling her nose.

Wilhelmina smiled in the back of her mind at the all-too-common phrase. Girls who said "he's like a brother to me" usually didn't have brothers of their own. Wilhelmina had two brothers, both monstrous little demons when they were young. Hubie, the youngest, had died of cholera as a child, and Berthold had died at 19 in the Great War.

Hildegard was hoping her mother wouldn't ask her any more questions about the boys at school. The fact of the matter was that some of the kids at Himmelberg school had moved well beyond "looking differently" at each other. Karl and Mathilde had some kind of experimental session a year ago, and Karl had gone off and told all the boys about it as excitedly as the Marys had run off to report the resurrection of Jesus Christ.

More and more kids were starting to "play doctor", as Henri called it, which Hildegard thought was gross and unappealing and showed Henri probably hadn't done much of anything, but there were plenty of her schoolmates who abided by the stern words of Father Schafer and their parents. As for Hildegard, she had pretty much seen it all back in Berlin. There wasn't any experimenting with any kids in Himmelberg she wanted to do that she wasn't already aware of.

"Well, be careful, Hilde," Wilhelmina cautioned. "Boys can be sweet and charming and lovely, up until the point they satisfy their curiosity, and then they will leave you brokenhearted."

"Yes, Mutti," Hildegard said evenly. Did she forget who she was talking to? Had her mother forgotten she used to be a prostitute, and Hildegard had to sometimes help her push drunken clients out of the door? The drunken clients were better than the leering, grinning, thinly-mustached men who would stick around long enough for Hilde to be forced to call them "Uncle", like "Uncle Heinrich," "Uncle Frank," and "Uncle Ernie". These she loathed with every ounce of her being. Otto, Hildegard had to admit, was the complete opposite of the Uncles. Otto was simply Otto.

"Let's get you a new dress for the Christmas party," Wilhelmina hugged her daughter around the shoulders from behind and kissed her on the cheek.

Christmas was always a jolly if busy time for the hospitable people of Himmelberg. Everyone wanted to host a Christmas party, but there were only 25 days in December until Christmas, and only 12 days of celebration of the Epiphany. The Christmas season culminated with the Dreikönigsfest, where three children from the village dressed up like the three kings—Caspar, Melchior, and Balthasar—who blessed the Holy Family with gold, frankincense, and myrrh. Hildegard, during her first year in Himmelberg, received the coveted role of Balthasar, the Macedonian king, meaning she got to paint her face and wear a turban. She and two other boys, Dan and Lars, went from house to house asking for money. Lars, the tallest of the children, wrote "C+M+B+1931" in chalk above the doors as a blessing from the Three Wise Men.

This year, the ski resort would be holding a Christmas party, and a gigantic Tannenbaum Christmas tree was hoisted into the square to commemorate the occasion. The whole town of Himmelberg gathered together, mittens wrapped around mugs of aromatic, spicy gluhwein, watching the steam from their cups twist up and intermingle with the falling snowflakes. Frau König had arranged a school choir to sing different German Christmas carols; each class sang a different song. The natural German sense of competition came out, and each class tried to outdo the other, singing louder and louder and making their parents laugh. Finally, all students came together, wrapped their arms around each other in a big circle, and swayed side to side as they sang "Stille Nacht", or "Silent Night."

"Stille Nacht, heilige Nacht

"Alles schläft; einsam wacht..."

The townspeople of Himmelberg began to sing along, and soon, the whole town square reverberated with German voices in unison. Hildegard noticed, while swaying, that one person was not singing.

Herr Zimmermann was standing very still, with tears streaming down his cheeks into his mustache, his mouth clamped shut.

"What's up with him?" Hildegard whispered.

"He's remembering The Great War," Felix whispered back. "He was there in 1914, you know, when the British and the Germans stopped shooting on Christmas night, and they all sang this song together."

Hildegard continued to sway for a moment, thought better of her idea, and decided to do it anyway. She broke from the circle of students and walked up to Herr Zimmermann, placing a mitten on his arm. He looked down into her face and smiled tearfully.

"That was the last night I had with my brother," he choked. "He was shot the next day."

Hildegard didn't know what to say. So she wrapped her arm around his and began to sway, continuing to sing. Frau Zimmermann, who had also begun to tear up, took his other arm. Johanna broke away too and took Hildegard's arm, and Felix took hers, and soon all the people of Himmelberg were linked together, arm in arm, their tearful voices rising higher and higher into the peaks:

"Da uns schlägt die rettende Stund'
"Christ, in deiner Geburt!
"Christ in deiner Geburt!"

For a moment, no one spoke. The only sound was the soft falling snowflakes on the icy cobblestones.

Then, Herr Zimmerman began to sing, in a clear, ringing tenor, "Das Deutschlandlied", the German national anthem:

"Germany, Germany above all,
"Above all in the world,
"When, for protection and defense,
"It always stands brotherly together...
"Unity and justice and freedom
"For the German Fatherland!"

The unified voices rang clear into the night, louder and louder, echoing in the valleys and peak of Mount Siegfried, echoing through the Alps. The song would be played again and again, louder and louder, in the halls of biergartens, at the start of each school day, at the beginning of every newsreel, and soon enough always accompanied by a flag of red, white, and black.

"Hey, Hilde, come here. I want to give you your Christmas present before we get to the ski lodge. I don't want Johanna to get jealous; I just picked up something for her at the Christkindlmarkt." Felix handed her a large envelope wrapped in beautiful robin's egg tissue paper with a purple ribbon.

"Oh, Felix, you shouldn't have!" Hildegard grinned, hastily unwrapping the present.

It was a portrait of her, in watercolor and oil pastel crayon. But it wasn't her… it was a forest sprite, or a valkyrie, or a faerie queen… this woman was far too beautiful to be Hildegard.

"Is this… this isn't me. She's too beautiful."

"Of course it's you, dummkopf!" Felix laughed, searching her eyes. "Do you like it?"

"Felix, I love it," she hugged him tight. "I'm going to have Mother put it in a frame, and then I'm going to hang it above my bed and hope the beauty spills down on me while I sleep!"

"You won't need much help," Felix chuckled, but it came out garbled and nervous.

"And it's a double present," Hildegard said, picking up the ribbon. "Can you tie it around my neck at the back?"

Felix obliged, his fingers trembling, and tied the thin velvet ribbon around Hildegard's neck. Felix noticed that when Hildegard came to Himmelberg, her childlike neck was scrawny, like a bobblehead's. Now, her neck sloped, swanlike, into broad shoulders. Like a woman's.

When had she changed so much? Had he changed as well? Did she notice the man's body he was growing into, or did time blindfold them as they grew up?

"Done," he placed his hands on her shoulders and left them there. Hildegard turned around.

"Thanks again, Felix," she smiled. "I'm going to take this back to the house. See you at the party!"

The ski lodge Christmas party would prove to be the social highlight of the season, much to the dismay of Frau von Braun and Herr Weissman, who were used to competing against each other, and to Frau Fischer, who liked to host enviable Christmas parties with a rotating guest list of 20 people, based on the townspeople who showed her enough respect.

Adding to the ski lodge's chicness were the outside families who had come to spend the winter holidays abroad in the scenic Alps. Among these exotic denizens were a Greek family from the embassy in Berlin, a Canadian couple, an American family, and one Belgian poet who looked very out of place but could be heard guffawing with glee down the slopes.

The American family's child, a prep school kid named Benny Woodford, bore an uncanny resemblance to Charles Lindbergh, the pilot who made it around the globe.

"We're related to him, somehow. On my mother's side. I've seen him at weddings and a few family get-togethers," Benny sounded flippant. He reminded Hildegard of when she first came to Himmelberg, trying to put on a good show of playing the chic outsider.

"He's a fascist, isn't he?" Lars said, "Charles Lindbergh?"

"What's a fascist?"

"It's someone who believes that the government shouldn't be run by weaklings," Karl said, "And that you should put the needs of your people first before trying to worry about every loafing country."

"Oh, I guess so," Benny shrugged. "I'm not much for politics; all I know about is democracy. Like what we have in the States."

"We have democracy, too, Benny," Johanna reminded him. "We have political parties in a parliament who vote on laws, and we have a chancellor."

"Is that like a president?"

"Kind of, but we also have a president, President Hindenberg. The chancellor is like the grand adviser who tells him what to do, because the chancellor is also the leader of the majority party."

"Oh, so kind of like the Speaker of the House."

Johanna shrugged unsurely. "I guess, I don't really know."

"The Speaker of the House isn't as powerful as the Chancellor," Lars said. "Remember, Johanna? We learned this in Frau Behring's class. The American system has three parts that balance each other out... the president, the judges, and the parliament. And none of them ever get anywhere because they're always pulling each other back when they try to go forward. No offense, Benny."

"None taken," said Benny, clearly offended. "But what's the point of having a President of Germany if the Chancellor just tells him what to do?"

"Exactly," Karl pointed at Benny. "That's why we're electing Hitler as Chancellor."

"Who's Hitler? Oh... is he that guy who screams a lot?"

"He doesn't scream," Karl said, affronted, "he speaks his mind. He doesn't go in for all that wishy-washy politician talk, where you say nice things and skirt all around the subject without ever actually saying what you're going to do. Hitler is a real German, and he speaks the German way—directly."

"I thought Hitler was Austrian," Johanna said.

"He was *born* in Austria, yes, but he's Bavarian, like us. If you listen to his speeches, he speaks with a Southern accent. He even fought in the Bavarian Army during the Great War."

"And who even cares about Austrian or German," Lars shrugged. "We're all Aryan, right? We all used to belong to the same empire centuries ago."

"*I* care," Karl replied, clearly repeating the opinions of his father as his own, as so many teenagers do. "The Austrians stabbed us in the back after the war, blaming us for something that was their fault. And you know who else feels that way? Hitler."

"Ugh, enough about Hitler," Ygritte rolled her eyes. "Politics bore me and it's Christmas. Can't we play a game or something?"

"Games are for kids," Louisa Schumacher said.

"I've got a game that isn't for kids," Irena smiled wickedly, producing a soda bottle. "Let's play Spin the Bottle."

"Gross," Ygritte, who was 13, said.

"I'm up for it!" Benny grinned. At which point the other girls in the group, and thereby following the boys, sat down in a circle near a broom closet, away from parents' prying eyes.

"Who should go first?" Johanna held the bottle up. "Irena?"

"Oh, I'm so nervous," Irena blushed attractively. "I couldn't possib—"

"How about Hildegard then?"

"Fine," Hildegard shrugged. Irena looked disappointed.

Hildegard took the bottle and spun it on the ground. The group *ooh'd* and *ahh'd* with mounting tension as the bottle whirled around, slower and slower, until it neared Henri, Lars, Felix...

And stopped on Benny.

"Lucky me!" Benny grinned.

"What do we do now?" Hildegard looked around.

"You go into that closet, and you have to kiss," Johanna giggled excitedly.

"Bah, you're so childish. Come on, Benny," she grabbed Benny's arm and hauled him into the closet.

37

Hildegard pulled the metal chain to turn on the light.

"Maybe… wouldn't it be better with the light off?" Benny suggested.

"You're right," Hildegard nodded, pulling the chain again.

In the dark, Hildegard felt Benny's warm, slightly clammy hands on her shoulders. She felt him pull her closer. Surprisingly, she felt her stomach become fizzy and bubbly like a soda. Is this what people meant by butterflies in the stomach? Her pulse quickened as she became aware of Benny's face gliding slowly towards hers. And then she felt his lips, unexpectedly soft and supple. She pressed her lips against his, becoming acutely aware that this was her first kiss. No kisses on the forehead from Mother or kisses on the cheek from little tykes, this was *real kissing*. Benny, apparently more adept at this than Hildegard, opened her mouth with his own and began sucking on her lower lip. This made her feel *very* good, and she wrapped her arms around him tighter. She began sucking on his lips, proud of herself for being such a natural kisser. It was probably genetic, she probably got it from her mother, who used to kiss other men professionally, and other stuff… God, no, why was she thinking about her mother with other men right now? Block it out, concentrate on the moment…

It was at this point when Benny's hand moved down to Hildegard's breast.

"Hey, what are you doing?" Hildegard stepped back.

"Oh, sorry. Wow, it's really pointy. I wasn't expecting that."

"That's because I'm wearing a bra, arschloch. Who raised you to go squeezing random girls' titties?"

"Sorry, sorry," Benny said, clicking the light on. "That wasn't right. It just… seemed like the next natural step."

"Well don't go assuming what the next step is until you get *my* permission, got it, dummkopf?" Hildegard adjusted the bra under her shirt and tucked it back into her skirt.

"Yes, ma'am."

"Okay, you don't have to call me ma'am. It was a nice kiss, before you got grabby. Now we have to go out and act like nothing special at all in the world happened. How's my hair?"

Benny reached out to smooth it down on the side. "Looks perfect."

"Okay. Take my hand. Let's walk out in three, two, one."

They emerged from the closet looking cool as cucumbers to the roaring applause of the boys.

"That's how *German* women do it, Uncle Ben," Hildegard said archly.

"Uncle *Sam*," Benny laughed. "Uncle Ben is a box of rice."

"Whatever," Hildegard chuckled and sat back down.

"How was it?" Johanna whispered as the group chattered away.

"It was... really nice. I wasn't expecting it to be... spicy?"

Johanna let out a belt of laughter and snorted, which caused everyone to laugh harder. Hildegard was grinning and turned to look at Felix, who was staring at her like she just shot his pet dog.

"Let's see, who should go next?" Irena said.

"I'll go," Louisa volunteered. She took the bottle and spun it so quickly, it clattered across the floor and hit Felix's shoe.

"Ohh, Louisa and Felix! Your turn!"

Felix stood up quickly. "This game is juvenile. I'm going home."

"Boo, big baby," Karl yelled. "Merry Christmas, Ebenezer Scrooge!"

Felix stalked out.

Johanna and Hildegard exchanged glances. "I'll go check on him," Hildegard offered.

"Make sure he takes his coat," Johanna said. "He always forgets his stuff when he's in a melodramatic mood."

Hildegard grabbed Felix's coat and hustled outside, careful not to slip on the icy cobblestones. She hurried to catch up with Felix, who was halfway down the road to the town square.

"Felix!" she huffed. "You forgot your coat!"

"You keep it," Felix grunted. "I don't need it."

"You'll freeze your ass off in this snow, dummy," Hildegard cut him off and threw it at him. Felix sighed in exasperation and pulled the coat on hastily.

"There, now leave me alone and go back to the party. I'm sure you're having *such* fun."

"Felix, what's with you?" Hildegard demanded angrily. "Don't be a priss, just come out and say it!"

"Fine!" Felix spun around. "You want to know what's bothering me? I wanted it to be *me*, not Benny, not some random Yankee-Doodle-asshole who... who got to share that special moment with you..." He blushed fiercely.

Hildegard raised her eyebrows.

"Why do you think I drew that picture for *you*, and not also for Johanna?" Felix said, opening his hands in a rhetorical gesture.

Hildegard sighed and rolled her eyes. "Felix, you dummkopf," she said, putting her hands on his shoulders and smashing her face into his. After a moment, she pulled her face away with an enormous *smack*.

"There, happy?"

Felix stared agape at her, as if he had seen a sign from The Madonna. "Does this... does this mean you'll be my girlfriend now?"

"Ugh, Felix! Don't overcomplicate it!"

"But why would you kiss me if you didn't like me?"

"A kiss isn't love, Felix. I'm not interested in love; I'm just interested in existing. But," she put her hand on his shoulder, "a friend means more to me than a boyfriend. Boyfriends come and go, Felix. A friend shares a piece of your soul."

Christmas was over, and a new year meant a new Germany. Adolf Hitler was officially elected Chancellor of Germany in January, and in three months, the first German democracy known as The Weimar Republic came to an end.

One month later, the Nazi Party quietly established a prison uniquely built for housing the opponents to the Nazi Regime: communists, socialists, political prisoners.

They called it Dachau.

The first concentration camp.

4

1934: Cinema

Over the summer, in addition to her chores on the Richter's property, Hildegard volunteered to help refurbish the movie theater. Otto had gone to oversee some business at the steel factory he owned, and Hildegard had asked him for a new book.

"We'll see," Otto said.

"I've read *Faust* four times already!" Hildegard protested. "And I've just about exhausted the school librarian. I want a challenge!"

"Hm," Otto grunted noncommittally.

"If you want a challenge, why don't you help scrub the grout in the bathroom?" Wilhelmina said.

"Can't," Hildegard said hastily, grabbing a peach from the fruit bowl, "I promised I would help Herr Weber install the new seat cushions today. Tschüss!"

Otto let out a guttural sigh out of the back of his nose. "Too much time in the theater."

"You know, I was in a movie."

Otto turned back to look at Wilhelmina. "Which one?"

"Oh, you wouldn't have heard of it. It was very artistic," Wilhelmina waved it away.

"Was Charlie Chaplin in it?" Otto asked seriously.
Wilhelmina laughed.

At the movie theater, Hildegard was unscrewing the moldy old seat cushions and hauling them out to the back alley. Herr Schumacher, a carpenter, was helping install the new seat bottoms, as well as patching up the roof.

"What are you going to do with the old cushions?" Hildegard said. "Are you going to burn them?"

"No, no. These are hard times for many people in the village. And although the seats may be warped and cracked, someone might appreciate the free lumber." Herr Weber said, attacking the large crate of new seat bottoms with a crowbar.

"Herr Weber! You're seventy-three years old, let me do that," Herr Schumacher hastily snatched the crowbar away from him.

"Why don't you use the wood from the seat bottoms to repair the roof?" Hildegard counted ten seats out and sat them by the first row to be screwed in.

"I can pay for a new roof. I'm old, and I'm not planning on taking my money with me."

Herr Weber was a fixture in the community of Himmelberg, the town's fantastical. Though not originally from Himmelberg, Herr Weber took his ailing wife up to the Alps for the warm seasons to "take the air," as was the 19th century cure for unprecedented Industrial Era pollution. Herr Weber was from money, rumored to be a distant relative of Kaiser Wilhelm himself. This was never verified by Herr Weber; the townspeople merely assumed he came from some kind of distant royalty because he always did whatever the hell he wanted, therefore he *must* not be from the socially-burdened middle class.

Eventually, Frau Weber died in Munich, at the age of 47. It was her express wish not to be buried in the family tomb, but at the top of

Mount Siegfried, where she felt truly at home.

The whole village, who had grown fond of their quirky summertime visitors, helped haul Freyja's coffin up to the very top of Mount Siegfried. Jakob Zimmermann, Matthias Schumacher, Otto Richter, Max Klein, Oscar Wolff, and Paul Kraus, Karl's father, had been pallbearers. They pulled Freyja's coffin up in a wagon led by two sturdy donkeys, and when the wagon would go no further, the six men shouldered the coffin a mile and a half up to the peak. The whole village was in attendance. Even Frau von Braun and Herr Weissman came to a truce that day, serving cold beer to all.

The Königs, Frau Peterson, and Herr Schmidt brought out their old alpen horns, long wooden horns like a tuba that stretched 13 feet long, and played in beautiful harmony. The sonorous quartet's melody softly drifted out over the hills, intermingling with the call of larks and warblers, and the piercing cry of a brown eagle as it soared overhead.

"Freyja, you clever girl," Herr Weber huffed, looking all around him. "You don't have to climb very much farther to reach the gates of heaven."

It was a spectacular view for a grave site. Surrounding Mount Siegfried were the soaring Alps, stretching up and up and up like dragon's teeth. Even in the middle of July, at the tippy tops of these colossal magnificent mountains, snow lay like whipped cream dolloped on the peaks. The snow stood out against the brilliant blazing azure sky, which yawned like a holy mouth across the horizon. The peaks swooped down into bright green meadows, nearly lime-green grass that was cropped close by lowing brown milk cows, trundling along with their clanging bells. The air was cold and crisp and fragrant with wildflowers, brilliant orchid purple and butter yellow. The meadows cascaded down and down into deep ravines, where thrillingly cold turquoise water cut clear paths through the oldest mountains in the world. It was as if the land itself was molded with special care by the hand of God.

A little plaque on a stone read: "Here lies Freyja Weber, a pure spirit whom God has taken into the air." It is there to this day, and it will be there long after the wars to come.

When the time came for Herr Weber to go back and handle family or business affairs or whatever usually pulled him back to the more cosmopolitan Munich, Herr Weber simply didn't go. He felt quite content to stay, and he had remained in Himmelberg for 13 years.

"You could probably just send the cushions off to be reupholstered, Herr Weber," Herr Schumacher said. "My cousin in Munich could do it for you; we've been cobblers and upholsterers since before Wagner."

"That's very kind, Matthias," Herr Weber smiled, holding up the bottom of a seat. "But, look, the damp has cracked the seat bottoms: we don't want Frau von Braun taking a seat and falling smack on her keister."

"I'd sure like to see it," chuckled Hildegard.

"Well... I hope you earn your money back," Herr Schumacher said uncertainly.

"Bah, I have enough money. Money can't bring back Freyja. But money can make you forget your troubles for a little while, and God knows we have plenty of them in Germany."

"Hopefully not much longer," Herr Schumacher said. In the paper four days ago, Himmelberg received word that President Paul von Hindenberg was dead from lung cancer. The town was decorated somberly with black crepe bunting hanging from the windows, and some townspeople were wearing a black cuff on their arm to show mourning for the President of the Weimar Republic.

Still, not everyone was in mourning. Many were hopeful that Adolf Hitler would provide the charisma and strong leadership to put Germany back on the map as a major world power.

"Or at least out under the thumb of the Allied countries, those backstabbers of the Treaty of Versailles," Herr Schumacher screwed in a seat bottom, making sure the hinges were oiled as he pushed it back and forth.

"I wouldn't put all my hopes in Adolf Hitler," Herr Weber cautioned. "I don't like this new title of his, Chancellor and Leader. We never had a *Führer* in our constitution before."

"The other parties are there to make sure he doesn't go too far," Herr Schumacher shrugged. "Anyway, it can't be worse than having a namby-pamby president who bends to anyone. Hitler won't let bastards like Brüning boss us around without the consent of the people. I read that he plans on having a vote—not of the party leaders, but every voter in Germany—approving of his title as *Führer und Reichskanzler.*"

"And if Germany votes no? What is he going to do, crawl under a rock?"

"Probably not, but it's a nice gesture."

"When you've lived as long as I have, my boy, you learn that politicians make nice gestures all the time, but their agenda is their own."

"You're just cynical. There are plenty of civil servants who work hard for the people."

"That may be, but I don't think Adolf Hitler will be a civil servant."

"Papa! I'm here!" Louisa's brother, Ralf, called. Ralf was a lanky 17-year-old.

"Excellent, Ralf. I need you to help me haul this lumber to the roof. Hold the ladder."

The seats were installed, the roof was thatched, and neon in the marquee was repaired. The movie theater's grand re-opening premiered with Josef von Sternberg's by-then classic, *The Blue Angel,* starring a slinky young Marlene Dietrich.

Hildegard watched, ensnared, as Marlene Dietrich sumptuously moved her way around the screen, reminding Hildegard of her mother at Babbel. Marlene Dietrich walked the same tightrope between angelface and femme fatale.

Hildegard felt her hair rise on her arms when Lola Lola, Marlene Dietrich's nightclub singer persona, said in a husky, velvet voice: "What's the matter, cat got your tongue?"

She practiced it in front of the mirror for weeks afterward.

"She reminds me so much of you," Hildegard gushed to her mother, when they were alone doing the dishes. "The way it was at Babbel."

"Bah, don't speak of that place. And that movie very much glamorizes what it's like to be a nightclub singer. Except for the awful little randy boys, that much is true. Last I heard, Babbel was closed down."

"Why?" Hildegard said, alarmed.

"Oh, management issues. Herr Meyerowitz was a Jew, and Otto says they're cracking down on shady Jew-owned businesses, like nightclubs. Anyway, we all know what went on behind those doors, and most of those people will have to go out and find a decent living in the new Reich. Like I did."

Hildegard was silent, drying the plates.

"You know what I *do* miss?" Wilhelmina smiled. "I miss being in movies. I was only in a few arthouse movies, but my greatest achievement was—apart from having you, dearest—working with my favorite director, Fritz Lang."

"What movie were you in?"

"Oh, it was a minor role in *From the Darkness Rising.* I played a moon priestess that tries to enslave the scientist astronaut. I wore a jeweled headband, and I did my best Theda Bara, and I had to point like this," she stood statuesque and slowly raised her left finger, pointing at the air in front of her, bulging her eyes and tilting her chin.

"We should show it at the movie theater!"

"Mein Gott, nein! I don't want anyone in Himmelberg associating me with my old life or poking around in my past. It would be infuriating to me and humiliating to Otto." Wilhelmina paused. "But I can give you some good recommendations, based on my old colleague's work."

The next film reel Herr Weber received was Fritz Lang's 1930 thriller, *M*. Hildegard went to see it with Wilhelmina. Wilhelmina explained the camerawork and what it was like doing multiple takes in a hushed voice. Afterwards, Hildegard went to the biergarten with her friends from school.

"My favorite part was watching Peter Lorre's performance as the killer. When he's about to pounce on the little girl, and she runs to her mother, and he has to control himself, but he can't stop whistling the song..." Hildegard sighed. "So suspenseful!"

"I thought it was great, really clever. I thought it was going to be a cop-and-robbers kind of movie, but when the underground gang of criminals band together to find the child killer, I thought that was a great twist," Johanna said.

"My favorite part was when the criminal carves a hole into the basement trying to find the child killer, and he comes out and the police have him surrounded, and he puts his hands up and says 'But I really *am* innocent this time!'" Lars laughed.

"It takes one to know one, I guess."

"I mean that's what's so interesting about the movie," Felix continued Johanna's thought. "It's not really about the killer, it's about the community. The major question of the movie is: how far would you go for justice, for payback? Would you break the law? If they had let the police do all the work, they wouldn't have caught him."

"Or maybe they would have caught him, but he wouldn't have been brought to justice, because of lack of evidence. That's always why criminals go free."

"Hildegard, my favorite part was also the child killer. I really liked how they cast a baby face guy and they never show him actually killing the little girls," Louisa said.

"Ach! What kind of filth are you talking about?" Frau von Braun said, refilling their beer. "Children shouldn't be watching that kind of pulpy trash!"

"It's *cinema*, Frau von Braun," Hildegard protested.

"Cinema my arsch," she blustered on, refilling everyone's drinks. "I remember when moving pictures were invented, and they were mostly nudie pictures of hussies!"

This caused the group to burst into suppressed snorts and snickers. As Frau von Braun lumbered off, Louisa continued, "They never show him killing little girls, and he looks so afraid as the gang hunting him down is closing in, you almost feel sorry for him. He's like a rat in a trap."

"Like a Jew," Karl said.

"He *is* a Jew," Hildegard corrected. "His real name is Laszlo Lowenstein."

"I guess that's where he got his inspiration," Karl laughed.

"I'll tell you what," Henri said, "If there were a sexual deviant in this town, and I found him, I wouldn't wait for the police to do anything about it. I'd rip his balls off right there in the street."

"Yeah, yeah," Johanna rolled her eyes.

"I'm serious," Henri said emphatically. "If you kill a child, you don't deserve to live. I think they should get the automatic death penalty, straight to the electric chair, and the parents of the dead child should get to flip the switch."

"The electric chair is too quick a death," Karl said. "They should have to suffer. They should be begging for death by the end of it."

"And not just child killers," Johanna said. "Rapists too."

"And elder abusers," Louisa said. "People who swindle other people out of their money instead of getting a decent job of their own."

"And tax evaders!" Lars joked, which broke the tension and made everyone laugh.

"One thing's for sure," Karl said. "*M* could beat any American movie: *Frankenstein, King Kong,* any of them. I bet Germany will overtake Hollywood by 1940!"

"Absolutely!" Hildegard agreed.

When Hildegard came home, her mother was fixing creamy asparagus soup.

"Otto is home; wash up for dinner."

"Yes, Mutti."

When Hildegard entered her bedroom, she noticed something that was not there before. Three books were stacked on her desk: *Candide,* by Voltaire; *The Prince,* by Machiavelli; and a red-and-black signed copy of *Mein Kampf,* by Adolf Hitler.

"You said you wanted a challenge," Otto said from the doorway.

"What are they about?"

"Philosophy."

"I love them already."

"The first two were hard to come by; many French books aren't available in the city anymore. And you should hold on to that signed copy; it will probably be worth something someday."

Hildegard hurried up to Otto and hugged him before he could move stiffly away.

"Thank you, Otto," she looked up at him and smiled.

"Okay."

When school started back, Hildegard was surprised by the change in curriculum.

"Fraulein Dansig?" Hildegard raised her hand. "We had German Literature last year. I thought 10th years were supposed to have World Literature?"

"Frau König has discussed this with the school board, and we all agree it won't hurt to have a deeper knowledge of a curriculum that is more closely aligned with German values and German culture," Fraulein Dansig smiled, handing out the required readings.

Hildegard looked down and read the syllabus:

The Sorrows of Young Werther, by Johann Goethe
Die Nibelungenlied
Simplicius Simplicissimus, by Hans von Grimmelshausen
Debit and Credit, by Gustav Freytag
Effi Briest, by Theodor Fontane
Mein Kampf, by Adolf Hitler

"What happened to the old books?" Felix asked.

"They're still in the library. We've created a new section titled *Non-German Works.* It's organized by country. You're welcome to continue to read world literature, but in the classroom, we want to make sure you are prepared for German citizenship, and the sense of loyalty it requires."

"Why do we have to be loyal to read a book?" Louisa asked.

"Who cares? Homework is homework," Karl shrugged. "We're still going to learn."

"Absolutely right, Lars," Fraulein Dansig nodded. "I don't want to discourage any of my students from broadening their minds. Why, the Führer himself has a library stocked full of classics from all over the world, like *Uncle Tom's Cabin, Gulliver's Travels,* and *Robinson Crusoe.*"

"If the Führer can read those books, why can't we?"

"You can," said Fraulein Dansig, running an exasperated hand across her forehead. "They're in the library."

"Can we start?" Irena turned back and cast a look at Hildegard. "Am I the only one who wants to learn something today?"

"Good point, Irena. Let's get ready to take some notes. Germany has a rich history of storytelling, dating all the way back to the middle ages. Many of the beloved stories people tell their children all over the world had their genesis right here, in the Black Forest of Southern Germany..."

Hildegard obediently scribbled down notes onto her journal. Irena and Karl had a point, she supposed. Reading is reading; learning is learning. If she wanted to learn about the outside world, she could always go to the library or have Otto procure more classics for her when he went into the city for business.

Meanwhile, at the city's university, college students dumped copies of Ernest Hemingway's *A Farewell to Arms,* Helen Keller's *How I Became a Socialist,* Leo Tolstoy's *War and Peace*—even German WWI veteran Erich Remarque's *All Quiet on the Western Front,* which describes the horrors of war—into a big pile in the campus square, and lit them aflame, raising their arms in a stiff salute.

5

1935, Part One: The Plot and the Poster

Gerda was absolutely hung up on Luka Lange. Hildegard could understand why: Luka was tall, tall, tall. The tallest young man in the village. When he walked into Frau Lehmann's grocery, he had to stoop over and tilt his head.

"So then Frau Neumann comes in here, and she's demanding a refund for the dress because she says it's unflattering and cheaply cut, and I say 'Look, Frau Neumann, I don't make the dresses, but if you hoisted those things up instead of letting them hang to the floor—'" she stopped; her eyes widened. "Oh, look, there's Luka Lange," she said, as casually as possible.

"Do you like him?" Hildegard smiled cynically, knowing the answer already.

"No," Gerda blushed, "I'm just—"

"I don't think he's going to come in here to buy a dress, Gerda," Hildegard arched an eyebrow.

"Ugh, you're right," she groaned, slumping over and plopping her cheek on her fist. "He's never going to notice me. I'm always in here and he's always out God knows where in the wilderness. He lives with his family out on a farm three miles from here. He's got, like, sixteen brothers and sisters."

"I guess you'll just have to be unrequited lovers, then."

"I guess so," Gerda slumped her head into her arms, her auburn hair spilling over. "It wouldn't be so bad, but I get so *lonely* here. There aren't any men in this town anymore ever since they reinstated conscription; now they're all off playing army and marching around in those stupid brown suits," she grumpily plunked her chin down on top of her arms.

"Why doesn't Luka join the army?"

"I don't know, I've hardly ever spoken to him," Gerda sighed, sitting up. "But I'm sure glad he's around to have something nice to look at."

"I'll see what I can do," Hildegard said, walking out.

"No, Hilde, don't go talk to him!"

"I'm not going to talk to him, I promise."

Instead, Hildegard talked to Luka's sister, who was in her class. Esther Lange had dark brown hair, and she didn't cut it into a shoulder length bob or curl it like the other girls. It was clean, brushed, and kept in a low ponytail, away from her face. She also wore plain clothes; Hildegard suspected she had never been into the dress shop and been attended by Gerda.

Hildegard sat next to Esther before class. "Hey, Esther, right?"

"Yeah," Esther pulled out her books.

"I'm Hildegard."

"I know who you are," Esther chuckled, turning her green eyes on Hildegard. "I remember the first day you came to Himmelberg."

"I don't remember you at the kid's table."

"I was there, but we left early. My family avoids drunkenness, so we try to steer clear of Von Breissman before they get too pushy."

"Von Breissman," Hildegard echoed, laughing.

"Yeah. They're always at each other's throats; I always expect them to crash into each other in a tangled embrace, like the movies," Esther giggled.

"Speaking of which," Hildegard said casually, bouncing the eraser on her pencil in a subconscious gesture of getting to the point. "I have a little gossip to share."

Esther raised her eyebrows, smiling.

"You know Gerda Roth? She works in the trachten store. I think she has a thing for your brother."

"Which one? I have six."

"Luka."

"Ugh, big dummy," Esther rolled her eyes. "He sure doesn't know about it. My father is always on his case about keeping his head out of the clouds."

"Oh, so he's a dreamer?"

"Yes, to a fault. He used to be in charge of the sheep. My parents thought: *Eh, why not make him a shepherd? He likes to be alone with his thoughts anyway.* But he always daydreams, and the sheep would be lost, and we would have to go out into the night calling for them. One time a sheep even wandered into Zum Hirschen. So, no more shepherd's duty for Luka."

"Maybe the army would be a good place to give him some grounding."

"He cannot join," Esther said, darting her eyes around the room.

"Why not? Does he have an injury?"

Esther took a beat. "It's against our religion to join the military."

"Oh. Are you pacifists?"

Esther thought about this. "I would consider us to be neutral. It's not like we believe in lying down like a dog and letting someone stab you. We believe in self-defense, but we don't believe the government should tell us when to kill. Only God has that power."

"So if God told you to kill me, right now, you would do it?" Irena said, turning in her seat.

55

"You're lucky God isn't telling her to smack you upside the head," Hildegard said.

"Hildegard, why are you always such a bitch to me?" Irena cried.

"Why are you always instigating?" Felix said from across the room.

"It's like you think your dad being the mayor makes you special," Henri added.

Irena recoiled. "I don't think that."

"You never hang out with us at the biergarten, and you always walk around like you're better than us," Henri continued.

Irena's lip quivered. "You don't understand what it's like, none of you do. You don't know what it means to have everyone always looking at you all the time, to have to be Miss Perfect because your father's career depends on being popular…"

"Yeah, that must be tough," Lars rolled his eyes.

"I always have to go to these stupid events with my family," Irena persisted. "I *want* to hang out at the biergarten, but Mother says it wouldn't be dignified, and you never invite me anyway."

Esther took a long look at her. "I understand, Irena."

Irena turned to Esther in shock. "*You* do?"

"Yes," Esther said. "You want to support your parents, because you love them, but at what point can you just be *you*?"

Irena quickly wiped at her eye. "That's… that's it *exactly*."

"Alright, young people, open up your textbooks to page 67," Herr Pfeiffer said, coming in from a smoke break with the other teachers.

"Today we're discussing quantum mechanics… one of my favorite topics. Many German scientists have made major contributions to the field of physics. Indeed, some scientists believe you may see a German man walking on the moon in your lifetime."

"I have, in that old Fritz Lang movie," Karl interrupted, and everyone chuckled.

"And it will all be thanks to the work of German scientists laying the groundwork," Herr Pfeiffer continued, ignoring Karl. "People like Wernher von Braun, Werner Heisenberg, Max Born, and my old colleague, Max Planck."

"And Albert Einstein," Felix added.

"Ehm... no," Herr Pfeiffer said.

"But you said that Max Planck—"

"Albert Einstein is a Jew, and he no longer is a German citizen, so he is not included in the list," Herr Pfeiffer said quickly.

"Will we be learning about Einstein's theory of relativity at all this year?" Henri asked.

"No, we will be focusing on German contributions to science," Herr Pfeiffer said, eyes darting toward the door. "You are German students, who will someday be inventing new theories and making progress not only for the good of the world, but for the good of Germany, so it's best to learn where you came from."

"But science didn't just come from—"

"I will not have any more arguments in my class!" Herr Pfeiffer said, raising his voice. The class sat back in their seats, anxious: Herr Pfeiffer never yelled at them before. "Now, if anyone has anything else to say about the course curriculum, you may head straight for Frau König's office and take it up with her. Am I clear?"

"Yes, Herr Pfeiffer," the class said in unison.

"I can't believe he yelled at us like that," Johanna said. "He's always been such a sweet old goof."

"People naturally get grumpier as they get older," Henri said. "It's certainly happening to my grandpa. All he yells about is damn Nazis, damn government, damn dry schnitzel..."

"Do you think they'll make him retire, like they did with Fraulein Varga?"

"No, they made her retire because she was whacko," Karl said.

Fraulein Varga was an ancient, witchy woman who dressed in bohemian clothing. She was actually Hungarian, and brought it up all the time, especially during lectures on the Franco-Prussian War. She wore long, fringed shawls that dragged on the floor, and she smelled vaguely of pipe smoke and cat piss.

Fraulein Varga had lived a bohemian lifestyle in Vienna, she described frequently, but never would say why she had taken a post in quiet, docile Himmelberg. It had something to do with the Great War; she lost a son or a lover or a brother or something, and she wanted to flee the memories of what was ripped away from her.

Fraulein Varga was in the middle of a unit on the Napoleonic Wars—"Listen, students, beware of Little Napoleon! Little men with big mouths who want to rule it all. So, too, did Julius Caesar... so always the tyrant!"—when she was politely asked to leave. The official story was that she had been "transferred to another school", but the students knew the score.

"I heard she was a secret Communist," Louisa said. "And when they found out, they arrested her."

"I doubt that," Felix said. "Anyway, I'd rather have a kook than Herr Schulz."

"I *like* Herr Schulz," Louisa countered.

"Of course you do; he's the youngest male teacher in the school," Felix raised an eyebrow.

As a replacement for Fraulein Varga, Himmelberg brought in a fresh-faced young college graduate from Berlin, Friedrich Schulz. He had blonde hair that looked like corn silk, which he kept combed slick to the side in a brassy sheen. He had blue eyes that were clear and piercing like the sky. He had a very white smile, and he had all of his teeth, and they were very straight. And he had a red cuff that he wore on his arm with a black and white circle, and a black swastika in the middle.

"I like your patch," Louisa said, blushing as red as the cuff as she touched Herr Schulz's arm.

"It's a swastika," Herr Schulz flashed one of his winning smiles. "It's an ancient symbol for good fortune and long life, and it stretches as far back as the Persian Empire. There are golden cups belonging to King Xerxes with swastikas on them."

"King Xerxes was the one from the Bible, right?" Lars said. "The one who married Esther?"

"Ooh, Esther!" Johanna cooed at Esther, who submerged her head into her history textbook.

"Yes, Lars. He was married to a Hebrew. He also squashed the brave 300 Spartans at Thermopylae, which was good fortune, but he met his end at the hand of his own son."

"I guess that's your luck when you're married to a Jew," Karl said, and Herr Schulz laughed.

"Haha, good one, Karl! You're right about that."

"Gosh," Louisa batted her eyes. "You know *so* much about history."

"That's why I became a teacher," Herr Schulz smiled magnanimously. "Now, let's begin our lesson, shall we? I understand Fraulein Varga was in the middle of the Napoleonic wars, but I'd like to take you back a few centuries to get a more complete picture of European history."

Herr Schulz pulled down a map of Europe and pointed with a meter stick. "Open your composition books and write, in large capital letters, five letters: A-R-Y-A-N. Aryan. These are our people. This is our heritage. The whole of German strength—all human culture, all results of art, science, and technology are tied up in the presence of the Aryan."

"I know that one," Hildegard said, looking up. "That's from *Mein Kampf.*"

"*Very* good, Hildegard! Excellent! Someone's been doing her reading," Herr Schulz winked. Louisa bit her lip and exchanged glances with Hildegard, mouthing the word *lucky!* "But where does the Aryan come from? The answer to that question goes back to over 1100 years ago: with the Vikings. These brave Norsemen of Scandinavia went—with just boats and axes and simple tools, mind you, and mostly brute strength—and conquered most of Northern Europe. The Vikings were in North America before the Pilgrims! So too, is American culture bound with the Aryan. In fact, the more you look into ancient history, the more you will see the influence of these proud predecessors of the Germanic people.

"The Vikings had red, blonde, and snow blonde hair, and blue eyes. So dominant were their genes that they went and changed the genetic makeup of the peoples of Europe. For example, what color hair do Irish people have?"

"Red?" Lars volunteered.

"Red, precisely! Ireland is known for their ginger-haired citizens. But did you know what color hair the people of Ireland had *before* the Vikings got there?"

The class was silent.

"Black! That's where we get the term 'Black Irish'. The Aryan Vikings were so strong and so virile, they went in, mated with every woman on the island, and changed their hair from black to red! How about that!"

Now it was the boys' turn to chortle and exchange glances at the word 'mated'.

"The Vikings' Aryan blood is so strong, it courses through the veins of most Europeans, with the exception of Mediterranean peoples, Roma, and of course Jews. This explains why Mediterranean peoples are inclined to laziness, Roma are inclined to thievery, and Jews are inclined to lying and debasing themselves. Meanwhile, Aryan blood is what inclines the German peoples to labor, progress, and community."

This statement made everyone sit up a little straighter in their desks, look a little prouder.

"And it is this blood, this gene, that the Führer wishes to strengthen in each of you. In you lies the key to our freedom from the bondage Germany has been in for the past 17 years. Only by tapping into this raw potential, this ancestral strength, the way the Vikings did, can Germany climb back to the global superpower it was, and deserves to be."

This elicited cheers and applause from the boys, which spread to the rest of the class. Herr Schulz smiled and put a hand over his heart, then waved his hands down.

"Alright, alright. This brings me to an announcement. When I was at university back in Berlin, there were special clubs for boys and girls like you. Or should I say, for young men and women. These clubs teach you how to harness this strength, but they also teach you the basics of German citizenship, which you are one year away from entering. I would like to introduce this club to the school children here, and I need your help in encouraging and recruiting the others."

He pulled out two posters and tacked them up on the walls on either side of the chalkboard. The posters showed a young man and a young woman, respectively. The young man was blonde and ruddy, almost a carbon copy of Herr Shulz himself, but he also looked like Karl, and Lars, and Henri, and Felix. This man looked out under a strong brow, grinning at the whole world ahead of him with very white teeth and an angular, masculine chin. He was also very fit and muscular. In fact, if he had dark hair and an S on his chest, he would be a dead ringer for Superman. The young man was wearing a brown shirt, very similar to the brown suits Hildegard remembered from her childhood in Berlin. He firmly gripped a pole, which was flying a red flag with a swastika on it. The red matched his ruddy cheeks, and the white background of the swastika emblem matched his pearly smile. At the bottom, in scripted black letters, was an inscription: "The German

Student: working for the Leader and the People."

The girl's poster was drawing whispers and gasps. The girl had golden braids, long and flowing past her shoulders, waving in the wind with the Nazi flag she carried. She too was bright and ruddy, like Cinderella gone camping, with tan skin and rosy cheeks that had been kissed by the sun. She was grinning hopefully with cobalt blue eyes at whatever bright future was ahead of her. In her strong, sinuous right arm she grasped a flagpole; her left arm was pointing, leading the way. Her svelte figure was robed in a dark blue skirt and a clean white button-up shirt. Hildegard noticed, as the boys were whispering and giggling, that the shirt was slightly see-through, and the young woman's brasier was faintly visible. She had pockets over her breasts, but the buttons on the pockets looked vaguely like perky nipples.

And, Hildegard realized with mixed feelings, the poster bore a strong resemblance to herself.

"She looks like you!" Johanna gasped.

"No, she looks like *you*," Hildegard deferred.

"No, my hair is white-blonde. *You* have golden hair. Look, you're even wearing braids today, like a little Bavarian angel," Johanna reached over and mussed up her hair. Hildegard chuckled and swatted her away.

"Hmm, could be, Fraulein Richter," Herr Schulz winked. "Maybe you and this *Jungmädel* are related?"

"I don't have any blood relatives alive that I know of, other than my mother. What's a *Jungmädel*?"

"The clubs are separated by gender. The boys are a part of *Der Hitler-Jugend*, The Hitler Youth. The girls are a part of the *Jungmädel*, The Young Maidens. The club is for 14-to-18-year-olds, like yourself. Although there are clubs for the younger kiddies too, called the *Jungvolk*."

"What do they do in the clubs?"

"Well, the *Hitler-Jugend* prepares boys to be men. You'll learn things like marching, camping—which I'm sure you already know a lot about, but the city slickers in Berlin were considerably lacking in outdoors skills—swimming, racing. And when you join, you get a special knife that says *Blood and Honor* on it."

"Sounds fun! Sign me up," Karl grinned.

"But that's not all. In the summer, you get to go to summer camp, and you march in parades, and, I really shouldn't be saying this," he leaned in conspiratorially, "you get excused from school."

A chorus of triumphant *yes!*es and cheers rang through the class.

"I know, I know, don't tell your parents. I was young too, not so long ago. Your youth should be spent doing more than wasting away inside and copying notes—which we're going to get back to in one moment, Lars, don't put that notebook away—it should be spent making friends and comrades, and it should be spent preparing you to be patriotic young men and women."

The class continued to whisper ("Are you going to sign up? I'm going to sign up." "Hell yes I'm signing up, if it gets me out of school!") as Herr Schulz went back to his lesson. Hildegard tried to keep her mind on her notes, but her eyes darted of their own accord continuously up the poster of the blonde girl with the braids. *That* girl looked like she could do anything. *Be* anything. She looked like she had her whole life figured out, under control. She also looked like a size D cup, Hildegard noted enviously.

Herr Schulz called Hildegard over after class. "Hildegard, are you going to sign up?"

Hildegard pursed her lips and hid a smile shyly. "I don't know yet."

"You should. The other kids in class look to you for leadership. You're a role model to them. It will make others want to join, too."

Hildegard blanched. "Really?"

63

"Sure, sure! You don't notice it, but you've got great leadership and untapped potential."

"Must be that Aryan blood, eh?" Hildegard winked.

"Yes, that must be it! But seriously, consider it. There's no pressure, Hilde, but I know everyone will have more fun if you're there. And I know it would make your parents proud, too."

Hildegard ran to catch up with Esther. "Esther, I've got a plan."

The two girls had joined in a holy pact of matchmakership: the plan was to smash Luka and Gerda together.

"I was thinking about what you said about Von Breissman: how you wish they would smash into each other in a tangled embrace, just like the movies. And then I had it! Eureka! We use the movies!" Hilegard opened her hands and gestured to the invisible array of romantic cinema that was before her.

"Brilliant! Luka will love it because he gets lost in his imagination," Esther grinned.

"And Gerda will love it because it's in the dark," Hildegard wiggled her eyebrows.

"What movie should we make them see?"

"I've got the perfect movie: *The Bride of Frankenstein.* I've been wanting to see it *so* badly. I know the other kids will, too, because we've pretty much rubbed holes in the reels of *The Mummy, Dracula, and Frankenstein,* we've watched them so much. *Everybody* loves a monster movie. It's a perfect pretense for being there! Plus," she added, wiggling her shoulders, "it's a romance. *Bride* of Frankenstein. Marriage. Kissing."

"And," Esther added, "I've heard that the best place to take a date is somewhere scary, like a haunted house, because their heart rate elevates and the brain confuses it with when you fall in love. A monster movie will definitely scare the two of them into falling in love."

"It's a perfect plan," Hildegard said. "Boo! I love you!"
Which made the two girls burst into tearful laughter.

Their plan ran into a hitch, however. On Friday night, Hildegard was appalled to see Herr Weber taking down the letters from the marquee.

"Herr Weber, what's going on?"

"Oh, Hilde," Herr Weber was clearly trying to mask his disappointment. "Here you are. I'm afraid we won't be able to show *Bride of Frankenstein* tonight."

"What?! Why? Is there something wrong with the film?"

"Yes," came Herr Schulz's voice as he walked out of the theater, carrying the round leather canisters that film reel came in. "It's American."

"But, Herr Schulz," Hildegard protested. "We... we had everything planned. We all love the Universal monster movies. We've been watching them for years!"

"Bah, that trash," Herr Schulz rolled his eyes. "American pop culture will rot your brain, Hildegard. You should watch something with a little more pulp; it's good for your character. Have you ever heard of German expressionist cinema?"

"Yes," Hildegard perked up. "I love Fritz Lang's *M.*"

"Me too! What a wonderful film. A German film. That's what we should be showing," he tilted his head up to Herr Weber. "Right, Herr Weber?"

Herr Weber smiled nervously.

"But Herr Schulz," Hildegard continued her protest. "We... we had plans. Certain people were supposed to come to this movie... everyone's coming to see it. It's a new movie, too, and we don't get many brand-new movies this far into the mountains. What will we do now?"

Herr Schulz cocked an eyebrow, smiling knowingly. No doubt he had overhead Hildegard and Esther plotting the meet cute. "I'll tell you what: I have the perfect solution to this problem. How about this: tonight, show an old movie. A *German* movie. Tell the 'certain' people who were supposed to come to the movie tonight to come tomorrow.

"I have a friend in Berlin, an old university buddy, who works at the *Reichsfilmkammer.* I'll ring him right now to get his hands on a brand-new movie that just came out. I'm very excited about it. And here's what I'm going to do for you, Fraulein Richter... I will drive up to Berlin myself and go get it, and I'll have it in time for the premiere tomorrow, say around 8:00. Does that sound like a good deal to you?"

"You would go all the way to Berlin, for a movie?"

"A very *good* movie," Herr Schulz nodded generously. "And this one is *really* new. They're premiering it in Berlin this weekend, and next week, all over Germany! And this little mountain town will have the scoop."

"That sounds wonderful, Herr Schulz! Thank you so much!" Hildegard beamed.

"You are very welcome. I'm going to ring Jergen right now," he walked toward his car.

"Oh, and Herr Schulz!" Hildegard called. He turned back. "It has to be an *exciting* movie. A movie that will make your heart race."

Herr Schulz laughed. "Hilde, I guarantee you this will be the most exciting, heart-wrenching, heart-racing movie you have ever seen."

Herr Schulz returned the next day, as promised.

"I can't believe Herr Schulz drove 8 hours *both ways* in one day just to get you a movie," Irena said, eyeing Hildegard jealously. "You're like his class pet, or something."

"Nah, you're the class pet," Hildegard said, directly lying through her teeth but not wanting to get into a tiff with Irena today. "He just did it because he felt bad for ruining our night."

He drove up in his sleek black Volkswagen, to the cheering of the crowd that had gathered outside the movie theater.

"Herr Schulz, I can't believe you made it on time!" Mayor Fischer said, looking at his watch. "A 16 hour journey, all for our children. What a teacher!"

"Actually, Mayor Fischer, it didn't take 16 hours. I traveled on the brand-new Autobahn, they just opened it. You can go any speed you want, so I decided to push this baby to her limit," he said, patting the boot of his car.

"How fast did you go?"

"177 kilometers per hour," Herr Schulz tried to cover his boyish grin. "I had time to lunch with my friend and have a beer in Munich."

"177 kilometers per hour! How thrilling, heh heh!" Mayor Fischer chuckled. "I hope they build the Autobahn near Himmelberg; then we will have even more tourism for the ski resort!"

"I hope so, too, Mayor Fischer," Herr Schulz opened up the boot of his Volkswagen. "And Herr Weber, I have good news. I was able to procure even more films from my friend at the *Reichsfilmkammer!* Now we'll be able to enjoy quality films in our little German paradise."

"Goody," Herr Weber said.

"And here," he handed Herr Weber the film canisters in their leather cases, "is tonight's entertainment. Leni Riefenstahl's magnum opus."

"What's it called?" Herr Schumacher asked.

"Triumph of the Will. It's brilliant. In fact, my friend Jergen swears by it: he told me to tell you all that, by the end of this evening, if you aren't absolutely thrilled with the movie, you can write to him, and he will personally mail you a check for your money back!"

The gathering crowd laughed.

"And I told him, I'll send you a postcard, so you can see what you're missing. Enough, let's go in: lights, camera, action!"

"Isn't that an American phrase," Felix said drolly, but far enough away so Herr Schulz couldn't hear.

"Shh, Felix," Hildegard cautioned.

"Do you have a crush on him, like everyone else?"

"No, dummkopf. But he went all the way to Berlin for a new movie and he's grading our essays by Monday. Have a little tact," she squeezed his hand.

"Hilde," Esther hissed, tugging on her sleeve. "I've purchased the tickets. Give this one to Gerda. She'll be sitting next to Luka. You and I will bookend them. We're sure to have success!"

The audience crowded into the theater and shuffled to their seats. Luka and Esther were already seated when Gerda and Hildegard plopped down beside them.

"Oh, looks like we're sitting next to each other," Gerda smiled. Luka looked up at her and beamed. "I'm Gerda."

"We've met before," Luka said, moving his coat which was draped over the armrest. "I remember you from school. You were the only girl in your grade with red hair."

"Oh," Gerda blushed, clearly pleased. "That's so nice of you to remember."

"It used to be bright red," Luka said, his eyes on her hair. "Like a ginger red. Now it's dark. Like amber."

Gerda fidgeted with a curl. "Yes, I used to be really insecure about it. The boys would make fun of me. But I don't care so much now."

"You shouldn't. You shouldn't worry about boys who make fun; they will make fun of everything that is different, which isn't even that funny or interesting. Hmm..." he said, coming to some kind of inward epiphany, "It's more interesting to be interesting."

"I agree," Gerda smiled. Hildegard leaned back in her seat and winked at Esther.

"This had better be scarier than *Bride of Frankenstein*," Karl said grumpily. He leaned back in his seat and addressed Hildegard, who

68

was sitting behind him. "What's this movie even about, anyway?"

"I think Herr Schulz said it was a documentary," Hildegard leaned forward.

"Awww!" Karl groaned, slumping forward. "Documentaries are boring! What a gyp."

"Just like a teacher to make us watch something educational," Lars grunted. "I'd rather watch toenails grow."

"Shh, it's starting!" Johanna hissed.

The movie opened up with a golden eagle, the Roman symbol of the empire, sitting atop a wreath of laurels, Apollo's symbol for peace. Inside the wreath was a swastika, the symbol of good fortune and longevity. Trumpets flared and drums thundered in a Nazi fanfare.

Suddenly, as the music reached a crescendo, the audience was soaring through the clouds, piled high like mounds of whipped cream. Then, the clouds broke to show an aerial view of Nuremberg, the medieval city of Bavaria, with its stretching Gothic towers and its exquisite cathedrals. Hitler's plane appeared on the screen, and the audience saw that this bird's eye view of the city was from his perspective, as if he—like a shining, golden eagle—were soaring above the heavens and alighting upon the steeple of the Frauenkirche, the Church of our Lady, to bless the citizens of Nuremberg with a visit. The shadow of Hitler's plane, cross-like, glided down the cobblestone streets, which were packed with people marching to the Zeppelin Field.

The city of Nuremberg erupted into applause and an echoing chorus of *"Heil!"* as Hitler's motorcade passed by. Hitler was filmed from over the shoulder, giving him an air of mystery, as he smiled benevolently and raised his arm in a salute to the passerby. Hildegard watched his profile carefully. He had a stern brow which cascaded down into a rounded, European nose, under which sat the famous mustache and a rather weak chin. Hildegard had to admit: if he didn't have the mustache, he would look like every other sausage-maker or paper-hanger on the street. He would look like anyone.

And he certainly didn't bear any resemblance to the poster of the fresh-faced brawny Aryan lad that hung in Herr Schulz's classroom. He was brunette, a little pale, and—like so many men in their mid-40s—beginning to lose the trim torso of his manhood. What was it about this man, who did not fit the mold of the typical Aryan, that inspired a whole city to erupt into cheers?

The film showed a group of Hitler-Jugend boys in tents at summer camp, playing around, wrestling, having a chariot race, doing flips on a trampoline. One boy did a particularly spectacular flip that made the audience murmur in approval.

"I hope we get to do stuff like that at camp this year," Karl whispered to Lars in the row in front of them.

"It sure beats the hell out of math," Lars replied.

The next scene showed German citizens marching in a midsummer parade, wearing their traditional trachten. The women were smiling and carrying maypoles, the ribbons billowing the breeze. Children smiled and waved from the sidelines. A blonde baby, like a cherub, cooed and clapped her hands.

Hitler smiled and shook hands with the people in the parade as they presented him with their bounty, bushels of wheat and fruit, with starry-eyed wonder. Then he reviewed the troops: rows upon rows upon rows of blonde German boys, with profiles as smoothly formed as the Alps. Each young man was clean-cut, attentive as a tiger, ready for action.

"We never fought in the trenches, nor did we hear the explosion of grenades," a young man said. "But nonetheless… we are soldiers! At the Somme! By the Danube! In Flanders!"

A flag was lowered somberly for the veterans of the Great War.

"Yawohl!" Herr Schumacher cried. Others murmured in agreement.

"Hitler was a veteran, too," Karl whispered. "He's a Southern man, like us."

Suddenly, the Nazi flags shot up at the sound of the drums. The young men chanted: "You are not dead. You are alive. You are us. You are Germany!"

This elicited applause from the people in the audience, which continued as Hitler took the stage.

"I am looking at a cross-section of Germany," he said clearly, rolling his R's as was typical of the Southern German-Austrian accent. "You young men and you young women are taking on everything we hope for in Germany. We want to be," he punctuated this with his fists, "ONE German people, and you, my youth, are to be these people. We want to see NO more class divisions. You MUST NOT let this grow up amongst you!"

"Amen!" came a voice in the audience.

"We want to see ONE Reich one day, and you must train for it! We want our people to love peace, but in order to have peace, you must be brave!" He raised his voice above the cheers of the young men and the growing applause of the audience.

"Whatever we do today, whatever we create," he continued. "We will all die someday. But Germany WILL LIVE ON... in YOU!"

Henri whistled and Lars and Karl cheered.

"It is because of you, the best of the German race, in proud self-confidence, have courageously and boldly claimed the leadership of this Reich and this nation, and every day we have more and more leaders growing among us," Hitler said, his eyes reaching out to the farthest people in the field, touching their eyes and their minds. "The German people are happy in that the constantly changing leadership of the Weimar Republic has been replaced by a fixed pole," at this, he extended a hand, to indicate the North Star of the Nazi party by which all Germans could now rely on to guide them, "a force that considers itself the representative of the best blood. Knowing this, knowing we have the best possible blood in leadership at this moment, we will fight to never relinquish this leadership again!"

The adults cheered and applauded.

"I *told* you," Frau Schumacher leaned over to Frau Zimmerman, clapping her hands. "A more direct form of government. No more bending over and taking it with these reparations."

"To merely believe in this new Reich, this new nation, is not enough," Hitler's raspy voice thundered across the fields. "Instead, we need every citizen to not only say 'I believe in the nation,' but also 'I will fight for this nation!'"

"Heil Hitler!" Herr Wolf cried, raising his arm. Others followed his example.

"In the past, our enemies have persecuted us and tried to remove what they view as undesirable from our Party. Today, *we ourselves* must remove the undesirables from our society. What is bad has no place among us!"

At this point, the audience was clapping and cheering so loud, it was hard for Hildegard to even distinguish what he was saying. She wished Herr Weber would spring for better quality speakers. But she did make out this sentence as Hitler reached the end of his speech:

"It is our wish that this Reich will endure, not for an age, but for millennia to come!"

The audience was fully on their feet, cheering, whistling, yelling, and chanting *"Sieg Heil! Sieg Heil! Sieg Heil! Sieg Heil!"*

"I have to go," Luka said, edging his way out.

"I'll come with you," Gerda said, searching for an excuse. "I'm going to get some more popcorn."

Esther and Hildegard grinned at each other.

Outside, Luka took a deep breath.

Gerda followed close behind him, closing the door gently. "Are you alright?"

"Hm? Oh, yes. He is... quite the speaker."

"Yes," Gerda said. "Although it can be hard to take him seriously." She mimicked Hitler, punching his fist in the air. "ONE nation, ONE people, ONE Germany!"

Luka looked at her, a little frightened. Gerda laughed. "Anyway, I don't go in for politics. All those politicians say pretty words, but they do what they want in the end. So who needs it?"

"Yes," Luka smiled, relieved. "Who needs it?"

"I wish they would've played a romantic movie... or something like that," Gerda's eyes darted toward Luka. "Do you go to movies often?"

"Not often. The last movie I saw was *The Four Musketeers.*"

"Well that was almost a year and a half ago!"

"Like I said, I don't go to movies much."

"Well, what *do* you like to do?"

"I like walking."

"Oh," Gerda smiled, sensing she was finally getting somewhere. "I like walking too." And, after a beat: "Maybe we could go for a walk together sometime."

"Perhaps so," Luka shrugged blithely.

The audience climaxed in cheers and applause, and then swept down into murmurs from the other side of the door, which grew louder as they got closer.

"Looks like the movie's over," Luka said.

Hildegard and Esther charged through the door, gaping at Luka and Gerda. They stared at the ceiling and the walls, attempting to recover their casual facade.

"Well, I'd better be going," Gerda said pointedly. "My house is this way." She gave Luka a very direct look.

"My house is that way," Luka said.

"Oh," Gerda said, disappointed. She extended her hand. "Well, it

73

was nice talking to you."

"I hope to see you around," Luka said earnestly, shaking it vigorously.

"You can always come see me in the trachten shop," Gerda gave a fetching smile.

"I don't go into the trachten shop much," Luka replied.

"Well, you could call me," Gerda said, trying the obvious. "I could give you my phone number."

"We don't have a telephone at our house."

"Well, I guess we'll never see each other or talk to each other again, will we?" Gerda cried, exasperated. "Hilde, I'm going home."

She stormed out.

"Good night!" Luka said.

Hildegard and Esther sighed and exchanged pained expressions.

"She *likes* you, vollidiot," Esther smacked his shoulder.

Luka raised his eyebrows, looking from Esther to Hildegard. "She does?"

"She's completely stuck on you," Hildegard nodded sagely. "Although I don't know how you're going to win her back now."

"I'll think of something," Luka said thoughtfully, and he left.

"I'd better follow him," Esther sighed. "Or this will be 'I-was-thinking-so-hard-I-let-the-sheep-wander-into-Zum-Hirschen' all over again."

"Our plan isn't foiled yet," Hildegard said. "Good night!"

"Did you like the film, Hilde?" Herr Schulz approached her outside of the theater.

"Very much, Herr Schulz," Hildegard smiled politely. "It was so thrilling!"

"I hope it was heart-racing enough for the *Bride of Frankenstein*-goers," he returned the smile. "But now I must ask you to return the favor. I'd like you to help lead the Jungmädel girl's camp this summer." He raised his eyebrows expectantly. "Surely driving 16 hours in one day would earn me your support."

"But weren't you going 177 kilometers per hour? It can't have been *sixteen* hours."

Herr Schulz's blue eyes flashed.

Hildegard cracked a smile. "I'm joking, Herr Schulz. Of course you can count on me! It's the least I can do."

Herr Schulz broke into a grin and pinched her cheek. "Ah, Fraulein Richter, you little devil! I'm glad to have your support. I know your father will be glad too."

Hildegard thought about telling him that her father was dead from pneumonia, but decided it wasn't worth the trouble. "Thank you. See you on Monday, Herr Schulz."

"Tschüss!"

On Monday, the students walked into Herr Schulz's classroom to find lyrics written on the chalkboard instead of the usual lecture notes.

"Good morning! I hope you had a restful weekend. Now, students, you see the song written on the chalkboard in front of you. I want you to copy it down into your composition notebooks, memorize it, and learn the melody, because we're going to be singing it every morning at the beginning of class to start the day."

"What *is* it?" Henri asked.

"It's an anthem. A new type of anthem for a new Reich," Herr Schulz said proudly. "It's called 'The Horst-Wessel Song.' I'm going to play it once for you, so you get the melody, and then I want everyone up and singing the second go round."

Herr Schulz put a record on a record player sitting on his desk and turned the needle back to start the record spinning. Then, he carefully lowered the needle onto the edge of the spinning record, and a chorus of voices charged out of the speakers. The students sat forward warily, listening.

"Now everyone, up, up, up! I want to hear you sing it loud and proud! Don't be shy, don't be worried about tone-deaf. Better to be a proud, tone-deaf German than a weak-willed traitor!"

All the students, including Hildegard, stood up and began singing. A few of them stifled giggles as they blundered their way through the melody. Hildegard looked around, grinning, until her eyes rested on Esther. Esther was seated, and she looked as if she had stomach pains.

"Fraulein Lange, up! I want to hear your voice!" Herr Schulz commanded.

"I... I can't," Esther said quietly.

"Do you have an injury, Fraulein Lange? What could possibly prohibit you from following directions in my class?"

Esther seemed to be grappling with some internal struggle, and after a moment, she looked up at him with bold, clear eyes. "I am a Jehovah's Witness, Herr Schulz. My religion forbids me from pledging or singing songs of allegiance to any country of man, because I serve the God of Heaven."

Herr Schulz's crystal blue eyes flashed, and then hardened in a way Hildegard had not witnessed before. He crouched down next to her desk and said in a murmur: "I don't give a good God damn about your religion. You'll stand when I tell you to stand."

"I *can't,*" Esther pleaded, tears welling in her eyes.

Herr Schulz straightened. "Then you'll just have to bear the punishment of being disobedient in class."

Esther took a quivering breath. "Fine."

"You'll have your knuckles rapped until the completion of the song."

"Yes, Herr Schulz."

"And we're going to start the song over, since we were interrupted by this little show of stubbornness."

"Yes, Herr Schulz."

Herr Schulz rotated the record back to its original position, chose a ruler, and pointed to the rest of the class. "Sing."

Hildegard sang with a nervous twist in her stomach, as "The Horst-Wessel Song" was punctuated by the swift *crack* of the ruler against Esther's outstretched hands:

"For the last time, the call to arms is sounded!

"For the fight, we all stand prepared!

"Already Hitler's banners fly over all streets.

"The time of bondage will last but a little while longer!"

Every day for three weeks, the eleventh-years would sing the song, and every day, Esther would control her winces as Herr Schulz whacked at her hands, emotionless, measured. Then, on the fourth week, she started coming late to school, and after a while, she stopped coming at all.

6

1935, Part Two: Camp Hitler

There were no Jews in Himmelberg, or at least there hadn't been any that anyone in town could remember, so nobody really talked about it when a series of laws were enacted after the Nazi Party Rally in Nuremberg. These laws would informally become known as the Nuremberg Laws:

1. The Reich Citizenship Law: All people who are considered to be German citizens have pure German (Aryan) blood. Jews, therefore, are not considered German citizens, because they come from somewhere else.

2. The Law for Protection of German Blood and German Honor: Since German citizens have pure Aryan blood, all future marriages and sexual relationships between Aryans and non-Aryans (Jews, Roma, African) are hereby illegal, to prevent intermixing and defiling future German citizens' bloodlines.

In order to prove their citizenship and bloodlines, citizens would have to produce birth records of grandparents, particularly baptism records. Other laws came out in the years to come:

3. The Law of the Alteration of Family and Personal Names (1938): In order to be more easily identified as a Jew, Jews must have a name

from a pre-approved list of Hebrew names. If a Jew does not have a name from the Hebrew Name list, they must change their name to Israel (men) or Sarah (women). All changed names must be reported to government offices.

4. Decree on Passports of Jews (1938): All passports of German Jews are hereby invalid. In order to have a passport (quickly becoming the only acceptable form of identification) validated again, Jews must report to a government office and have their passport stamped with a J.

5. Police Regulation on the Marking of Jews (1941): In order to appear in public, Jews six years old or older must wear a yellow star on their clothing at all times.

Hildegard had to admit: the Nazis certainly knew how to put on a show. Himmelberg wasn't as poor as the other nearby mountain villages, because of the tourism it brought in from the ski resort, but it had nowhere near the resources to put on the dog-and-pony show that *Triumph of the Will* exemplified. But, not to worry, Herr Schulz reassured the camp counselors, Der Führer would take care of everything.

A large army truck rolled in one June morning, full of fresh graduates from the Hitler-Jugend and Jungmädel. These delegates were here to help coach Hildegard's group in how to mentor their own branch of Hitler-Jugend, as well as the Jungvolk.

Frau Fischer was set to host them for a welcome tea, but Irena and Ygritte begged their parents to let them handle it.

"*Please*, Mutti," Irena pleaded. "A tea would be a social nightmare. These kids are real Aryan fighters; they're training to be strong men and women... a tea would be the exact *opposite* of what the Führer wants from us!"

"Well, Pauline, she may have a point," Mayor Fischer wiped his brow. "It is a summer camp, after all. And they're big kids, not socialites."

Pauline Fischer *humphed* in disapproval.

"Let us take them to the biergarten," Irena said calmly, "and you foot the bill."

"*I* foot the bill?!" Mayor Fischer exclaimed.

"Yes, and think about what nice things these delegates are going to be saying about Himmelberg when they report back to Commander Baldur von Schirach." Schirach, it was known, was the commander of the Hitler Youth, who had connections to Joseph Goebbels. It was like having the ear of St. Peter: not the ear of God Himself, but one step over.

"Fair enough, very well," Mayor Fischer said. "But keep an eye on those boys… I don't want a bunch of angry fathers knocking on my door claiming these young recruiters took liberties."

"Daddy, that's what the Jungmädel is all *about*," Irena laughed, kissing her fuddy-duddy father on the cheek. "How else are we going to make an army for the Führer?"

The delegate for the Jungmädel was a girl named Else Knopff, and she looked like a taller, beefier version of Johanna. She was only one year older than the rest of the girls in Hildegard's class, but she carried herself with the confidence of a 30-year-old.

"I'm not going to lie to you, girls," Else leaned in. "Our job is harder than the Hitler-Jugend. The boys are being trained to be soldiers, and we have to take on the burdens of ensuring a stable homelife for future generations."

The boys were ecstatically showing off their new Hitler Youth knives: each one had a five-inch nickel-plated blade, which had *Blood and Honor!* scrawled on it. They pretended to stab each other with them.

"Not like you could stab anything with them, really," Felix said sourly.

"You're just jealous you didn't get one," Karl said. "That's what you get for not signing up."

"I didn't sign up because I don't think the idea of being bossed around like a trained monkey is a fun way to spend my summer," Felix said curtly. "Anyway, if all I get out of it is a dull blade, it doesn't sound like a good deal to me."

"It's dull because you have to sharpen it yourself, dummkopf," Lars pulled his out. "That's our first step as initiates. It symbolizes the self-made man."

"You're not men, you're boys," Felix said.

"Next year, we'll be eligible for conscription, and when we go and fight for our country, we'll return home as men. And then we'll make women out of these girls," Karl laughed to Henri.

"I'm sure they're waiting with bated breath," Felix rolled his eyes, ambling off.

Hildegard turned back to the girls' table. Else was finishing her second mug of Weissbier. "Do we get knives?"

"Sadly, no," Else wiped the foam from her upper lip with the back of her hand. "But we get something much better in the long run: we get to provide the Führer with a new generation of Aryan babies."

Hildegard sat back, trying to mask her disappointment.

"I know, I know. At first I was disappointed, too. And my parents nearly hit the roof the first time I got pregnant. But here's the thing, you have to look at the bigger picture: we're not working for a better Germany; we're working for a better *world*, right?"

"Right."

"Well, how are we supposed to keep this thing, this social experiment of the Third Reich, going? The Führer won't be around forever to guide us, God bless him. How are we supposed to create a whole world of Aryans from one country of people? We have to start *now* in order to have enough time to pass the baton on to the future."

"What did your parents say the first time you got pregnant?"

"My mother went off her lid, screaming at me. My father was all 'I didn't fight in the trenches of Belgium just to raise a harlot!' You know how fathers are. Anyway, I talked to my Bund leader about it, and she alerted the Gestapo, and the Gestapo explained everything to my parents, and now they don't have a problem with it anymore."

"What's the Gestapo?" Louisa asked.

"They're Hitler's police force. And let me tell you, they're loads more efficient than the regular police force. My hometown's streets have never been cleaner nor more orderly ever since the Gestapo moved in. We don't have any robberies, no more gypsies begging or pickpocketing, and no more sneaky Jews."

"I guess we don't need the Gestapo," Hildegard shrugged. "We don't have any Jews or gypsies here. We don't even have a jail; just a locked room at the courthouse."

"Don't worry; they're coming. Hitler wants to make sure everything is running smoothly. You'll have some Gestapo in your town soon enough. I hope, for your sake," she winked at Hildegard, "they're handsome."

"And unmarried," Irena giggled.

"Sure, unmarried too, why not?" Else shrugged good-naturedly, waving over Herr Weissman. "Another, bitte."

In order to officially be inaugurated into the Hitler Youth, candidates were required to pass a bravery test, which the delegates called a *mutprobe*. This culminated in a high-jump from a diving board. The school's swimming pool wasn't nearly deep enough to do a high-jump safely, so the Himmelberg kids marched with the delegates up to Lake Wotan, which was partially surrounded by twenty-foot cliffs, back when it had been a quarry for Mad King Ludwig II.

"Blut und ehre!" each boy screamed, reciting the oath on his dagger and jumping.

"Blut und ehre!" each girl screamed, not to be outdone by the boys.

"I can't believe you just *have* this," Else looked around admiringly. "The beauty of the Fatherland, all around you. You know, this is what Hitler means... when he wants us to test our bravery by jumping off a high-board, he *really* wants this, like the Vikings jumping to Valhalla... and you're already doing it as a part of your everyday life!"

"We don't have much else to do here," Hildegard shrugged as she unlaced her shoes.

"But you will. Soon, all of Germany will be like you. Solid, wholesome, salt-of-the-earth people. We're going to get back to the basics: farming, working the land, being one with the soil."

"Did you have a farm back in your hometown?"

"Nah, we lived in an apartment."

"Then trust me," Hildegard laughed, "working on a farm isn't all it's cracked up to be. A lot of ruined shoes and smelling like pig shit."

Else threw her head back and laughed. "Hildegard, you're a pip! Now go on, show us what you've got."

Hildegard peeped over the rocky cliff at the swimming figures below.

"Come on, Hilde, don't be chicken!" Lars shouted up.

Hildegard took a few steps back.

"I told you she wouldn't do it," Irena said in a low voice.

"Blut und ehre!" Hildegard shouted, taking a running start and plummeting to the aquamarine waters below. The water was icy cold and invigorating. As she drifted up, she heard the cheering of her comrades get louder and louder as she reached the surface.

"Well done, Hilde! 8 out of 10 points!" Karl laughed.

"Only 8 out of 10?" Hildegard raised her eyebrows. Suddenly she felt a pinch on the back of her thigh. "Hey!"

One of the recruiters surfaced in front of her, grinning.

"Knock it off," she frowned, splashing him.

"You'd better lay off, Brenner," Karl cautioned. "She's Felix's girlfriend."

"Felix is not my boyfriend," Hildegard protested.

"Sure, sure," Karl chuckled. "I've seen the two of you in the back of the movie theater before, and it sure didn't look like friendship to me."

Hildegard felt her face redden and she wanted to sink under the water and bury herself under a rock. She had proved her courage by jumping off a twenty-foot cliff, but right now she felt as cowardly as a snail.

She wished she could produce feelings of love for Felix, as easily as a magician produces a rabbit out of a hat, but she doubted these feelings would ever come. She had talked herself into the idea that she would just wind up marrying Felix someday, because she got along well with him, but this future seemed hardly satisfactory. Maybe there was a future for her in the new Reich.

The next morning, the children of Himmelberg lined up for registration, gawping at the summertime splendor around them. Bright red, white, and black pennants were draped across high flagpoles. Soon, tents were pitched in neat little rows. The nickel-plated knives gleamed cheerily in the rising sun, also arranged in orderly rows. The Jungvolk and Hitler-Jugend would not receive them until they passed their mutprobe.

Hildegard suggested providing the Jungmädel with a conciliatory prize. "If you want these girls to buy into the program, Else, they need to see that the Führer thinks that they're every bit as special as the boys."

"I suppose you're right," Else said. "We usually don't have this problem because the boys and girls are separated. And the girls' mutprobe is less rigorous than the boys', normally. But, considering our lack of resources in the country, I suppose it looks bad if girls are meant to jump off a cliff and receive nothing."

"And," Hildegard added, "it ties into what you were saying yesterday. If you want people who are hard workers and tied to the land... well... girls do every bit of work out here as the boys."

"And probably more so, since the boys will be going off to war soon," Else pondered. "But what can we do? They didn't send us with anything for the girls."

"I'll think of something," Hildegard said.

She went home and Wilhelmina, with her artist's soul and Depression-era penchant for thrift, had a wonderful idea. Wilhelmina went to every home in Himmelberg and collected enough can lids for each girl in the camp. Then, she went to Gerda and bought yards of velvet ribbon, like what Felix wrapped Hildegard's present in years ago. Hildegard retrieved Johanna, Louisa, Irena, and Ygritte, who came with their mothers. The women worked into the wee hours of the night with screwdrivers and hammers, punching a hole and carving little designs into each of the can lids. The basic design was a heart with the letters JM (for Jungmädel) inside it, and little designs around the edge of the can lid.

"Then you loop the ribbon through the lid like this, and there you have it! Medals of courage," Wilhelmina smiled. "Pretty good for a last-minute prize, eh?"

"I don't think it's very fair that the girls don't get *any*thing," Pauline Fischer said. "If they want them to settle down and become mothers, you think they would give them a cooking knife, at least."

"Yes," Irena said. "Theirs says *Blood and Honor,* ours says *Blood Sausage.*"

"Or *Blood and Tampons,*" Ygritte said.

85

"Ygritte, don't be disgusting!"

"What? We've seen more blood than they have; why do they get a dagger?"

"Because they're going to go fight for their country, darling," Pauline said.

"Else mentioned that yesterday," Hildegard said thoughtfully. She turned to her mother. "Who are we going to war with? I thought we just had a war."

Wilhelmina took a moment to compose her words. "Well, it's always good for a country to be ready for anything. A country with no military defense will not remain a country for much longer. How familiar are you with The Treaty of Versailles?"

"That's when the Allied countries stabbed us in the back and forced us to pay reparations," Louisa piped up.

"Yes. But that's not all we had to pay. We were forced to give up lands—crucial lands, you see—to Belgium, Czechoslovakia, and Poland. We also had to give up the land bordering the Rhine River—the Rhineland—to the Allied powers."

"So... we're going to get them back?"

"That's what Otto thinks will happen."

"We're going to provide a little German payback," Johanna said with an ironic smile. "And then we'll show the rest of the world what happens when you disrespect Germany."

When Hildegard presented the medals to Else, a smile grew on Else's face that stretched from ear to ear. "Wunderbar, Hilde! You're a genius!"

"It was my mother's idea," Hildegard lowered her head humbly, smiling.

"Then genius must run in the family. I'm going to tell my supervisor about you. I mean it. I think you have a future in the *Frauenschaft*, the Nazi Women's League," she said, playfully punching her on the shoulder. "I'll take these. And look... I'll let you give them out, since they were your idea."

"Can Johanna, Louisa, and the Fischers do it too? It was a group effort."

"I think that's a wonderful idea."

So the recruiters and the teenagers and the Himmelberg children all hiked around the ravine to Lake Wotan, up to the quarry cliffs. Most children jumped off the cliffs without a hitch, because they had done it before (some of them had done it the previous week to cool off), but there was one girl who was too afraid.

"Come on, Suzanna! All your friends are down there!" Johanna encouraged her. Suzanna shook her head, breathing heavily.

"You don't want to be the only girl who didn't jump, do you?" Louisa asked. The kids began chanting her name from below. This did not assuage Suzanna's fears, but seemed to heighten them. Tears of anxiety welled in her eyes.

"Suzanna," Hildegard bowed down to meet her eye level. "What if you and I go together? I'll hold your hand the whole way down."

Suzanna lifted her head. "All the way?"

Hildegard smiled. "All the way. The Jungmädel are sisters. Sisters stick together."

Suzanna took a breath. "Okay, let's do it."

Hildegard and Suzanna held hands and approached the edge of the cliff. "Don't think about the splash, think about the wind you'll feel when you jump," Hildegard said. "Oh, and straighten your legs. That way you'll dive straight through."

Suzanna looked green around the gills, but nodded.

"Ready? One... two... three!" Hildegard yanked Suzanna with her, and they fell down, down, down into the lake. Hildegard said a silent prayer to God: *please, let her be able to swim. I didn't ask her if she could swim!*

Hildegard surfaced, looking around quickly for Suzanna amongst the cheers. Then, Suzanna surfaced a few yards away. "That was *amazing!*" She beamed.

"See? It's never as hard as you think it's going to be. Your nerves are your biggest enemy."

"Am I a Jungmädel now? Am I a sister?"

"Yes, indeed!"

"I've never had a sister before," Suzanna grinned.

"Me neither," Hildegard said, spitting a thin stream of water at her between her teeth.

At the medal and knife ceremony, held separately by gender, Hildegard made sure to award Suzanna her medal. "You're one of us now," Hildegard winked. "Officially."

The rest of the day was divided up into outdoor activities: hiking, learning to march, playing volleyball, running relay races, running human chariot races, running blindfold races to fetch paper letters that spelled out "Heil Hitler," learning "The Horst-Wessel Song," and finally, as the sun went down, telling campfire legends of German mythology, like the Nibelungenlied.

Also during the week were lessons on German history and the importance of the Aryan. Brenner, the boy who pinched Hildegard, was particularly good at telling the story of Hitler's life. The children sat, enchanted, as he told the story of the Führer's tragic childhood and the bereavement of his dead mother and brother, his steel-minded and selfless acts of courage during The Great War. When he got to the part where the Führer was wounded by mustard gas after a devilish plot from the invading Brits, the children audibly gasped. When he got to the part where Hitler learned to love peace and find peace within himself as an artist and a vegetarian, the young preteen girls clutched their hearts and the heart-engraved medals they wore.

"You're really good at that," Hildegard nodded in respect to Brenner during dinner.

"Thanks, my uncle was a priest," Brenner laughed. His uncle, he did not mention to Hildegard, was currently in Dachau with six other Catholic priests for protesting the Third Reich.

On Thursday, Irena gave a lecture to the girls about how Hitler needed as many Aryan babies as possible to make a wonderful new world of peace and brotherhood.

"I can't wait to have babies with Hitler," Suzanna confided to Hildegard.

"*For* Hitler, Suzanna," Hildegard laughed. "Adolf Hitler is nearly four times your age."

"I'll just have to be his Schmuckstück, then."

"Suzanna!" Hildegard chided, laughing.

At the end of the week, Otto returned from his steel factory with presents for all the kids at camp: helmets for the boys, emblazoned with a swastika, and combs for the girls, which had an attractive and feminine swastika-and-laurel design that branched around the comb.

"Steel lasts longer than tin," Otto said.

"Otto, you absolute treasure!" Hildegard cried, standing on her tiptoes and kissing him on the cheek.

"Okay."

"No, you're not getting away that easily, Herr Richter!" Johanna grabbed him by the sleeve, giving him a kiss on the other cheek.

Every female camp counselor lined up to kiss Otto on the cheek, and through it all he looked as if he'd like to throw himself off a cliff. And, to add to insult to injury, all the camp counselors crowded around him for a photo: the girls showing off their beautiful combs, the boys wearing children's helmets that were too small and sat like bowlers on the tops of their heads. The spectacle made everyone burst into tearful laughter, and even Otto himself cracked a smile.

1936

Hildegard's final year in school, as so many senior years are, wasn't nearly as memorable as she thought it would be. Most of the boys skipped classes for Hitler-Jugend activities, including the Reichsparteitag, the Nazi Party's giant week-long extravaganza full of parades, speeches, and shows of glory.

Hildegard spent her time helping out with the Jungmädel. She enjoyed taking the girls on hikes, organizing after school activities and charity drives, and being a role model for the other girls. This was her last year in the League of German Maidens, although Herr Schulz encouraged her to apply for an internship at the Nazi Women's League.

"But the best thing you can be for the Führer," Herr Schulz smiled, "is a wife and mother. Don't work too long… you don't want to waste your childbearing years!"

Herr Schulz presented Hildegard, Johanna, Louisa, and Irena with special stoles and red-and-black cords to wear at graduation. The stoles had the Hitler Youth badge in brilliant gold thread sewn on the back. Lars and Karl also received stoles. Henri was not present for graduation because when he turned 18 in April, he immediately enlisted in the Wehrmacht, the armed forces of the Third Reich. Lars and Karl (albeit a little begrudgingly) had to stay behind: Lars to help on the family farm, and Karl to help his father (who was missing an arm from the Great War) in the butcher shop.

Hildegard, the typical high school senior, spent most of her time wishing she could get away. "I'm just so *bored* in Himmelberg!" she groaned to Gerda as she folded scarves.

"Tell me about it," Gerda said, then her eyes darted to the window. Hildegard turned around. "Is that Luka?"

Gerda nodded solemnly. "He passes by the window. He started passing by once or twice a week, but now he passes by multiple times a day."

Hildegard cocked an eyebrow, half-smiling.

Gerda rolled her eyes. "But he never comes in, and when I go out for my lunch break and say hello to him, he turns like this," she turned on her heel, "and walks in the opposite direction."

"Aw, he's probably nervous."

"He's a fool," Gerda said with finality, "And I'm done with fools. I would move out of this one-horse town to Munich, but my grandmother needs me here."

"Well, *I'm* glad to have you here."

"Bah, you'll leave me too soon enough, Fraulein Hitler Aryan Maiden of the Mountains," Gerda said sardonically. "Which reminds me. I have a graduation present for you."

She lifted a black box tied with blue ribbon out from under the clerk's counter. Hildegard grinned and untied the ribbon, lifting the box. Inside was a forest green silk scarf, embroidered with starry white edelweiss. The scarf was looped through a silver heart pendant engraved with a scripted, looping *H*.

"I ordered it specially made from Austria," Gerda said proudly. "It reminded me of last year, when you made those medals for the little girls."

"Gerda, you angel!" Hildegard hugged Gerda from across the counter. She tied the silk scarf around her neck, knotting it at the back.

"Now you look like a real Bavarian woman," Gerda smiled, then stepped back. "Ach, that's what I told your mother six years ago! Mein Gott, you look exactly like her now."

"I'll take the compliment," Hildegard said. "There goes Luka again." "I need to go do inventory," Gerda left the room. "Call me if a customer comes in."

Hildegard went to go visit Esther that afternoon. She walked three miles through the hills to the Lange's house. It looked like the typical German farmhouse: white stucco walls on the first floor and wood on the second, with a large sloping roof to keep off the snow. Flower boxes bursting with red geraniums accented the small balcony on the second floor. Hildegard knocked on the door, and Mrs. Lange's voice was nervous on the other side.

"Who is it? We have all our papers," she barked.

"It's Hildegard Richter, Mrs. Lange," Hildegard responded. "I'm a friend of Esther's, from school."

Mrs. Lange opened the door slowly, looking her up and down. "Oh, Hildegard," she said, her eyes resting on the swastika-emblazoned Hitler Youth pin she wore on her shirt pocket. "Please come in. I'll call Esther."

Esther came in, sweaty from chores, and stopped in her tracks when she saw Hildegard sitting at the kitchen table. "Hilde," she said. "What are you doing here?"

"I came to check on you," Hildegard said.

Esther's eyes darted through the windows. "What for?"

"Because you weren't at graduation, silly!" Hildegard laughed. "I've barely seen you this year!"

"Oh," Esther said, sitting down shakily. "Yes. I dropped out."

"Why did you do a silly thing like that?"

"I... was needed here. Besides," Esther got up, pouring a glass of water, "there wasn't much I was getting out of Himmelberg School anyway. Can I get you a drink?"

"Yes, please. It's quite a hike up here, but wow, what a view!"

"Yes," Esther said simply. "Although we may have to move."

"What! Why?"

"We... our landlord may be getting new tenants."

"Well, that's a shame. Maybe you could be a tenant for Otto. He has all this land and this gigantic barn, and he's getting older. And his tenant farmer is as old as Methuselah."

Esther cracked a smile.

Hildegard sipped her water and leaned forward. "Look, Esther, there's another reason why I came here today."

Esther looked anxious. The color drained from her face.

"It's about our plan last year, to get Luka and Gerda together."

Esther's eyes widened. She broke into a smile and breathed a sigh of relief. "Oh, is that all? Yes, our great matchmaking scheme. It didn't work out too well the first time."

"Are you aware that Luka has been walking by the trachten store every day, multiple times?"

"No, but it doesn't surprise me. He hasn't been himself for the past year. He's been distracted—well, more distracted than usual. Of course, it's been a hard year for all of us. We just assumed..." her eyes drifted down to Hildegard's pin. "We assumed it was something else."

"Oh, I'm sorry, Esther. I wish you would have told me you were having a hard time."

Esther gave Hildegard a strange look. "Yes... it's... you never know who you can trust."

"Well, you can trust me. Come over to our house any time, and we'll talk."

Esther smiled sadly. "Yes, I'll do that. Some time. Next time."

Hildegard stood up. "I'd better be going; I don't want to disrupt your chores, and I need to help with dinner." She hugged Esther. "It was nice seeing you again."

Esther returned the hug. "Nice seeing you."

Hildegard exited through the front door and made her way around to the road leading to the Richter's house. As she passed by the side of Esther's house, she noticed a large black stain on the white stucco walls. It looked like a burn mark: like there had almost been a house fire, and it had been put out. She felt relieved that Esther and her family were alright, and the fire had not spread, but wondered why Esther had not mentioned the house fire in their conversation.

Hildegard turned and walked to the road. If she had been to the back of the house, she would have seen the large red swastika spray-painted on the white stucco that Esther was in the process of scrubbing out.

When Hildegard returned home, she found dinner was already prepared. Fresh mountain trout, delicately fried, lay steaming over mounds of hot potatoes tossed with parsley, bacon, mustard, and vinegar.

"Ooh! My favorite! What is all this for?" Hildegard exclaimed.

"A little graduation celebration," Wilhelmina smiled, pulling out a chair for Hildegard. "For our only daughter. We're so proud of you, Hildegard. You've grown into such a beautiful woman, and we're proud of the difference you're making in the community."

Hildegard hugged her mother and Otto, then sat down at the table. The three Richters joined their hands in prayer.

"Thank you, Heavenly Father, for Hildegard. Thank you for her golden presence in our lives," Otto prayed in his deep baritone. "Thank you for our Führer, please bless him and guide him to make our paths straight. Please bless this food to the nourishment of our bodies, and us to Your service. Amen."

"Amen," Hildegard said, picking up her fork.

"So," Wilhelmina smiled, looking at Otto, "Otto and I have a graduation present for you." She paused for suspense. "We know you've been wanting to get out of Himmelberg for a while, so we're taking you on a little vacation." She grinned. "Otto has tickets to the opening ceremony of the Olympics!"

Hildegard dropped her fork in disbelief. "In Berlin? We're going to Berlin?"

"We're going back to Berlin!"

Hildegard shrieked, jumping up and kissing her mother and Otto, and squeezing him around the neck. "Aah! I'm so excited! Thank you, thank you, thank you, Otto! I have to go pack!"

"But... you haven't finished your trout!" Wilhelmina called.

"And it's in August," Otto said.

"I have to pack!" She scampered up the stairs.

Being back in Berlin was a surreal experience for Hildegard. They had left Berlin when it was cold, snowing, and there was nothing to eat. But the Berlin of 1936 was flourishing, in the same way Hildegard felt she was flourishing. As Otto drove the Richters along the tree-lined Friedrichstrasse, Hildegard felt her old connection to the city, even though Berlin and Hildegard had greatly changed.

For one thing, Nazi flags were absolutely everywhere. Anywhere one could stick a flagpole, there was a Nazi flag. The city was positively draped in red, white, and black. And Brandenburg gate, the column-lined colossus modeled after the Athenian acropolis, had ten 25-foot-long red drapes with the swastika emblem hanging above, fluttering and snapping in the breeze like the wings of a cardinal. Originally meant to invoke the arts-loving iconoclasts of Athens, the city had transformed itself into the stalwart, militaristic Spartans.

The family strolled down the verdant, lush Tiergarten. They found a bench under a sprawling oak tree, flipping through a program highlighting German Olympians.

On the opposite side of the pathway was a bench marked "JEWS ONLY." An old man was sitting on it, reading a book. He was wearing a black hat and had a gray beard. He didn't look like the monstrous depictions of Jews that Hildegard had taught to the young girls in the Jungmädel. There were pigeons cooing and waddling around him. He reached into his pocket and pulled out a flat brown cracker, snapped a piece off, and crumbled it between his fingers. He deftly tossed the crumbs out to the pigeons, then turned the page.

"Hey, Evolutionbremse! Get out of here!"

A rock hit the old man on the side of the head. Two little boys and a girl, about 10, ran up, shouting invectives at him.

"Get lost, you dirty Jew!" the little girl screamed.

"Little girl, it's not right to scream such things at your elders," the Jew said.

The little girl spit at his face and kicked him in the knee. The boys returned with more rocks and began hurling them at the Jew. "I said beat it, you goddamn dirty bastard!" one boy screamed. The old man made a hasty retreat, and the children went back to playing, running off and laughing and shrieking.

"We'd better go," Otto said, standing up.

Hildegard walked over to the bench as Otto and Wilhelmina continued down the shaded path. The Jew had run away without taking his book. It lay in the dirt, pages splayed. Hildegard picked it up: it was a copy of Kafka's *The Metamorphosis*.

It's none of my business, right? She flipped the book over. *It's not my fault he was sitting out here with... isn't this on the banned book list?* Curiosity overtook her. She read the first line of the Jew's book:

"Gregor Samsa awoke one morning from uneasy dreams to find himself transformed into a monstrous vermin."

The massive zeppelin *Hindenburg* loomed overhead. People exclaimed and pointed, cheering and applauding as it floated above the stadium, flying a massive Nazi flag.

The trumpets flared, and Hitler and his entourage entered the field. The crowd exploded into cheers. *Sieg Heil! Sieg Heil! Sieg Heil!* A woman sitting next to Hildegard was screaming in rapture, jumping up and down, with tears of joy streaming down her face. Hildegard was screaming herself. She couldn't help herself: you sit there and stare at the same picture for six years, you memorize every line on someone's face, you imagine what it would be like talking to him, being close to him, and then, suddenly... there he is! In the flesh! You and he are breathing the same air, crossing paths for one moment of your lives! Yours, so insignificant, so agrarian, and his, so exceptional, so powerful, history-making! Hildegard's voice rang out with the rest: *Sieg Heil! Sieg Heil!*

The other countries made their entrance, in one long parade: Australia, Bolivia, the United States of America, Iceland, Egypt...

"Those damned backstabbers have a lot of gall, showing their face here," a man behind her said, glaring at Austria, Belgium, and France and they walked in, carrying their flags and smiling. "We'll show them a thing or two."

"We'll show all of them," the woman with him said. "We'll show them the strength of the Aryan race. These mixed race countries, they're no better than mutts, and they're competing against purebred greyhounds!"

"Especially the blacks," another woman said with disgust. "How can they even stand to bring them here? They'll dirty the facilities!"

"The Americans segregate the blacks in their own country, why can't they do it here?"

"Oh really? They segregate them?"

"Sure, sure. They can't go to the same schools, drink from the same water fountains, swim in the same pools. They even make them go to the back in the movie theaters and on buses."

Hildegard thought of the old man reading *The Metamorphosis* on the bench marked *JEWS ONLY.*

"Well, let's hope it stays that way. Anyway, why did they even bother bringing them? It's not like they're going to beat our athletes. Look how scrawny they are!"

In the span of three days, Hildegard watched Black Olympian Jesse Owens win four gold medals and break Olympic and world records, beating out German favorite Luz Long in the long jump.

"God DAMN it!" the man behind Hildegard cursed, throwing down his paper program.

Hitler did not shake hands with Owens, or indeed any of the Olympic medalists, after the reported snub caused the Olympic Chairman to tell Hitler he should shake hands with all medalists, or none at all. However, Owens disclosed that, while passing the Führer's box, Owens waved at him and Hitler did a little wave back. The Alabama native and record-breaking Olympian medalist would return home to a ticker tape parade, but no word or note of congratulations from President Franklin Delano Roosevelt, much less an invitation to the White House.

Owens would report later: "Hitler didn't snub me—it was our president who snubbed me. The president didn't even send me a telegram."

A strange thing happened that set a bad taste in Hildegard's mouth. She bought special Olympics souvenirs—a program for Felix, and a Jesse Owens medal for Johanna, who was the only girl in Himmelberg who could attempt a long jump—but, on her way out of the stadium, she was stopped by a man in a black military uniform.

"What's this?" he said, taking her bag.

"Souvenirs," Hildegard said, reaching for the bag. "From the Olympics."

The man had a red swastika arm band, and there was a skull on his military peaked cap. Hildegard recognized this, based on Else's descriptions, was the uniform of a Gestapo officer. He pulled the program out of the bag. Jesse Owens' face was on the front cover. He looked up at Hildegard and sneered.

"This material is being confiscated; it is inappropriate for German girls to be carrying this filth." He ripped the program in two and chucked it and the bag in the trash.

"But I just bought that—"

The Gestapo officer smacked her lightly across the cheek and shook his finger at her. "I don't give a damn if you bought it, Fraulein. You would do well to treat an officer of the Führer with more respect."

Otto came up behind Hildegard and put his hands on her shoulders. "I am a Party member, Herr Officer."

"If you were a *real* member of the Nazi Party, you wouldn't allow your family members to be buying merchandise that does not glorify the Aryan race," the Gestapo man shot back.

"We will know better next time. Hilde, let's go," Wilhelmina pushed Hildegard and Otto, whose normally calm gray eyes were blazing, away. "Otto, please."

"You'd better go when your hausfrau calls you," the Gestapo gave a cynical twist of a smile, "Herr Tee-Trinker."

Otto's knuckles were white as he gripped the steering wheel on their way back to the hotel. Hildegard's face was red and warm, and not just because of the slap. Her stomach felt as if it was on the floor of the car, between her shoes. *I thought parents were supposed to protect their children,* came a sullen voice. Another: *What could they have done?*

"I'm ready to go home," Hildegard said, rubbing her cheek.

"Me too," said Otto.

"Me three," said Wilhelmina.

It was a stormy summer day in Himmelberg. The town had been

suffering a heat spell, so everyone was glad for the rain. It would be the first of the fall storms. Children shrieked and splashed in their galoshes outside.

"And then he *slapped* me," Hildegard told Gerda. "For talking back."

"He actually *slapped* you?" Gerda's eyebrows rose.

"I know, I couldn't believe it. The police never *slapped* us back when we lived in Berlin. I mean, maybe a drunk vagrant or a gypsy or something, but never a law-abiding German citizen!"

"I hope they don't come to Himmelberg," Gerda said, concerned.

"Me too. Well, I have to go. I'm going to help Herr Weber polish the marquee letters."

"Oh, take a raincoat, Hilde, that umbrella is too flimsy—"

Suddenly, Luka Lange burst through the door. "Gerda!" he yelled.

Gerda jumped back, eyes wide. "Luka?"

Luka was sopping wet. His boots were muddy and his shirt was soaked through. It was clear he had been out in the rain for a while, but he didn't have an umbrella or a rain jacket, so Hildegard guessed he might have just walked out into the deluge. In his hand grasped a bunch of drooping, waterlogged wildflowers, which may have at one point resembled a bouquet. His eyes were terrified, like a rabbit in a trap.

"Luka, you're soaki—" Gerda began, but she stopped as Luka took five enormous steps with his long legs, bonking his head on the ceiling light as he crossed the room. He shoved the drooping flowers into Gerda's hands.

"These are for you."

Then he grasped Gerda by the shoulders, took a breath, stooped down and pressed his own face into hers.

Hildegard tried to use all her Hitler Youth army training to become invisible and stealthily backtrack out the door. Before she left the trachten shop, she flipped the sign on the door from *Open* to *Closed.*

100

Then she grinned and punched her fist in the air in celebration, running to the movie theater, jumping in every puddle she could along the way.

7

1938: The Stranger

In 1937, four things happened.

First, as Else predicted, the Gestapo did indeed come to Himmelberg. It wasn't long after the Olympics that men in black uniforms appeared.

The story of Hildegard's slap had by that point spread all over town, so the Gestapo received a lukewarm welcome at first. Pauline Fischer finally got the tea party she had been wishing for, and hosted the men for a formal welcome luncheon. The luncheon was really an excuse for her to use her new bone china, which was encircled with a gold ring and a golden eagle carrying the swastika in its talons.

Some Gestapo were stern and suspicious, like Officer Voigt. Others were friendly and courteous, like Officer Jäger, who helped carry Frau Schumacher's groceries to her car.

Irena's wish was also granted in the young, handsome Officer Engel. Officer Engel could sometimes not complete his duties patrolling the square because he was constantly barraged by teenage girls. Officer Engel was solidly Irena's territory, however. It was all over the day Officer Engel bought Irena an orange and vanilla popsicle; the battlefield was won. The coup de gras was when, as vanilla ice cream leaked out from under the popsicle and ran down Irena's arm, Officer

Engel caught the dripping ice cream with a swipe of his finger and popped the finger in his mouth.

By the same token, Luka and Gerda had become An Item. Esther pressured Luka to propose fast ("She's waited forever for you to make a move, dummkopf, don't lose her now!"), but Luka and Gerda were waiting for Gerda's grandmother to pass. Frau Roth was not Gerda's last living relative—her father had been killed in The Great War, and her mother had remarried, was living in Poland, and was emotionally unavailable—but she had practically raised Gerda, she liked to remind her almost daily, and was letting her live rent-free, and her father, God rest his soul, would be turning—yes, rolling!—in his grave if he knew she was carrying on with a Jehovah's Witness.

"Why can't you go for a nice Catholic boy, darling?" Gerda's grandmother pleaded with her, cataract-ridden eyes searching for the red-haired beauty as she clutched her quilt.

"Because all the nice Catholic boys are off playing soldier, Oma," Gerda curtly replied, tucking her blankets in around her. "Now eat your soup."

Not that there was much of a congregation left anyway. Hitler—though raised in a Catholic family, baptized, and confirmed in the Church, albeit by the skin of his teeth—was letting slip his real views on religion. Hildegard read in *Mein Kampf*: "Hence today I believe I am acting in accordance with the Almighty Creator: by defending myself against the Jew, I am fighting for the work of the Lord."

"I don't understand... wasn't Jesus a Jew?" Felix asked Father Schafer.

"Yyye-es," Father Schafer replied, eyeing Officer Voigt, who was passing by the church door.

"You are mistaken," Officer Voigt replied. "The Messiah was an Aryan. Our Führer says that Jesus was an Aryan fighter, and he was crushed by the Proto-Bolshevism of the Jewish puppet government."

"His execution was spurred on by the leaders of the Jewish community, yes, but because He allowed it. To make a new Way for Gentile and Jew, and all who believe, Herr Officer," Father Schafer said, becoming heated.

"Convenient," Officer Voigt smiled thinly. "When someone loses a game, and he says 'Oh, I meant to lose on purpose.' Sounds like a sore loser to me."

"This is not a *game*, Herr Voigt," Father Schafer said, red in the face. "This is the salvation of mankind! This is the Holy War that is being waged around us, the forces of good and evil!"

"I'm not concerned with invisible wars, Herr Schafer," Officer Voigt sniffed. "I'm only concerned with real ones, being waged by Bolshevik agitators and Communist anti-patriots." He turned to Felix and Hildegard. "My advice, children, is to not fill your head with made-up stories from thousands of years ago, but instead learn the values of National Socialism: power, integrity, steel-mindedness."

"We're not children," Felix shot back, but Hildegard pinched him behind the back.

"Oh?" Officer Voigt raised an eyebrow. "Then why haven't you enlisted?"

"He has a heart condition, Herr Officer," Hildegard interjected before Felix could start. "He's very sensitive about it."

Officer Voigt looked coldly at Felix and turned away, continuing his patrol. "Leave sensitivity to the women, young man," he shot at Felix over his shoulder. "There is no place for weakness in the Aryan race."

Hildegard breathed a sigh of relief as Officer Voigt turned the corner.

"Lying is a sin, Hilde," Felix muttered. "You know very well I don't have a heart condition."

Hildegard turned to Father Schafer. "Mea culpa, Father."

"I think, under the circumstances, one Hail Mary will do," Father Schafer smiled.

But fewer and fewer people were showing up to Mass on Sunday to listen to Father Schafer plead with his flock to show the fruits of the spirit—love, joy, peace, patience, kindness, goodness, faithfulness, gentleness, and self-control—because they did not like the anti-patriotic implications of his sermons. "If Jesus walked among us today, in 1937, would you recognize Him?" he asked an audience of now twenty people. "Or would you condemn Him as an outsider, a liberal fanatic, a vagrant who should be out working the fields or serving His country? Christ has no country, only the Kingdom of Heaven!"

This remark reduced the congregation to almost nothing.

Father Schafer was not the only one chafing at the presence of the newcomers. Herr Schulz had acquired a new movie, *Der Ewige Jude*, a documentary about the insidious presence of the Jewish people in the ghettos of Poland. *The Eternal Jew* was the brainchild of propaganda minister Joseph Goebbels. The movie poster, which Herr Schulz had volunteered to post all over town, showed a shifty-looking, unshaven, long-nosed man with a unibrow coming out of the shadows, squinting his beady eyes. The entire poster was bathed in a sickly, pus-colored yellow, making the Jewish man's skin look pallid and corpse-like.

"What a creep!" Karl said, staring at the picture.

"He looks like he's coming for your children," Louisa said grimly.

"Reminds me of Frankenstein's monster," Felix said.

"Frankenstein was *green*, dummkopf," Karl, the Karloff aficionado, corrected him.

"I was talking about the descriptions in the book, vollidiot," Felix rolled his eyes. "And it's the Creature. Frankenstein was—"

"I know, I know!" Karl waved his hand dismissively.

The movie showed Jews in the ghetto, praying in shabby surroundings, while cockroaches crawled up the walls. *"The Jews do not care about cleanliness,"* the narrator informed the audience.

Jews were shown sweeping streets and clearing rubble. *"Rarely do Jews participate in useful work, and when they do, the German government is making them do it. The Jews are lazy... they do not like doing the work."* A petite Jewish woman hauled a boulder the size of an ottoman out of the road.

"No, I don't imagine anyone would," Felix snorted.

"Felix, shut up!" Karl threw popcorn at him.

"Karl, quit throwing popcorn. Don't make Herr Weber sweep up after you," Hildegard hissed. Karl grinned and threw one kernel at her.

"The Jews are a people without farmers or workers: a race of parasites," the narrator continued. *"Wherever the body of a nation shows a wound, they anchor themselves and feed on the decaying organism."*

"It's true," Johanna whispered. "My father says Jewish shops started popping up like pimples all over Nuremberg after the Great War, when nobody could afford to stay in business." Then she shrieked as the movie showed rats swarming out of storm drains. "Ugh, rats! I can't *stand* rats."

Then Louisa screamed. "A mouse! A mouse just ran across my shoe!"

This caused all the girls to shriek and cry and stand on their seats, while the boys laughed and the panic spread to the audience, who pushed their way out of the rows and into the aisles and out of the auditorium.

Karl pointed as the mouse scurried down the aisle. "Look, a Jew!" he laughed.

Lars jumped over the seats and cornered the vermin, stomping on its head as it squeaked and squelched. "Got it!"

Herr Weber came out to dispose of the mouse and sweep up the popcorn. "Hilde," he directed. "Go put on something else. A musical, or a comedy, or something. Anything that isn't so disgusting."

"Herr Weber, what's wrong?" Herr Schulz asked.

"I'm not playing this movie," Herr Weber said angrily. "It's turning my customers' stomachs. It's not art, it's silly propaganda, and it has no place in this theater."

As Hildegard ran upstairs to the projection room and dislodged the film reel, the last thing she saw on *Der Ewige Jude* was the narrator introducing *"the Jew Peter Lorre, in the role of a child murderer."* Peter Lorre clutched at his hair, his eyes bulging out of their sockets. *"With the notion that not the murderer, but his victim, is guilty."*

A week later, Herr Weber would be dead. Ygritte witnessed the whole thing, pale-faced and wide-eyed. "I saw him. He was on the ladder, taking letters off the marquee. He clutched his heart, like he was having a heart-attack, and he fell off the ladder and died. That's what I saw," she repeated steadily to the police and later Hildegard.

Hildegard was inconsolable, ridden with guilt. "I should've been there," she sobbed into Felix's shoulder. "I should've been helping him!"

"He shouldn't have been on that ladder by himself; he was nearly eighty, what was he thinking?" Felix pondered.

"He was all alone," Hildegard choked. "I can't get over it... he shouldn't have been alone."

"No one should be alone when they die," Johanna sighed. "And yet so many of us are. At least he's with his wife now."

Karl, Lars, Felix, Luka, and two boys from Ygritte's grade, Ollie and Bruno, carried Herr Weber's casket up the mountain. Herr Kraus, Himmelberg's coroner, mortician, and gravedigger, had a hard go at digging the grave shaft, because it was November and the ground was hardening. The people of Himmelberg who were still spry enough to make it up to the peak of Mount Sigfried huddled around the grave, pulling their wool coats tighter around them as they shuffled from one foot to the other in the frost.

"People will shun an outsider. Herr Weber came from outside of this community, but he was one of us. I am reminded of the words of St. John the Baptist, who was also a fantastical, who chose to live in the wilderness and eat wild honey, rather than the comforts of home, proclaiming the coming of Christ: 'He who is coming after me is mightier than I. I baptize with water; He will baptize you with the Holy Spirit, and with fire.'"

So indeed were many of Herr Weber's film reels baptized with fire. The Gestapo went through the archives of the projection room, and threw out anything not on a pre-approved list. Most of the movies that were left were propaganda films. Soon after, the movie theater closed.

Meanwhile, far down below the German border, a failed government coup and civil war raged in Spain. This led to two warring groups: the Popular Front (comprised of communists, socialists, leftists, and liberals) and the Falange (comprised of conservatives and fascists). The right were wealthy landowners, businessmen, military personnel, and staunch Catholics. The left were union laborers, urban workers, and the educated middle class who thought of themselves as "enlightened to the people's woes".

In the middle of this conflict, fighting on both sides, were the guerrera, the people of Spain. By 1937, the Spanish Civil War had become a bloody conflict, rife with executions, murders, and assassinations. It wasn't enough to have an opposing political opinion. Spanish citizens had to be willing to die (and, more importantly, kill) for their beliefs.

500,000 Spanish refugees fled. Traveling north up the Iberian Peninsula, many were displaced in France. Some continued even further east and north, especially those who tended toward fascism. A few of these families passed through Himmelberg, but few stuck around.

In December of 1937, six days before Christmas, Otto suffered a stroke. He remained in the hospital for five days, unconscious. Wilhelmina sat by his side, clutching her rosary, counting each bead. Hildegard sat at the end of her bed and stare at the photograph, taken two years before, of Otto smiling with the camp counselors.

"Don't leave me alone, Otto... don't leave me alone again, I can't bear it this time... I can't bear it without you..." Wilhelmina whispered to her rosary.

"I'm not going anywhere," came Otto's voice, and Wilhelmina looked up, and one side of Otto's face was smiling at her.

Otto would lose the use of his right arm and the right side of his face. With great difficulty did he succeed in learning to walk again, but he would walk with a cane for the rest of his life. This would cement, in Hildegard's mind, her decision to not pursue a career with the Nazi Women's League or an administrative position at the Bund Deutsche Mädel.

But groundskeeping would be significantly harder to do now that Otto's tenant farmer had passed. "We need a young man to help us with all this," Otto said.

"I can do it myself," Hildegard said fiercely.

"But you shouldn't have to. We'll hire a young man."

The only issue was there weren't many young men to hire. Some graduates of the Hitler Youth were sent on an internship year, working the fields, but this would be someone who would be needed full-time; someone reliable. So, in the spring of 1938, Otto hired a Spaniard named Miguel Benaroya.

"Why would you hire a Spaniard if you wanted someone reliable?" Hildegard asked. "All these Spanish refugees are here one day, gone tomorrow."

"Hilde," Wilhelmina warned. "This is Otto's family property; he has the final say."

"*I'm* Otto's family," Hildegard countered. "I'm his daughter."

"That may be, but the Spanish refugees are fleeing a Civil War. They have nowhere to go. The Christian thing to do would be to help someone in need."

"The *German* thing to do would be to hire a German boy."

"There are no German boys. They've all gone off to be soldiers."

Hildegard opened her mouth to retort but found nothing. "Fine," she huffed.

As if to prove Otto's point, to Hildegard's chagrin, Miguel was exceptionally large and exceptionally strong, able to handle the chores Hildegard strained to do. He stood over 6 feet and was positively covered in dark hair. He had dark brown hair all over his forearms, and a dark beard (unlike the traditional clean-cut, clean-shaven German look), and a mop of black curls covered his head. Miguel's defining characteristic, however, was a bandage that covered his left eye.

"How did you lose your eye?" Hildegard asked him, point blank, over dinner.

"Hilde!" Wilhelmina exclaimed, putting down her fork.

Miguel held up a conciliatory hand to Wilhelmina with a slight smile. He looked at Hildegard with his good eye. "I was in the guerrera in the civil war. I fired an old musket, it blew up in my face, and shrapnel got lodged in my eye. The doctor had to cut it out."

Otto looked up, holding his fork in his left hand. Wilhelmina had taken to pre-cutting all of Otto's food, to spare him the humiliation of having his wife cut his food for him at the dinner table. And to spare him further humiliation, she pre-cut everyone's food. And to spare him from further-further humiliation, she covered everything in gravy now. He put his fork down and wiped his mouth, which sometimes had a dribble on the right side.

"Which side did you fight for?" Hildegard asked, stabbing a chunk of her rehbraten.

"For the Nationalists," Miguel continued. "My father was a member of the Falange, what you would call in Germany the National Socialists. We had a vineyard in Madrid, but the Communist bastards—perdóname, Frau Richter—of the Popular Front bombed it to ashes. 200-year-old vines, reduced to cinders. I lost my parents, I lost my sister, I lost my eye... there's nothing left for me there," he said bitterly.

"I'm sorry for your loss," Hildegard said, embarrassed. Miguel nodded.

"Well, you can find a new home in Germany," Wilhelmina said graciously. "We're all fascists here."

Early in the morning, Hildegard set out to milk Valkyrie, only to find Miguel there, already milking. "That's *my* job," Hildegard said.

"My apologies," Miguel said, releasing Valkyrie and opening up his hands in a 'don't shoot' gesture. He stood up so Hildegard could sit on the stool. Hildegard gave Valkyrie a reassuring pet, smoothly running her hand across the heifer's front haunches. Then, she began to milk.

Miguel leaned on the other side of Valkryie, looking down over the cow's sloping spine at Hildegard. "You don't like me very much, do you?"

Hildegard looked up at him. "What makes you think that?"

"You haven't been very nice to me since I got here," Miguel smiled archly.

Hildegard rolled her eyes. "I'm German. Germans are plain, hard-working people. We don't laze around all day, drinking wine and yelling at each other like the Spanish."

"I'm hard-working."

"You're not working now," Hildegard muttered.

Miguel laughed. "Good point." He grabbed a shovel and began shoveling manure into a wheelbarrow. "How old are you, Miss Overseer?"

"Nineteen."

"Ay, still a baby."

"I'm not a baby!" Hildegard turned around. "I'll be twenty in September."

"Just a baby."

"How old are *you*, Rip Van Winkle?" Hildegard snapped, color rising in her cheeks.

"Twenty-six."

"So if I'm a baby, what are you, a toddler?"

"Old enough to know better," Miguel said to himself, turning back to his work.

"You know why I don't like you?" Hildegard crossed her arms, leaning back on Valkyrie. "Because I know your type. My father is not as he was before, and we need someone *reliable* to help us. I don't see *reliability* in you."

Miguel rested an elbow on the tip of the shovel's handle. "Baby, when you're old enough, you'll learn that no one is reliable. You can't pin all your hopes and dreams on one person; you can only rely on yourself."

"Don't call me—" at this moment, Valkyrie ambled off, and Hildegard tumbled backward off the stool and into the bucket of milk.

Miguel burst out laughing, doubled over, his hands on his knees. "Perfect timing! Here, let me help you up." He extended a hand.

"Don't touch me," Hildegard threw the bucket aside, glaring. She stormed off to go catch Valkyrie, Miguel's hearty laughter following her out.

"Ugh, he's the *worst!*" Hildegard groaned at Zum Hirschen.

"I'm sure," Johanna said into her beer foam.

"Felix, why can't *you* just be the groundskeeper?" Hildegard pleaded with Felix.

"And spend my days shoveling cow shit? No thank you. I already have a job at the hardware store."

"Mixing paint? You'd rather be inhaling paint fumes than the open air?"

"Yes, I'm inhaling paint fumes now so I can save up enough to inhale paint fumes in Munich at the Academy of Fine Arts," Felix said. "Why don't you come with me?"

"I have to stay with Otto," Hildegard repeated doggedly.

"I can't wait to beat it out of this town," Felix said disgustedly. "I'm so sick of these Gestapo, following you wherever you go, asking you questions that's none of their damn business."

"Hate to break it to you, Felix, but there are plenty more Gestapo in Munich," Johanna said.

Felix vented his angst: "Why can't it be the way it was before? Why can't we just live our lives free of all these people bothering us? I'm so sick of hearing about Gestapo, and Nazis, and Jews, and refugees, and transports... I just want to live my life."

"Me too," Hildegard said, lost in her own thoughts. "I'll tell you what, though. I'm going to find a way to get him back. I'm going to pay him back for laughing at me."

Eventually, by following him and with careful planning, Hildegard did find a way to get Miguel back. Every day, Miguel sliced away at the hay field from sunrise to noon, when he would wash up and go into lunch. Miguel would continue slicing away with his sickle until 3:00, when he would jump in the cow pond and swim for ten minutes to cool off. Hildegard hid behind a bush at 2:50, waiting for Miguel's footsteps. She ducked her head, concealing herself, listening for the *splash* as Miguel jumped in and paddled to the middle of the pond. Then, she emerged from the bush, crept through the grass, behind the cows and their clanging bells, until she found Miguel's clothes, neatly folded on a rock.

"*A-ha!*" Hildegard cried triumphantly, snatching the clothes up.

"Hildegard!" Miguel cried, sinking in the water to cover himself.

"We'll see who's laughing when you have to walk all the way—" she began, but something fell from the bundle of clothes and winked golden in the sunlight.

"Hildegard, wait!"

Hildegard bent to pick it up. It was a necklace. A thin leather cord held a small golden amulet, no bigger than Hildegard's pinkie fingernail. Two triangles crossed over each other, forming a star with six points. Hildegard recognized it from *Der Ewige Jude* as the Star of David.

"Are you…" Hildegard peered down at the star, looking up at him incredulously. "Are you a *Jew?*"

Hildegard thought about running for help. She had seen and taught plenty of propaganda that cautioned German girls against cavorting with Jews, especially Jewish men. In the Jungmädel, Hildegard read a book about a German girl's mother who makes an appointment for her to see a Jewish doctor. But the German girl remembers her Jungmädel training and escapes before the Jewish doctor can rape her. The children sang songs about old Jewish babayagas, disguised as elderly grandmothers, who came out of the swamp and ate children alive.

But Hildegard remembered the old Jew who had been stoned by the children in Berlin, the look of surprise and hurt on his face. And she was looking at Miguel now. Before swimming, he had removed the bandage that covered his left eye. There was a red scabby hole where his eye should have been; it looked like he hadn't been to see a doctor about it in years. His right eye was light brown, almost hazel, and it was filled with terror. It wasn't like the rabbity fear that Luka had in his eyes before he kissed Gerda. It was a primal terror.

"Please," Miguel's whisper, barely audible, came across the water to her.

"Why are you in Germany?" Hildegard murmured, eyes wide.

"There's nowhere else for me to go," Miguel said helplessly. "No one else will take in a refugee."

Hildegard pursed her lips. She felt all the blood rush to her head as the weight of the impending decision sweltered upon her. She looked down, carefully refolding Miguel's clothes and placing them on the rock. She stuffed the necklace in the middle of the clothes, where it wouldn't be seen. She gave Miguel a final look, then turned on her heel and walked into the fields.

From that point on, Miguel ceased teasing Hildegard. In fact, Miguel said almost nothing at all to Hildegard. But he expressed his thanks for Hildegard's silence in small gestures. Hildegard would go to feed the chickens in the morning to find them already fed. She would duck into the chicken coop to collect eggs, only to find them collected and resting in a basket nearby. Even Hildegard's favorite chore, milking Valkyrie, would not be completed, but Valkyrie would be tied up, waiting, with the bucket and stool ready.

Even at lunch, when Hildegard asked Wilhelmina to pass the salt, the shaker would already be in front of her before she finished her sentence.

"Thank you," Hildegard murmured, picking up the saltshaker and allowing her eyes a moment to dart in his direction. Miguel nodded curtly, not looking at her, stabbing at his veal schnitzel.

Otto cleared his throat. "Miguel, no more for today. Hildegard will finish the work. I have something for you to do in town."

"I can go into town for you—"

"It is man's work. Miguel must go into town."

"Why am I always—"

"Hildegard." Otto turned his clear eyes on her.

Hildegard sat back with a *hmph*. "Yes, Otto."

Hildegard whacked away at the wheat field in the late August heat. Sweating, she mopped at her face and under her chin, squinting as a figure came down the road and made their way through the swaying wheat. The late afternoon sun was behind them, and Hildegard shielded her eyes with her hand to see as they approached.

It was Miguel. He was grinning from ear to ear at her. His bandage was removed, and in place of the gaping red hole, a brown left eye was looking at her.

"What do you think?" he said, beaming.

Hildegard stared at it.

Miguel tapped on it. "It's made of glass. Your father arranged everything, didn't tell me anything. He just told me to go to the doctor to pick up something for him, and the doctor sat me down and looked in my eye and had me choose from a leather case of glass eyes. They're from Austria! The doctor said your father ordered them weeks ago."

Hildegard smiled proudly. "That sounds like Otto. He's incredibly thoughtful and always so generous." *Does Otto know?* Hildegard wondered. *Did he hire Miguel on purpose?*

"I don't know how I'm going to repay him," Miguel said with a worried sigh.

Hildegard looked up at the cerulean sky, thinking, then down at Miguel. "Stay," she said. "Stay and help him."

Miguel nodded, understanding. "Let me take that for you," he said, reaching for the sickle.

"No, no, I'll finish up here. You go in and show my mother. She'll be so happy to see it."

"Good idea." Miguel turned and walked a few paces away. He stopped. "Hildegard."

Hildegard turned and looked at him. He was staring at her.

"Thank you," he said pointedly.

Hildegard went back to cutting the wheat, thinking about Otto. *He did it to make Miguel a whole man again,* she thought. *He did it because he no longer feels whole himself.* She thought about Otto, and Miguel, and all the men in Himmelberg, and all the men in Germany, and then she imagined millions of men, ordinary men walking around Europe, caught up without a choice, feeling so alone in their lack of wholeness, walking around in their own private crucibles.

August sank into September, Hildegard's favorite month, because it was the beginning of Oktoberfest and her birthday month.

While the famous official Oktoberfest celebration of Munich had its roots in the early nineteenth century, Oktoberfest celebrations in Bavaria stretched back before Christianity, like the midsummer fests high up in the Aryan origins of Scandinavia. The wheat would be harvested in late August and early September, and brewed into a sweet, caramelly, malty, yeasty märzen by mid-September, the start of Oktoberfest. The people of Bavaria would eat and drink and cavort for 17 days, until around October 3rd.

"Are you coming with us to Oktoberfest?" Hildegard asked Miguel. He looked at her carefully with his one good eye. His right eye was light brown, and his left eye was a darker brown. He told the Richters that the doctor had twenty shades of blue eyes, but only five shades of brown.

"I'm not sure," he said vaguely. Miguel had been to town a few times for grain and seed and larger purchases, but it was mostly Hildegard and Wilhelmina who went for groceries. Everyone knew there was a refugee living in Himmelberg, but no one knew much about him.

"I hope you will," Hildegard said. "The first time we came to Himmelberg, the town threw a big dinner for us. It was a bit intimidating at first, being welcomed by all those people, feeling everyone's eyes on you, but they mean well and they're happy for neighbors."

"But," Wilhelmina said, "If you're going to celebrate Oktoberfest, you're going to need to look the part."

Miguel emerged from the dressing room of the trachten store, looking humiliated. "I look ridiculous," he huffed, turning around to grimace at himself in the mirror. He was wearing lederhosen, the folksy knee-high leather breeches of southern Germany.

"Oh, surely it can't be more ridiculous than those silly matador outfits in Spain," Hildegard waved a hand.

"Those are *traditional,* not silly," Miguel said defensively.

"So are these. I think you look perfect. What do you think, Gerda?"

Gerda hadn't heard. She had a far-off look on her face, and her brow was furrowed.

"Gerda?" Hildegard said, concerned. "What's wrong?"

Gerda looked up. "Hm? Nothing."

"Trouble in paradise?" Hildegard smiled. "Anything going on with Luka?"

Miguel, as if on cue, disappeared into the dressing room.

"He wants to marry me," she whispered.

"That's wonderful!"

"But there are so many problems," Gerda continued. "My grandmother forbids it, his mother wants him to marry a Jehovah's Witness girl, and I'm a Catholic," she said.

"So? Just get married without their approval. Plenty of marriages are inter-denominational."

"How many *happy* marriages, though?" Gerda asked. "And that's not all. We'll have nowhere to go. His family keeps getting death threats."

"What!"

"Yes, Luka told me. People will throw messages tied to rocks through the window. Someone tried to set their house on fire."

"Have they alerted the police?"

Gerda leaned in. "Luka thinks the police are the ones who are doing it," she whispered, frightened. Hildegard's eyebrows rose.

"So why don't they move? Maybe they can move into town, so they won't be so isolated."

"They've tried. No one will take them in. No one will accept a family of Jehovah's Witnesses. Nobody wants to bring trouble on their own households."

It was true. Hildegard thought about Otto, who was already harboring a Jewish refugee, knowingly or unknowingly. Could he risk more? How much could Otto, a respected member of the Nazi Party, be expected to give? When would his generosity give out?

"I hear, up north," Gerda said in a low voice, "they are putting these people away. They make the Jews all live together in ghettos. They force them out of their homes, and make them live together in these big apartment buildings, sometimes multiple families in an apartment."

"That's awful," Hildegard said.

"Yes, but at least they're together! At least they have a place to live! I talked with Luka about it. He said that he has family in Berlin; he hasn't heard from them in months. They've been taken away, to a farm or something, an indentured labor type of situation. I said maybe we could go there—"

"They're called concentration camps," Miguel said, emerging in his regular clothes. He was looking at Gerda. "You don't want to go there."

Gerda looked up at him, unable to speak. So Miguel continued.

"There were a few in Spain when I left. They're not like indentured servitude or working on a farm. It's worse than prison. It's worse than anything. Gerda, take my advice. You should shoot yourself before going to a concentration camp."

He stalked out, the bells on the door clinging behind him.

Oktoberfest was here, although it looked a little different. Normally, the town would be decked out in pennants and bunting and ribbons and streamers of blue and white checkered print: the flag of Bavaria. This year, blue and white mingled with red and black and swastikas. The Führer, a Bavarian Southern boy and celebrator of Oktoberfest himself, had the idea that this year, Oktoberfest should not just be a celebration of Bavarian pride, but of German pride. Of Aryan pride. Of National Socialist pride.

Still, the large, fluffy pretzels were steaming, the sauerkraut was sour and punchy, and the bratwurst were sizzling in large flat pans of beer. Frau von Braun and Herr Weissman were at it (and at each other's throats) again, in competition for who could make the best Oktoberfest brew.

"As if you could possibly compete with my märzen!" Frau von Braun crossed her meaty arms over her significantly shelf-like bosom.

"Bah, who wants that old tired-out recipe? You serve it all year round!" Herr Weissman waved her off.

"I serve it all year round because people request it year-round! Paulaner could not do better!"

"Take your Paulaner knock-off and serve it to the pigs, you old cow!" Herr Weissman shot, dodging as Frau von Braun chucked a glass mug shaped like a boot at his head.

"So," Lars turned back to the group, as if nothing had happened, "Miguel, what kind of wine did you make in Spain?"

Miguel paused. "A... special type of wine. It was so delicious," he smiled thinly, remembering, "that the recipe was said to be passed down and blessed by God Himself."

"I'd love to try it!" Louisa exclaimed.

"I don't think you'd like it. Too sweet for German palates," Miguel grinned.

"Sweeter than a Riesling?"

"Much sweeter."

"Well, it's practically just grape juice, then!"

"Basically," Miguel laughed.

Frau von Braun placed a bratwurst in front of Miguel. "Miguel, you must try one of Herr Kraus' pork sausages, fried up in my Braunbrauen."

Miguel stared at it, then flashed a charming smile up to Frau von Braun. "I'm afraid, Señora, that sausage disagrees with me," he patted his stomach. "But I'd love some more of those spongy balls."

Frau von Braun turned red and giggled like a schoolgirl. "Knödel, meine liebe! Spongy balls, hehehe!"

"Would you show me how you make them… the knödel?" Miguel said. "My mamá was a brilliant cook, not unlike yourself."

Frau von Braun wagged a finger at him. "Nein, nein! A magician never reveals her secrets. But I'll be back with a whole bowl for you." She went off, chuckling to herself.

Karl smiled bemusedly at Miguel, raising an eyebrow. "Careful, there, Mr. Spaniard, or you'll have a new wife by the end of Oktoberfest."

"You certainly have a way with women," Louisa smiled, unconsciously squeezing her shoulders together as she rested her elbows daintily on the table.

"Hardly," Miguel rolled his eyes good-naturedly. "Where I come from, I've had bigger things thrown at my head than a glass boot. I've had practically the whole kitchen thrown at me," he glanced at

Hildegard quickly. "Even a milk bucket."

Hildegard cracked a smile, snorting into her beer. Felix caught the look and frowned.

"So, Miguel." Felix bit into his bratwurst. "How long will you be with us in Himmelberg?"

Miguel swallowed a draught of beer. "I'm not sure. Until the civil war is over in Spain. But I have nothing left to go back to."

"Are you a deserter, then? Why not stay and fight for your country?" Felix probed.

"I did," Miguel looked at him directly. He tapped his glass eye with his knife. "That's how I got this."

"You've seen combat?" Karl leaned in eagerly. "What's it like?"

Miguel said somberly: "Hell."

"Ah, so you're a pacifist," Lars said, jutting his chin towards Felix. "Like our boy Felix here."

"Ideologically, before the war, my whole family and I were fascists."

"*Were?*" Felix repeated.

"I'm not knocking fascism," Miguel said quickly. "I'm just telling you, having been in battle… war can rip everything you hold dear away from you." He looked at Karl with a sad wisdom in his one good eye. "Your family, your home, your sight… I'm just saying, if you're going to fight a war, make sure you're fighting for something worthy. Something you truly, actually believe in, to your core, to your very soul. Because, at the end of all of it, your cause may be all you have left."

Louisa broke the tension. "Hey, aren't all you Spaniards supposed to be really good dancers?"

Miguel looked at Louisa, bemused. "Charmers, dancers, fighters… you put a lot of pressure on me, Louisa!"

"Well, I'm about to put more pressure on you. How about a dance? I can show you how to do it German-style."

"Yes, Miguel, Louisa's great at doing it German-style," Karl chuckled lowly. Hildegard kicked him under the table.

A group of people began to circle up in the stadtplatz. Frau König and the Alpenhorn Four brought out tubas and accordions and began to play. Some of the other townspeople from neighboring villages also came to celebrate, bringing their drums, violins, and other musical instruments. Everyone was enrobed in lederhosen, green or gray felt Tyrolean hats, or full-skirted dirndls, swishing and swaying as the women spun around the square.

Miguel and Louisa joined the crowd, holding hands and twirling and spinning within the group. It made Hildegard happy to see Miguel smiling and comfortable within the dizzying swirl of people. She turned to Felix.

"Want to join them?"

Felix huffed and glowered at her. "*Now* you want to pay attention to me?"

Hildegard sighed, exasperated. "Don't be such a priss, Felix." She swung her leg over the bench to let herself out. She walked over to her parents' table. Wilhelmina was dancing with Mayor Fischer, who for a good show offered himself to every lady over 30 who was not otherwise engaged. Otto sat, hand on his cane, tapping along to the music. His dancing days were over.

"No dancing for us, eh?" Hildegard sighed, plopping down next to him and putting her head on his good shoulder.

"I don't mind it," Otto said.

"No, you never were much of a twinkle-toes, were you?" Hildegard giggled.

"It's not so bad," Otto continued, uncharacteristically chatty. "But there is one thing I regret."

"What's that?"

"I wanted to dance with you on your wedding day."

Hildegard looked at him. His eyes were glassy and wet. She kissed his cheek at the corner of his eye to prevent a tear from falling down into his mustache. "You will."

"What do we know about this Miguel, anyway?" Felix said the next day at the biergarten. "He looks like a Jew to me."

"He's Spanish, dummkopf," Hildegard said.

"But he has curly black hair all over him, like a Jew."

Hildegard stared at Felix. Since when did Felix become so concerned about Jews? He had always been contrarian about antisemitism. But Felix was always contrarian about everything.

"He's Mediterranean. Aren't they all kind of... swarthy?" Lars asked.

"*Swarthy* is a good word for it. He's certainly not Aryan," Karl said.

"So what, we're supposed to hate everyone who isn't Aryan? Anyone with brown hair? Lots of people in Himmelberg have brown hair," Louisa said defensively, toying with her brunette locks.

"No, but all I'm saying is... look, it all goes back to history, right? The Vikings, they conquered all of Europe, and they were Aryan. That's where our ancestry lies. So everything that makes us strong, makes us ruddy, makes us powerful... it's all from them. It's why we're stronger than, say, the French. Right? Because the French are descendants of the Gauls. So, logically, it follows that anyone with Viking blood, blonde or not, probably blonde..."

Everyone waited for him to finish. Karl took a breath, and said: "Is stronger than someone without it. There, I said it. So sue me. But you must admit I have a point. It all goes back to history."

"Didn't the Roman Empire conquer Europe first?" Hildegard asked, trying to cover her cynical smile. "I mean... they weren't Aryan. And they conquered Asia and Africa, too. They were... what's the word, swarthy?"

Karl glared at Hildegard, readying his retort.

"The Führer has brown hair," Louisa interrupted.

"I'm not saying it's a blonde thing," Karl said, irritated, "I'm saying it's a German thing."

"That, at least, we can all agree on," Johanna smiled. "Prost!"

"Prost," Karl said, raising his glass and meeting eyes with Hildegard.

"Prost," Hildegard smiled.

Best not to argue with Karl. He's always been so gregarious, and everyone's entitled to their own opinion. It's not like I can really convince him of anything, once he sets his head to an idea. It's just the way he is. Her eyes drifted toward the market and found Esther.

"Esther!" she called.

Esther looked up and waved nervously at the group of blonde-haired, trim-cut youths. Hildegard waved her over. "Come sit with us!"

"I don't know if that's a good idea," Esther glanced down at her grocery basket. "I'm supposed to be back to help with supper." Her voice became quiet, like a mouse's, her eyes on their beer steins. "And... I don't... I can't—"

"Come on, Esther, we all know your family doesn't drink," Louisa said, waving Frau von Braun over. "We'll order you some blackcurrant juice; it's still your favorite, right?"

"Stay with us for just a little while," Hildegard hugged her shoulders and plunked her down. "We miss you!"

"I miss you too," Esther said, her voice tight with an emotion Hildegard couldn't name. Esther squeezed her arm, like she used to. But her hands were trembling.

October chilled into November. The leaves—vermillion, gold, and hunter green—changed, withered, and fell. The frost set in. The ground became hard, embittered.

In Paris, a 17-year-old Jewish boy named Herschel Grynszepan learned his parents, Polish Jews who had emigrated to Germany before the Great War, had been deported. On the morning of Monday, November 7th, Herschel walked into the German embassy and shot German embassy official Ernst von Rath. Herschel immediately surrendered himself to the French police. There was a postcard in his front pocket: "May God forgive me... I must protest so that the whole world hears my protest, and that I will do."

It was all the excuse the Nazis needed to bring their fist down on the Jewish communities of Germany.

Heinrich Müller, the chief of the Gestapo and the SS, directed the Hitler Youth and SA to take "the most extreme measures" against the Jewish people. On the evening of Wednesday, November 9th, the men and boys smashed the windows of 1,400 synagogues and 7,000 shops. Torahs and holy scrolls were lit aflame. Gravestones were torn up and defiled. Women were raped. 30,000 Jewish men were arrested and sent to concentration camps. 91 Jews were murdered.

It was called Kristallnacht, or Crystal Night, because the broken glass littering the cobblestone streets of Germany's cities gleamed like facets of crystal under the streetlights.

Though there were several accounts of non-Jewish Germans trying to help their Jewish neighbors, British reporter Hugh Greene was an eyewitness to the scene in Berlin:

"Mob law ruled in Berlin throughout the afternoon and evening and hordes of hooligans indulged in an orgy of destruction. I have seen several anti-Jewish outbreaks in Germany during the last five years, but never anything as nauseating as this. Racial hatred and hysteria seemed to have taken complete hold of otherwise decent people. I saw fashionably dressed women clapping their hands and screaming with glee, while respectable middle class mothers held up their babies to see the fun."

Kaiser Wilhelm II, former King of Germany, stated: "For the first time, I am ashamed to be German."

While some stated this was the beginning of the Shoah, in Hitler's eyes, the Holocaust was well under way.

8

1939: Secret Birthday

It was the last day of January 1939. The people of Himmelberg listened in their homes, in Zum Hirschen and Zur Rentier, to the sounds of their Führer's voice at a Reichstag meeting. For two and a half hours, Hitler called out Allied countries who criticized Nazi Germany's pogrom of terror towards their Jewish citizens, yet were unwilling to take in Jewish refugees themselves.

"For hundreds of years Germany was good enough to receive these [Jews], although they possessed nothing except infectious political and physical diseases. What they possess today, they have by a very large extent gained at the cost of the less astute German nation by manipulation. Today we are merely paying [the Jewish people back] what it deserves."

Hitler had a message to the countries he intended to invade: there would be no mercy from him, for they showed no mercy to Germany in the Treaty of Versailles. "Thanks to the brutal education with which the democracies favored us for fifteen years, we are completely hardened to all attacks of sentiment." No appeals to man's better nature, Hitler made it clear, would be tolerated... revenge was a dish he intended to serve cold.

The speech would be heretofore known as The Prophet Speech, because of Hitler's forewarning of his intentions for the children of Israel and the world:

"In the course of my life I have very often been a prophet, and I have usually been ridiculed for it. [The Jewish race laughed at me] when I said that I would one day take over the leadership of the State, and with it that of the whole nation, and that I would then among many other things settle the Jewish problem. Today I will once more be a prophet: If international Jewish financiers should succeed in plunging the nations once more into a world war, then the result will not be the Bolshevization of the earth, and thus the victory of Jewry, but the annihilation of the Jewish race in Europe!"

In other words, the "Final Solution" to "the problem of the Jewish race" was clear to Hitler: annihilation.

"What's he saying?" Louisa asked. Hildegard, Felix, Johanna, Karl, and Louisa were crowded around the radio. "Is he saying we're going to have another war?"

"You're damn right, we are," Karl said excitedly. "You heard him... we're going to finally have payback for those backstabbing Allied countries. We're going to get it all back."

"We're taking back the Sudetenland?" Hildegard asked. "I can't believe it. We're actually going to take it back? What will the other countries do?"

"Nothing, if they're smart," Johanna said.

Louisa bit her lip. "I hope it will be a nice, peaceful takeover. Like the Austrian Anschluss, when they elected to join with Germany. Everyone's happy and unified. Aryans with Aryans." She was no doubt thinking of her father and how he lost his brother in the Great War, how there were so many men under the ground, instead of walking around Himmelberg, enjoying middle age. "Hopefully there won't be any bloodshed."

Karl grasped her forearm. "Bloodshed will be a part of it, Louisa. War is a part of life. But the Führer is working towards something that will ensure peace for hundreds of generations to come."

"I don't see why they can't just settle this with another treaty," Felix asked. "Why not re-write the Treaty of Versailles?"

"Do you think the Allied countries would be willing to participate in that? It's not very often in history that the victors willingly give up the spoils of war," Johanna countered. "It usually takes another war to settle things out."

"We just had a world war," Hildegard said, brow furrowed, staring at the radio.

Would Karl and Lars be here much longer? Would Felix? How long before he would be forced to sign up for the Wehrmacht? She thought of him, shivering in a trench, bleary eyes looking at the glowing red horizon, rattled by the rumble and roar of tanks and planes and grenades overhead. She felt a deep stab of fear.

Karl shrugged. "Maybe the war's not over yet. Maybe this Depression was just a break, an intermission."

"Some break," Johanna said.

Otto had left for his steel factory and hadn't been home in months. He spent his time between Berlin and his steel factory in Munich, cranking out tank parts, bullet casings, rifle stocks, and any other materiel the armed forces of the Wehrmacht could think of.

He came home for Easter and to oversee planting. Miguel and Otto sat at the dinner table while Wilhelmina ladled creamy green asparagus soup into bowls, and Hildegard served.

Otto asked the blessing, and Hildegard stole a glance at Miguel. He had his hands folded like a Christian, but he was deftly touching the medallion under his shirt. *Is he saying a different prayer?* She wondered.

He's praying to the same God; but are his prayers different from ours? She wanted to ask him about it. She wanted to ask him so many questions about what Judaism was really like, so she could sort of what was true and false.

The Führer said that Jews were a parasite upon Germany; sucking the blood of the economy of Europe out like a tick on the cleft of a thigh, buried deep with its head burrowed into the skin of Aryan culture. And that seemed true, based on what Johanna said about her father struggling to find work. Herr Schumacher said the Jewish department stores made it difficult for small family-run stores to thrive, but Otto was always talking about supply and demand and how businesses had to change with the needs of the market. If department stores were the way of the future, then whose fault was it that small German shops were struggling? Wasn't that the tenets of capitalism, the opposite of Bolshevik Communism? So were the Jews capitalists or communists?

And what good would war do for the economy, anyway? Wilhelmina explained that war creates jobs—Otto needed more workers at the factory to produce these on-demand military items at a faster rate—but, based on her time in Berlin, Hildegard knew that war also creates scarcity. And, if the world was in the middle of a Great Depression, wasn't there already enough scarcity? How much more could the people of Europe take?

Wilhelmina broke through Hildegard's thoughts. "I saw Lars and Louisa in town today. Are they together?"

"Hm?" Hildegard looked up. "Oh, yes. It's all very new, but we all knew it was bound to happen. Lars has been stuck on Louisa since eleventh year, when we were all in Hitler Jugend together."

Miguel looked strangely at her. "What is *Hitler* Jugend?"

"It's like scouts. Did you have a scout program in Spain?"

"Yes, but it was more of a community thing. Is it required of German children?"

"It is now," Hildegard said. She heard that parents could be jailed for refusing to sign their children up for the Hitler Youth. This troubled her.

"Hildegard was very good," Wilhelmina said proudly. "She was in charge of the little girls in the Jungmädel. Practically ran the whole program by herself. The higher-ups wanted her to make a career of it."

"But it wasn't for me," Hildegard said. She looked at Miguel, trying to relay a message she herself didn't quite understand. "Not anymore."

"All the same," Otto said. "It would have been better than sitting here all day."

Hildegard looked hurt. Hadn't she stayed in Himmelberg to help him, help with the farm? She was hardly sitting around. What did he want from her? A career? He had never pushed her towards anything, always let her make her own decisions. And the Führer had made it very clear that he wanted German women in German homes having Aryan babies, not out chasing professional employment.

This is what she told herself, but a deeper part of her knew a truth she wasn't willing to admit, but had just admitted it to Miguel: she had outgrown the Hitler Youth. There were parts of it she enjoyed and found worthy of her time, but there were other parts that didn't sit right with her. The Hitler Youth encouraged children to spy on their parents and report to bünd leaders if they were saying anything anti-Nazi. When she made the choice to leave, a part of her felt relieved.

"I'm not *sitting here* all day," Hildegard said sourly to Otto.

Otto looked at her. "I'm saying it's high time you started something of your own. A career, or a family. You could be married by now, with your own home."

"Isn't being your daughter enough for you?" Hildegard shot back. "I stayed *for you*. I stayed *to help you*."

"But I won't be around forever," Otto countered. As if to prove his point, he hauled his right arm up onto the table, crossing it under his left hand. "You must find someone. You could marry Felix."

"I don't *want* to marry Felix. I've said it a thousand, *thousand* times. He's a friend, and I don't love him in that way."

Miguel, looking as if he'd like to slip under the table and bury himself under the floorboards, reached timidly for the salt. Hildegard snatched it and plunked it down next to his plate.

"But he could take care of you."

"Why do I need taking care of?"

"Because there's going to be war," Otto said, coming to his main point. "I want you to be safe and taken care of."

"If there's going to be war, Felix and all the other men will be conscripted anyway. And I'll end up a war widow, just like Mother," she angrily gestured to Wilhelmina. "We had to scrimp and scrape for 12 years before you came along. And do you know why? Because everyone was *dead*. Because of a stupid war. Because one man shot another important man and *this* man's country was friends with *that* man's country, so *this* man has to die in the mud and leave a child fatherless because of *that* man's country, and he doesn't even understand their language!"

"You may disagree with it, Hildegard," Otto said evenly, "but there will be war. It's coming, whether you like it or not. You must prepare."

"*I* must prepare?!" Hildegard raised her voice, her chair scraping across the wooden floor as she stood. "*You're* the one who has been away from Mother for three months! Who's going to take care of her, if not for me? *You're* the one who's been supplying the army with bullets and tanks and God knows what else! What are you thinking?! Those bullets are going to kill boys! To slaughter another generation! And *you're* making it happen!"

"*Hildegard!*" Wilhelmina said sharply. Hildegard knew she had wounded Otto; she saw it on his face. But her need to say it had outweighed her conscience, and now she felt ashamed that she had hurt him. Embarrassed and angry, she stomped out of the dining room and upstairs.

She sat on the edge of her bed, trying to regain her composure, staring at the picture taken four years ago at the Hitler Youth camp. Otto was grinning, but you couldn't tell underneath his bushy mustache. His raised lower lids of his clear gray eyes betrayed his smile. He had gone to his steel mill and made beautiful and fitting presents for the campers and counselors, emblazoned with swastikas, and for a long time Hildegard thought it was because Otto wanted these young men and women to have something official, to show their pride in the Party he belonged to. But over time she realized that the purpose of the gift was to make them believe in something they wanted to feel. The helmets: to feel brave, valued, and protected. The combs: to feel beautiful, special, elegant. How many boys and girls had Otto seen grow up feeling like dirty street urchins, barely getting by? He was so sparse with his words; gifts had always been his way of communicating his real feelings towards the people he cared about.

A knock came at the door. Hildegard muttered, "Come in."

It was Miguel. He leaned against the wall, arms crossed.

"Have you come to chide me?" Hildegard looked up at him daringly. "To give a lecture to the baby?"

"No," Miguel said, cocking an eyebrow. "I came to talk, but if you're going to act like a teenager, I'll go."

"Fine," Hildegard shrugged curtly.

"Fine," Miguel turned to go, but thought better of it. "I just wanted to say I agree with you," he said, unconsciously touching his glass eye. "I don't want war either. I went through hell to get here trying to escape war," he sighed. "It seems to follow me wherever I go."

Hildegard was silent.

"It disturbs me," Miguel went on. "Your friends talk about how ready they are for war, but they don't know. They can't remember the last one; they can't understand. But it's even more disturbing to hear the older generation talk about it, because they *do* remember."

"It's like their memory is mixed up," Hildegard agreed.

"Right," Miguel nodded. He took a breath. "Hildegard, don't leave it like this with your stepfather. I left things badly with my father. We were *always* fighting. He wanted me to become someone great, I didn't even know what I wanted, and I resented him for pushing me before I figured it out. The last time I saw him, I told him to go to hell. I apologized because my mother asked me to, but I didn't mean it. Not with my heart. In my heart, I was still cursing him. And then some Popular Front guerreras shot him and my mother while I was off fighting for the Falange guerreras. And the Falange guerreras never thanked me for fighting for them instead of being there to protect my parents. Or for losing my eye for them. So all I got out of it was a dead father and unspoken words."

Someone cleared his throat behind Miguel. Otto was standing unsteadily, leaning on his cane. He was huffing with the duress of hauling himself up the stairs, somewhere he rarely visited anymore since he and Wilhelmina moved to the suite downstairs.

Miguel nodded to Hildegard and ducked out into the hallway, tromping downstairs to help Wilhelmina clean up. Otto sat down with Hildegard on the edge of her bed, the bed practically launching Hildegard into the air with his weight.

"You think I don't remember the war," Otto said. "I remember it like it was yesterday. It lives in my mind. I don't talk about it. I don't ever want to talk about it again."

"Then why are you doing this?" Hildegard asked.

"Because I want to protect you and your mother. It's not just about the money. There are bridges I have crossed without knowing I crossed them, and I am not on the steady ground that I thought I would stand on when I reached the other side. I joined this party because I believe in the cause, I believe in my country. But, every day..." he paused, searching for words. "I want you and your mother to be protected. To not be harassed."

"But how can you live with it? With knowing what you're supporting?"

"I can live with it. As long as you're alive, I can live with anything."

The next month, a ship full of 900 Jewish refugees called the SS *St. Louis* left for Cuba. These German Jews had applied for US visas, and hoped to sanctuary in Cuba only until their US visas were granted. But when the SS *St. Louis* approached the shores of Havana on May 27th, they were barred entry. The SS *St. Louis* then crossed the 90 miles of Caribbean ocean to Florida, hoping to directly appeal to President Roosevelt, but once again they were barred entry. With nowhere else to go, the SS *St. Louis* was forced to turn back, where they had to dock at Antwerp. 254 of the 900 refugees were killed.

As Hitler said: "France to the French, England to the English, America to the Americans, and Germany to the Germans."

Three months later, Hitler made a second speech to the Reichstag. He opened by claiming that, in the same way that Germans living in Czech-owned Sudetenland were being "persecuted", there were Germans living in Danzig, located in previously-German Prussia, now a part of northern Poland, who were also being "strangled". Hitler claimed that, despite critiques of bulldozing other countries and ignoring diplomacy, he had given several "warnings" and had tried to sue for peace with Poland.

This was not exactly the case. Poland had not directed attacks against the former Prussians of Danzig. Yet the exact same day as the speech, Germany officially invaded Poland. Faithful to a treaty promising protection from Axis powers, Britain and France declared war on Germany two days later.

On September 3rd, 1939, World War II officially began.

One month later, after Poland buckled under German control, Otto came home again. The steel factory was still merrily underway, churning out more bullets and submarine hulls for the Wehrmacht, but Otto had hired new foremen under Nazi guidance to help tend shop while he was away.

On October 11th, President Roosevelt received a letter signed by Albert Einstein warning him that German scientists were currently trying to produce an atomic bomb, and that America should develop one as a preventative measure, with Einstein's help. This would eventually turn into the top-secret Manhattan Project. On the same day, Otto approached Hildegard in the kitchen.

"I'm sorry for missing your twenty-first birthday," Otto said.

"Oh, it wasn't that special," Hildegard, a German girl who had been drinking beer since she was 16, said. "I just went out with my friends. Mother made me a bienenstich cake."

"I haven't given you your birthday present yet," Otto said. With effort, he got up from his chair, grasping his cane, and limped over to the kitchen cupboard. In the corner nook where two walls of cabinets met, there was an empty space. Otto beckoned Hildegard over.

"Reach up behind the cabinet, in the corner."

Hildegard looked at him strangely. She hoisted herself up onto the kitchen counter, reaching behind the cabinets into the enclosed nook. She was surprised to find a small shelf had been installed, on which rested a leather case.

"Pull it down. Be careful; it's heavy," Otto commanded.

Hildegard pulled the leather case down, all too familiar with the rounded shape. Inside, she knew, were six spools of film.

She looked up at him. "A movie?"

He nodded, glancing out the window.

The tape with the title had been stripped off. The leather case looked battered and beaten, as if it had been through hell to get here.

"When I was in Berlin, at a Party meeting, I happened upon a pile of items that were confiscated and going to be burned. I paid the man who was unloading the contraband 200 marks to 'forget' about this item." He looked at her clearly. "We're not supposed to have this, you understand. We will 'forget' about it too, after we see it."

"What is it?"

"An American movie. *The Wizard of Oz.*"

Hildegard's eyes widened, and she broke into a grin. "*The* Wizard of Oz? The new one? It's only been out a month! I can't believe it!" She hugged it to herself. "How will we watch it?"

"As far as I know," Wilhelmina said, coming in, "there's only one projectionist in Himmelberg."

Hildegard grinned.

Meet at the movie theater at midnight. Come through the stage door entrance. Don't let anyone see you. Burn this note when you get it.

Hildegard covertly delivered this to Felix, Johanna, Esther, Luka, Gerda, Ygritte, Louisa, Karl, and Lars.

Irena was not invited because she had a special mission: distract Officer Engel, who was on duty that evening.

"With pleasure," Irena cocked a smile.

The invitees staggered their show-up times to divert suspicion. The lights were kept off in the lobby. "We shouldn't attract too much attention, if we keep just the projector on," Hildegard said.

"Do you want us to help you?" Felix said.

"No," she smiled. "For my birthday, I want everyone to sit back and enjoy."

"I feel like I'm going to one of those Communist resistance meetings," Louisa giggled nervously.

"Don't joke about that," Karl said, frowning at her. "We should barely even be doing *this.*"

"Karl, I'm surprised at you," Felix smiled sardonically. "Normally you complain about *me* being the spoil-sport."

"You *are* a spoil-sport," Karl glared at him. "I'm just saying... we need to be careful. We shouldn't even be watching this American trash. It's all a product of Hollywood Jews."

Johanna groaned. "Good grief, Karl, even the Führer watches American movies."

"Laurel and Hardy movies are his favorites," Hildegard giggled.

This seemed to temporarily assuage Karl's concerns.

It was odd how quickly time ate up the structures of man. The theater has been closed less than a year, and already it was showing signs of wear, reverting back to its moldy, drafty, leaky state before Herr Weber had purchased and renovated it for the town. As Hildegard entered the locked projection room with her old key, she coughed on the dust and damp that hung in the air.

"I hope you still work," she said to the projector. "Have you forgotten my face?"

She loaded the film spool onto the feed platter and into the projector. Then, she attached the film reel's square holes into the teeth-like sprockets of the projector. She checked the tensile strength of the cambers, which held the film and kept it from bunching up. She checked the loud speakers and turned the projector on.

Nothing.

"Where's the picture?" Karl shouted up.

"Shh!" Johanna hissed.

Hildegard's heart sank in disappointment.

Miguel knocked on the door and let himself in. "Something wrong?"

"The film won't play," Hildegard said, gesturing to the obvious. "I mean, there's no picture."

"Is it plugged in?"

"Of course it's plugged in!" Hildegard said irritably.

"Okay, let me check the fuse box," Miguel said, and he disappeared.

She looked pitifully at the projector. *Pleeease* play for me. I'm sorry. I'm sorry I abandoned you."

And suddenly, the film blazed forth in a blast of sepia light. The few people who had come to see the movie yelled appreciatively.

Miguel came loping back from backstage and entered the projection room quietly. "Phew!"

"Thanks," Hildegard unbound the second reel.

"It was just a blown fuse," Miguel said, pulling up a chair next to hers. "It was an easy fix; he had replacement fuses in a box lying nearby."

"Not surprising," Hildegard chuckled, "Herr Weber thought of everything. He was always prepared."

"I would've loved to see this place full of people," Miguel looked down at the scant amount of people, couples cloistered together, who were brave enough to come to the screening.

"Oh, a few years ago, this place would've been packed. I remember when *Frankenstein* came to Himmelberg. *Everyone* loved it. It gave some of the younger kids nightmares, but I saw it again and again. Karl used to do this crazy impression of the monster—" she stuck her arms out and crossed her eyes, grimacing.

"Is that where Karloff comes from? Boris Karloff?"

"Exactly!" Hildegard grinned. Her grin faded. "It seems an eon ago. Everything's changed. Nobody... nobody's allowed to say what they really think any more. Nobody's allowed..."

"I know what you mean," Miguel said.

"Say," Hildegard said, trying to change the subject. "Did you know

Dorothy is supposed to be much younger? She's supposed to be twelve, but the actress playing her is close to my age."

"Still a baby."

"Not so much a baby anymore," Hildegard said, almost to herself. Miguel thought she was a baby, but she could probably shock him with everything she had seen by the time she was Dorothy's supposed age of 12. She had lost her innocence long ago. And her mother had lugged them all the way out here to the tippy-top of the mountain wilderness, hoping to reclaim some of that innocence, and here it was being taken away from them again. And Herr Weber was dead.

They sat in uneasy silence, watching Dorothy bicker with Auntie Em then barrel out to the wide open fields (as wide open as a closed set and a painted plywood backdrop would allow) of rural Kansas.

"Some place there isn't any trouble," Dorothy said ponderously, tossing pieces of donut to yippy little Toto. "Do you suppose there is a place, Toto? There must be. It's not a place you can get to by boat or a train. It's far, far away... behind the moon... beyond the rain..."

And then Judy Garland began singing what would become her signature lullaby, "Somewhere Over the Rainbow." And even though she was 17 years old, she sounded as sad as a woman who had lived a lifetime of misery. Millions of Great Depression Americans saw their own troubles reflected in a sad young girl, and at this moment, so did Hildegard. Her hand went to her cheek and she was surprised to see she had been crying.

Miguel was looking at her.

"I miss him," Hildegard choked, "I miss everything."

Miguel reached out and took her hand in his; he squeezed it tightly.

They sat there in silence, watching Dorothy's life be literally blown apart by a tornado, watching her past and present whirl by in a dizzying carousel. And when Dorothy slowly opened the door of her sepia farmhouse into the first-ever full-color cinematic splendor of the land of Oz, only then did Miguel and Hildegard release each other from their grip to sit forward.

"Ach! Mein Gott!" Hildegard heard a voice cry out. It was Otto's.

"Wunderbar! Wunderbar!" came another voice.

"Wunderschön!"

People began standing in their seats and applauding. Hildegard and Miguel exchanged grins, and then they too began applauding. They were so enamored with the brilliant yellow road and the dazzling ruby slippers, they completely forgot to change to the next film reel.

After the movie, Hildegard bid quiet farewells and thanks to her covert party-goers.

"We're driving home," Wilhelmina said. "You stay here and be with your friends. But be quiet!"

"Miguel, stay with Hildegard," Otto directed.

Hildegard thought about retorting "I can take care of myself," to Otto, but considering he had procured such an exciting birthday gift for her, Hildegard respectfully nodded.

Esther approached her. "I'm going home," she hugged Hildegard, then gave her a strange, sad look. "It was nice seeing you. You've always been a friend."

"Of course I am," Hildegard laughed, her eyebrows furrowed with confusion.

"I'm... I may not be... I may be going to visit some family soon, and I may not be back."

"Where are you going?" Hildegard asked.

Miguel put a hand on Esther's shoulder, shaking his head.

Hildegard huffed. "What's with you two? Are you in cahoots with each other, or something? Planning some secret vacation?"

Miguel turned to her and said plainly: "No, and that's the point. The less we know, the better it will be for Esther. And the safer it will be for you."

The gravity of the situation settled on Hildegard. "Esther... I..." She couldn't find the words.

"It's alright, Hildegard," Esther gave her a tight hug. "I hope to see you again soon," she whispered.

Hildegard found the tears coming up again, and she fought to keep her composure. "Auf wiedersehen," she said with a melancholy smile.

Felix and Johanna walked Esther home, and Karl and Lars headed off to more mischief. "Miguel," Lars whispered conspiratorially, "over in Krün, there's a little house, and the girls in there, they'll let you—" he reached up and whispered in his ear. He leaned back, eyebrows raised. "You in?"

"I have my orders," Miguel chuckled. "But maybe I'll meet you after."

The Fischer's house was on the same road out of the stadtplatz as the Richter's. It was high up on the hill. "Mind if I join you?" Ygritte said.

"The more the merrier," Hildegard said, and the trio began their moonlit walk home. Hildegard looked up. "Not much of a cover for a covert operation," she said.

"The stars are so much brighter here than Madrid," Miguel said.

"That's because there's nothing out here to block the light," Ygritte said drily. "*Everything's* better in Germany. If Hitler has his way, the whole world will look like Himmelberg."

"That doesn't sound so bad," Miguel replied.

"Doesn't it?" Ygritte said, lighting up a cigarette. "Mind if I smoke?"

Hildegard let out an impressed laugh. "Ygritte, I didn't know you were a smoker."

Ygritte looked at her for a long time. "There's a lot that you don't know."

After an awkward beat, Hildegard sighed. "I guess you're right." It was true: Esther was going off to who knows where, Otto was bribing

Nazi officials for contraband, even Miguel seemed to be acting aloof. Why should he call her a baby when everyone insisted on keeping everything from her?

She tried to change the subject. "Ygritte, please make sure to thank Irena for me. None of this would have been possible without her help."

Ygritte chuckled bitterly. "'Help' is a choice word. She wants to get married, that's certain. Mother made her start wearing a diaphragm, but I catch her stuffing it into her underwear drawer all the time. She thinks she can paint him into a corner. As if," Ygritte was acidic, "as if any of us..."

She stopped walking, staring at Hildegard with pursed lips. "Hildegard, I have to tell you something."

Hildegard exchanged glances with Miguel. "Does Miguel need to be here?"

"It doesn't matter. I... I've got to tell you. It's been eating me up like a cancer." She took a deep drag on her cigarette, then she threw it like a dart on the ground, snuffing it out with the toe of her shoe.

"That day I saw... I saw when Herr Weber died."

Hildegard's stomach dropped. "Yes... he had a heart attack."

"He didn't have a heart attack," Ygritte shook her head, eyes wide. "He was on the ladder. He was pushed."

Hildegard blanched. "What?" she said in a low voice.

"He was pushed," Ygritte repeated emphatically. "Officer Engel pushed him. He toppled over on the ladder, and... and his... he was bleeding from his head, I think his skull was open. He was gurgling, and he was looking at me... and he just... he died. He wasn't there anymore. He was just an old dead man."

"My God," Hildegard whispered. She put a hand to her throat.

"And Engel told me... he told me..." Ygritte fought to keep from choking on sobs. She took a breath, looking down. Then she looked up with fierce blue eyes. "He told me, 'Your sister likes me. She wants to go off to quiet places with me. It would be a shame if I got a little too rough with her. What would your father think? What would the *community* think?' That's what he said. Exact words. So I told the lie Officer Voigt told me to say. And since Officer Voigt was in charge of the case, he closed it."

The pit in Hildegard's stomach was rolling and bubbling, heated by Hildegard's boiling blood. It threatened to come up, like a spew of hot lava. "I think I'm going to be sick," she murmured.

"That's how I feel every day," Ygritte said, and she walked away up the road to her house.

Hildegard continued down the road in silence, breathing heavily, trying to process the evening. She felt dizzy, and she stumbled. Miguel caught her and helped her over to the side of the road.

"Put your head between your knees and breathe deeply," he directed, crouching beside her. "It will help ease the panic."

Hildegard let her head sink between her knees, feeling the fabric of her skirt against her cheek. "First I'm a baby, now you'll say I'm a cry-baby," she mustered a weak laugh.

"I wasn't going to," Miguel said gently. He hesitated for a moment, then he rested his hand on her back. "When my grandfather died, I felt the same way. And when my sister died... the Popular Front set off a bomb, and my sister was crushed under the building." He sounded dead. "She had been going to pray. She was lighting a candle for my parents. And she was under the cement wall for hours, being crushed... and then she just gave out."

"I'm so sorry," Hildegard said, looking up. "I can't believe those awful people would bomb a church."

"It was a synagogue," Miguel said, looking honestly at her. "They didn't care about a Jewish place of worship. We don't count."

He ran a slow, exhausted hand through his hair. "I wanted to die after that. I thought about killing myself every day. I would look over a bridge and just think… all I have to do is just trip. I could just let my feet do it, just stumble over this bridge, and then all this pain will be over. It wasn't even in my heart; it was in my body. My skin hurt. My veins hurt. My eyes hurt."

Hildegard felt embarrassed. Here she was, crying over a mentor who wasn't even her blood relative. Her mother was alive, Otto by a miracle was still alive, Felix and Johanna and Louisa and Karl and Lars were still alive. Miguel had left everything behind, had no one. "How do you stand it?" she whispered.

Miguel sat down beside her, pulling his knees up to his chest, and resting his bearded chin on his hairy arms. "I was going to do it. I had made a plan to do it. I didn't care I was the last of my line, I didn't care about the family property, what was left of it. But then I thought of my sister, and what she would think if she saw me in heaven. Would she be relieved? Would she approve? No, she would be disappointed. She would have resented the fact that her life had been taken, and I didn't live mine. So I decided to fight. I'm going to survive," he tilted his head and looked at her. "But I miss her every day."

Hildegard breathed out and leaned back to look at the stars. "Let's go home."

"Good idea," Miguel said. "I don't want to be on the road if there are any more Gestapo."

"If I hear the word Gestapo one more time, I really am going to be sick," Hildegard frowned. She looked at Miguel. "Aren't you going to Krün with Lars and Karl?"

Miguel laughed. "No, I wasn't serious about that. Those kinds of kicks don't appeal to me anymore."

"Any*more?*" Hildegard smiled with her eyebrows raised.

"When I was Karl's age, I was also… I did a lot of things because I was curious," Miguel remembered fondly. "And because I wanted to piss a lot of people off."

Hildegard laughed. "Like what?"

Miguel chuckled, shaking his head. "Oh no, your father would never let me in his house if I told you."

"Well at *least* tell me what Karl and Lars were going to see."

Miguel looked at her. "It's not ladylike."

"Obviously, it's a brothel. No one will tell me. Come on, tell me." She beamed up at him.

Miguel sighed to the sky. "Alright. Do you remember blowing bubbles as a kid? Well, there's a woman in Krün who..." he leaned in and whispered in her ear.

Hildegard burst out laughing. "Why would you pay to see that?"

"I told you," Miguel said. "Curiosity and pissing people off."

"Pissing *something*, if she's not careful," Hildegard said, approaching the house.

"Hold on, we need to burn the film," Miguel said, retrieving the film from the boot of the parked car.

Hildegard *hmphed* in disapproval. "It seems a terrible shame. Just a waste."

"Yes, but we can't be caught with it. Safer to burn it than to keep it in the house where it could be found in a raid." He grabbed the kindling and matches that Otto had left at a safe distance. "Your father's already risking enough."

As they watched the first color film burn to cinders, Hildegard turned to him. "Does Otto know about you?"

Miguel chewed his lower lip. "I don't know. I've never said anything about it to him. Some days I think he does, some days I think he was just being kind and taking a man off the street." He adjusted the small medallion distractedly, shoving it further into his shirt. "This was the first town I came to that didn't have a sign or something up. *Jews, turn back now. No Jews here. Jews, don't let the sun set on your back.* I went to

147

Switzerland, to the Basel Border, and they turned me back because I didn't have the right documentation. I snuck into Germany, thinking, *This will be fine. They're fascists here.* So when your father asked me about myself, I told him I was a fascist, and I was in."

"Well, keep it that way," Hildegard kicked at the ashes, making sure there were no bits of film reel left. "Just keep to yourself but keep saying those fascist opinions, and nobody here will bother you. Now that we're taking back the Rhineland, all of this will calm down. We're going to get back to normal soon, I just know it."

Hildegard was making pretzels. First, she heated some water on the stove and whisked yeast into it. Then, she added salt, butter, and flour into the warm, foamy water. She mixed it with a wooden spoon until it was sticky, then with her hand. Hildegard's favorite part of the process was spreading flour over the counter, turning the dough out, and kneading it. Similar to milking Valkyrie, who was well into middle age, Hildegard enjoyed kneading bread because the repetitive motions calmed her mind and allowed it to wander.

"Making bread?" Miguel's voice broke through her thoughts.

Hildegard looked up. "Pretzels."

"Why isn't the oven on?"

"You have to boil them in baking soda first," Hildegard took a long rope of dough, and with a swift twist of her wrist, curled the ends of the ropes into a knot and looped it through the circle, creating the signature pretzel shape.

"So that's how you do it," Miguel crossed his arms, leaning over the countertop onto the floured surface.

"Be careful, your arms are in the flour."

"I don't mind," he traced a finger through the flour.

"Yes, but I'll mind if I bite into a nice, steaming pretzel only to pull out one of your arm hairs."

"Yes, Fraulein Overseer."

"So we're back to teasing now," Hildegard said under her breath. Hildegard noticed that, ever since the night of the screening, when he held her hand and touched her back, Miguel had refrained from touching her. Indeed, he refrained from being in the same room with her. He would dodge her as she passed by like she was holding a poisonous snake.

There was a knock at the door. Hildegard wiped the flour from her hands on her apron and crossed the kitchen to look in the peephole.

She turned back to Miguel. "It's Officer Engel," she hissed, alarmed. "You should go."

Miguel crossed the kitchen and grabbed a knife out of the drawer.

"Are you crazy?" Hildegard shook her head. "That will provide a perfect excuse to arrest you."

"I'm not leaving," Miguel said, stuffing the knife into the back of his shirt.

Another knock, this one brisker, more demanding.

"*Hide!*" she hissed.

Miguel slowly shook his head. But he backed into the kitchen, out of eyeline.

Hildegard opened the door. "Oh, Officer Engel. May I help you?"

"Ah, Fraulein Richter. Just the woman I wanted to see."

Hildegard's stomach dropped. She forced a smile. "Oh, really? Is everything alright?"

"Of course, of course." He paused, smiling blithely. "May I come in?"

Hildegard felt a drop of sweat run down the cleft of her back. "Of course, where are my manners?" She opened the door. "Please, come in."

Officer Engel stepped inside, blue eyes sweeping the room, smile unfaltering. "I forgot to wish you a happy birthday," he said, eyes

149

finally resting on her.

Oh, God. He knows.

Hildegard smiled thinly, eyebrows raised. "Oh, thank you, Officer Engel. But my birthday was some weeks ago."

"Yes, I remember. I was on duty when you and Irena and the rest of your friends were celebrating in Zur Rentier." His eyes drifted over to the kitchen. "Hello, there."

Miguel was holding a glass of water, sipping it, his eyes on Officer Engel. He nodded his head with a jut of his chin. "Hello."

"I don't know if we've been formally introduced. I am Officer Hans Engel."

"I'm Miguel Benaroya. I'm Herr Richter's tenant farmer."

"Benaroya," Officer Engel cocked an eyebrow. "That's not a German name."

"No," Miguel continued sipping his water.

"It sounds… Italian? Spanish?"

"Spanish," Miguel said.

"If you don't mind me asking, what's a strong Spanish ox like you doing on a farm like this? You could be off fighting in the war."

Miguel tapped his eye. "I am half-blind, so I am ineligible for military service."

"How did you lose your eye?"

"Fighting leftists," Miguel said coolly. He had been ready to give his answer.

"Ach, good for you." Officer Engel said, taking a seat. "You wouldn't happen to have your papers on you, Miguel?"

"What's all this about?" Hildegard said impatiently. "Did you come all this way to wish me a belated happy birthday?"

"No," Officer Engel said, his lips upturned slightly, as if he had reached checkmate. "I came down because, as I was making my rounds, I noticed some people leaving the theater last night. It was very late."

"Oh really? Who did you see?" Hildegard said, keeping her breathing normal.

"I saw Esther and Luka Lange," Officer Engel said. "I know they are Jehovah's Witnesses, and perhaps they were having a secret meeting." He shook his head, pityingly. "It is illegal, you know, for Jehovah's Witnesses to have Bible studies. And yet they are determined to do it."

Hildegard was silent. The gears of her mind were spinning, overheating. And Officer Engel could see it, she knew. He was playing chicken with her. He was daring her to deny it.

"I assumed they must have contacted someone with a key," Officer Engel continued, "because I saw no signs of a break-in."

"You assumed right," Hildegard said. She crossed the kitchen to where her set of keys were hanging up on a hook. As she retrieved them, Miguel shot her a pleading look. She shook her head at him as subtly as she could, and turned around, holding up the key. "I have the key to the theater. I let them in."

Officer Engel arched his eyebrows, as if he couldn't believe he had wrenched a confession from her that easily.

"But you're wrong about the Bible study," Hildegard continued. "I invited them for a private screening."

"Of what?" Officer Engel's eyes narrowed.

"*Triumph of the Will,*" Hildegard said, her heart racing. *I hope my cheeks aren't red,* she prayed, *I always blush when I lie. Please God, in Your infinite mercy, whiten my face!* "It's my favorite movie. Were you here, Officer Engel, when it premiered?"

"No," he said suspiciously. "I don't believe I was."

"Well," Hildegard smiled benevolently, "it was quite a spectacle. Herr Schulz drove all the way to Berlin to get it for me. We had a big premiere; the whole town came to see it." She continued, laying it on thick. "I've always been fond of it, you see, because it reminds me of my time in the Hitler Youth. Did you know I was the head of the Jungmädel?"

"I did not."

"Oh, I'm surprised Irena didn't tell you," Hildegard said, pressing her luck. She felt emboldened. "I was in charge of *her*. And the other female counselors of the Jungmädel. I have a picture of the two of us together at the first Hitler Youth summer camp; would you like to see it? It's upstairs."

"That won't be necessary," Officer Engel frowned.

Hildegard smiled primly. "Some other time, then."

Officer Engel pushed his case. "You're *sure* it was *Triumph of the Will*, then?"

"Yes," Hildegard said, the heat rising in her cheeks. "You must know, Officer Engel. It's one of the few films left in there, after you and the Gestapo cleared it all out. After Herr Weber died."

Officer Engel rose slowly and took a leisurely step toward her. Miguel put his water cup down and stepped out into the living room. Officer Engel's eyes flicked over to Miguel.

"I believe I asked you for your papers, Herr Benaroya."

Miguel's big hands curled into fists.

Officer Engel slowly reached for his belt.

"His papers are here, Officer Engel," Otto said, lumbering into the room with his cane. He limped over to the secretary, unlocked it, and produced fresh white papers, clean and crisp. "I just had them re-authorized in Berlin," he said, holding them up.

Officer Engel stalked over to Otto and snatched the papers. He perused them like a hound dog sniffing out blood. He handed them back, masking his disgust. "Everything seems to be in order," he said, narrowing his eyes at Otto.

"Yes," Otto said. "We want to make sure we are following policy."

Officer Engel's face pivoted toward Miguel. "It must be nice," he sneered, "having friends who are so high up in the Nazi Party."

"I am a fascist, just like you," Miguel countered.

"I'm sure," Officer Engel said. "Well, I must be getting back to my post. And, if I were you, Hildegard, I would refrain from any more midnight screenings."

"I didn't realize I needed permission from the Gestapo to have a birthday party," Hildegard shot before she could stop herself. Otto put a hand on her shoulder.

Officer Engel narrowed his eyes. "Take my advice, fraulein. Live your life as if you need permission from the Gestapo to do anything. Then, you will have nothing to fear. Better to ask for permission than beg for forgiveness."

"Good advice," Otto said. "Thank you, Herr Officer."

Officer Engel turned on his heel and stalked out.

Miguel let out a sigh of relief and removed the knife from the back of his shirt, returning it to the kitchen drawer. He crossed to the secretary and looked at the papers. He looked up at Otto. "Thank you, Herr Richter."

Otto pulled Hildegard closer to him. "Thank *you*, Miguel. For protecting her."

Before Hildegard could say anything, Miguel spoke her thoughts. "She can handle herself." With a nod to both of them, he left the house and crossed toward the barn.

Otto turned to Hildegard. His eyes were very afraid. "You must be more careful."

"Yes, Otto." Hildegard nodded.

"No more backtalk."

"Yes."

"I'm calling my foreman," Otto said. "I'm going to stay in Himmelberg. At least until we're rid of these Gestapo."

"Maybe you could pull some strings," Hildegard offered. "Have him transferred somewhere else?"

"When you cut off the head of a sea serpent, two more grow in its place," Otto said, walking out of the room.

Hildegard heard the pot hissing and realized that the baking soda water was boiling over. She turned the heat down, then went back to twisting pretzels. As she passed the counter, she saw what Miguel had been drawing in the flour.

Hilde.

The next day, when Hildegard thought the coast was clear, she went to the trachten shop to warn Gerda and everyone else at the screening of what had happened.

"I was able to lie to him, but if he asks you what movie you saw, you need to say *Triumph of the Will,* got it?"

"Got it," Gerda said, troubled. "Thank you. For protecting Luka and Esther."

"I don't know how I was protecting them; I was telling the truth. Well, sort of. I mean, they weren't having a Bible study."

"No, but it would've been easy to just blame it on them. They *do* have Bible studies. They just haven't gotten caught yet," Gerda chewed a fingernail.

"Well, that would be lying. It would have been easy, but it would have been wrong."

"Yes," Gerda said uncertainly.

"Gerda," came a voice from the storage room. *"Gerda!"*

Gerda and Hildegard crossed to the back of the store. It was Luka. He looked as if he had been dragged through the dirt, and his right eye was swollen and bruised.

"Oh my God, Luka! What happened to you?"

"The Gestapo came to our house last night," Luka said. Hildegard crossed the store and locked the front door, turning the *Open* sign to *Closed.* She assumed Gerda had given him a key to the back door, for who knows what purpose, and that's how he let himself into the closet. He looked at Hildegard. "They know. They saw us."

"Did you tell them anything?"

"No," Luka said, indicating his eye. "That's how I got this. But they think we were having a Jehovah's Witness meeting."

"I told them we were watching *Triumph of the Will,* and I burned the evidence of *The Wizard of Oz,*" Hildegard said in a hushed voice. "I think you're safe."

"No, Hildegard, that's the point," Luka looked at her, terrified. She remembered the look in his eyes when he got the nerve up to woo Gerda, but now this look was so similar to Miguel's the day she found his Star of David necklace. "We'll *never* be safe. Not while the Gestapo are here. Not ever, I think." He took Gerda's hand urgently. "We're leaving. Tonight. Gerda, I want you to come with me."

"What?!" Gerda's eyes were wide.

"Gerda, please. I need you. Please, come with me."

Gerda shook her head. "You... I can't... I can't just *leave* everything, Luka."

"I know. I know I'm asking a lot. I know your grandmother is still here, and she wouldn't approve. But please. Come with me. We can be married."

Hildegard wished she were an invisible fly on the wall. Her heart was breaking for Luka, because Gerda did not look hopeful at the prospect. She and Esther had worked so hard to get them together, and Luka had come so far out of his shell... but did any of that matter, when it was life or death?

"Luka," Gerda's eyes were filled with tears. "I..."

"We'll find a way," Luka pleaded. "None of it will matter, as long as we're together."

"I *can't,*" Gerda cried. "I *can't,* Luka!"

She pulled her hand away from him. Luka looked as if she had put a knife into his stomach. He stepped back.

"Then this is goodbye."

"Luka, please. Please try to understand."

"I do," Luka said somberly. "Goodbye, Gerda."

He gave her back the key and let himself out the back door. Gerda collapsed into sobs, and Hildegard held her. *I should have told him to hug Esther for me,* she thought.

In the end, it was for the best that Gerda did not go with the Langes. Because of their large family, with multiple babies who fussed in the night, the Jehovah's Witnesses heading for the Swiss border did not make it very far before they were caught by border patrol. After a night in jail filled with terror, interrogation, and torture, the Langes admitted they were Jehovah's Witnesses. The official policy was to police them onto a train and send them to a concentration camp, but it had been a long night, and policies were broken all the time, especially with escapees. The border patrol officers marched them out to the back of the building in a line, took aim, and shot them all at the same time, with the exception of the little ones, who were shot in the second round, as their mother and sisters who were holding them collapsed to the floor. The Langes were driven into the forest, where a mass grave full of other escapees lay. Luka and Esther's bodies were stripped naked and dumped in, where they lay side by side, and covered with dirt.

9

1940, Part One: Parade

It was May.

Himmelberg was dripping with flowers. In May in the Alps, every bright and glorious flower bloomed fiercely, and color was at its zenith. Golden sunflowers tilted their faces toward the sun. The tulips planted in the stadtplatz were like red and yellow teacups. Cherry trees are full of crepey, blushing blossoms, billowing like puffs of cotton candy and fluttering like butterfly's wings when the breeze pushed the petals off their dark branches. It was the end of strawberry season, when the little teardrop-shaped gems hung voluptuously from their runners, shaded from the luxuriously soft late spring sun by emerald-hued leaves, branching over them like umbrellas. The strawberries were so achingly juicy and red, when you bit into its soft flesh, magenta-colored juice would run down your fingers, and your hands, and onto your shirt, and you were so enraptured you didn't care about the stains. The people of Himmelberg, during the strawberry festival, would walk around looking as if they had been riddled with bullets, for all the strawberry juice that stained their clothes.

Hildegard and Miguel were hard at work in the fields, tilling the soil for planting corn in the west field. The east field was green with ripening wheat, while the field to the south of the house lay fallow for a season. Hildegard guided the family's draft horse, Falco, as it pulled the plow, and Miguel pushed the plow into the soil. There had been a tractor, but it was donated for the war effort. Then they would pick strawberries and snap tender white asparagus stalks at the base of their necks, and they would talk.

Hildegard forcefully ignored the signs her body was sending her. The buzzy, nervous feeling she got in her stomach as they talked, as if her gut had been replaced by a smooth, papery ball teeming with wasps. She found herself looking forward to their early morning chores, working in the fields, mentally preparing herself for what she would ask him about today, visualizing the conversation. But when the time came, her nerves overcame her and she pretended to act aloof and arch, to appear older and wiser than she felt. And, to her great dismay, she couldn't stop herself from watching him in the late afternoon from her window. She would be doing some mundane thing, brushing her hair or sweeping the floor or changing linens, and her eyes would wander out to wherever he was in the fields. One time, he caught her looking down at him. He looked up and waved, and she turned red and hastened out of the room, inventing a new chore for herself.

He's a Jew, dummkopf, she lectured herself. *He's a son of Israel, a cursed race.* But every day she believed it less and less. He was a Jew, he was different from her, but it was exciting. *You only want him because you can't have him, you insipid teenager,* she continued her inward berating. *And you don't want him. You* don't *want him. It's not even an infatuation. It's just a friendship. A perfectly normal friendship.*

With a Jew.

He wouldn't talk about his Judaism with her, not ever in public, nor in the fields, but he would talk about Spain. He would tell her about his journeys around Spain, before the Spanish Civil War, and how he ran with the bulls in Pamplona, and about watching a bull be gored by a matador and the cheer of the crowds.

"I think that would make me sick," Hildegard said.

"Do you get sick at the sight of blood?"

"No," Hildegard said defensively, "but I don't think I could watch someone impale a bull just for the sake of impaling him."

"If it makes you feel better, sometimes the bull gets to do the impaling. I saw a man impaled through the thigh by a bull once."

"Ugh. It doesn't make me feel better, actually. And the matadors are the ones who are enraging the bull, poking and prodding it before the match? It doesn't sound like a fair fight."

"I don't think it's supposed to be a fair fight. It's… it's supposed to represent a larger battle. Between good and evil. Man and beast."

Hildegard turned and looked at him. "And you don't see the irony in that?"

Miguel raised his eyebrows.

Hildegard bit her lip, realizing she had gone too far. But there was no backtracking now. "I feel as if… sometimes… no, all the time. Like Hitler is the matador, and the Jews are the bull."

Miguel rested his arms on the plow, thinking.

Hildegard patted Falco, smoothing the glistening chestnut fur on his flanks.

Miguel approached her, and said in a low voice. "I understand what you mean. I think people in Himmelberg hate Jews because they don't know any Jews. Ignorance leads to hate. But you're right… Hitler is a matador. Because the matador knows his enemy. The matador instigates and provokes the bull to learn the bull's weaknesses. And, when he has the bull cornered, that's when he strikes." He looked at her earnestly. "That's what I'm afraid of."

Hildegard was aware of his closeness. She watched in disdain as her arm hairs stood on end, and she rubbed them, trying to calm her skin down.

Miguel continued, looking at her intently with his one hazelnut-colored eye, the other one dead and brown and glassy. "But I'm not just a Jew, Hildegard. My blood is old and eastern and passed down from Abraham, but it's not solely my identity. Do you feel that being descended from some horn-helmet Viking with blonde braids and a red beard entirely comports who you are?"

"No," Hildegard squeaked.

"I am a *man*," he stepped toward her. "I have interests, skills, hobbies, desires, dreams. I have a heart..." he looked down at her. "Why are you rubbing your arms like that?"

"I'm... cold."

Miguel raised an eyebrow. "But you're sweating."

"I... I'm not feeling well. I'm going... inside." Hildegard stepped back and walked quickly to the house, arms swinging robotically in front of her.

Henri was home on leave, to the delight of the people of Himmelberg and the envy of Karl and Lars. Mayor Fischer had a dinner in honor of the town's first member of the Luftwaffe, the air force branch of the Wehrmacht.

"Henri, you lucky bastard," Karl clapped him on the back, shoving a stein of Weissbier in Henri's hands, "what's it like?"

"Amazing. Thrilling. Being up in the air, doing tail spins, hitting those Polacks and Frogs... pap pap pap pap pap!" He mimicked the report of air fire, shaking his fists like he was at the controls.

Hildegard smiled bemusedly at Henri. He was a man now, just turned twenty-two, but he was still boyish. Is this what Miguel thought of her? Acting like a kid? Maybe twenty-two was still a kid, just in a grown-up body. She didn't know what made a twenty-two-year-old a kid and a twenty-eight-year-old an adult, though. When she turned twenty-eight, would she feel like an adult? What was the age when becoming "older and wiser" magically happened?

"God, I'm so jealous. I would enlist right now, today, if it weren't for my father's butcher shop."

"Bah, your father can hire a boy. We need all the men we can get. You'd be climbing the ranks in a cinch, Karl. You *look* like the perfect SS Officer."

Karl, whose hair was white-gold and whose eyes were a piercing blue, beamed with pride. "You think so?"

"Sure. And Karl, the girls? They would be all over you. They see us coming in our uniforms and their legs just *open*, Karl. You wouldn't believe it."

Karl groaned, laughing. Louisa smiled politely and hugged Lars' arm tighter around her.

"Ach, sorry Louisa, I forgot. I've been away for so long! When is the happy day for you and Lars?"

"Next month. June 25th."

"Lars, take my advice: sign up for the Wehrmacht after the honeymoon. The benefits, the career, it would provide a good life for you and Louisa. Louisa, wouldn't you like to be an officer's wife?"

"Not if her husband's dead," Felix said. Hildegard nudged him, but she sent him a look that said *I was thinking the same thing.*

"Ah Felix, still a pacifist, eh?" Henri said patronizingly.

"No, I just think all of this is getting out of hand," Felix said defensively. "People have gone Nazi-crazy. It's all anyone talks about here."

"And why shouldn't they?" Johanna said. "We're proud of Germany and our might. It seems like every day we take control of a new country."

"And that doesn't scare you?"

"No, it doesn't," Johanna bit back. "It shows our strength. I'm proud of my country," she looked Felix up and down. "Though I can't say the same for you."

"Johanna," Hildegard put a hand on her shoulder, "please. Let's all remember we're friends." She hugged Felix and Johanna to her, and looked at Henri. "Henri, we're all very proud of you. You signed up to serve your country when we were all just kids, and that takes incredible bravery and patriotism. I think," giving a warning glance to Felix, "what Felix is saying is that he's concerned for Lars' safety. His father died in the Great War, as did mine."

"We're actually calling it World War I now, Hildegard," Henri smiled forgivingly. "This is World War II. And I completely understand. But there are plenty of opportunities to rise in the ranks of the SS without facing combat. I hear, and this is very hush-hush, you understand," Henri leaned in conspiratorially, "I hear that Hitler just gave orders to build a new work camp."

"So Lars can find a career as a prison guard?" Felix asked sardonically.

"Is it like Dachau?" Johanna asked. Dachau was a prison, everyone knew about it as it was right outside of Munich, but few people knew what went on inside. "For political prisoners?"

"This one's going to be even bigger than Dachau," Henri said in a hushed voice. "Like nothing we've ever seen before. A new prison for a new Reich."

"Where is it?"

"Poland."

"Ugh!" Louisa said, disgusted. "I don't want to move all the way out to Poland for some career opportunity!"

"Keep your voice down," Henri commanded. Hildegard could see the military had made him more commanding, more sure of himself. He glanced around and sipped his Weissbier. "The reason why it's in Poland is because there are so many Jews there," he said, his lips curling. "They're swarming there like a nest of rats."

"I *hate* rats," Louisa grimaced. This conversation was going from bad to worse.

"But it's not for Polish Jews. It's for *all* of them," Henri grinned. "All the Jews in the world!"

"Wow," Karl said, impressed.

"We're finally going to be rid of them," Johanna breathed a sigh of relief. "Keep them locked up, like mice in a cage, that's where they belong."

"Not for long," Henri said coyly, taking a long draught of his beer. His eyes drifted over to Miguel, who was sitting with Wilhelmina and Otto. "Who's that?"

"That's Mi*guel*," Johanna said archly, eyes darting to Hildegard. "Herr Richter's tenant farmer."

"Miguel? Is he Spanish?"

"He's a refugee," Hildegard spoke up, feeling the heat in her cheeks rising. *It must be because I'm lying*, she thought. "He left Spain during the Spanish Civil War. He saw combat, like you."

"Why isn't he back in Spain? The civil war's over," Henri said, looking at Miguel strangely. "What is he waiting around here for?"

"He has nothing left there. He likes it here."

"And the girls like him," Johanna said, winking at Louisa.

"He's awfully hairy."

"He's Mediterranean," Hildegard said and excused herself. "Does anyone want another beer?"

"Ask Miguel if he has any of that Spanish wine," Johanna called to Hildegard's back. "Since you're so thirsty."

Hildegard blushed and ignored the comment; she wove her way through the crowd, carrying four steins of beer. She approached Otto, Wilhelmina, and Miguel.

"You look like the typical German girl," Miguel laughed. "They have

German beer posters in the clubs in Madrid, with a blonde girl in a peasant dress, holding four beers like that." He took two mugs from her, handing them to Otto and Wilhelmina. Hildegard handed one to Miguel. "And she had her hair braided like that, too," he smiled.

During town celebrations, the women of Himmelberg would braid their hair into two plaits, weaving it above their heads like a crown. And in the spring and summer, they would weave ribbons and flowers into the braids, to make it look like they too were trees in bloom. Like Daphne, fleeing the amorous advances of Apollo.

"Maybe we could go into business together," Hildegard grinned. "You can be the poster-boy for Spanish wine, and I'll be the poster-girl for German beer."

"And we'd need an Irish girl for whiskey."

"And a big Kossak for vodka. With our powers combined, we'd have Europe drunk out of their minds in a single night, and we'd be rich!"

Miguel laughed. Hildegard felt that nervous buzzing in her gut and took a gulp of beer to calm her nerves. It did not make it better. She glanced at Otto and Wilhelmina, who were conversing with the Schumachers.

"Are you going back?"

"Back home?"

"Back to *your* home." Hildegard said, searching his eye. "Now that the civil war is over."

"I've been thinking about it," Miguel said in a low voice after a long pause. "I don't know as much as I'd like to about what conditions are like; the radio doesn't give much news about countries that aren't being invaded at the moment," he surreptitiously looked around to see if anyone was listening. "I've heard that the fascists have taken power, but I'm afraid..." he paused. "I'm afraid that before long, it may become like... like it is here."

"But still, you would be with your countrymen. You would be safe.

Safer. Maybe. What's stopping you from going?"

Miguel pursed his lips and stared at her, as if the answer were obvious.

"Ladies and gentlemen!" Herr Fischer boomed over the microphone on the stadtplatz stage. "Damen und herren! May I have your attention please! Our hometown hero, Henri, has honored us with a visit, and he has prepared a special speech!"

The townspeople of Himmelberg began to clap for Henri. Hildegard and Miguel turned to see Henri approach the stage.

"Thank you, Mayor Fischer. I am honored to stand in front of you today. I am honored to serve my country, and my Führer, as we make the world a better place. An Aryan place. We are providing stability to a continent racked with economic turmoil for the past two decades, due in large part to the parasitic Jewish race."

Karl, Lars, and Johanna began to boo. Others joined in.

"When I joined the Luftwaffe, I must admit," Henri shrugged good-naturedly, "I was in it for the glory. But training with my command has developed in me a new sense of leadership. I feel a bond of brotherhood with my fellow soldiers that is second only to the bond I feel with my kinsmen, with you, the people of Himmelberg."

The townspeople applauded appreciatively. There were whistles and cheers.

"We are in the midst of vanquishing those who would stand against us in France," Henri said, pounding a fist into his open hand. "But I am *sure* that a swift victory awaits us! The Führer assures us that France will buckle under the might of our Aryan warriors in less than a month, in the same way that Poland too came under the reign of our glorious leader!"

"Heil Hitler!" Herr Schumacher saluted, raising his right arm.

"Sieg Heil!" Frau König joined in, raising her arm, her husband as well.

"In a matter of weeks, the Rhineland will once more be brought back to the bosom of the Fatherland!" Henri raised his fists victoriously.

"Sieg Heil! Sieg Heil! Sieg Heil!" More and more townspeople were raising their arms. People began cheering and yelling excitedly, and soon the whole stadtplatz of townspeople were on their feet, saluting and chanting.

"Which is why the Wehrmacht needs manpower more than ever. If you are young and able, I *urge you...* fight for your country! Fight for your Führer!"

Hildegard looked over at Karl and Lars. Their arms were around each other's shoulders; they were nodding excitedly to each other.

"And," he spread his hands out over the chanting crowd, quieting them. "And... I have a special message for you. I was sent on leave, with other Bavarian soldiers, back to our hometowns. But only a certain number of us were permitted to leave, you understand," he said, building the suspense. "For, as you know, last month was the Führer's birthday. He is so proud of us all, but particularly his fellow Bavarians, in fighting for victory on the shores of the Rhineland, that he is planning on making a journey to Paris..." he grinned impishly at the crowd, on the edge of their seats, "and he is stopping in Himmelberg!"

The crowd erupted into frantic cheers, screaming and saluting. Johanna and Louisa were jumping up and down, holding each other, shrieking like girls. Herr Wolf was chanting *Heil Hitler!* with both arms raised in reverent prayer, tears streaming down his face. The cacophony unified into a thunderous, pulsing *Sieg Heil! Sieg Heil! Seig Heil! Sieg Heil!* And it continued well into the wee hours of the night.

For the next month, Himmelberg was absolutely in a tizzy preparing for the Führer's visit. Henri went back to the front, and Hildegard never saw him again. (Henri would be killed in 1944 on the beaches of Normandy. His plane would be shot down by Norman Harlow, a sergeant in the 82nd Airborne Division. Coincidentally, Benny Woodford—who played spin the bottle all those years ago—would also be there, and in fact flew close to Henri's plane as it crashed into the English Channel, but neither of them would have recognized each other, even had Henri not had more pressing issues at hand.)

"What an honor that the Führer would visit our little town!" Wilhelmina said, grinning.

"He won't come," Otto said, reading his newspaper.

"Don't you think so?"

"No," Otto turned the page. "I doubt that they would go around spreading to every possible spy in Germany that Hitler will be making a tour of small towns on his way to France. It sounds like a decoy plan."

"Ah, you spoilsport," Wilhelmina chided, kissing him on the cheek.

"I think there will be a parade," Otto said, "but I don't think Adolf Hitler will grace Himmelberg with his presence."

"Are you going to rain on *that* parade too, or just mine?"

Otto shrugged his good shoulder.

Every inch of Himmelberg was draped in red. It looked like a giant berry exploded all over the town, staining every wall, except every wall also had a swastika on it, like ants crawling over a rotten fruit.

Hildegard had gone into town with Wilhelmina to buy groceries. Ever since Henri's speech, Miguel preferred to hang back closer to the house, where he wouldn't attract attention from the Gestapo, and where his visas and papers were within arm's reach. On the way to the butcher's shop, Hildegard passed Felix, busy painting a mural on the side of the slaughter house.

"What do you think?" Felix said, wiping his forehead with the back of his arm, unwittingly smearing paint across the bridge of his nose. He looked at it proudly. "Mayor Fischer is paying me 600 marks to do it, plus money for the paint, because the parade will pass this way."

"I love it!" Hildegard, on cue, exclaimed. Whenever Felix showed her anything, it was Hildegard's duty to always say she loved it, it was a work of genius, it would put Michelangelo to shame. "It will put the Sistine Chapel to shame. What is it?"

"It's a mural. Of Himmelberg. And Germany. And Hitler. And the triumph of the Aryan race," Felix said, indicating various spaces with his paint brush. "Obviously it's a work in progress, but I was inspired by that poster of Hitler, you know, the one where he's leading the people and he's hoisting the flag in the air, and the eagle is flying overhead. So he's going to be doing that here, and we're going to be marching behind him."

"Oh, so we're Hitler fans now, are we?" Hildegard crossed her arms in mock curiosity. Felix winked at her and rubbed his thumb against his forefingers, indicating that he had been paid well. Hildegard looked down at the rough pastel sketches of ugly mongoloid faces at the bottom of the mural. "What's that?"

"Oh, those are the Jews. Right here, we're going to be tromping over the Jewish race. It's going to be like chiaroscuro, light and dark. We're all going to have golden and white hair, and they're going to have curly black hair, looking ape-like. I know Louisa will be disappointed that there are no brunettes in the group, but..." he shrugged.

"There's one brunette," Hildegard pointed to the very tall, muscular and vigorous visage of Hitler.

"Exactly." He climbed down from the step stool and beckoned her closer. "Hey, did you hear that Irena's pregnant?"

"No!" Hildegard's hand went to her mouth. She tried to look surprised so as to not reveal Ygritte's secret.

"Yep."

"With...?"

Felix nodded knowingly. "And, from what I heard at the hardware store, Mayor Fischer's been trying to put pressure on him, but Engel doesn't like being bullied. I think he's got big plans for his career that reach beyond Himmelberg."

"Well, let's hope he achieves those plans sooner rather than later and gets out of here."

"I'd rather have Engel than Voigt."

"That's true," Hildegard said. *But it's not true. I don't want any of them here. Engel's a murderer, and Voigt is just as corrupt. How long will it be before they push* me *off a ladder?* She looked at Felix, climbing up the step stool. *Or Felix?* Her stomach twisted. *Or Miguel?*

"Felix?" Hildegard said.

He turned to look down at her.

"Be careful."

"It's only a three-foot ladder."

"I mean," Hildegard waved her hand in a circular motion, "*be careful.* During this parade… be a good German. Don't give them an excuse to hurt you."

Herr Wolf turned the corner, carrying a package wrapped in white paper. "Heil Hitler!" He greeted them, smiling, with a raised right arm.

"Heil Hitler," Hildegard returned the gesture, trying her best to smile. She and Herr Wolf looked up at Felix. Hildegard gave him a pleading look. Felix exhaled through his nose, raising his right arm.

"Heil Hitler."

Herr Weissman turned up the volume on the radio. "If those British bastards want a fight, we'll give it to them. We'll push them back, and push them back, until we push them off their island. They'll be swimming across the Atlantic to America if they don't comply."

"And then we'll take America, too!" Karl said.

"Jawohl! Here, here!" Herr Weissman said, filling up Karl's stone

169

mug with beer. He sat down at their table, leaning in towards Hildegard. "Hilde, what do you think of my place? Do you think the Führer will be proud?"

"I think he would be absolutely proud," Hildegard smiled.

"No, not *would*. He's going to need a place to stay, right? He can't go traipsing around Bavaria all day and night. So, what do I do? I'm renovating the whole place to make it perfect for him. He'll have no choice but to stay at *my* place. And I'm going to have a plaque that reads 'Adolf Hitler, Führer and Father of the Third Reich, found rest at this critically-acclaimed establishment.' Won't that beat the bricks off of that old heifer von Braun's dump!"

"Is the goal to make Hitler feel comfortable, or to beat Frau von Braun?" Hildegard chuckled.

"Why not both? You can have it all. Look at Hitler: he wants Poland, he takes it. He wants France, he takes it. He wants England, he's cracking his knuckles, getting ready to pounce. There you go!" Herr Weissman slapped the table to prove his point, making everyone's beer shake and slop out of their mugs.

"Which is why I wanted to talk to you, Hilde," Herr Weissman said. "I know Otto has connections at his steel mill. And I was thinking: maybe it's time for some new steins. Some stainless steel steins. Some stainless steel swastika steins! Do you think he could do me a favor? I would pay him back, of course, I could pay him back double with the tourism I get once the Führer stays here."

"I can talk to him," Hildegard said, "but I should warn you... it may take more than steins to impress the Führer. I heard Frau von Braun has replaced all her quilts with Nazi flag bedspreads. She has a sister in Munich who made them special. And they're stuffed with down."

"What!" Herr Weissman exclaimed. He stomped over to the door, causing everyone's beer to slop and spill some more, threw the door open, and bellowed: "Hey, you cow!"

Frau von Braun opened the upstairs window and leaned out, her shelf-like breasts swooping over into the flowerbox. "What do you want, you old coot?"

"Are you ripping off my idea?"

"I didn't realize being patriotic was *your* idea," she mock-bowed, her arms open. "Next time, you'll have to get a patent on patriotism. Then you'll *really* be making money off of Hitler!"

"Go to hell, you witch!"

"I would throw a glass at you," she smiled victoriously, producing one as if she had been carrying it around all day just in case of this moment, "but I just ordered some new glass steins from Munich that came in yesterday. They have *swastikas* on them."

"How dare you!" Herr Weissman shook his fist at her. Frau von Braun cackled in triumph and slammed the window shutters. Herr Weissman wheeled on the twenty-somethings, who were clearly entertained. "Did *you* tell her about this? Is there a spy in this place?" He pointed an accusing finger at them. Hildegard and the rest put up their hands innocently, shaking their heads.

"Never, Herr Weissman!"

"Wouldn't think of it, Herr Weissman!"

"I've read that the Führer is a wheat beer man, Herr Weissman!"

Herr Weissman crossed his arms. "Good. And it will stay that way, once he comes to *my* place. *My place!*" he hollered toward the door, as if Frau von Braun were listening on the other side.

As Herr Weissman left to tend other tables, Louisa and Lars resumed a heated argument. Hitler would not be coming to Himmelberg before his trip to Paris, but he would be passing through afterward on June 25th. This was the day of Lars and Louisa's wedding, and everything—all of their vendors, even their venue—had been re-booked for the Führer's visit.

"I don't see why we need to change the date. Hitler won't be needing a chapel; it's not like he's going to visit the church."

"He might... it's been around since the 15th century," Lars weakly offered.

"So has every church in this area," Louisa snapped. "And I can't even get my bouquet, because they're using all the red roses for a Nazi flag flower arrangement that's supposed to take up the whole stadtplatz."

"So use white roses," Johanna suggested.

"I can't... that's a part of the flower arrangement too!"

"Why not yellow roses? Or sunflowers?" Hildegard asked.

"Oh, Hildegard," Louisa shook her head at her incredulously. "*Yellow?* The color of *Jews?*"

"I didn't realize the color yellow was illegal," Hildegard huffed. "I've always liked yellow."

"Then help yourself to all the yellow roses and sunflowers and daisies you want," Louisa pinched the bridge of her nose. "Lord knows there are plenty of them at the florist."

Frau König and Herr Schulz were practicing with the Hitler Youth band as Hildegard left Zur Rentier.

"Now, make sure you march straight, children. Kick your knees up and point the toes. It's all about creating a nice, strong line. Albert, I don't hear you in the back. We want to play so loud, the Führer hears us from a mile away. From the top. And one, two, three, four!"

The children banged their drums and blasted on their flutes and trumpets and tubas with all their might. The Hitler Youth members who were not in the Fanfarenzug, the marching bands, carried banners and flags and goose-stepped as rigidly as their little legs could muster. Hildegard noticed they were all blonde children. Then, upon a second glance, she saw the brunette children had been moved to the back. Like Felix's mural. It was an ombré arrangement of hair color: the snow-white, tow-headed children in the very front, the golden haired in the middle, and so on.

Two girls a few grades below Hildegard, Georgina and Helene, were arguing about Herr Schulz' choice to award Brigitte the honor of Maiden of the Mountains. This title came equipped with a flower crown, a dirndl, and the honor of awarding a large bouquet of red and white roses to the Führer.

"I don't see why Brigitte should do it," Helene sulked. "*I'm* more Aryan."

"Brigitte has lighter hair," Georgina said.

"Yes, but she's Swiss, originally. *My* people have been in Germany for generations. I have more right to the crown than she does!"

A family of Italians had come up from Lake Como to climb Mount Sigfried and were staying at Frau von Braun's inn. Herr Voigt was checking their papers, eyeing them suspiciously. "You wouldn't happen to be related to any *Jews*, now would you, Herr Pioletti?"

Hildegard hastened by him so she wouldn't be stopped as well. She felt a panic rise within her. *I have to get back to the house. I have to get back to the house. I have to get back to the house.*

On her way, she noticed that Herr Schumacher and Herr Zimmermann were hammering in a new sign next to the one welcoming visitors to Himmelberg: *Juden sind hier unerwünscht.*

Jews are not wanted here.

On June 25th, a beautiful, sunny day in Himmelberg, when the bees buzzed in the wildflowers and the birds were calling, the tanks of the Wehrmacht rolled through the rocky terrain of the Alps, and Hitler was returning from a visit to Paris to celebrate the fall of France.

Hitler, an artist and a vegetarian, was dazzled by Paris. Hitler was rejected twice by the Academy of Fine Arts in Vienna in his youth, but he produced hundreds of paintings in his lifetime. Mostly watercolors, he enjoyed painting landscapes that were pretty as a postcard, though critics described them as "innocuous and trivial". He also enjoyed painting dogs. In Paris, he drove down the tree-lined boulevard of the Champs Elysees, and he visited the artist's quarter of Montmartre, the bohemian paradise of Paris, with the pristine white Sacré-Cœur topping the hill like a swirl of whipped cream plopped on a banana split, a diamond in a diadem.

He also visited the tomb of Napoleon. Napoleon, like Hitler, stood well under 6 feet, with blue eyes and dark hair. Napoleon, like Hitler, captured the city of Vilna on June 24th. Napoleon, like Hitler, tried to invade Russia in the winter, which led to a staggering military loss and eventually the demise of his great empire.

"This was the greatest and finest moment of my life," Hitler said of the trip. It would be his only visit to Paris.

The people of Himmelberg masked their disappointment that Hitler would not in fact stop in Himmelberg but would be passing through. However, they were cheered that Hitler's second-in-command and chief of propaganda, Joseph Goebbels, would be honoring them with a visit. If you can't win gold, you might as well settle for silver.

Goebbels, Hildegard noted with interest, looked like a turtle. He had a high, wide forehead that ended in arched eyebrows and heavily-lidded eyes, as if he were surveying everyone from a throne (which, someday, he hoped to inherit from Hitler). He had a downward-pointing nose and mouth, and when he pointed to the air and raised his fists, he resembled a parrot.

"My fellow Volk, I look upon you, the sons of daughters of a glorious Aryan race, and I see hope for a new generation," he said, his eyes swooping over them under his sleepy lids. "I am so grateful to have the ear of our glorious Führer, and I know his golden heart will glow when I tell him of the kindness and generosity of the people of these mountains."

The crowd of people—townsfolk from Himmelberg and men and women of the surrounding villages that covered Mount Siegfried—cheered and applauded.

"I look into your eyes and I see that most noble of virtues... I see patriotism. I see a love for your country... paralleling a mother's love for her child, or our Führer's love for his people. I see that the same red German blood that beats in my heart beats in yours as well," he smiled magnanimously, putting his hand over his heart as the cheers grew louder and louder. "I look across this crowd and see the shining golden hair of a pure Aryan race." (Goebbels himself, like Hitler, had dark hair.) He stretched out his hand above them. "I see a brighter and better future ahead of us, with you in the lead!"

"I wonder if he was inspired by my mural!" Felix turned to Hildegard, excited by Goebbels' words and applauding along with the crowd.

Goebbels punctuated this with his fists, mimicking knocking over each sentence with the swipe of his hands, sweeping to the left and right: "We have taken back the Sudetenland, we have taken back the Rhineland, we have seized Czechoslovakia, we have seized Poland, we have seized the Nordic countries, and Netherlands, and Belgium, and now France is under our fist! We have paid these treasonous, lying, disloyal countries back, blow for blow!"

"Sieg Heil!" Herr Zimmermann raised his arm.

"Heil Hitler!" Karl cried.

"Heil Hitler!" Johanna shouted.

"Soon, the snakes of Great Britain will be crushed under our foot, and then the Bolsheviks, with all their mighty terrain, will have no choice but to bow to our eternal Reich. Today France, and tomorrow... the world!"

The crowd erupted into cheers and began to chant again: *Sieg Heil! Sieg Heil! Sieg Heil!*

"But, my Volk, there is something that threatens to snuff out the shining sun of our beautiful future," Goebbels warned, his voice drawing low. "The insidious presence of the Jews."

"Boo!" Karl jeered. The crowd joined in.

"We have done our best to negotiate with them," Goebbels continued. "We have offered them treatises, given them shelter in ghettos, and still they continue to squirm under our feet. They creep in and grow like rot, and as long as the Jewish race is present in Europe—indeed, the world—the foundations of our great Empire are bound to crumble."

"Damn them!" Herr Wolf cried. "Damn those hateful Jews!"

"There is no further option," Goebbels said, pointing his fist in the air. "The solution is clear… we must wipe out the Jews from the face of the Earth! It is the only way to save our country, to save your children, to save the world!"

"Kill them!" Johanna shouted.

"Kill them!" Karl shouted.

"Kill them! Kill them! Kill them!" the crowd began to chant. The *Sieg Heil*s and the *Kill them*s intermingled into one thunderous chant, like the beating of a war drum.

Hildegard looked around at her fellow townspeople. Frau König, the woman who promised she would ensure Hildegard's safety at her school ten years ago, was screaming at the top of her lungs, her eyes wide, blazing and rat-like. Herr Schumacher, who had helped Hildegard and Herr Weber fix up the theater, was punching his fist in the air, chanting *Kill Them!* so hard that spittle was flying out of his mouth like a rabid dog. Herr Zimmermann, the man who had cried over his brother and Hildegard had comforted him on a snowy Christmas night, was chanting and slashing his extended right arm in the air, like a soldier slashing a saber.

Who the hell are *these people?* Hildegard wondered in disgust.

She looked over, and Otto and Wilhelmina were there too, with their right arms raised, somberly chanting *Sieg Heil! Sieg Heil!*

She let herself melt into the crowd, walking backwards with her right arm in the air, until she was out of town and storming down the road back home. *Her* home. Himmelberg was her home. It had taken a while for her to accept it, but it was more her home than Berlin; that time was too long past. The people here were kind and neighborly and accepting... how had this happened? How had the seeds of hate been planted so deeply in their hearts?

She stomped past the approaching parade, past the Fanfarenzug, the little brown-shirted boys that were waving their flags and banging their drums and tooting their horns and goose-stepping their way past childhood into the front lines. She stomped past the young boys who had just signed up for the Wehrmacht, boys she had taught in the Hitler Youth; she might as well have tied the noose of their little black ties around their necks. She pushed past the men and women from Bavaria, crowding together to watch the show, with tears of pride and joy in their eyes as they watched their children march by, off to war, off to certain victory, off to a land where there was no bloodshed, only golden Aryan sunshine. When the crowd erupted into shrieks and screams, there was mass chaos and a tumult, and she was nearly pushed out into the road when Adolf Hitler's motorcar passed her by.

He was standing there, zooming by like Apollo on his chariot, with his arm extended toward the crowd. His eyes rested on her. They were bright blue, tired, but clear. And cold.

It was the second and last time they would be in the same place at the same moment.

She continued down the road as the motorcade puttered by her, brought up in the rear by roaring, rumbling tanks. Attila the Hun crossed these mountains to vanquish the Roman Empire with elephants, and now Hitler was doing the same thing with these colossal panzer tanks.

"Keep out of the way, woman!" a Wehrmacht officer shoved her to the side of the road.

Hildegard stumbled into the ditch and crossed up the road to the barn. She turned to watch the parade. Five years ago, she would've given her left hand to march in this parade with the Hitler Youth. She had completely bought into this ideology. But she hadn't thought it would get this far... not *this* far! And how much further would it go? Where would this road end that this parade of bloodlust marched toward? Would it end in victory? Or would it drop off, too late, down into Hell?

It was all too much for her. It made her feel sad, it made her feel bitter, it made her feel helpless, and finally it made her feel angry.

Blindingly angry.

"Hey, you assholes!" Hildegard shouted, picking up a rock to hurl at a passing tank. Before the stone could leave her fist, a hand snatched her arm and pinned it down. Someone had their arms wrapped around her, pinning her arms down to her sides, and hauled her kicking into the darkness of the barn.

Hildegard panicked and began to scream for help, and a hand clamped over her mouth. She looked down at the hand, and saw it was connected to a dark, hairy arm. It was Miguel's.

"Are you crazy?" he hissed. "Are you trying to get yourself arrested?"

He kicked the door closed, and the latch clunked down over the handle. The two of them stood tense, breathing in the dark, waiting for someone to bang on the door and demand to be let in. They hid by the wall, eyes wide and staring fearfully at the door to their left.

A minute went by.

Was it an hour?

Nothing.

Hildegard became very aware of how close Miguel was to her. He had never been this close before. She could feel his heart pounding into her shoulder blade. She could feel the warmth of his body, like a brick baking in the sun. She could smell him.

She felt her pulse quicken under his hand, faster than a moment ago, when they had waited for a Nazi or a Gestapo to come barreling in with an arrest warrant or a club or a gun. She began to struggle. He lowered his hand.

"Let go of me," she gasped.

"Don't go out there," he warned.

"Let go of me!" She struggled to release herself from his grip. He really was as strong as an ox. There was nothing she could do. She had never been pinned like this. He pivoted her and pushed her back against the wall, holding her by the shoulders.

"Don't go out there," he repeated in a low voice. And then his mouth crashed into hers.

It all happened very fast. He opened her hungry mouth and searched it with his tongue. Her arms encircled his corded neck, running through his hair, and he grasped her face, the small of her back, her waist, her hips. She could feel him, and she could feel herself bucking against him, like a cat purring against the door, trying to get in. And then she was pulling at his shirt, and reaching for his belt, and clutching at the bones of his hips, and his buttocks, like two firm peaches. And he was undoing the laces, tugging them, snatching them away, about to break them. And off went her dirndl, hastily dumped on the floor. And the brasier followed. And her underwear was bunched somewhere next to her ankle. And his palms and his lips and his teeth and his tongue were at her breasts, and she was swimming in a feral heat, drowning in it. And suddenly he hoisted her up, his hands were under her hips, and her legs were locked around his waist, and he was inside of her, thrusting, urgently, like a train engine inside of her, revving fast and faster, charging, pushing, and she cried out.

Outside, the parade went on.

They were hiding in the hay. There was something wrong about just putting on their clothes afterward, it made it feel dirty and cheap, so they grabbed their wrinkled clothes and ducked under a pile of hay that needed to be baled to the upstairs loft. It was scratchy, and there might have been mice scurrying around in the dark, and the warm, dusty smell made Miguel sneeze, but Hildegard felt like she was on a cloud. She felt as if she were in an opium dream, as if she had a morphine injection inside her thighs, and it was spreading to the tips of her toes and up to her ears.

"I wish I could see you," Miguel murmured, for the parade had passed, and the noise and cheers and *Sieg Heils* had died down. "I wish it hadn't been in the dark."

"I liked it," Hildegard said, rubbing her hand up the cleft of his thigh and further up the hair of his stomach.

"All the same," he said. "I wish we didn't have to hide. I wish it could've been in the morning. In my bed. So I could've seen you, every inch of you. That's the way I think about you." He stopped, embarrassed.

She pushed aside some hay to see him better. "You think about me?"

"Of course," Miguel looked down at her. "I think about you all the time. When I was out in the fields, I would think about what we're doing right now. What it was like to feel you. But I wish I could see you."

"Wish granted," Hildegard said, standing up. The hay fell and fluttered down around her. A ray of waning golden sunlight streamed through the cracks of the barn door and hit the side of her face. She stepped into the sunray and looked at him, smoothing her hands from her ribcage down to her hips.

He sat up and looked simply at her, his elbows on his knees. After

180

a moment, he said, "I know this seems like convenient timing, but I want to tell you I'm in love with you."

She smiled at him and squeezed her hands over her torso, hugging in the feeling. She understood. It could've been just a romp in the hay, and he had alluded to many romps before her, but he wanted her to know it was different this time. And it didn't seem believable, because that's what they all said, so he wanted her to know he was sincere.

"We probably shouldn't do this again," Miguel looked down, scratching his neck. "I'm a Jew. If someone finds out, I wouldn't want anyone to think you—"

"I'm exhausted with bending and twisting myself for what people think," Hildegard said. She knelt down beside him, straddling his leg, tracing a finger over his beard. "When did you first fall in love with me?"

Miguel looked at her and smiled archly. "When you fell backwards into that bucket of milk."

She pushed him down playfully, then climbed over him. "Let's do it again."

"People are probably wondering—"

"I told you, I don't care about people," she said, the inside of her leg feeling his growing hardness, and she reached down to touch it. "I want you."

"Te quiero," he murmured, and then he was over her.

Lars and Louisa were married on June 28th, 1940. There were pink roses. The whole town was invited to their wedding celebration and threw rice as they exited the church. Then there was wine and cake and dancing.

It wasn't the traditional zwiefacher, where couples swirled and spun together with joined hands, but regular old band music, ragtime and waltz and swing, dances that Americans made popular and Germans participated in and pretended not to notice the taboo appropriation.

Miguel approached Hildegard and took her wine glass from her, setting it on the table. "Let's dance."

"I was just about to ask Hilde," Felix protested.

"You can ask her for the next dance," Miguel said. "I'm terrible at German dances; this one is simple enough so I won't step all over her feet."

The two of them swayed together in a foxtrot, out of earshot from eavesdroppers.

Miguel looked at Hildegard for a moment and cocked a smile. "You're blushing."

"No I'm not."

"Your cheeks are red as a beet. You're going to give us away."

"Then don't put your hands on me like this."

"I'm afraid," he leaned close to her ear, "that's not an option."

Hildegard felt that familiar heat coming on, and she looked around for prying eyes. "Let's get out of here. Let's go somewhere."

"Where?"

"Lars' father's orchard," she said in a low voice. "They won't leave here until late in the evening. Nobody will be around."

"Which one of us should go first? We can't leave here at the same time."

"You go first. Don't let Karl or Lars rope you into a round of drinks; it will never end."

"Don't let Felix rope you into dancing; same answer."

"Are you jealous?" Hildegard teased. The music ended, and everyone stopped dancing to applaud. Miguel let his hand slip from her shoulder blade to the small of her back, his eyes communicating his reply. Then he released her, applauding. Hildegard stepped on her own shoelace, snapping the cord. She and Miguel nodded to each other, trying to keep up the farce of platonic friendliness in front of a crowd that wasn't paying attention to them, and Miguel ambled off. Hildegard sat down at a chair as Felix approached.

"Miguel stepped on my shoe, the big oaf," Hildegard smiled and rolled her eyes.

"Take it off and dance barefoot."

"On this dirty cobblestone? What, do you want me to get tetanus?"

"Gerda can probably get you a new shoelace from the shop."

"I don't want to bother…" Hildegard's eyes drifted over to Gerda. She was pale, and her eyes were bleary and she was staring off into space. She was slumped over the table, and taking a shaky sip of wine, which slopped over the side. Hildegard looked up at Felix. She took his hand and squeezed it. "I need to go talk to her."

"But you said—"

"Go dance with Johanna," Hildegard beckoned. "She's upset that Karl's been drinking instead of asking her."

"Mmm," Felix nodded, looking at Johanna. "We're all of us fish in a barrel now."

"Thanks, Felix. I'll come back later," she said before he could elaborate on that comment.

Hildegard approached Gerda and sat down. "How are you, Gerda?"

Gerda looked miserably at Hildegard. "I haven't heard anything from him. It's been nearly a year and I haven't even received a postcard."

"Well, maybe he can't write, wherever he is," Hildegard shrugged. *Or he doesn't want to… after you shot him down.*

"Maybe he moved on to someone else," Gerda said, tears welling in her eyes.

"I don't think anyone could get over you, Gerda," Hildegard said, trying to make her feel better. *Not so quickly, anyway. Not while he's running for his life.*

"It would be easier to believe that," Gerda suddenly clutched Hildegard's hand with a vice-like grip, her eyes wide and fazed. "It would be easier to believe he got over me, he's found new love, and he's happy. What if... what if he was taken?" She lowered her voice to a whisper. "To Dachau?"

Hildegard sighed and squeezed Gerda's hand with her free one. "All we can do is hope he's safe, I suppose."

Gerda relinquished her grip on Hildegard and went back to her wine. She stared into it, uncaring, dead to the world. The conversation was over.

Hildegard patted Gerda on the back, trying to be a comfort to her, but she was impatient. What could she do? Gerda made her choice. She had her time, and now Hildegard wanted her own. She got up and eased out into the alley.

"Going somewhere, Hildegard?" came a voice from the darkness.

Hildegard jumped and spun around. It was Herr Schulz. It smelled as if he had just finished taking a piss. Hildegard made a mental note to step carefully in her broken shoe.

"Oh, Herr Schulz! You frightened me!" she laughed, giving him a playful punch on the shoulder.

"Well, what are you doing skulking in alleys?" he returned the playful punch, which felt strange and awkward. Also hypocritical.

"I've broken my lace, and I'm going to get a new one from my house."

"Allow me to escort you."

"No, Herr Schulz," she tried to flippantly wave off the offer, "really. My house is right over there. Please enjoy the party." Would there be no end to these obstacles obstructing her from getting Miguel alone?

"You must be careful at this time of night," Herr Schulz cautioned. "It's not safe for women to go walking around alone."

Hildegard giggled, trying to cover her discomfort to disarm him and leave her alone. "Who should I be afraid of in this tiny German town?"

"Non-Germans." Herr Schulz gave her a pointed look.

Hildegard weighed the odds of passing off ignorance. There was only one foreigner in Himmelberg; he knew she wasn't stupid. He taught her, after all. She was his protégé, in a way.

"I hope you're not speaking of Miguel, surely?" she asked seriously.

"He is not from here originally; you must be careful with whom you spend your time, Hildegard." Herr Schulz crossed his arms. *Was he always this patronizing?*

"My father hired Miguel because of his good character, Herr Schulz." Hildegard stated matter-of-factly. "He has been a good caretaker of our property for two years. I hope that would give him *some* credit."

"I see," Herr Schulz was politely unconvinced.

"Plus," Hildegard said, in one last attempt to win him over. "He is a fascist. Did you know he fought for the fascists in the Spanish Civil War?"

"Then he should go back to where he came from," Herr Schulz said, showing his cards. He flashed his old toothy smile. "But I cannot control Herr Benaroya. I can only offer counsel to one of my greatest pupils."

"Thank you, Herr Schulz," Hildegard bowed her head. "I will take this into consideration."

As she dodged past him, walking into the alley, she heard him call: "There's always a position open for you, Hilde, at the Women's Nazi League! You could be something yet!"

"I have to stay with my father," Hildegard said automatically, and she turned the corner, hurrying down the road to the orchard.

You could be something yet, bah! Hildegard thought indignantly. *I am something. I'm not a screw-up because I didn't want to climb some ladder leading to nowhere. Who does he think he is, anyway? Who does he think he is, that he talks to me that way? Wasn't he the one who encouraged me to become a wife and mother?* An image, like a prophetic vision, flashed in her head, married to Miguel, with a child. She nervously shooed it away. *Don't think about that now.* Hildegard Benaroya. *Stop it, get a hold of yourself...* she stopped. *How did he know his last name?*

How did Herr Schulz know Miguel's last name?

Miguel has been here for two years, of course he would know who he is, don't be silly.

But they've never had a conversation. I've never seen the two of them together.

That doesn't mean he wouldn't know him.

Know him, yes. But know his last name? I don't know the first names of some of the people in this town, and I've been here for ten years. Why should Herr Schulz, a schoolteacher, be aware of a tenant farmer who mostly keeps to himself, living on a property on the outskirts of town?

Herr Schulz is a spy.

Hildegard remembered when Herr Schulz was sent to Himmelberg. Bright and shiny and the very image of the Hitler Youth poster. She remembered Herr Schulz leaning in towards a circle of youngsters at camp.

"And remember, kids, you can always come talk to me if things are bad at home. If you hear your mommy or daddy talking about the Führer or Germany in a way that makes you feel funny, especially if it goes against your Hitler Youth training, I'm always here to listen and help."

And she remembered the tilt of his face the day *Bride of Frankenstein* was supposed to premier. The day he suggested that the people of Himmelberg watch a movie that was more *German.* "Right, Herr Weber?" he said, in that same cloying tone of voice.

Maybe he's not a spy. Maybe he's just a regular old racist xenophobe.

But Herr Weber is dead.

Would Miguel be next?

How long would Miguel be safe here?
How long before he, too, would have to run?

10

1940, Part Two: Blessings

After, they lay propped up against a peach tree, slowing their ragged breathing. Hildegard could hear her heart beating in her ears. She was reclining between his legs, and his arms were around her shoulders, lazily cupping her left breast.

"I think," he panted, "this tree has seen enough."

She gave him a playful slap on the arm, and the gesture reminded her of playfully slugging Herr Schulz.

(Did he make dirty post-coital jokes with his lover, whoever she was? Did he even have one? Or was his love life wrapped up in some homoerotic-anxiety-driven desire to please his Führer and his government? Or was he some kind of robot, perfectly engineered by Nazi scientists to charm schoolchildren, with a microphone built into his pearly white teeth to record nay-sayers? Did he roll into his teacher's apartment, turn the lights off, and shut down? Did he have a heart? Did any of them have a heart?)

"What's bothering you?" Miguel asked, sensing her thoughts.

She craned her neck back to look up at him. "When are you leaving?"

He tried to force a bemused chuckle and failed. "I didn't realize I *had* to leave."

"It's not safe here."

"Why? Because the town's been covered in swastikas?"

"You weren't there," Hildegard continued, "you weren't there when Joseph Goebbels made his speech. It was all about killing the Jews. And everyone went along with it." She remembered it, her stomach icy. "No... they didn't just go along with it. They were *into* it. It was as if... as if he had awoken a sleeping dragon. It had been there, underneath, dormant, all along."

"You think your friends would kill me? They know me. They ask me to come drink with them. Karl asked me for advice today. You think he would really kill me?"

Hildegard pushed her knees up to her chest. "That's what I'm afraid of."

"I'm his neighbor."

"You're a foreigner," Hildegard turned around to face him, holding his hands. "And soon they're going to find out the secret. Or even if they don't, this... this madness won't stop at Jews. Today, it will be Jews and Jehovah's Witnesses and Communists. Tomorrow, it will be foreigners. The next day, it will be anyone without blonde hair. Anyone who can't prove they're Aryan."

"I guess that rules your Führer out."

"Miguel, *please!*" She shook his hands like she was reining in a horse. "I couldn't bear it if something happened to you."

Miguel stood up angrily. He shoved on his pants and buttoned them, staring at her hotly. "So you just want me to go? Go back home to where I came from?"

Hildegard felt her eyes welling up, and she told herself not to cry. She swallowed her heart back to its place in her chest. "I want you to be safe."

Miguel let out an exasperated sigh of irritation, and snatched up his shirt and shoes. "Grow up, baby," he said coldly. "I'm not safe anywhere. I could go to Antarctica and someone would force me to wear a star. It's only a matter of time."

And he stormed off.

They avoided each other after that. Miguel would plow the fields alone. Hildegard would weed and prune and water the garden alone. They didn't speak to each other at dinner. They didn't look at each other. Hildegard would go and drink with Johanna and Felix, and Miguel would go to his room. And Hildegard would wake up in the morning, groggy and grumpy, and she would stare at the ceiling, she would force herself to not look out her window, because she knew he was down there, in the early morning, staring up at her. *If I shut him out, if I cut him off, maybe he'll give up and go. Like Luka. Maybe he'll be safe.*

Then she thought of Gerda, with her empty eyes and her unbrushed hair, shakily reaching for a glass of wine.

I think I'm going to be sick.

Felix, Karl, Johanna, and Hildegard were crowded around the bar of Zur Rentier, listening to the radio as a reporter delivered news of the first Luftwaffe bombing of Britain. People in the bar cheered and whistled.

Hildegard took a long draught of beer. She was on her third stein. She found after stein number three, she developed a nice buzzy feeling that would enable her to sit in a public space with all of these people and smile and laugh without wanting to scream.

"Slow down, Hilde," Johanna said, concerned.

"M'fine," Hildegard said, plopping her cheek on her hand. If she was lucky, the fizzy, swirling feeling would carry her long enough so she could trundle along home, flop into bed, and pass out so she didn't have to be at dinner with Miguel.

"She's celebrating," Karl said, clinking her drink with his own. Hildegard wrinkled her nose and smiled thinly at him.

"In fact, I'm buying the next round," Karl said.

"Oh, Mr. Moneybags!" Johanna grinned. "What makes you so uncharacteristically generous this afternoon?"

"Because," Karl stood up, staring at his spread fingers on the table and then looking slyly up at them, "I signed up for the Wehrmacht. I'll be shipping out next week. Soon, you may be listening to this radio, and it'll be me out there, bombing the hell out of those Brits."

"What!" Herr Weissman said. "Good show, lad! Good for you! Nein, nein, nein, nein, your money's no good here! I'll buy your drinks for the rest of the night!" He sent the rest of the group a sideways glance that said: *But the rest of you hoodlums will have to pay.*

"What does your father think about it?" Johanna said quietly.

"He'll be fine. He'll find someone."

"Who?" Felix asked. "There'll be no one over the age of 17 left in this town."

"Oh?" Karl sipped his beer. "Are you planning on joining?"

Felix took a breath. "I'm applying for an internship. In Berlin. Painting propaganda posters. There were some higher-ups at the parade who saw my work and encouraged me to do it."

Johanna smiled at Felix. "Oh Felix, that's wonderful!"

Felix smiled at her and looked at Hildegard.

"What about Munich? What about the university?" Hildegard said, disappointed.

Felix shrugged. "I won't need the university, if I get this internship. I'll be skipping to getting the credentials I need to really go places."

Hildegard sat back. "But you don't believe in the National Socialists," she said.

Karl grasped her arm. "Keep your voice down."

"No," Hildegard woozily snatched her arm away. "Never mind. I'm happy for you. I hope you all get what you want under the glorious new empire," she raised her voice. "I hope Felix becomes the next Pablo Picasso, and I hope Karl becomes the next Rrred Baron, and I hope you all come back alive, so Johanna can get married too, otherwise we're going to be two old unmarried crones, working all the leftover farmland."

Johanna blushed. "Hilde..."

"What's stopping you from getting married?" Felix said bitterly.

Hildegard swung around on Felix. She cupped her hands on the sides of her mouth, so he could hear her better. "This war, Felix. This stupid war."

"Hilde!" Karl commanded. "You need to go. Go home. Before you say something you regret."

"Why? Is someone listening? Oh that's right, you're *all* listening." Hildegard fumbled with her money, turned, and wobbled out the door.

She was zigzagging down the road, regretting the last stein. She severely miscalculated this time. She thought about finding a place to sit down, but she was afraid of passing out in the middle of the street, to Otto and Wilhelmina's shame and dismay. But she was too drunk to go home now; it would be humiliating. She couldn't go to the orchard, or the cow pond, or the fields, because they would make her too sad. Where could she go?

An arm looped through hers. It was Felix.

"You didn't think I was going to let you stumble around Himmelberg drunk, did you?"

Hildegard breathed in relief.

"Let's go to Zum Hirschen. Frau von Braun will give you some water. She might even let you sleep it off, out of pure spite."

"Can we just walk a little while? I need some fresh air."

"Sure."

They walked in silence.

Then, Hildegard said: "I made an ass of myself."

"Yes, you did," Felix chuckled.

"I'm sorry. I shouldn't have said it in front of Karl."

"Nothing can faze Karl, especially now."

"But I shouldn't have said it. It's just... everyone is so..."

"I know," Felix said, squeezing her arm. *Not here, not in public,* he was communicating to her.

"So... you're leaving too?"

"Maybe," Felix shrugged.

"Everyone is leaving," Hildegard said miserably.

"I'll tell you a secret, Hilde," Felix tilted his head toward her. "We all would have left here eventually. War or no war. Life moves on, we move on. We're not feudal villagers, as much as the Führer would like us to be. We would've gone our separate ways."

Hildegard looked at him. "That was very wise."

Felix half-smiled. "Occasionally, I can pull a nugget of wisdom out."

"Ach, come in, come in, Hilde!" Frau von Braun bustled out the door. "You poor thing! You shouldn't drink too much of that swill; it's not good for you, the way he makes it."

"Oh, God," Hildegard murmured, pinching the bridge of her nose.

"Come inside, and I'll give you some water. We'll flush it right out. And then, you dear lamb, you can come sleep it off upstairs. Did I tell you I have new bedspreads?"

"I wouldn't want to be sick all over the swastika sheets," Hildegard murmured.

"Ha ha, swastika sheets! Come inside, Hilde. We'll get you feeling better in no time." She handed her a glass. It had a swastika on it.

Two weeks passed.

"The corn is ready," Otto said, reading his paper.

"You don't think it's too early?" Hildegard asked.

"No. We're going to harvest some now and send it to Stuttgart to be canned. For the war effort."

"You should make cans in your factory. Why send it to Stuttgart when you can cut out the middleman?"

"Because the Wehrmacht is paying me very well to make army materiel in my factory," Otto replied. Hildegard thought she detected a little sassy undertone in his voice, *I don't need to make cans of corn when I could make tank parts, thank you very much,* but decided she was imagining things. "But it's not a bad idea," he continued grumpily. "The Wehrmacht has so much free labor churning out parts from those concentration camps, I'll soon be out of a job."

"How many camps are there?"

Otto looked at her. "Hundreds."

Hildegard's heart felt thick, as if it were turning to stone. "Hundreds," she repeated in a whisper. "Oh my God."

Otto turned the page of his newspaper with his good hand.

"Do people know? I mean... do they talk?"

"People see what they want to see." He looked up at her. "Go pick the corn."

"Alright," she walked out, turning back. "You're sure you don't want Miguel to do it? He usually handles the fields, and I work the garden."

"No. I have another task for him."

Hildegard nodded and headed out the door, grabbing a burlap bag. *How much longer will there be two of us to do this work?* she wondered, gazing out at the vast fields before her. *Soon he'll leave. Could Mother and I manage it? Would Otto hire a boy from town? Are there any boys left?*

She was tearing off ears of corn, dark green with singed brown silk streaming out of the top. *When this war is over, the first thing I'm doing is convincing Otto to buy back his tractor,* she thought, itching her forearm.

If this war is ever over.

Would it ever be over? Would it ever end? Would it end in oblivion? How long would it take to go back to normal? Could that normal ever be achieved, the innocence of her teenage years, or were they all too far gone? Had they damned themselves? Had *she* damned herself?

What would life be like, with Miguel gone?

Would she ever get over it?

She allowed herself, within the privacy of the claustrophobic walls of corn stalks, to break. Her face squenched into a mask of agony, and hot tears leaked down the sides of her nose and under her chin. She took a shuddering breath, inhaling the fresh, green scent of the corn stalks, and she heard the sandpapery sound of them rustling together.

She opened her eyes and saw Miguel, holding an ear of corn, about to stuff it in a bag slung over his shoulder. He was staring at her, surprised and hurt.

"I'm sorry," she choked back a sob. "I love you."

"I'm not going anywhere without you," he said.

"Okay."

"Okay."

He made his way through the thick rows of corn to her and pulled her into an embrace. He cupped her face and kissed her deeply and kissed her tears, too. She buried her face in his chest and through his shirt, she could feel the golden star. It was between them, but she wouldn't let it separate them. Not if she could help it.

There followed the days when all lovers become careless. Hildegard and Miguel would separately wake up early in the morning to finish their work, talking about anything, anything except the war. He would tell her more about Spain and his mother and his bar mitzvah, when he turned thirteen and read the Torah in front of his family and friends and God.

"You *pissed* yourself?" Hildegard laughed.

"All over the temple floor. I was so nervous and I couldn't go right before because Rabbi Zaccuto kept lecturing me, because in Hebrew class I couldn't remember the aliyah. So I had a very full bladder and I was stepping from left to right, trying to chant the haftarah blessing, and I knew I wasn't going to make it. And I saw Rabbi Zaccuto had a goblet of wine sitting on the pulpit, so I faked a clumsy attempt to gesture, and I spilled the wine all over myself, right as I let it all go."

"Did it work? Did they believe you?"

"I think they politely pretended to believe me. But I also spilled wine all over the Torah."

"Oh, no!"

"Yes," Miguel said, "Rabbi Zaccuto was furious. I guess it gives a new meaning to the phrase, 'full of piss and vinegar.'"

Hildegard let out a honk of laughter. "I wish I could have been there."

Miguel shuddered. "I don't. You wouldn't have liked me when I was thirteen. I wasn't the charming young gallant you see before you today. I was spoiled, nervous around people. Chubby."

"I would've been seven; I would've thought you were dreamy. Do you still remember it?"

"What?"

"The... hafa... the chant."

"The haftarah blessing? Every word. We sing it every week for Shabbat."

"Like the Doxology? 'Herr Gott, Dich Loben Alle Wir'?"

"What is that?"

"It's a blessing, kind of. A prayer of praise."

"How does it go?"

"*Herr Gott, dich loben alle wir*

196

und sollen billig danken dir
für dein geschöpf der engel schon
die um dich schweben um deinen Thron,"
Hildegard sing-songed. Miguel bemusedly applauded. She opened her arms and rang out: "Aaaaaaah-men!"

"Beautiful."

"No, I'm a terrible singer."

"I meant the song." She threw an ear of corn at him. "No, I'm serious. That's very beautiful. The part about God's creations, the angels, hovering around His throne."

"I'd like to see you do better," Hildegard retorted.

"I wish I could," Miguel said sadly. "Everything I do is so secret. I cannot worship God without peeking one eye open or looking over my shoulder."

Hildegard cocked her head. "I have an idea."

After they finished their work, Hildegard told Wilhelmina she was going for a hike. "I'm taking Miguel to Lake Wotan; can you believe he's been here for two years and he's never been up Mount Siegfried?"

"Won't that be nice," Wilhelmina said. Was she being coy? Did she know? Did she know about Miguel, or what her daughter and her tenant farmer were doing in the corn and the barn and the orchard? Could a woman sense it in another woman? Could a mother sense when her daughter had been officially plucked?

Hildegard found an excuse to make when Johanna swung by. "I can't go out today; I'm needed at home."

"We never see you anymore," Johanna said, concerned. "Are you alright?"

"I'm fine. And you see me all the time; I was there for Karl's send-off."

"Yes, but you weren't *really* there. What's with you?"

"I'm fine," Hildegard squeezed Johanna's arm reassuringly. "I'm great, actually. I... I haven't been myself recently. But I'm feeling much better."

"I'm glad," Johanna said unsurely. "Don't disappear on me."

"I won't. I promise."

Miguel huffed as they reached the top of the cliffs of Lake Wotan.

"Don't have a heart attack on me, old man," Hildegard called over one shoulder.

"I'm not an old man, little girl. I'm in my prime."

"You're nearly thirty. Practically decrepit."

"Twenty-eight is not..." he stopped, marveling at the view. "Dios mío!"

He gazed out at the dazzling landscape before him. The limestone cliffs swept down and crashed into the brilliant turquoise waters of Lake Wotan. Spindly pines flanked the edges of the cliffs, and Mount Siegfried climbed higher and higher out of sight into the clouds to the left. To the right, the glorious vista of eastern Bavaria swept out before them. Himmelberg was a tuft of crumbs below them, and the rolling green hills were crisscrossed in a patchwork of different shades of green, the bountiful farmland ready for harvest. The sun was still high above them, warming their shoulders even in this altitude with its clean, bright light.

"Are you sure we'll be safe up here? Didn't you say kids come up here all the time?"

"Yes, but they're all in school right now. And even Herr Schulz won't take them hiking now; he's in the middle of fourth period. We have a few hours," she added sultrily. She was watching him, admiring his figure. How many women had been here in this moment, like this, with him? How many women had watched him, in secret, while he was lost in thought? Was there someone in Spain who had asked him to speak his thoughts, who yearned to know what went on in that mind of his? Was she also blonde and blue-eyed, or like him, a dark-haired beauty? Was she strong and impetuous, or a shy waif? Hildegard didn't begrudge any of the girls who came before her, oddly enough. What was there to be jealous of, except that they got to know him in a time before war? War had brought them together. In a sick way, she was grateful.

He turned to look at her with his hazelnut-colored eye and smiled. From this angle, she couldn't even tell he had a glass eye. He was beautiful. God had thread him together with as much care as He did this lake.

"Go on," she said. "Sing the chant. No one's around for miles."

Miguel took a deep breath, and sang out in a beautiful, clear voice: "*Baruch atah, Adonai Eloheinu, Melech haolam, tzur kol haolamim tzaddik b'chol hadorot, HaEl hane-eman, haomeir v'oseh, ham'dabeir um'kayeim, shekol d'varav emet vatzedck.*"

The song reminded her of a bird in a gale, flapping its wings and rising and dipping with the wind, curving around the clouds. She applauded when he finished and watched him hastily swat a tear away from his eye.

"What's wrong?"

"It's just... I haven't... I haven't been able to sing out in so long. Always in private. Always under my breath. I feel as if I'm suffocating my faith." He took a shuddering breath. "I feel as if God is drifting away from me."

She took his hand. "He's here. He's all around us. Whatever they're doing below," she gestured to Himmelberg, "He's still here. He's waiting."

"For what?"

"Isn't that a part of Judaism?" Hildegard shrugged. "Contemplating the unanswered questions."

He stared at her for a beat, then he smiled. It was a new kind of smile, one that she had not seen before on his face. Or indeed, on anyone's face: no one had ever looked at her in this way. It made her nerves feel twisted and electric, but her heart felt light, and it was easier to breathe. "I love you," he said, taking her hand.

"I love you, too," she smiled.

"No, I..." he looked at her. "I don't know how to explain it. I'm in love with you, but... I *really* love you. In this moment."

"I know what you mean," she grinned. "I can't explain it either." *It's not coming from my body, or even my heart, it's coming from my soul.*

He pulled her in quickly and began kissing her. They moved into the thick brush of the woods and she prayed to God to please not let a little troupe of Hitler-Jugend or a deer hunter accidentally happen upon them. She wasn't sure if God was listening. She and Miguel weren't married, after all. But she *felt* married to him... she felt as if they were already one before they had even met, and all this chaos and war was just pushing him down the road to finally meet her.

Was this in Your plan? All this chaos? Do You have an endgame?

Or is it all the handiwork of Man?

It was getting cooler. Fall was coming again. Another harvest, another Oktoberfest, another November, another Christmas. It was 1940: how many more seasons would they have to spend in this war? Hildegard milked Valkyrie and prayed: *let it end soon.*

"Hildegard," Miguel said in a low voice, slipping in through the barn doors.

"You'll have to wait until later," Hildegard smiled wickedly at him, turning back to her milking. "My mother's around here somewhere."

"Your mother's gone into town for groceries, and your father's gone with her." He looked out the door, and Hildegard could indeed hear the sound of the motor chugging away down the road. He came in and closed the latch over the door. "I need to show you something."

"I don't think there's any part of you I haven't seen," Hildegard turned and crossed her arms expectantly. Miguel pulled her up and led her to a dark corner of the barn. She began undoing the buttons of her shirt.

"Not today," Miguel said, grabbing a shovel. "Well... not right now." He cleared a pile of hay aside and plunged the shovel into the dirt. "I told you there was nothing left for me in Madrid," he said over his shoulder, tossing the dirt aside. He stamped his foot on the hilt of the shovel and plunged it in again. "But I didn't exactly come to Germany with nothing." He tossed the dirt aside. "My family... we're winemakers, but we're not farmers. We were wealthy landowners. There were quite a few heirlooms in our house, and we weren't about to let those Popular Front bastards go stealing our valuables in the name of wealth distribution..." He tossed the shovel aside and knelt down to dig in the dirt.

He pulled out a cloth sack. It looked like an old shirt that had been tied together by its corners. "I came all the way from Spain with these sewn into the inside of my shirt, and I buried them here for safekeeping." He sat cross legged on the ground and gestured for her to join him. She sat down with him, and he took her hand, staring seriously at her with his brown glass eye.

"I can't find my necklace. The one with the gold star on it."

She jumped up, looking for the needle in a hay pile. "Where did you see it last?"

He pulled her down. "I can't remember. I've looked everywhere. It's too late now; someone's going to find it."

"We'll find it first. We'll comb every inch of this place."

"It won't matter. Hildegard, you were right. Eventually, someone will find out about me. There's a whole sign that I have to pass on my way into town reminding me I'm not wanted." He took her hands in his. "I want... Hildegard, if something happens to me..."

"I won't let it," Hildegard said fiercely.

"Cállate and listen," he said firmly. "If something happens to me, I want you to know where these things are. I want you to take care of them. They're the last pieces of my family."

Hildegard nodded grimly. "I will. I promise."

Miguel untied the satchel, handing it to her. She examined each item delicately and respectfully.

"This gold watch has been in my family for five generations," Miguel said, taking it from Hildegard and turning it in his hands. "The engraving, see here? *Elisha Benaroya*. This was my great-great-grandfather. He was a Sephardic Jew who lived in North Africa during the late Ottoman Empire." He handed it to her.

"So much history... in one little pocket watch," Hildegard murmured.

"And the gold chain? You see the detail? It's from Algeria. And the mirror is from Portugal. It was my grandmother's, pure silver. I walked through three countries with Abuela's heavy silver compact clunking against my chest," he smiled ruefully. "I hope she's happy."

"This is *beautiful*," Hildegard gasped, holding up a ring. The ring had tiny vines and flowers growing up the side, and it held a striking opal which caught the light and flashed pink, green, and blue.

"It was my mother's," Miguel said. "Her wedding ring."

"She had exquisite taste," Hildegard held it up to a scant ray of sunlight streaming in.

"It's yours if you want it," Miguel said carefully.

Hildegard laughed at first, then she paused as his words sunk in. She looked at him. He was staring at her, his good eye riddled with anxiety.

"I don't understand," Hildegard faltered.

"Yes you do." He shifted his position so that he was on one knee, even though she was sitting right next to him. He took her left hand

and put the ring on her finger.

"But… I'm not Jewish. Would she approve?"

"Hildegard," he looked at her. "It was always going to be you."

The blood rushed to her head and was thumping in her ears, and she barely heard what he said next. He took a deep breath. "I know the difficulty of what I'm asking. It's illegal. I may be condemning you to prison. And, if I'm being honest… this place has been a home to me when my home was burnt away. But now… a life with me would mean your home would not be your home for much longer. But I've stayed this long because I can't tear myself away from you. It would be like losing my other eye, it wouldn't be a life at all…" He realized he was speaking faster and faster. He sighed. "I'm asking you, formally, if you want to by my wi—"

"Yes," she said, and she tackled him.

She was sitting with her friends in the biergarten, but she might as well have been sitting in the clouds. She promised Johanna she would come out for her birthday, but her mind was on Miguel. When would they be married? She longed to tell them. If their life were normal, she would ask Johanna to be her maid of honor, and maybe Felix could be the best man. No, he would hate that. Maybe he would do it, though. And Otto could walk her down the aisle, and she would wear a white wedding dress and a long veil. In fact, right now, she and Johanna and Wilhelmina would be driving to Munich to look at wedding dresses. And maybe Gerda. Actually, if Gerda knew Hildegard was planning on buying a store-made wedding dress, she would lose her temper. She would be the way she used to be.

But if there were no war, she and Miguel would not be together.

Actually, that wasn't true. It was the Spanish Civil War that brought Miguel here. What would the world be like, without antisemitism? Without this constant judgment, this desire for a homogenous society?

Miguel could live here in peace. They would be married, and the Langes would still be here, instead of wherever they were right now.

Hildegard's heart sank.

They would have written by now, wouldn't they?

"Hildegard, did you hear me?" Felix asked.

"Hmm?" Hildegard looked up.

"You haven't been listening at all, have you?" Felix was disappointed.

"Sorry," Hildegard giggled nervously.

"We were talking about your ring," Johanna said patiently.

"Oh," Hildegard smiled and looked down at it. She was wearing it on her right hand. Miguel had cautioned her to wear it concealed on a necklace, like his missing star medallion. She knew the dangers of wearing the ring, but she wanted it not to matter. She wanted to honor the engagement, even if she couldn't tell the truth.

"Why should I have to conceal it?" Hildegard puffed. "I'm proud of it. I'm proud of you."

"I appreciate that," Miguel said, "but we still need to be careful. When someone asks you where you got it, lie."

"Where did you get it?" Johanna asked.

"Esther gave it to me," Hildegard lied, "before she left."

"I've never seen you wear it," Johanna said.

"Are you sure? I'm pretty sure I've worn it around before."

"No, I would remember a ring like that," Johanna said, eyeing it impressively.

"It looks like a wedding ring," Felix said flatly.

"It does, doesn't it?" Hildegard said, wiggling her finger. "But it's not. She bought it off a gypsy a long time ago and it was too small for her finger. I'm pretty sure it's not even a real opal."

"Not if she bought it off a gypsy," Johanna laughed.

"And she knew that I always liked it, so she gave it to me as a goodbye present," Hildegard continued, surprised at how easily the lie was flowing out. "I don't wear it when I'm out drinking because I'm afraid I might lose it," she willed herself to give a self-effacing laugh. "Remember last time?"

"Yes, you were reeling!" Johanna grinned, rolling her eyes.

"It was lucky Felix was there to rescue me, otherwise I would have been spread-eagled in the street with my skirt up, like Frau Müller that one time!" Hildegard laughed. "What a slosh!"

"Yes, lucky," Felix echoed.

Miguel was making his way down the road to the next town, Krün, where there was purportedly a brothel that the boys from Himmelberg liked to frequent in secret. He had heard other secrets about Krün: namely, that there was still a rabbi in residence, although he was laying low, no longer holding Shabbat services.

They had, a week ago, snuck out in the middle of the night and made their way to the cathedral to see Father Schafer. He stopped her in the middle of the road.

"Wait," he said. "I want to do this, but…"

She looked at him with trepidation.

"I'm not getting cold feet," he laughed nervously. "I just… I want to do this right. I want to be *really* married to you. I want God to recognize us as married, and I want a rabbi's blessing." He looked at her helplessly. "Being up there on the mountain, when I sang the haftarah blessing… it felt like I was right, you know? In my soul. For the first time in a long time."

Hildegard took his hand. "I understand. When you find a rabbi, I'll be ready."

So he was in Krün, looking for the rabbi. Maybe, if he was lucky, they could get married in a synagogue. But he would get married in the barn as long as it was done properly. He approached the town's border, and his eyes widened. He saw the rabbi.

He was hanging from a flagpole. The Nazi flag flapped in the autumn wind, snapping over his stiff body. His beard had been burnt off. His eyes were bulging upward and cloudy gray. He was missing his shoes.

He was wearing a sign that read: *Juden essen ihre Jungen.*

Jews eat their young.

Shit. Miguel stared up at the hanging body. *Shit, shit, shit, shit. I have to get out of here.*

"Hey! You!" a voice called.

Miguel turned in fear. He willed himself to stay calm. He had nothing to hide. He was just a man taking a walk. He was not a Jew. He did not eat his young.

"Yes?" Miguel mustered, coolly enough.

"Where are you from?" A young man, a teenager really, approached him. He was wearing one of those brown monkey suits all the kids in Himmelberg wore.

"Himmelberg," Miguel replied.

"No, dummkopf, I mean where are you *from?*"

"Originally? Spain."

"Then why don't you go back to where you came from?" he laughed.

"I'm a citizen of Germany now," Miguel lied.

"You don't look like a citizen." He peered up at the rabbi. "You look like him!"

"I'm not a damned Jew." *Adonai, please forgive me. Don't turn Your back on me, the way I turn my back on You. Let me leave this godless country. Let me be close to You once more.*

"Hey, Officer Behring!" the kid called, waving a Gestapo over. Miguel's heart sank. *I failed the test of faith, and this is my reward.*

Officer Behring, a man not much older than the brown-suited kid in shorts, strolled over.

"Doesn't this guy look like a Jew?"

"I'm from Spain," Miguel repeated obdurately. "I fought in the

Spanish Civil War. I'm a fascist."

"Papers, please."

Miguel, thankful for his foresight, produced them. He never left the Richter property without them. The Gestapo officer looked up. "You're not a German citizen."

"No," Miguel said uncertainly.

"I heard you. You said you were."

Miguel remained silent.

"So, you're a liar, then?" the Gestapo officer began chuckling.

Miguel allowed himself one moment to imagine what life had been like before he lost his eye. There had been people like this in Spain, and he had clobbered him. There was a point in his life where he was so full of anger, like a set trap was his rage, that at a moment's notice, he would have pummeled these snickering little shits into the ground until they were a grease spot under his boot. But if he indulged himself now, the only thing he would be is dead on the side of the road. Hung up like the rabbi, with a slur of his own scrawled on a sign around his neck.

"I didn't realize I had to report to Hitler Youth," Miguel said through gritted teeth.

"You have to report to anyone in uniform," the Gestapo shot back. "You're a refugee. You don't have the same privileges."

"And soon enough," the Hitler Youth grinned, "you won't have any privileges at all."

Miguel took a breath. "Thank you. I'll know better next time. May I leave?"

"Sure," the Gestapo smiled.

"May I have my papers back?"

"Sure," he continued to smile. He handed them to Miguel. Before Miguel could take it, the Gestapo jerked the papers back, with the same shit-eating grin, and tore the papers in two. He crumpled them up and tossed them into the ditch. "Just remember... I can do anything I want." He laughed. The Hitler Youth boy laughed too. "Now get the hell out of here."

Miguel swallowed his pride, like a horse pill, and forced himself to stoop in the ditch to retrieve his papers. The two boys continued to laugh at him, then grew bored and went away. Miguel walked down the road, willing himself not to run. Running would look suspicious.

He was getting the hell out of here, alright. Getting the hell out of Germany.

Hildegard floated home. Wilhelmina was boiling potatoes for tonight's supper. Otto was in the garden, limping through the orderly rows of autumn squash, examining them like a general in a passing revue. She looked in the fields for Miguel. She looked in the barn. She looked everywhere, except his room, which was in a guest house near the kitchen. The old tenant farmer had lived in his own house in the village, but since Miguel had so little, he was paid partially with free food and board.

She wandered into his room to find him packing. He had a small rucksack, and he was shoving a pair of socks inside.

"What's going on?" she whispered, shutting the door behind her.

"We have to go," he said quickly. "Tonight. I have to leave Germany. I heard there's a pass we can climb, we can go to Switzerland... they're sending people away, but it's our only chance."

"I'm sure Otto can—"

"Hilde," Miguel said sadly. "If you come with me, it would be only me."

The gravity of his words sunk in. She would have to leave her mother and father. Tonight. She hadn't been away from her mother ever in her life. Not even out of the same town. And after tonight, she wasn't sure when she would see her again.

"I know I'm asking too much of you," Miguel said somberly. "To leave your family. And, if you want to stay here, I understand."

Hildegard considered this. What would her life be like, without Miguel? She thought of Gerda, who stayed for safety, who had refused to run because of fear. Fear of what? Discomfort? And now Gerda sat all day, with her empty eyes and her empty wine glass, and she trudged around Himmelberg like a tumbleweed, like a ghost. She barely even showed up for work anymore. What had she considered so valuable in Himmelberg that was worth leaving love behind for? Hildegard shook her head. She did not want to end up like Gerda.

"No," she said. "I'm coming. I'm coming with you."

Miguel pulled her into a fierce hug and kissed her deeply. "I want you to go pack light, only what you can wear and run fast in. Right now. Try not to be seen by your parents. We can't let them know where we're going, otherwise we would be hunted down quickly. And it's safer for them if they don't know. Meet me at the woods that border the corn field in half an hour."

Hildegard hugged him and hastened out the door. She walked as casually as possible into the house and up to her room, mentally plotting her escape. How would she be able to sneak past her mother? Where would she find the courage to leave her? Would her mother be alright tomorrow, knowing that her daughter was no longer there? Would she be sick with worry? Would Otto come looking for her? She changed out of her skirt into some slacks, pulled on a raincoat and a pair of thick socks, and laced up her hiking boots. She looked around the room. What could she take with her that wouldn't weigh her down? What could she afford to leave?

She reached for the steel comb on top of her dresser that Otto gave her five years ago. Then her eyes fell on the swastika resting like a nest of coiled snakes in the middle of the silvery vines. Her fingers curled away from it, and she left the comb where it lay.

She quietly slipped down the hallway into Otto and Wilhelmina's old room, which had a small balcony. She climbed out over the balcony, her legs dangling seven feet above the ground, and let herself drop with a *thud*. Then, she picked her way carefully through the brown corn stalks towards the woods.

Meanwhile, Miguel was digging up the valuables in the barn. He didn't know how far he could run with them, since they were no longer sewn into the inside of his shirt, but he would shove them in the bottom of his pack and hope for the best. If he had to sell his great-great-grandfather's watch to a border officer at Switzerland to look the other way as he and Hildegard passed through, so be it.

He wrenched the bundle of valuables free from the dirt and turned around, and Otto was there, leaning on his cane, staring at him. He shifted the cane to the crook of his arm and with his good hand dug something out of his pocket and tossed it to Miguel. Miguel caught it, already knowing what it was before he opened it in the palm of his hand.

The Star of David necklace.

There was no going back now. No more hiding like an animal in the dark. Miguel met Otto's eyes and looped the necklace over his head.

"I'm leaving tonight," he said. "And Hildegard is coming with me."

Otto was expressionless, as always.

Miguel continued: "I wanted to do this the right way. I wanted to ask your permission for her hand. I wanted you to give her away in a church. I cannot provide that now. But I can provide for her. I love her."

Otto held up his hand.

"It's better this way," Otto said. "I want you to take her somewhere safe."

Miguel smiled gratefully. He could've kissed that colossal man on his sandy walrus mustache, but there was a knock at the barn door. Otto pointed up to the hay loft. Miguel nodded and obediently climbed the ladder to the second floor.

Otto opened the barn door to Officer Engel's opaque smile. "Good evening, Herr Richter."

Otto kept his breathing steady. "Evening."

"I've been looking all over this premises for you," Officer Engel twirled a black gloved finger in the air. "Your wife told me you came in here."

"Yes."

"What for?"

"It's my barn," Otto said defensively.

"Yes," Officer Engel chuckled. "I know that. I mean... don't you have a tenant farmer here to do all your barn work for you?"

"Miguel is not here," Otto said.

"Oh?" Officer Engel raised an eyebrow, circling in. "Do you know where he might be?"

"No." Otto said. "It is outside of working hours. I am not Miguel's keeper."

"Pity," Officer Engel said, stepping with one long leg into the barn past Otto's hulking frame, "because, in fact, Miguel is the reason I am here to talk with you."

Otto said nothing. So Officer Engel continued, his blue eyes boring into Otto's gray.

"Are you aware," Officer Engel said, "that you are hiding a Jew on your property?"

Otto said: "No."

"It has been reported that Miguel is a Jewish refugee. And you've been hiding him."

"Do you have any proof?" Otto said.

"Look at him," Officer Engel snorted incredulously.

"You have given me no evidence that he is a Jew," Otto said. "Only that he is not Aryan. And, last time I checked, Officer Engel," Otto took a threatening step towards him, "it is not a crime to not be Aryan."

"For now," Officer Engel's smile was a sneer. A rattlesnake.

"If you have no proof," Otto said, taking another step, "I suggest you get the hell off my property."

"Unfortunately, Herr Richter," Officer Engel said, producing a paper, "I don't need proof to bring someone in for questioning. There are police cars waiting nearby, should you resist. I came prepared with my *own* paper this time," he smiled thinly, "an arrest warrant."

"He's not here," Otto growled.

"I saw him run in here," Officer Engel said in a low voice.

There was a moment of silence.

Then, buried in the dusty hay, Miguel stifled a sneeze.

"Gesundheit," Officer Engel whispered triumphantly.

Otto shouted, "Run!" and shoved Engel to the ground. Engel hit the dirty floor, and turned like a viper, firing a shot at Otto's head.

Otto was dead before he collapsed to the ground. Something papery and thin slipped out of the inside pocket of his jacket. It was a pressed edelweiss, starlike and white, before it was stained with his leaking blood.

Around the time Engel fired the shot, Miguel had leaped out the barn window and was barreling through the corn. He landed badly on his leg, by a miracle it wasn't broken, but he was aware that adrenaline was pumping through his veins and soon he would begin to feel the effects. Even now, a shooting pain was stabbing up his foot with every leaping step he took. He found Hildegard in the woods and yanked her along.

"We have to run," he hissed. "Run as fast as we can."

"I heard a shot; I was afraid you were dead!"

He looked at her. She had been crying. Her eyes were wild with fright. Should he tell her? When could he break it to her? When was the right moment to say "I'm sorry, but your father's dead, and your mother will be all alone"?

Was this the right thing? Should he tell her to go back, go hide in her room, while he gave himself up? How far could he get on this leg, with Engel fast on their trail? It had all gone wrong before they even had a chance to begin.

That was when he heard the dogs.

There was the sound of yelling in German. That hoarse, harsh German yelling from male voices that he had come to dread and fear. They were finally here for him. His time had run out. His luck had run out. *Please, my God,* he sent up a prayer desperately. *Let us get out of this alive.*

A shot rang out, and Hildegard shrieked. He spun around, fearing the worst. *If she dies, I'm going to kill myself right now.* She was holding her arm, attempting to rise.

"I'm fine. It only grazed me."

He picked her up and, with all his strength, hurled her to the ground so she wouldn't get up. Then he crouched over her, attempting to shield her from any more bullets.

"No!" she yelped. "No, no, no! Not yet!"

"Listen to me," he hissed. "They're going to take us. Don't do anything stupid. Do what you have to in order to survive, do you promise?"

"No, Miguel!" She struggled to free herself. He had her pinned, just like the first time they were together. How long ago was that? A lifetime ago.

He wanted to tell her he loved her, he loved her so much, but the dogs overtook him and a German Shepherd's jaws clamped down on his leg. He cried out in agony, curling up over her, willing himself to be like a boulder over her.

213

Then he was wrenched away by two uniformed officers who were shouting in German.

Hildegard was screaming and screaming, she wasn't even using words anymore, she wasn't even thinking in words anymore, just terror and panic.

Then she was clubbed across the head.

11

1940, Part Three: Where There's Smoke

At first, it was like she was waking up from a nap. She had been dreaming of Miguel, he was singing on the cliffs, and then he jumped down and splashed into the water. And she jumped after him, but she was falling, falling, falling, and was she drowning? Was she in the water? Where was he? She couldn't find him in the water...

A hood was ripped from her face, and a blinding white light shone in her eyes. A gloved hand walloped her on the side of the face. She cried out.

"Hildegard Richter. Please confirm that is your identity."

"Yes," she whimpered, trying to gauge her surroundings. All of a sudden, the beating across the head with a club she had received in the woods came back like a hand clenching the back of her brain. She groaned.

"Are you aware of why you are here, Fraulein Richter?"

"For taking a walk in my father's woods?" she shot back and received another slap across the mouth. Her hands were handcuffed to the back of the metal chair she was sitting on, so she could not reach up and wipe away the blood.

Don't do anything stupid, Miguel's voice came up from her memory.

"Try again," the man behind the light advised.

Hildegard was silent.

She could see the man's profile turn to the other officer in the room, giving him a curt nod. He unlocked the handcuffs of her right hand and forced her hand to the table. Before she could protest, the man produced a pair of pliers, clamped them over Hildegard's fingernail, and tore the whole thing off. Hildegard shrieked in agony.

"Why are you here?" the man asked calmly over Hildegard's cries of pain.

"I'm a German citizen, I'm Aryan!"

Off went another fingernail. She screamed again.

"You only have ten fingernails, fraulein, and we have all night. After we've ripped off your last nail, we'll begin chopping the fingers off."

"I don't understand; I'm not a Jew!" she shrieked. *Do you even hear yourself? You coward.*

"No, but you were consorting with a Jew, weren't you? Do you deny it?"

Off went another fingernail. Hildegard yelped. The pliers clamped down on her thumbnail.

"*Do you deny it?*" the man yelled.

"No!" Hildegard moaned. *Just tell them what they want to hear; they already know.* "No, I do not deny it. I was consorting with a Jew."

"Do you know it is illegal to have inter-racial relations with non-Aryans, especially Jews?"

"Whatever the fine is, I'll pay it!" Hildegard heard her own shrill voice, and was disgusted with herself. "My father is a rich man, he will pay you anything!"

"Your father is dead," the officer replied with satisfaction. "For hiding a Jew and for assaulting an officer."

"He... you're lying," Hildegard said, anger rising in her.

"I assure you, I am not. He attacked Officer Engel, and he was shot."

Don't do anything stupid.

She heard the words in her head, even as she spat a blood-filled wad in the direction of the interrogator. She bid goodbye to her thumbnail, only to be met with a fist to the eye that sent her reeling backwards. Her head hit the cement floor with a *crack.*

She regained consciousness as she was being lifted back into position.

"If you're going to shoot me, just get it over with," she said tiredly. How long had she been in here? An hour? Five minutes? Had she even lasted that long? She used to tell herself she wouldn't crack under pressure, she used to imagine standing bravely up for her beliefs. Of course, back then, her beliefs were the same as the men currently ripping her fingernails off.

"I'm not going to shoot you," the anonymous man had a smile in his voice, "but I am going to send you somewhere where you'll learn some manners. Think of it as a finishing school for Aryan girls who misbehave, Fraulein."

Shit. He's sending me to prison.

Well, it's better than being shot.

She would come to realize the irony of that statement very soon.

Hildegard Rothschild was a French-Jewish twenty-year-old woman in the underground resistance movement in Strasbourg. She had a short pixie cut, a long equine face that made her look like a doe sniffing the air, and a maroon beret that was simultaneously chic and serious. When she was only fourteen years old, she was distributing anti-Nazi pamphlets tucked into bread loaves. She had successfully helped four Jewish families out of the ghettos and across the border to Switzerland. She was finally caught, after numerous outmaneuvering of Gestapo and many escape attempts, in a bunker with several other Communists, planning a raid on a Rhineland outpost.

217

Hildegard Rothschild's papers arrived in the hands of SS Officer Hartmann around the same time that Hildegard Richter's papers appeared on his desk. It had been a late night; he hadn't had much sleep. He and his wife had been fighting. She wanted to take their son Friedrich and their teenage daughter Leona to live with her god-awful mother in basically Denmark, and SS Officer Hartmann had spent four hours arguing down the point that Basically Denmark was no safer than Very Safe and Guarded Munich. This recent desire to move was brought on by the very same underground movement that Hildegard Rothschild was a part of, coincidentally: a bomb exploded near Leona's school. So not only was SS Officer Hartmann having to deal with a damned bomb going off and the possible outcomes of a guerilla attack on the premises; he was also having to stamp all these orders to move Jews and Communists and asocials and Gypsies and homosexuals and everyone else on this godforsaken planet into various concentration camps.

So he accidentally mixed up the papers, so sue him.

And that's how Hildegard Rothschild found herself detained in Ravensbrück, the all-women concentration camp in northern Germany, and Hildegard Richter found herself on a train to Auschwitz.

Right around the time SS Officer Hartmann confused the papers, Hildegard was sitting in a cold, dank prison that smelled of piss. It smelled of piss because there was a puddle of piss in the corner. This was appalling to Hildegard's sensibilities and German values of cleanliness and order. She was wondering if the puddle of piss was another form of torture. A mental ripping of fingernails.

"What did you do?" an old woman asked her. She could have been a gypsy or some vagrant. Maybe she was a petty thief.

"I took a lover. He's a Jew," Hildegard said, exhausted, her head aching from the club to the head and the punch to the eye and the concrete concussion.

"Big boy?"

Hildegard opened one eye. "Yes."

"Hairy? With a beard?"

Hildegard sat up quickly. "You know him?"

"I saw him. Here."

"Where? Is he here now? Where did they take him? What did he look like when you saw him? Was he alright?" She scooted over to where the old woman crouched on the stone floor.

The old woman cracked a mostly toothless smile. "I can tell you that, but what will you give me?"

Hildegard was disappointed. Of course, she forgot. She was in a prison. Prison was full of criminals. Criminals were selfish. "I have nothing to give," she said, affronted. "They took everything of value from me when they arrested me. I don't even have most of my fingernails on this hand," she showed her hands, attempting to rouse some pity.

"What about that ring?" the old woman pointed a gnarled finger at Miguel's mother's ring.

Hildegard snatched her hand back. *Idiot. Watch yourself when you sleep; she'll probably take it when you're not looking.* "This I cannot give. It was his mother's. His whole family's dead."

The old woman shrugged, turning away. Hildegard sighed in exasperation, returning to her corner the farthest away from the piss puddle.

"You want my advice?" the old woman said at last. "If it's really his mother's ring, if it's that important to you... swallow it."

She would regret not taking the old woman's advice the next day. She thought about swallowing the ring, but was afraid she would choke on it, so kept it hidden in her underclothes so the old woman wouldn't steal it. But the next morning, when she was jerked up from

219

her sleeping position on the floor, the ring fell right out. An officer, probably the one who delivered that punch to the eye a few days ago, picked it up.

"That's mine," Hildegard protested.

"Is it valuable?"

"It's only sentimental, it's not even a real opal," she lied. "Please... it's all I have left."

The Nazi guard smiled. "I'll keep it safe for you, Fraulein. My wife thanks you for the gift." He examined it. "Maybe my mistress."

Hildegard willed her stomach to stop churning and kept her anger down below her head. As the guards roughly pushed her out of the prison cell, she turned back to the old woman in one last desperate attempt.

"His name is Miguel," she called to her. "Where did they take him? Was he alright?"

"What do you think?" the old woman snorted. "He looked like hell."

And she was shoved into the blinding light.

She was being shuffled through a crowded line of people. Mostly families. They gave her strange looks and edged away from her. *It makes sense. I'm the one who spent who knows how many days in a prison with the stench of piss on me.*

A chic woman was in an expensive coat. There were people gathered on the sides of the chain-link fence, lined with barbed wire, that led to the trains.

"You won't need that where you're going!" someone in the crowd jeered at her.

The woman kept staring ahead. These, Hildegard could tell, were people that ten years ago would have been shining her shoes. Now that the shoe was on the other foot, she wasn't going to give them the satisfaction.

Then, a uniformed officer approached her and ordered her to take her coat off. It was a beautiful coat. Fox fur, with tails sewn along the hem of the sleeves. It was the kind of coat Marlene Dietrich wore. The officer was yelling at her and threatening her.

"Faster, faster!"

"What do you want with me?" she asked, frightened. He slapped her across the face. The crowd cheered and laughed. Then he took the coat. For some reason, he also took her suitcase.

"Am I going to get those back?" the woman asked, and the realization dawned on her. She had been robbed. But it wasn't robbery. It wasn't robbery when you were a Jew.

Hildegard approached her. "They took my wedding ring, too."

"You should have swallowed it," an older woman murmured behind her.

"Hilde!" she heard a voice cry. She searched the crowd on the other side of the barbed wire fence. Felix was clutching at the fence on the other side, calling desperately for her. "Hilde, over here!"

She pushed her way through the line and made her way to him. "Oh, God, Felix! Felix, I don't know where they're sending me! I don't know where I'm going!" She clutched his fingers through the diamond-shaped holes in the fence.

"I'm going to talk to the guard, I'm going to get you out of here," Felix said, pushing through crowds as the line surged forward.

"Raus! Get away from there!" a guard yelled at Hildegard, advancing towards her.

"Felix," Hildegard said, "Felix, please take care of my mother. I don't know what's happened to Otto. They said they shot him. Take care of my mother—"

"I will," Felix grabbed her fingers desperately and kissed them. "Hilde, I love you. I love you so much. I'm so sorry, I never meant for this to happen, but I'm going to make it right, I promise—"

Hildegard snatched her fingers away. "It... it was *you?*"

Felix had a ferrety fear in his eyes. He looked like he had been caught.

Before he could backtrack, Hildegard put the pieces together. "It was *you. You* called Engel. *You* told him."

"Hilde, Miguel was obviously a Jew... I didn't like what he was doing to you... it's not normal, it's not decent."

"No," Hildegard breathed heavily, anger rising. "You didn't like that he and I were together. You've always wanted me for yourself, and if you can't have me, then you'd sell me off to a concentration camp, is that it, Felix?"

"Hilde, it's not like that—"

"Go fuck yourself, Felix," Hildegard said coldly, then the guard clubbed her across the shoulder.

"Get back in the line!"

Hildegard walked back into the line, ignoring Felix's pleas for forgiveness, ignoring the jeers and *awws* of the surrounding crowd. She pushed her way to the front.

Ten years. He's been my best friend for ten years. And he sold me out to the Gestapo. Wasn't he supposed to be the smart one? The one who rose above all this madness? But he's cruel and selfish, just like everyone else in this country. In the whole world. Then, a memory of Miguel, shoveling manure in the barn, saying: *"You can only rely on yourself."* But that was two years ago. *You have me, and I have you. I'll find you.*

"Name?" a browbeaten man in spectacles asked. He had a large yellow star sewn into the shoulder of his coat.

"Hildegard Richter," she said. *If Miguel is still alive, he's on this train. He* must *be.*

"I don't see..." The man searched for her name.

"There," a supervising guard pointed.

"That's not—"

"Put her on the train! Quickly! Keep it moving!"

Hildegard was shoved onto the train, pushed into the tumult. It wasn't even a train, exactly: it was a cattle car full of about forty people. More and more people were shoved onto the train... there must be a mistake.

"There's too many people in here!" a man called.

"Tell them to stop loading! We're going to be crushed!" A woman was struggling to keep her children together. The toddler in her arms began to shriek and wail nervously, sensing something was wrong with that innate sixth sense all children seem to have.

More and more people. It was stifling. There wasn't any room to move. There wasn't any room to breathe.

Then, yelling from outside the car. The cattle car doors rolled shut and were locked from the outside. People were gasping for air.

They stood there for an hour. Hildegard knew because a man kept checking his watch and saying "When are we going to leave? It's been an hour!"

"Are you so willing to leave your home behind?" an old man with a long beard said near him.

The man with the watch huffed. "This became no longer my home seven years ago. If we're going to move, then let's move."

And then, as if by magic, the train lurched. They all sighed in relief as they heard *chug... chug... chug* under their aching feet.

Hildegard would hear those sighs of relief over and over and over again in her head on her first night in Auschwitz.

And she would curse herself for getting on the train.

The train ride, all in all, would take about 12 hours. There were several transfers, but since Munich was a large city, the cattle cars were already stuffed with about 80-100 people inside. The dimensions were roughly 25 by 10 feet. So there was about two square feet of space for each passenger. It felt like half a foot of space, as people were in their coats and clutching rucksacks and what few possessions they still had that weren't ripped away from them.

The stench of sweat, body odor, and piss and shit was overwhelming. There was a bucket in a corner for 100 people. It was overflowing. There was also vomit on the floor where a pregnant woman, overwhelmed by the smell, became sick.

"That's disgusting," the man with the watch said irritably. "Can't you make your way to the corner, like everyone else?"

"If you say one more damn thing," the pregnant woman's husband snapped, "I'm making my way through this crowd and I'm going to beat your nose off. Shut the hell up."

Some people echoed their support. It was the heat, the hunger, the stench, the crowd, the suffocating lack of air ventilation, and the fear of the unknown that was already turning them on each other. Children were crying and wailing, women were crying, but Hildegard willed herself to be optimistic. *If I'm on this train, then Miguel's on this train,* she thought, and hope fluttered in her chest. *Wherever they send us, at least we'll be together. If I can find him, maybe we can find a way to escape. I don't care if they send us to Timbuktu. I don't care if we have to live on a deserted island. We'll be together.*

"I hear they're sending us to a work camp in Czechoslovakia," a young man said. "They're going to re-settle us."

"Why would they re-settle us in the Sudetenland, when they just got it back?"

"Search me," the young man shrugged. "Better Czechoslovakia than this shit-hole."

"Watch your language, there are children around," a mother scolded.

"What do you think they will do for the mothers and children? Will we have to work too?" the mother with the crying toddler said, straining her voice over his shrieks.

"Surely not. Maybe it will be like it was in the ghetto, where everyone works, and we get to be by ourselves."

"That doesn't sound so bad."

"You're all a bunch of idiots," a man in a newsboy hat scoffed. "Hitler has made it perfectly clear that he wants us gone."

"So? He's getting rid of us."

"He'll never be rid of us," the man said under his breath. "Until he's *rid* of us."

Some people passed out from the heat. Others attempted to slump down out of exhaustion and find a place to sleep for a few hours. The people who were in the corner closest to the bucket were obliged to stand.

Hildegard's stomach rumbled. She hadn't had a proper meal in days. When was the last time she ate? She had something resembling cold muesli in prison, but it was a very small bowl. Before that... before that she and Miguel were preparing to leave right as Wilhelmina was boiling potatoes for dinner. What ever happened to that meal? Was it still untouched, cold? When did Wilhelmina discover Otto's lifeless body, his gray eyes staring blankly at the ground? Had she eaten since then? Was her mother in jail too, imprisoned for unknowingly (knowingly?) hiding a Jew? God forbid... was Wilhelmina on this train?

Please God, Hildegard prayed, *please take care of my mother.*

And then she passed out.

When she woke up, her first thought was: *did I get piss all over me? Or was that from before? It won't make much of a difference; we all smell rank now.* She wondered if the chic woman who had her coat stolen was in here somewhere.

The train slowed, and slowed, and slowed. Then it stopped.

Yelling in German from outside.

"Everybody out! Quick! As fast as you can! Everybody out!"

People attempted to gather their belongings, only to have them roughly taken and tossed aside when they exited the train. A guard told a woman next to Hildegard that they would receive their belongings later.

"Thank goodness we marked our names and addresses on them," the woman told her husband. "Children, put your coats on, it's cold outside."

She was pushed outside into the open air. She thought the fresh air would smell better, but it smelled worse. What was that god-awful smell? It wasn't like urine or feces or body odor. It was like nothing she had ever smelled before, but it stuck in her nostrils and made her want to vomit.

It was a cold November night in Poland. The air was biting. The dogs were, too.

German Shepherds all around were barking and yowling and snapping at people's heels. A dog bit an old woman's ankle. She cried out in fear and confusion. Children began to cry and hugged close to their mothers.

"Shut those children up! Keep moving!"

Hildegard looked around to get her bearings. They had passed through a gate. It was about ten at night, but the moon was shining and there were floodlights all around. The train had entered through and stopped a hundred yards from a gate, which was shut and locked. The gate was a long brick building. The gate's center, which the train passed through, had a high guard tower. The floodlights swooped everywhere, endlessly, blinding, disorienting. The masses of people, a little under a thousand in all, surged forward, away from the barking and snarling and snapping dogs.

"Men to the left! Women to the right!" a guard yelled.

"Men to the left! Women to the right!" a guard further beyond echoed.

The crowd looked at each other in confusion. People were being ripped away from their loved ones. There was chaos, screaming, and then tears. Crying.

"Don't worry, Benjamin, Mommy will see you on the other side," a woman waved at her husband and young son. She pulled her daughter, a little girl who looked about five, close to her. "Stay close, Bilhah. Branja, come with Mutti. Hold your sister's hand."

"Ezra! Ezra!" the pregnant woman shrieked as two Nazi guards ripped her and her husband apart.

"Chana! Chana! You bastards, don't touch her!" Ezra reached out for Chana, and he was clubbed across the back of the neck as he tried to push his way to her. "Chana! *Chana!*" This man had threatened to beat another man's nose off several hours ago, and from the looks of him he could've done it. He was crying now; Hildegard saw tears leaking down his face. "CHANA!"

"Ezra! I love you!" she screamed as he disappeared into the crowd of men veering to the left. *"Ezra!"* She held her swollen belly and crumpled to the ground.

It broke Hildegard's heart. It reminded her of what she and Miguel (and who knows how many others in this crowd? God, *all* of them?) had endured a few days ago. It made her ache for Miguel. She never even got to tell him she loved him. An idea struck her.

"Miguel!" she called. "Miguel Benaroya! Have any of you seen Miguel Benaroya?" she shouted at the group of men as they were being split. None of them heard her; all were entranced in their own private agony of being ripped away from the most important people of their lives. Her eyes searched the crowd. "Miguel!"

"Get up! Keep going!" A woman guard was blowing a whistle. She drew her nightstick and advanced toward Chana, who was beside herself.

227

Hildegard turned back and scooped up Chana, helping her to her feet. "Don't let them beat you, don't let them hurt the baby," Hildegard said.

"Meyn Got, hern meyn sfilus," Chana sobbed. "The father of my child is gone!"

"You'll see him later," Hildegard lied as they pressed forward. "See? Look… we just have to go to different facilities. Look, there, in the distance? See where the men are going? You'll see him later."

Chana continued to sob, holding her belly.

They were stopped by a man with a kindly-looking face. His hair was slicked to the side, and he had bright, sparkling eyes. He was in an SS uniform, complete with a death's head emblem on the military cap, and he had a baton that he was waving to the right and left.

"Don't cry, Mother, this part will be over soon. Go that way, and you will be taken care of." He pointed to the right with his baton.

Chana tore herself away from Hildegard's grasp and wandered blindly with the other women going to the right. She joined a crowd of mothers with their small children, elderly women, and women who looked sickly. *Perhaps they are going to a sick ward,* Hildegard thought.

The man with the baton looked Hildegard up and down and smiled politely at her. "What is your profession, Fraulein?"

"I work on my father's farm," Hildegard responded.

The man examined her hands. "Your hands are rough from hard work," he smiled benevolently at her, giving her a wink. "That's very good. Go to the left."

The woman behind her with the small daughters stepped up to the officer. "I am a farmer's wife."

"Very good, Mother. Go to the right."

"The right?" the woman said, confused.

The officer knelt down and ruffled Bilhah's curly dark locks. His eyes drifted over to the other sister.

"Ah! You are twins!"

"Yes," the woman said warily, hugging them to her.

"Are they identical twins?" the officer asked.

The woman looked to the left, then looked to the right. The gears in her head were turning. "Is that good?"

"It's very good, Mother," the officer smiled and nodded. "We love twins in Auschwitz. They will be given special care. Would you like to send them with me?"

Tears had appeared on the woman's face, but her expression was a mask of grim understanding. She nodded silently.

The officer raised his gloved hand and flipped two fingers toward him. Another uniformed officer appeared.

"Yes, Dr. Mengele?"

"Take these two to the kindergarten," Dr. Mengele smiled, giving Branja's cheek a quick stroke. "Say goodbye to Mutti; you will see her later," he gently took the hands of Bilhah and Branja. They began to scream and shriek and cry for their mother as they were dragged away by the other officer.

"Be good," the mother murmured, and she was pushed along to the right.

Hildegard continued on in the line to the left. She looked around. What was the difference here? There were so many different types of women. Big women, small women, blonde woman, brunette women, young teens, women in their thirties, a few women in their forties. She looked carefully. No. Not many women in their forties. Some mothers with teenage daughters. No mothers with young children.

No older women.

No mothers.

No children.

It was then that she connected the smell in the air with a memory. A long time ago, a pig had gone missing from the farm. Otto, Wilhelmina and Hildegard searched high and low for it, but to no avail. A few days later, they smelled it. It was all around. An impermeable wall of stench.

They followed the stench, retching and gagging, until they finally found the pig's corpse. It had been gutted and dragged off, probably by a wolf. Chunks of flesh were missing, but it was swollen in the sun. Maggots squirmed in its cloudy eyes. The flesh had taken on a greenish-gray tint. Its tongue lolled out of its snouted mouth, and it was swollen and purple. The sight of it was enough to make her vomit, but the stench would live in her memory, in her clothes, in her hair, for days afterward. It was putrid, like garbage sitting out in the sun for days, but also faintly sweet, which made it even more sickening. It was like sewage but worse. It was an unholy smell.

The smell of Death.

Hildegard's eyes snapped up to a building with a chimney. The chimney was fully ablaze, burning like a gate into the deepest layer of Hell. Flames spewed out of the chimney, and a thick, greasy smoke that blotted out the stars and the moon sludged its way into the chilly night sky.

Her eyes drifted down, and in the darkness, she could see people going downstairs into the building. It was the line of women who had gone to the right. In fact, she could see Chana's gibbous silhouette as she waited in line, step by step, as if she were waiting to check out at the counter with a bundle of groceries.

Once Chana was inside, she was relieved by the nice warm atmosphere, as compared to the frigid November air of Poland. Compared to that, it was like a sauna in here. It also reminded her of a sauna because the antechamber was like the room you change in before going to a public pool.

"Right this way, ladies," a female guard beckoned. "Please strip down and leave your clothes here. You are going to take a hot shower and be de-loused before your registration begins."

"Meyn Gott, I can't remember the last time I had a hot shower," a woman said, relieved, to another woman. "How many days were we waiting for deportation?"

"I haven't had a hot shower since May, when we came to the ghettos," the woman replied, stripping off her skirt and leaving her shoes neatly on top of her clothes pile.

Chana took off her dress and her underwear and her brasier. She was insecure about her body and its changes during her pregnancy. She watched for nine months in revulsion as her perfect breasts, like beautiful grapefruits, swelled and sagged and drooped over the sides of her growing belly. Ezra would hold her in front of the mirror and tell her every day, every morning, all the time: "You are just as beautiful today as when I met you. You are even more beautiful... because you are growing our child!" But she would still feel helpless and insecure. Would her figure ever return? She wanted to be beautiful for Ezra. She wanted to be a woman who men would slap Ezra on the back for: "Bah, Ezra, you lucky fellow. You have a beautiful wife!"

She looked around at the other wives and mothers and elderly women. All of their breasts were sagging, all of them tried to hide themselves with their crossed arms. And, almost at the same time, they all realized they were thinking the same thing about themselves. There were nervous giggles, nervous laughter, feelings of relief. *We are all equals here. We are like how God made us in the Garden of Eden,* Chana thought. She looked at a naked mother, holding her children to her. They were comforted in her presence. *Soon,* she thought with a smile, *that will be me.*

They were ushered into a cement room with spigots and pipes. It was to be a group shower, it appeared. They were crammed in, but there was more space in the shower room than the cattle car, thank God for that.

The door shut.

It was locked.

There was a sucking sound as it was hermetically sealed.

The women looked around in confusion.

Then the lights shut off.

A few shrieks of fear.

Suddenly, a hatch opened from the ceiling, and a canister of something dropped down to the floor. It rolled near Chana. It had a name stamped on it: Zyklon B.

The canister leaked a gaseous substance into the air. The women screamed and ran away, charging into the corners, trying to get away from the smell. They began coughing and choking and clawing their fingernails at their necks.

The stronger women pushed past the weaker ones, climbing on top of the fallen dead bodies, scratching their fingernails into the wall, trying to reach a gasp of air, raking their fingers into the cement until they were bloody. The screaming continued.

The children were screaming.

There was a porthole where SS officers could watch the show. They would report later that they knew Zyklon B had done its work when the screaming stopped. They would wait five minutes to clear most of the gas, and then they would send in prisoners wearing gas masks to haul the bodies out.

Chana's body was swollen and bruised from where the crowd of women trampled all over her. There was a dent in her stomach. Four of her fingers were broken, and her arm was coming out of its socket. A male prisoner picked her up as gingerly as possible and dragged her outside. Her dark chestnut hair, which was glossy and beautiful like a horse's mane, was shaved. It might be used for a wig, but more than likely it would stuff a mattress. Three of her teeth, which had gold fillings, were removed.

Then, her corpse was dragged over to a dumbwaiter, where it was lowered into another room, the crematorium. There were three furnaces waiting. Prisoners called Sonderkommandos loaded her body onto a slot, like a human-sized coin acceptor on a vending machine or arcade game. Then, the slot was shoved into the furnace. The Sonderkommando, whose name was Israel Oslovski, had to shove Chana's stomach down to fit into the space of the furnace, which was called a muffle.

"God forgive me," he prayed. She was so beautiful. She was the fourth pregnant woman he had to burn today. He knew he would be burning with them in Hell soon, for all the bodies he helped exterminate. Cremation, according to Jewish Talmudic law, was forbidden.

The furnaces were made by Topf and Sons, an oven-making company. A small family business started in the 1880s, it was led by two brothers who, like Otto, joined the Nazi Party for possible business connections. By the next year, forty percent of Topf and Sons sales were to the SS, as the Final Solution pushed ahead with the building of several large-scale extermination camps. An engineer named Kurt Prüfer, who worked for Topf and Sons, would eventually invent a four-story crematorium with a conveyor belt, so four thousand corpses could be burned in one day. After the war, Kurt Prüfer would be sentenced to twenty-five years in prison. Neither Topf brother would ever be brought to justice in court. Although one brother, in his suicide note, claimed: "I was always decent."

Zyklon B was a cyanide-based pesticide invented in 1919 by Fritz Haber. A recipient of the Nobel Prize for Chemistry, Haber was also known as "the father of chemical warfare."

He was a Jewish scientist.

For Hildegard, the real registration process began.

First, their hair was shorn from their heads. It was the first step in a never-ending line of humiliation. Hildegard watched helplessly as her golden hair, the Aryan hair that had earned her such praise amongst Hitler Youth leaders and Nazis alike, fluttered to the floor.

"Rapunzel, let down your hair!" the barber joked. Was she making fun? A cruel jest? Was she trying to make her feel better? Hildegard didn't know. She wanted to be stony-faced, to preserve her dignity. But she ended up crying, like all the rest.

They had to strip down. They left their belongings behind. Most of them, like Hildegard, had their jewelry taken from them long ago, but the few stragglers were forced to give up any valuables they were smuggling. They were given real showers, but they were not warm, comfortable showers, as the others had been promised. Then, they were plunged in a disinfectant liquid. It stung, and whatever lice that had burrowed in were temporarily eliminated. But they would soon return, as the bunks were crawling with all manner of vermin.

Hildegard was given a work dress that reminded her of a hausfrau. She was given clogs that were too big. *Better too big than too small,* she thought, and the optimism she felt at that thought disgusted her. It was November, and very cold, but she was neither given leggings nor socks. She stumbled forward in the line to the next building, where she could hear buzzing, like a swarm of wasps.

In the next building was a tattooist. Tattooing, like cremation, was also expressly forbidden in Talmudic Law. A Jewish tattooist held a makeshift tattoo gun, which was a series of stamped numbers made from needles, held it in a flame, dipped it in blue ink, and stamped numbers into each woman's left arm.

A Polish woman, seated with the same record book as the brow-beaten man with the yellow star, indicated for Hildegard to step forward.

"Name?"

"Richter."

"Loena Richter?"

"No. Hildegard Richter."

The woman paused. "There's a Hildegard Rothschild."

"That's not me."

The woman looked up at her. "What did you do?"

"I'm sorry?"

The woman was beginning to lose her patience and therefore her temper. "What did you do to end up here? Are you a Jew? Communist? Asocial? Jehovah's Witness? Gypsy?"

What should she say? *I slept with a Jewish man.* What would that mean in here? It was illegal. Would she be shot, here, after coming so far? She looked around. What had these other women done to make them guilty of going to prison? *Nothing,* a voice said inside her. Another voice: *Don't do anything stupid.*

"I... I suppose I'm a political prisoner."

The woman wrote down her name and gave her a number and a red triangle. Hildegard was pushed over to the tattoo table.

"Give me your number," the tattooist said without looking at her.

She handed over the number. Her arm was clamped on the table and the needle stamps went in. She had heard Karl and Lars talk about tattoos before, and how they didn't really hurt on fleshy areas of the body, but close to the bone and nerves, it was torture. This tattooist clearly hadn't been privy to this conversation; he dug into her arm.

"You're hurting me," Hildegard complained.

"Then hold still," the tattooist said, as if he had heard that sentence eleven million times before.

Soon, it was done. Hildegard looked down at the blue stain on her left forearm.

A64390.

The women had to sew their triangles to their uniforms. Hildegard sat naked, sewing the red triangle on the left side of her shirtdress, next to the lapel. A woman passed around handkerchiefs, which were more like old dishrags. "This will keep your head warm," she said.

"We're like freshly-shorn lambs," a woman murmured.

"Ready for the slaughter," another woman said.

"Hush! Haven't we endured enough today?"

Hildegard tied the kerchief around her buzzed head. What would Miguel think of her now? If she saw him, would he recognize her? *Is he alright? Did he go to the left or the right? He went to the left, he's fine. Don't think about it; just focus on the next task. He's fine. He's fine.*

She continued to sew.

She was also given a badge with her number on it.

"Memorize your number," a woman guard shouted. "From now on, you are no longer your name. You are the number on your arm. You are equals. You are nothing. You have no identity. You would do well to remember that," and she walked out.

Hildegard was bobbing and swaying with exhaustion as she stood in formation with the other women. It was muddy outside, but the freeze had come and was beginning to harden the ground.

What will Mother do, now that the ground has hardened up? Did she harvest the rest of the wheat? Did someone help her?

Is she even still alive?

Finally, they were ordered to march. They marched into a long wooden house full of wooden bunkbeds. The barracks reminded Hildegard of stables: the bunkbeds weren't really beds at all; they were brick walls with spaces about seven feet wide. Each space had a double-decker bunk, leaving three areas for sleeping, counting the floor. Thin layers of straw took the place of mattresses. There were a few threadbare blankets. (In later years, blankets would be unheard of.) Women fought over them.

"Silence!" a woman shouted. She too was in a prisoner's uniform, but it had pockets. She also had socks. And boots.

"I am Bruna, your Kapo. I am in charge of this block. There will be no more fighting. If I hear even a peep out of you, I will not hesitate to beat the shit out of you, understood? Line up by your bunks! Five to a bunk! Go!"

The women scrambled to a bunk, lined up.

"You are in Auschwitz-Birkenau," Bruna said. "Auschwitz is a labor camp. Tomorrow, you will receive your labor assignments. Wake-up time is 4:30 in the morning. You will receive a bowl and a spoon: guard them with your life. If you are stupid enough to have your items stolen, don't come whining to me. Lights out in two minutes."

The women climbed into bed. Hildegard climbed into the top bunk. "You're lucky," the woman next to her whispered. "The top bunk is farthest away from the rats."

The lights went out.

It was then that the emotions of the day finally hit Hildegard like she was being slammed into a wall. Like she was being slammed to the ground. Like when Miguel picked her up and threw her down and covered her with his body to protect her from the bullets and the dogs. If only they left one day earlier... where would they be now?

Was her mother alright?

Was Miguel alright?

Were they alive?

Would anyone be around to bury Otto's body, or would he be tossed into an unknown grave?

Hildegard began to weep. Others around her began to as well, their loved ones also on their minds. Soon, the room was like the story of Egypt after God stretched His hand out and killed the firstborn children... full of wailing and gnashing teeth.

"Shut up! Shut the fuck up!" Bruna yelled, swatting on the lights.

"What do you want from us? Can't you see what we've been through?" a woman in a bottom bunk cried to her. Bruna stared at her incredulously and pulled out a nightstick. She walloped the woman across the face. There was a spray of blood and a dull *crack*. She had broken her nose.

Bruna waved her nightstick around the room. "Anyone else have anything to say to me?"

The women were silent.

Bruna put her nightstick in its holster. "Listen to me now, and listen well. Whatever your lives were before Auschwitz, they don't exist anymore. Whoever you were before you left this train, she isn't real anymore. The only thing you have is a body and a number. You're fucking scum. You're a bug, and no one in this place will hesitate to squash you. And if I hear one more sniffle, I'm coming up to your bunk to beat the shit out of you myself." She turned off the light.

Hildegard curled up, her back against the stranger next to her, and willed herself to sleep, her body shaking with silent sobs.

12

1940, Part Four: Kanada

At 4:45 in the morning, they lined up outside in the appelplatz, the large open space between all the bunkers. They were given small metal bowls, like dog bowls, and a spoon edged with rust. They shuffled from side to side, trying to keep their blood pumping in the frigid cold.

"We're going to freeze to death in the winter," a woman murmured.

"I think that's the idea," a woman behind Hildegard said.

Hildegard approached a large cauldron of coffee. It was slopped into her bowl. It looked like tea. She sipped it; it was very bitter. It didn't taste like coffee. It tasted like some kind of root, maybe chicory? She was also given a crust of bread, about two inches thick. It was tinged with mold.

"Mine has mold on it," she said. The woman passing out rations only laughed at her.

Hildegard's stomach rumbled. She hadn't eaten in days. She nibbled delicately around the mold, then hunger overtook her and she devoured it in one sitting.

"Don't eat it so fast," a woman her age said. "They only give you a small bowl of soup for lunch after this. That's all."

239

"That's it?" Hildegard asked incredulously. "Are they trying to starve us to death?"

The woman looked at her plainly.

After breakfast, they stood in line for two hours, in formation, for roll call. Women would lock their knees and slump down into the dirt, only to be beaten awake. Sometimes with clubs, but mostly punches.

"A64387!"

"Here!"

"A64388!"

"Here!"

A64389!"

"Here!"

"A64390!"

"Here," Hildegard said.

Another half hour of that, and the women were ordered to march through the appelplatz. In the cold morning light, Hildegard took another look around this new place which was to be home. It was immense. It was, she would find out later, larger than 5,000 football fields.

Auschwitz I was the organizational headquarters of the camp. Auschwitz II, called Birkenau, was 835 square miles of flat Polish land, with hastily-built barracks that stretched toward the horizon. Birkenau was the main killing center for the Final Solution, with four gas chambers and four crematoria. A small town, Oświęcim, was nestled nearby. On the other side of Oświęcim was Auschwitz III, called Buna, a series of factories and warehouses that benefited from free prison labor.

In Auschwitz, as well as several concentration camps, there was a sign above the gate, surrounded by electrified barbed wire: ARBEIT MACHT FREI, it read.

Work will make you free.

Free from what?

She would ask herself this every day as she passed by it.

They were given work orders. Hildegard, a political prisoner and non-Jew, was sent to work separating and organizing prisoner's belongings, repurposing them to be shipped back for German use. This building was called Kanada. For some reason, Polish people equated Canada as being the land of riches, so the nickname stuck.

"You're lucky to be in Kanada," a woman whispered next to her as they opened suitcases and dumped out their contents. "If you're clever, you can sneak things."

Hildegard didn't care about sneaking other people's property. Right now, the only thing on her mind was food. Unless there was a non-moldy piece of bread in all this paraphernalia, it didn't concern her.

She opened suitcase after suitcase after suitcase. Their names and addresses were marked in white paint or chalk. Who were these people?

They were probably dead.

She dumped out a small suitcase. It had a child's clothes inside and small red shoes. They fit into the palm of her hand.

Best not to think about it.

"Children's items are to be processed in that room," a Kapo directed. Hildegard carried the suitcase to the next room over and saw a mountain of baby clothes, baby hats, baby shoes, baby bonnets, baby blankets, toys, prams... it was fifteen feet high, and it engulfed the whole room.

Don't think about it.

She dumped the suitcase, turned around, and walked slowly out. "Faster!"

At noon, they were served soup out of what looked like an aluminum trash can with handles on each side. They were organized by their triangles. Hildegard got to go in front of the yellow stars and in front of the purple triangles.

"That's not fair!" a woman yelled. "We've been waiting in line longer; we haven't eaten in days!"

"Shut up!" a female guard yelled at her, slapping the woman across the face. She grabbed the woman's bowl and hurled it like a discus across the yard. "Now go fetch your bowl, dog."

The prisoner crossed the yard to get her bowl. She crossed the yard, and she wasn't glaring at the female officer, she was glaring at Hildegard. Hildegard wanted to snap, "What do you want me to do about it? It's not my fault you're a Jew," but she held her tongue and looked ahead.

"Now go to the back of the line," the guard ordered.

The woman obediently went to the back of the line. The guard followed her all the way to the back, then shot her in the head right as the woman turned around. She fell backward, a hole in her head, her bowl skittering across the yard.

The women screamed and backed away from the guard.

"You are prisoners. There will be no backtalk when I give directions, or you'll end up like her. Understood?"

"Yes, ma'am," the women whimpered.

"Back in the line!"

They ran back into position.

When Hildegard's turn came, a Kapo slopped a foul-smelling liquid into her bowl. It appeared to be soup... if soup had died and this is what came crawling out of its grave. A few rotten potato peels and a shriveled turnip floated in a broth that somehow managed to be both congealed and watery at the same time. That was because it wasn't actually broth, the nourishing liquid made from the proteins of rendered animal bones, it was water with hulled oats and rye flour mixed in. It was slimy and gritty, and it tasted sour and rotten.

Hildegard managed to swallow it down, but she threw it up later behind the warehouse of Kanada.

She wearily trudged back to the appelplatz.

"Don't worry, you get used to it," a woman her age said, walking away.

"Wait!" Hildegard said. The woman turned back. "That's the first kind word anyone has spoken to me in this camp. Thank you."

The woman looked at her wearily. "Kindness will kill you in here. You want to live past a few months? You have to toughen up. You are a blister. Make yourself a callous."

She walked away.

At the end of a long day of work, they marched slowly back to their blocks. Thousands of women, wearing exactly the same thing, all in kerchiefs, all in clogs and no socks and no coat, not so much marching as trudging in rhythm.

"This reminds me of *Metropolis*," Hildegard murmured.

"What?" a prisoner nearby said.

"*Metropolis*, the Fritz Lang film."

"Who gives a shit," the prisoner gruffly replied. "Don't talk so loud; you'll attract a Kapo."

Hildegard kept to herself, embarrassed, and continued marching in silence until she heard a voice behind her.

"I remember that film," the voice whispered. "*Metropolis*. They used to show it on Silent Movie Night. Fritz Lang."

"He's my favorite!" Hildegard whispered. "I'm Hildegard."

"I'm Riziel," the voice replied.

"Both of you, shut up," the woman to her left growled between her teeth. "I'm not kidding. A Kapo will come over here soon."

They marched silently by the block of medical barracks. There were shrieks of pain and agony inside, similar to the sounds Hildegard made a few days ago when she had her fingernails pulled off. What was going on in there?

She passed by an office with a plaque: DR. MENGELE.

Here too, there was screaming. But of a different kind.

There were children inside.

They gathered again for roll call at 7 o'clock. A gong rang, just like it did at 4:30 AM, for morning roll call and to go to work. A phrase rose up to the banks of Hildegard's memory: "Ask not for whom the bell tolls, it tolls for thee." What irony. Who was the person in charge of the gong here? Did they choose a gong on purpose, because it sounded like the toll of Death? Or were they making this up as they went?

What disturbed Hildegard the most was, though there were thousands of people milling around, marching in line, performing seemingly useless tasks, waiting for death, it appeared the Nazis had thought of everything. Everything had a rule or a procedure. Everything was tidy, just like a typical German schoolhouse. And yet there were rats, and no stalls in the toilets, and they couldn't wash their clothes. All of this was on purpose. How could there be so much forethought co-existing with so much barbarism?

The young woman, Riziel, approached her after they had been given their crust of bread. This bread was black, and had a smear of margarine. Joy.

Is someone milking Valkyrie? Will there be butter for Mother tomorrow?

"Save half of that for tomorrow," Riziel said. "I heard we only get lunch and dinner from now on." She stared with consternation at Hildegard's fingers. "What happened to your hand?"

"I had my fingernails pulled off," Hildegard said. In the outside world, she would have been embarrassed and tried to hide them in her pocket. But she didn't have a pocket. She didn't have anything. After seeing that pile of baby clothes today, she didn't have anything left.

"Here? At the offices we passed by?"

"No, in the Munich jail."

Riziel looked at Hildegard's red triangle. Riziel had two yellow triangles sewn to her shirt, forming a Star of David. "Are you a Communist?"

"No," Hildegard said. "I was... I had a lover. He's Jewish. We were running away and we were caught." *Don't think about it don't think about it don't think about it—*

"Oh, I'm sorry," Riziel grasped her shoulder. The gesture shocked Hildegard, and she began crying. She couldn't help herself. Riziel pulled her into a hug.

"I don't know where he is," Hildegard said. "I don't know if he's here, or where they took him. I don't even know if he's alive!"

"Well, what was his profession?"

"He's a tenant farmer."

"What did he look like? Would he pass the selection, or go to the right?"

Hildegard thought. "He would pass. He's big, and he's strong." *And in 1938, when he first came to my town, the girls would exchange glances as he passed by. We were all wondering the same thing about him. Was he as strong as he looked? Could he make it count? The same greedy eyes that devoured you wanted you served up on a platter, even though you were their neighbor, even though you were kind to them, and funny, but not like Karl or Lars, you were funny in your own cynical way, your own grown-up way. Everyone liked you, yet underneath their hearts they were teeming with jealousy for you. Why did you bury yourself in this nest of vipers?*

Riziel snapped a finger in front of Hildegard's face. "Were you thinking about him, just now?"

Hildegard blushed. "Yes."

Riziel grinned. She was missing a tooth in the back of her smile. She had a long, narrow face and dark eyebrows. Hildegard guessed

245

that before Riziel came here, she had long, beautiful dark hair. "I do the same thing when I think about Moishe."

"Your lover?"

"My husband," she chewed a fingernail. "He's tall and skinny. Like a beanpole. We weren't tenant farmers. He was a scholar; he spent all day studying the Talmud and the Kabbalah, arguing with scholars over existential questions. That means nothing to these brutes. I wonder... I worry if he..." Her voice wavered, and she stopped talking.

It was Hildegard's turn to return the kind gesture. She barely knew this woman, yet how did she feel closer to her than Johanna?

Riziel wiped her eyes hurriedly, putting on a brave face. "We're just going to have to find them," she said, almost to herself. She turned her dark eyes, like two black marbles, on Hildegard. "There's a way to pass information around this camp. There must be. We'll find them. We'll find them."

After two hours, the gong sounded again. Time for bed. The women washed up in the sparse facilities. Hildegard approached Riziel's bunk.

"Can I sleep here with you? I don't want to be by myself."

Riziel patted the wooden slats. "We'll pretend we're schoolgirls at a sleepover. We'll keep pretending about everything. That's how we'll get through it."

Someone snorted cynically near her, rolling over and crossing her arms.

The woman who was supposed to be sleeping next to Riziel approached after washing up. She looked ready to pick a fight.

"My bunk is up there," Hildegard pointed. "Away from the rats."

The woman immediately left.

Hildegard curled up and faced Riziel.

"We're going to get through this," Riziel whispered determinedly. "We just have to beat the bastards at their own game."

"Shut up," someone hissed nearby.

"Good idea," Riziel nodded. "Good night."

As much as Hildegard pretended she was camping (she was back in 1935, when she was a young and beautiful idiot, and she was sleeping on the grass under a tent at the Hitler Youth summer camp), the wooden slats were still uncomfortable. She was still in Auschwitz. But she had hope.

4:45 in the morning. A Sunday. What luck! They didn't have to labor on Sunday. They just had to clean. It would be like a spring cleaning day at home.

"What goes on in Dr. Mengele's office?" Riziel asked an older woman nearby. Hildegard let Riziel ask the questions. Hildegard was a red triangle, and Riziel was a yellow star, so while Riziel attracted ire from the guards because of her race, she had sympathy from her fellow inmates. Hildegard attracted at best ambivalence from the guards, but from her fellow prisoners, she was treated with cold indifference because she got to cut the line. Anyway, Riziel just had one of those friendly faces. Even with a severely shaved head and a handkerchief, she looked trustworthy.

The woman glanced around for a listening Kapo. "Torture."

"Why? In God's name, why is he torturing children?"

"He calls it 'science experiments'. Something about trying to populate the Earth twice as fast with little Aryan bastards. That's what the twins are for... to see if you can force a blonde woman with blue eyes to have two at a time, through 'science.' Personally," she went back to her mopping, "I think he has a proclivity for them."

Riziel grunted in disgust. Hildegard's gut swam in guilt. It sounded so evil to her now, but she had to admit: a few years ago, she would have been the lynchpin of that movement. She was a blonde woman with blue eyes. If she had moved to Berlin to pursue a career in the Nazi Women's League, where would she be now? Would she be analyzing these "test results" from Dr. Mengele, rounding up a group of silly naïve Aryan girls, injecting them with some secret formula? *Don't worry how we learned to do it, girls, that's the power of German engineering!"*

"Have you ever observed him with them?" The woman leaned in, leaning on her mop. "He's so nice to them. He wants them to call him 'Uncle Joseph', the sick son of a bitch. He gives them sweets and lets them sit on his lap, like a grinning crocodile with an open mouth, and then *snap!* He bites."

Another woman sidled up. "You weren't here a few months ago. There was this Roma kid: a little boy who looked just like him. He called him his son, took him everywhere he went. He even bought a little Nazi uniform for him and paraded him around in it. Next day? Shot the boy point blank in the appelplatz."

"What a monster," Hildegard murmured, horrified.

The woman turned a cynical eye on Hildegard. "They're *all* monsters. They're men."

"Not all men are monsters," Riziel said, deflecting the attention to her. "My man is not a monster. He's an angel."

"Oh?" the woman said pithily. "And where is your angel now?"

As fate would have it, Riziel would see her angel the very next day. A group of men marched by the throng of women under the gates, always reminding them: WORK WILL MAKE YOU FREE.

Hildegard saw a spectacled head above the crowd of men, bobbing along. He reminded Hildegard of Luka, a tall man with an introspective look. He sensed her staring at him; their eyes met. Then he averted his eyes, and they rested on Riziel. They lit up.

"Riziel!" he called.

"Moishe!" Riziel shrieked. "Moishe! Moishe! You're alive!"

They rushed at each other, snatching one moment to grasp each other's hands. They were beaten away from each other before they had the chance to embrace.

"Get back in line, you fucking dog!"

"Back in line! Keep marching!"

"Riziel, I love you!"

"Shut up!" a Kapo clubbed him in the mouth. Moishe turned and grinned a bloody smile at her.

Riziel continued marching, grasping Hildegard's hand. "Oh my God, oh thank God, God thank you, he's alive! He's alive, Hilde!"

"I'm glad, Riziel," Hilde whispered, smiling.

"If Moishe is alive, yours will be too," Riziel said.

After cleaning, Bruna approached Riziel and pulled her to the side. "Is that your husband?"

"Yes," Riziel said warily. What new insults would come today?

"I can organize it so that you can see each other," Bruna said, appearing benevolent.

Riziel's eyes lit up. To "organize" something was camp slang for stealing and secretly passing around, any covert operation. "What will it cost me?" she asked suspiciously.

Bruna smiled. Riziel was a smart girl; she had seen right through to the end. "Your bread. And you'll have to steal something valuable from Kanada. For me and for your husband's Kapo."

Riziel pursed her lips. "Is this some kind of trap? I could be killed if they caught me stealing."

"So don't get caught," Bruna shrugged and walked away.

The next day, they woke up at 4:30 and washed themselves with a sliver of hard soap in the barrack's trough-like sink. Riziel washed in between her legs, a determined look to her face.

Hildegard and Riziel and the rest of the block stood in line for roll call, which took two hours. Riziel's finger was tapping against her leg.

They marched to Kanada, past the screams and cries of the torture block.

Hildegard and Riziel were seated side by side, sorting watches and jewelry. Riziel's hand scooted deftly to the edge of the table, subtly sliding the watch off the edge. It landed with a *plink* in her lap.

"Don't do it," Hildegard murmured between her teeth, not moving her lips.

"Why not?" Riziel said, quickly sliding the watch in between her legs.

"It's stealing, for one," Hildegard said in a low voice. "Those people are probably dead."

"If they're dead, they're *my* people. And they would rather have their items help a Jewish woman see her husband than be sold back to some German asshole."

"If it falls out, you'll be shot," Hildegard muttered.

"It won't," Riziel said, giving a wicked side-smile at Hildegard. "Ask my husband. I've got the tightest pussy in town."

This made Hildegard burst into laughter, and Riziel laughed too.

"Stop laughing! Get back to work!"

"Yes, ma'am," they both said, going back to sorting.

At the end of the shift, they marched back to their bunks for dinner. Riziel walked carefully, only moving her legs below the knees.

"Why are you walking like that?" a woman nearby said.

"I have stomach cramps," Riziel replied. "I think it's the soup. I'm going to skip my bread for tonight."

"Can I have it?"

"She already said she would give it to me," Hildegard lied for her.

They passed the male group, and Hildegard's eyes drifted to Moishe. He had a stern look on his face. He was staring straight ahead. Why wasn't he talking to Riziel? Then it occurred to Hildegard: his Kapo probably told him the same thing. The Kapos were getting double the stolen items.

After roll call, Riziel went back to the barrack. She heaved a sigh of relief as she unclenched after hours of marching and standing. She was beginning to shake.

Bruna hastened up to her. "Give it to me."

Riziel wearily stood up, and the watch plinked out on the ground. Bruna hastily picked it up and shoved it in her pocket. One of the special privileges of Kapos was they wore a different uniform, which included pockets.

Bruna opened the pocket and examined the watch. "This is a man's watch!"

"Yes, that's for the male Kapo," Riziel huffed, sitting wearily down on the bed.

Bruna smacked her upside the head. "You stupid girl, why didn't you get something for *me*?"

"I wanted to ask you what kind of things you like," Riziel said lightly. "I see all kinds of things in Kanada."

Bruna's eyes sparkled greedily. "Find me something... pretty."

"If you want pretty things," Riziel said cunningly, "could you organize a skirt for me? With pockets, perhaps?"

Bruna's eyes narrowed, and she smiled thinly. "You're my kind of girl. Clever."

"Here's what you should do: don't give the watch to the male Kapo. Give it to a seamstress or a tailor. Have them make me a skirt with a secret pocket, like this," she drew it in the dirt, then looked up at her. "Then I can get you pretty things whenever you want."

Bruna stared hard at the drawing, memorizing it, then rubbed it out with the sole of her shoe.

"I want to see my husband every day," Riziel said.

"Not every day. The best I can do is once a week."

"Then I will only smuggle items twice a week."

"You're giving *me* orders?" Bruna's face got red.

"No, I'm being realistic. If you can only let me see Moishe once a week because it will arouse too much suspicion, it will certainly arouse suspicion if I'm walking around clinking and clanking every day." She extended her hand. "Deal?"

Bruna took it begrudgingly.

The next week, Riezel had her new skirt, Bruna had a necklace that she wore under her work dress, and Riziel and Moishe were reunited in each other's arms.

Hildegard found Moishe to be a kind and loving person, even in Auschwitz. Auschwitz seemed to bring out the worst in everyone: in Riziel, it was cunning; in Bruna, it was greed; in Hildegard, it was cowardice. But Moishe stayed the same.

"That's because he's a man of unbreakable principles," Riziel said admiringly, rolling her eyes at him in a *what are going to do with him!* sort of way.

Moishe was liked by many in his block. He had a quiet, unassuming way, and volunteered to help when he was needed. But his kindness was running him ragged. Already skinny, his cheekbones were so prominent after the first two months of his tenure in Auschwitz.

Hildegard, who sometimes accompanied Riziel as a lookout, begged Riziel for help finding Miguel. "Maybe we could switch skirts, and I could carry something for a Kapo, and he could tell me something about new transports from Bavaria."

"Are you sure you want to take the risk?" Riziel asked Hildegard, narrowing her eyes and crossing her arms.

"Hildegard, don't worry about it," Moishe said. "I'll see what I can do."

"What are *you* going to do? You don't work in Kanada. Are you going to smuggle nuts and bolts up your asshole?" Riziel put her fists on her hips. *She doesn't want him to risk his safety,* Hildegard saw.

Moishe pursed his lips and gave Riziel a stern look. "I said I'll handle it."

Riziel stomped back to the block. "Ooh, that man! He makes me livid. Like a brick wall."

"My father was like that," Hildegard said, smiling wistfully. "Never said anything. It was what he did that counted." *Like consort with Nazis,* she thought bitterly. Then she thought of that fight they had a few years ago. He said he would do whatever he needed to keep her safe. *Would you sell your soul, Otto?*

"What happened to him?"

"He was killed by the Gestapo. For hiding a Jew," Hildegard said dully.

"Miguel?"

She nodded.

Riziel pulled her into a side hug. They plodded down the road, arm in arm, Bruna following at a distance behind them.

The next week, Moishe brought someone with him. "This is Dmitri," he indicated. "He knows everything. Hildegard, he may have the answers."

"Bread first," Dmitri grunted. Moishe handed his crust of bread over; Dmitri devoured it.

"Moishe, no!" Hildegard was horrified. "I could have given my bread!"

Moishe gave Hildegard one of his stern looks, holding up his hand. "Keep Riziel safe. Keep being her friend."

Riziel was blushing. She was trying to look put out at her husband once again sacrificing his comfort for others, but not far underneath she was glowing with pride.

Hildegard turned to Dmitri. "Do you know of any prisoners here named Miguel?"

"No," Dmitri said through a mouthful of bread.

"Maybe it was under a different name. Like Michael?" This was pronounced *Migh-hay-el*, the Yiddish way.

"There are thousands of Michaels," the prisoner said, licking the crumbs off his fingers, not looking at her.

"But there's only one Miguel," Hildegard snapped, drawing his attention. She gathered her patience. "He's missing an eye. He's big, a juggernaut. And he's a Spaniard. That *should* be enough to jog your memory," she piped.

The prisoner gave her a long look.

Hildegard settled down.

"I've been here since this place opened months ago," Dmitri said. "I work in the administration building. And I've never heard of a Spanish Jew named Miguel. It's all Poles and Germans here."

Something broke in Hildegard. Hope, maybe? She felt nothing. She didn't feel agony, or worry, or loss, or pain. Nothing.

"Cheer up," Dmitri said sardonically. "It Hitler gets his way, your boy will be here soon enough."

Hildegard turned away from Riziel and Moishe and walked away, numb.

But he's not here.

They didn't send him here.

Miguel is dead.

13

1942: Scum

Two long years. They had felt like an eternity. Hildegard couldn't remember what her life was like before Auschwitz. Was there a time when she used to eat three meals a day? Was there a time when she pushed away a bratwurst boiled in beer, with sauerkraut and a foamy weissbier on the side, and protested that she couldn't eat any more? She couldn't imagine this time. She only cared about her soup and bread. It no longer made her sick; she slurped it down quickly. One time she tried to make it last, only to find it had been stolen.

She had given up all hope of Miguel. She heard the stories, whispered among the women at night, as they hovered over the bucket of coal in the middle of the barrack that served as their scant source of heat.

"My cousin and her family tried to escape to Palestine... a neighbor saw them leave the barn. They never even made it out of the village."

"I heard in Hungary they made them dig their own graves."

Oh God... Esther. And Luka. The babies...

"How did you hear that? How could it be true, if no one lives to tell these stories?"

"Why shouldn't it be true? All of this escapes belief... these Nazis

255

think of the worst possible crimes to commit, the most inhumane acts, because the world could never understand it. But here we are. Trapped in She'ol."

"One thing's for sure... if you haven't heard from anyone, they're most assuredly dead."

Miguel.

It had been two years, and she had given up searching for his face in the new transports. He wasn't coming. He was gone.

Riziel was still alive, but most of the older women were dead. They froze to death. The winter killed them off. Especially those who had no one, whose sons and husbands were killed in the snow and burnt in the fires.

Much of the contraband was passed through Oświęcim. If you were clever, like Riziel, you could organize a link of dried sausage or hard cheese from the village. One time, at Christmas, Riziel was bold enough to smuggle a bottle of wine she found in a suitcase to Bruna. This was in exchange for a conjugal visit with Moishe, previously unheard of.

Afterward, Hildegard clutched her hand, grinning. "How was it?"

Riziel shrugged. "It was... fine."

"Fine?" Hildegard giggled. "Only fine?"

"I don't know, Hilde," Riziel sighed. "It's not the same. It's not the same as being in bed with your man, and he's all yours, and you're in your house that you bought together, and you have nothing to do all day but make love. It's not the same when it's cold and you're both starving and skin and bones from malnourishment, and there's a Kapo standing ten yards away, keeping watch."

"Bah," Hildegard grumped and lay back on the wooden slats of the bunk. "You're the only one in this block who's had a solid fuck, and all you want to do is complain. You're no fun."

Riziel laughed and lay back. She stared at the ceiling, which had snow leaking through several spaces in the roof. "I'll tell you what," she said somberly. "I'm never going to take it for granted again. When we get out of here, I'm going to make love to him every day."

The expansion of Auschwitz meant the arrival of droves of SS officers. They were crawling all over the place. Many of the guards were young men, while the officers were men in their late thirties and forties, who had made a career of the SchutzStaffel.

By 1942, the population of Auschwitz had ballooned to a million. Hundreds and hundreds of people were transported every day, and the furnaces of Birkenau were always going, day and night. As a way of further culling the weeds, SS Officers would use any excuse to shoot a prisoner. Hildegard once saw a prisoner shot for marching out of step. She saw a female SS officer beat a prisoner to death for not having her spoon and asking for another.

Hildegard noticed, without surprise, that the female SS were more cruel than the males. It wasn't that the male SS were kind or humane; it was there was a distinct sort of pettiness in every punishment the female officer doled out. What was it that made them so cruel? Was it an Aryan woman releasing her frustrations of not being able to move up in her career in the same way as a male on a scapegoat? How did they hire these women? Did they ask them if they had been bullies at school? That's what Hildegard thought of them. Was it something in the Aryan blood? Or was it women's nature?

At noon soup, a male guard began following her around.

"Hey, look at her!" he called to his fellow guards. "That's not a Jewess, that's a baby doll!"

The only modicum of similarity to a baby doll was perhaps Hildegard's shaven head, with a few blonde locks jutting out of her handkerchief. In the winter, because the lice were less likely to be rampant, sometimes they were allowed to grow their hair a little longer than a spiky stubble, to keep their heads warm. So in that way, yes, she did look like a blonde baby.

But if Hildegard had looked in the mirror (there weren't any at Auschwitz), she would not have recognized herself. Years of malnutrition had hollowed her rosy cheeks out. Her skin was pallid and sagged on her face, the baby fat of her cheeks all eaten away. Her face ended in a sharp, pointed chin. Her head bobbed on a skinny neck. Her collarbones rose like oars resting on a canoe. Her rib cage was like the black keys on a piano. What was left of her beautiful, perky breasts (the kind that only a twenty-year-old can have) was now withered away. Her hair was no longer shining and gold, but a dull brassy color. Her dark blue eyes bulged out of her sockets, making her look like a hungry, mangy dog on the street.

"China baby! Come back here!" the guard called.

Oh, God.

"I said halt!" he commanded.

She stopped.

"Turn around. Come here and speak when you're spoken to," he said, sternness in his voice.

Little soldier, you haven't been here for very long. The rule is that prisoners don't speak. Ever.

She kept her eyes to the ground.

"Look at me."

She looked up.

He looked like her. He looked like Herr Schulz. He looked like any of these Nazi drones, the typical blonde hair, the typical blue eyes, very white teeth, very fit. Not strong. Not naturally big and tall, like Miguel. Just a boy who had spent the last ten years in a gymnasium rather than in school. How old was he? He must have been her age. Maybe younger. How old was she, again? What was her name, again?

"What's your number?"

"A64390."

"Oof. Too many numbers for me," he laughed to his friends. Were they friends? Or did they all have to stand together? Did they sign up for the war together, like Karl and Henri? Congratulations, little soldier, you're a prison guard, not a general. "I'm going to call you china baby."

Hildegard stared at him.

"Would you like to suck my cock, china baby?"

She tried to mask her revulsion.

The guard burst into snickers. His lackeys followed. "I bet you would. I bet a strong German cock would put a smile on that sad face."

A whistle blew. "Line up!" a female guard called.

The guard smiled and waved her away. "Run back to your line, china baby!"

Hildegard turned and walked away, thanking God for every step put between her and that pig, praying that this wouldn't be one of those times when guards got bored and shot prisoners as they walked away with their orders.

She told Riziel about it later.

"Don't go anywhere without me," Riziel warned her.

"Why? Are you going to scare them away?" Hildegard snorted.

"No, but there's safety in numbers."

"Not in here."

After dinner (could a crust of bread be called dinner?) Bruna told Riziel that Moishe was waiting for her.

"But I haven't..."

"You'll pay me later," Bruna shrugged. "It's now or wait 'til next week."

Riziel obediently walked off.

After ten minutes, Bruna told Hildegard to go fetch her back. Hildegard walked, hugging her arms in the snow, hastening her step.

She knew where to walk to avoid the guards at the watchtowers. She passed by Block 16. She was almost to Block 23, their meeting place. Suddenly, she was clubbed across the back. She yelped, and her mouth was covered with a gloved hand. She was dragged into an empty block. The door shut behind her.

She was having flashbacks of when she and Miguel were taken. Had they been found out? Were Riziel and Moishe hanging somewhere on the appelplatz, as they occasionally did to ward off prisoners who got ideas? Was she next?

"China baby," the SS guard said.

Shit. Shit shit shit...

"We never finished our conversation today," he smiled and unbuttoned his pants. "About you sucking my cock."

The others laughed.

"Do you want to suck my cock?"

Miguel flashed through her mind. *Don't do anything stupid.*

She looked up at him. "Not particularly."

He punched her in the eye. Another joined in, kicking her in the ribs. Then he kicked her in the back, and she cried out.

"Let's try it again," the SS officer said. "You're going to suck my cock, and you're going to swallow it, and you're going to thank me at the end. Or I'll get Hans here to step on your face. And he's got big boots." He bent down, pulling his pants down at the same time. "Are you going to be a good girl, china baby?"

Hildegard wanted to say, "Fuck you, fuck your lackies, just go ahead and shoot me, you fucking Nazi asshole," but the instinct to survive took over. She couldn't will herself to say it. She nodded her head. *Miguel, please forgive me. If you're in heaven, turn your face away and try to understand.* She thought she was going to vomit. Maybe if she vomited all over this boy's penis, he would shoot her in disgust, and she wouldn't have to do it.

"Put it in your mouth."

She did.

"Now suck on it."

She did.

"Harder."

She did.

"Harder."

She did.

It didn't take him long to finish. The power excited him.

"Now swallow it."

It was like the soup. She gagged. The others laughed.

"Now say thank you," the officer chuckled.

Hildegard looked at him, and tears began to well in her eyes. "Please... just kill me," she whispered to him, sending a plea into the blue eyes that were so like hers. The SS officer's expression changed. To... what? It wasn't guilt. It wasn't pity. It was... something. Recognition, perhaps. Recognition that she was a human being.

"Me next," Hans said, pulling his pants down and rubbing his shaft. "I'm going to fuck you right up the ass," he leered at Hildegard.

Kill me, she silently pleaded.

The SS guard buttoned up his pants. "Leave her alone."

"But you said—"

"What are you, a fucking faggot, rubbing yourself off in front of me? Pull up your pants. I said no." He looked at Hildegard sternly. "Get the fuck out of here."

Hildegard jumped up and ran out the door. She bolted all the way back to her block, where she forced herself to vomit. She wanted to plunge herself in the disinfectant barrel. She wanted to sit in that acidic substance until her skin melted away, and her nerves, and her heart, and her brain, and eventually her skeleton. She didn't think she would ever be at peace again.

She trudged into the room. Women were getting ready for bed, climbing into the bunks. Riziel was sitting up, looking for her.

"Where were you?" Riziel said. "I was worried about you; I've been looking for you for ages!"

I was only gone for ten minutes.

It only took ten minutes.

Her eyes found Bruna, who was watching her like a panther.

She knows, Hildegard thought with revulsion and anger.

She set me up. He paid her to do it.

As if reading her thoughts, Bruna produced a small flask from her pocket, smiled smugly at her, and drank out of it.

The flask had a swastika on it.

The next day, the officer found her again. Her heart sank from her stomach down to her shoes. *God, why did You allow this to happen to me? Why did you send this devil to torment me?*

"China baby!" he called, jogging up to her.

God, please. Strike me down. Strike me down now. She looked at the electric fence. If she ran for it, she could electrocute herself. And she would be dead. And she would be with Miguel. And this demon would not touch her again. She tried to make her feet move toward the fence.

"Come here, let's talk alone."

She moved a foot toward the fence. Another foot. *Keep going... it's now or never.*

"Where are you going, silly girl?" he laughed charmingly, grasping her wrist and dragging her over to an empty area. The fence receded: twelve, thirteen, fourteen steps away.

She stared at the fence. She couldn't bear to look at him. Worse than looking at him was living with herself. She had to look at the inside of her mind every god-awful second.

"I never got to thank you," he put a gloved finger against her cheek, "for last night."

She looked up at him incredulously. Was this man a lunatic? He raped her last night. HE RAPED HER—

"My friends can be such brutes," he laughed, rolling his eyes, the same way Riziel laughed and rolled her eyes talking about Moishe's killing kindness. "I'm sorry that Hans was such a pig."

She stared at him.

"Don't you say anything?" He grinned at her, flashing beautiful white teeth.

She looked around. Where was Riziel? Where was Riziel?

He caught her face in his hand and squeezed. "I'm talking to you," he growled.

"I'm sorry," Hildegard said automatically, and she hated herself for it.

"I forgive you," he smiled, the 200-watt smile back on. "What's your name?"

"Hildegard."

"Oh, beautiful! My nanny was named Hildegard." *How disgusting was that?* He put a gloved hand on his chest. "I'm Ernst," he bowed slightly, as if they were at a country social dance. "Ernst Langstrom."

Hildegard chewed her lip, and then she gave him a curt nod.

Ernst extended a gloved hand. "I'd like to start again. We didn't get off on the right foot."

She shook his hand, acutely aware that people saw it. Guards saw it. Prisoners saw it.

"I'd like to get to know you better," he said.

She looked visibly pained. Was he going to drag her behind a warehouse this time, or just do it in the open? As if sensing her thoughts, he put up two hands. "No funny business this time, honest to God, I just want to get to know you better. What's a beautiful Aryan girl like you doing in a hellhole like this?"

Honest to God. What an ironic statement. What should she tell him? *"Well, Ernst, if you must know, I fucked a Jew."* If she said that, he would think she was a whore, and then he would do whatever he wanted to her. But hadn't he done that anyway?

"I'm a political prisoner," she said in a small voice.

"Political prisoner? Are you a Communist?" he poked at her red triangle, which was above her breast.

She shook her head.

"Good," he smiled.

Riziel had found her. She had crossed her arms tightly around herself, and she looked anxious.

"Is that your friend?" he said softly, smiling still.

Hildegard nodded.

"Go on, then. We'll talk later. Goodbye, Hildegard!" he waved.

Hildegard walked away quickly towards Riziel, feeling her eyes get wet. She joined Riziel, and Riziel turned with her, matching her quick pace.

"Who was that?" Riziel asked.

Hildegard shook her head. "A guard."

"What did he want?"

She tried to keep herself from vomiting. "To talk."

"Do you know him?"

Hildegard wrapped her arms around herself for comfort, rubbing them to make it appear as if she were cold, which was the truth, because it was December. Riziel grabbed Hildegard by the shoulders and stopped her. The sudden move made Hildegard flinch, reminding her of last night.

Riziel looked into her eyes and Hildegard averted her own eyes away, willing herself not to cry, knowing Ernst was still watching. She forced herself to meet Riziel's gaze, only to find tears were running down Riziel's face, freezing on her cheeks.

She understood.

Ernst tried to talk to her the next day as well, while she was walking to work.

"China baby!" he called and waved.

Hildegard looked straight ahead, swinging her arms and legs in rhythm.

"Hildegard!" he called again.

God, please, not in front of all these women. It will make it worse.

He fired a shot in the air. "Halt!"

The group of women jumped and came to a stop.

He dragged her out of the line, calling over his shoulder, "stay there." Bruna was unsure of what to do; she looked around at other Kapos, marching their blocks by to their various work stations. She looked at a guard posted nearby. He didn't tell her to do anything. So they waited.

Ernst dragged her, his hand tight around her wrist, behind a shed. He slammed her up against the wall, his wrist still clutching her purpling skin. It reminded her of the first time she and Miguel were together, and she felt disgusted linking the two memories.

"You think you're too good to talk to me?" he said, his face red. "You're a goddamn prisoner. You're a criminal. You're a piece of scum, compared to me." He slammed her against the shed wall again. "You're ignoring me now?"

"No, I don't think that," she said quickly, her mind racing for an excuse. She met his eyes, trying to look convincing in her lie. "It's just... we get in trouble when we talk while we march. I've gotten in trouble for it before; I didn't want to be disciplined by my Kapo." Then, to consummate the farce, she mustered with all her strength a charmingly apologetic smile. "I apologize."

Ernst let go of her wrist. She held it gingerly to her chest.

"So you *do* want to talk to me?" he said suspiciously.

"Of course! Of course I do." *You're disgusting, Hildegard.* "I just... it's just..."

"Just what?" he snapped.

"The... my block is waiting for me. We have to go to Kanada. Will you get in trouble for detaining me? I don't mean that in a disrespectful way, I just... I don't want you to get in trouble."

Ernst looked out from behind the shack. Bruna was staring at him. The whole block was staring at him. "Eyes front!" he barked. They immediately turned around.

"I see your point," he said, bridging his fingers together and resting them on his lips. "I'll figure something out. You may go."

Hildegard slunk back to her place in line, followed by the eyes of a hundred women, and Bruna, whose cheeks were red from anger and embarrassment at having to detain her block.

"Forward! March!" she yelled, and they marched on.

Bruna gave Hildegard a shove on her way in. "Tell your boyfriend not to make me late again, or it will be your ass."

Something broke in Hildegard. The bile of hurt and anger rose up to her throat. "What do you want me to do about it? *You* sent *me*. You sent me right to him, and I know it was on purpose."

Bruna made to hit her, and Hildegard dodged, going on quickly. "And if you hit me now, I'm going to tell him about what's under your shirt." Feeling bold, she poked at the pearl necklace. It rattled incriminatingly.

Bruna's eyes were filling with fear, yet she punched Hildegard in the stomach. Hildegard doubled over, the wind knocked out of her. "You do that, and I'll tell him it was your little friend who's been stealing, not me," Bruna was breathing hard.

Hildegard regained her breath, and she stood up straight. There was a poison in her veins. "Maybe he'll believe you. But he likes me better. I'm the one who sucked his cock." She smiled cruelly. "Thanks to you."

Bruna had nothing left to say. Hildegard turned away and marched off, plopping down on her work bench and sorting through a large pile of eyeglasses.

Matters were made worse at lunch. Ernst was waiting at the soup line. He beckoned Hildegard to come to the front of the line with two fingers.

"A64390!" the Kapo in charge of the soup called.

"Here," Hildegard replied, coming forward.

"This one gets to come to the front of the line," Ernst instructed. "And she gets double rations. Understood?" He turned his back away from the prisoners, grabbed the Kapo by his gaunt shoulder, and leaned in. "Take care of her, and I'll take care of you. Got it?"

The Kapo nodded, dumping an extra serving into Hildegard's bowl. Ernst smiled warmly at Hildegard and winked. Then he walked off.

Hildegard looked up at the Kapo unsurely. "Thank you," she mumbled.

The Kapo didn't say anything. He had his orders.

She turned around and walked back down the line, only to find that every female prisoner was glaring at her. She searched for Riziel's face, hoping for a supportive look. Riziel's eyes flashed, but then she masked herself with a wan smile: *Come back and let's keep going.*

But the brief emotion in Riziel's eyes was unmistakable.

Disgust.

In the evening, she was called again. She received two crusts of bread. She shoved one under her shirt for Moishe. *Are you buying back Riziel's friendship by taking care of her husband? How would she take that? Would she be pleased, or would she tell you she didn't need your damn charity?*

She reported to the guard's barracks. It was near ARBEIT MACHT FREI. She stared at it. She allowed herself one moment, one single moment, to stand still of her own accord.

Work will make you free. What a cruel joke. If you work hard enough, you'll starve and overwork yourself to death, and that's the only way you're getting out of here. You're never getting out, not unless it's through a chimney. How long would it be before she too would make her escape into the smudgy gray air?

Let it be soon, she heard a small voice inside say.

"What are you doing here?" an SS barked. "Go back to your block at once!" He pulled at the holster of his gun.

"I called her here, Commandant Hoess," Ernst said, emerging from the officer's barracks. "I'm in need of a new secretary, and I require someone to run messages for me from here to the other camps."

Officer Hoess looked at him quizzically. "You don't want a male for that position?"

"No."

Officer Hoess took a beat, then shrugged. "Boys will be boys," he chuckled.

The phrase made Hildegard's skin crawl.

Ernst handed Hildegard a notepad and pencil and beckoned her to follow him into the barracks. *Who is this ruse for, exactly? Why give me a notepad and pencil? Why not just make me wear a sign around my neck that reads "whore"?*

"I bet you're wondering why I was able to talk to Commandant Hoess like that," Ernst said from over his shoulder, smiling slightly. She wasn't. She didn't have the faintest idea who Commandant Hoess was, but perhaps it could be valuable information for later. She continued to follow Ernst down the very clean and tidy halls. A female prisoner was scrubbing the floor, and Ernst stepped right through it. Hildegard tried to edge around where she had scrubbed, and the female prisoner noticed the clogs, and she looked up at Hildegard. *She knows what I'm doing here.*

"My uncle is a big-wig in the Nazi Party," Ernst said with more than a tinge of pride. "He works for Joseph Goebbels. He got me a job here," he looked around, surveying the halls. "It may not be long until I myself am running the place," he sighed, then winked at her, grinning impishly. "Stick with me, baby."

"I saw Joseph Goebbels once," Hildegard volunteered. *Keep him talking about Nazis. Maybe you can convince him that you don't belong here. Maybe he can use his uncle's connections to get you out.*

"Oh really?" Ernst was interested. He leaned against the wall, arms crossed.

"Yes," Hildegard said. *And I left in disgust.* "He gave a speech after the Führer drove through our town after the taking of Paris. He was an excellent speaker."

"I thought you said you were a political prisoner," Ernst said patronizingly, unlocking the door to his room. "What are you doing, talking about the Führer? Trying to butter me up?"

"No," Hildegard lied evenly. "But if you want to know, I saw the Führer. Twice," she added. *Beat that.*

He opened the door for her, and she stepped in. His was a small room, but orderly. The floor was swept. The sink was immaculate. The two twin beds were neatly made, with tight corners ending in 90 degree angles. Hildegard felt herself start to cry.

"Why are you crying, china baby?" Ernst put a comforting hand on her shoulder.

"I haven't seen a mattress in two years," she said. "I had forgotten what it looked like."

"Oh, you poor thing! Why don't you jog your memory? Sit down," he beckoned. She looked at him unsurely. He put his hands up. "I promise, I'll be a gentleman. You sit on that bed, and I'll sit on this one."

She obediently sat on the bed. The springs creaked as she sat down. This mattress was military-grade and wouldn't pass muster in the Richter household, but right now it felt like sinking into a cloud.

"May I get you a drink?"

A drink? How about a meal that isn't moldy or rotten?

He poured some pear schnapps into a small glass for her. She took it and sipped it carefully, then began coughing and spluttering as it burned down her throat.

Ernst laughed. "Aw, you're a lightweight."

Little boy, two years ago, I could drink you under the table. I haven't had anything other than coffee since I was twenty-two.

"I guess I'm not used to it," she put it on the table. "It's been a long time since I had schnapps."

"When's the last time you had it?" he refilled her glass and sat down next to her, pushing it into her hands. "Go on, drink up. It'll warm your bones in this awful Polish cold."

She took another sip. It was immediately going to her head, making her feel sick. "Well... it was in 1936. When I saw Hitler," she nodded to her earlier comment. "My father took us to see the Olympics. We went to a café, and we had peach schnapps in the Tiergarten." She smiled at the memory. "My father was a member of the Nazi Party, too," she said to him.

"A Nazi?" He was confused. "I thought you were a Pole, or something. Or a Communist, and you were just lying about it."

"No," Hildegard said, her mouth feeling warm. "He was a Nazi. He made tank parts and bullets for the Wehrmacht. And I was a little Nazi too, for a little while. Just like him. I was the leader of the Jungmädel." She looked at him. "They wanted me to join the Nazi Women's League, but I didn't. I stayed with my father. For the father and the Fatherland," she giggled. *Shit.* She looked down at her drink. *I haven't even had that much. Keep your wits, moron.*

Ernst laughed too. He was closer now. "But I still don't understand... what's a beautiful Aryan maiden like you doing in a hellhole like this?" He took off her kerchief, admiring what was left of her blonde hair.

Hildegard turned to him. How honest should she be, now? What would make him stop prying, and what would get her out? Maybe he was more sympathetic than he seemed. "My father was hiding Jews," she said. Partial lie. Twenty-five percent true.

"Oh, Hildegard," he said sorrowfully. It was like she told him he was an opium addict. "The Jews are a spineless, deceitful race. They prey upon the kindness and virtues of Europeans; they have been for centuries." He took her hand. "But I forgive you for that." He kissed it.

She managed a smile. She was going to be sick.

"I know you've done wrong, but now that you're here, I'm going to take care of you. I fixed it with administration this afternoon... you're going to be my personal secretary." He put a hand on her thigh and gave it a squeeze. "That way we can get to know each other better, and no one will bother us."

Hildegard closed her legs tight automatically. "Does... does that mean I have to move blocks?" *Please don't make me leave Riziel. She's the only kind person I have left in my life.*

Ernst sat back, insulted. "Look at all the trouble I've gone to for you. I make sure you're fed, I give you a better job, I let you lap up my liquor, I let you sit on my bed instead of out in the fucking snow." The anger was rising in his voice. "Doesn't that mean anything to you? Aren't you going to be the least bit grateful?"

"I am grateful," she said helplessly.

"Then why don't you show me how thankful you are." It wasn't a question. It was a command.

Her head was swimming. *I've already sullied myself,* she thought miserably. *What does it matter. If I lie back and close my eyes, it will be over soon.*

So she did.

She tried to think of Miguel and imagine it was him instead, to take her mind off of it. But it wasn't the same. This was toxic as sewage, and when she and Miguel were together, it was as pure as an untouched spring. She didn't want to confuse the memories. She couldn't bear to think of Miguel. It made her too sad, and she would start crying, and then Ernst would become angry. She didn't know if she could ever face Miguel in her memories again. What would he think of her?

Afterward, Ernst lay back in bed. "You'd better go, before lights out. I wouldn't want you getting shot by a guard thinking you're trying to escape," he laughed playfully, kissing her on her parched mouth.

Hildegard put on her clothes, stepped into her clogs, and reached for the door.

"I'll see you bright and early tomorrow, china baby," he smiled at her, his hands propped up behind his head.

I hope a guard does *shoot me on my way back,* Hildegard thought. *Or I could just walk into the fence.*

But she didn't. She went back to her bunk and ignored the stares as she climbed up next to Riziel. She lay on her side, trying to push out the hot liquid that clung stickily to the inside of her legs, knowing that was a useless endeavor. Riziel didn't say anything.

Hildegard produced a crust of bread and pressed it into Riziel's hand. "This is for Moishe," she whispered. "But if you don't want to be my friend anymore, I understand."

Riziel grasped her hand tightly, and the crust of bread was crushed flat between them.

The next day, Hildegard followed Ernst around, doing little errands for him and taking little notes. She struggled to hold the pencil in her hand. She looked at her terrible penmanship, not recognizing it. How long had it been since she had written anything down? 1940? Two years? What was the last thing she wrote down? Her signature on a receipt? A grocery list?

"Did you hear what I just said?" Ernst said, eyebrows furrowed.

Hildegard looked up. "I'm sorry. I was just thinking about the last time I wrote on a piece of paper. I think it was a grocery list in 1940."

Ernst stared at her, then laughed. "I love the way your mind works. All the silly little details you can just bring up from the depths of your memory." He pinched her chin in his fingers and gave her a kiss on the forehead. "I find it absolutely charming."

She managed a smile.

"Now, the commandant at Buna has a list of materiel needed for Commandant Hoess. You're going to go get it for me. You will be accompanied by an armed guard. There's a block leaving for Buna right now, so you'd better hurry."

It was a cold winter day. The sky was dark gray and smudgy, and the snow covering the ground was crisp and white. In Himmelberg, on days like today, they would go up to the ski lodge and buy a ticket to be taken to the top of the mountain. Then they would ski or toboggan down, shrieking with delight. The children would be playing outside on a Sunday afternoon, throwing snowballs or building a snowman. There would be mulled wine bubbling away merrily in a pot in every house, filling each room with its spicy, deep fragrance.

She passed by a few German children, the progeny of the officers who took up residence in the abandoned village of Oświęcim, who threw snowballs at the prisoners marching by. They cheered and laughed when they knocked their hats off. The prisoners looked ahead. Hildegard tried to glean the hats as she walked behind them with the armed guard. Then she too was hit by a snowball.

"Bullseye, Jew!" a little girl yelled.

The armed guard began yelling at them in German and shaking his finger at them, for they had almost hit him and his new leather boots. The children ran away in fear.

Buna (also known as Auschwitz III) was about six miles away from Auschwitz I, in the village of Monowice. As Hildegard approached, the gigantic factories and warehouses, with their flowing chimneys (no crematoria here, just pumping out regular industrial-grade pollution) really did remind Hildegard of *Metropolis*. She wondered where Fritz Lang was right now. (He was currently in Hollywood, safe and warm under the palm trees, filming a movie called *Hangmen Also Die!* which was based on the assassination of Reinhard Heydrich, the SS mastermind behind the Final Solution.)

Before she went to find the commandant, she passed out the fallen hats to the bare-headed prisoners. They wearily smiled their thanks. No talking here. She placed a hat into the bony, gnarled hands of a prisoner, looked up into his eyes, and recognized them.

It was the Empress, stripped of makeup and wigs and corsets, but unmistakably Empress Varvara. He was gaunt and sickly and older, but this was absolutely the same performer from the lurid days of Babbel.

"Empress?" she whispered.

He looked at her in fear, recognition on his face.

"It's me, Hildegard," she smiled. "Wilhelmina's daughter!"

"I'm afraid you must have me confused for someone else," he plastered on a polite smile that showed all of his teeth. "I don't know anyone by that name. I am Franz Muller. Always have been."

"But I know—"

"I am Franz Muller," he said, desperation in his voice, looking around nervously. He snatched his hat and walked away quickly.

Hildegard's heart sank. She went to go find the commandant.

The commandant's list wasn't ready, so she had to walk around Buna with him, taking notes about each warehouse. The process lasted three hours. She prayed Ernst wouldn't be angry.

"Stay here," the commandant told her in the tire factory. "I just have to talk to the clerk upstairs, and you should be ready."

Hildegard obediently waited, watching him climb the stairs of the factory to the office, thinking about how many times Otto had done the same thing in his steel factory.

Then she heard something: *"Psst!"*

She turned around. Franz was hiding behind some tires, staring at her. He beckoned for her to come over.

"Hildegard Appelbaum," he smiled tearfully. "You've grown up!"

She hugged him, and he returned the hug, squeezing her tight and kissing her forehead. They laughed at their affection: twelve years ago (twelve!) Franz wouldn't be caught dead hugging a little girl, and Hildegard begrudged Franz from hogging the limelight away from her mother, with all of his little quips and cutting remarks about her real parentage.

"I'm glad to see you," she said.

"How's your mother?" he asked.

"I don't know," she shrugged. "I've been in here since 1940."

"My God! And you're still alive?"

"Barely," Hildegard smiled sadly.

"I know what you mean," he sighed. "They say Buna is the best place to get stationed, because you're away from the crematoria. But people still only last a few months around here." He looked at her. "Why are you here? What's a pretty German girl like you doing in this shithole?"

The line was so similar to what Ernst had purred into her ear last night before climbing on top of her. It made goosebumps appear on her arms. "I fell in love with a Jew. We were trying to elope. We were caught." It came out bluntly. But it felt good to tell it to someone who knew her from long ago, someone who knew her as she was.

He squeezed her hand. "Hildegard, whatever this place does to you, whatever they make you think about yourself, it's not your fault," he said kindly.

The gentleness of his words made tears prick up in her eyes. God, would she ever stop crying? Hadn't she cried her tear ducts dry? She pulled out her crust of bread from under her shirt.

"Please, take this. Franz, take it. You showed kindness to me when I was a child; let me show some kindness to you."

"You weren't such a child then," Franz sighed. "A 12-year-old girl in a cabaret, Jesus Christ, what was your mother thinking..."

"She was surviving. That's what we're all doing," Hildegard said, again extending the bread. Franz hesitated, then took the crust with trembling fingers, shoving it in between his thin, parched lips. Lips that, it seemed an eternity ago, were overlined with rouge to give them a more fuller, feminine look. Now The Empress Varvara Alexia Zlovitzskia looked like a corpse walking.

"Save some for later," Hildegard suggested.

"It won't do any good. You shouldn't have wasted this on me. Hardly any of us make it through selection. We're the lowest of the low, not even the prisoners like us, because of what we are." He began shaking, maintaining the last modicum of composure. "I'm always made to go to the back of the line, when they see the pink triangle, they shove me backwards. There's nothing left for me, just watery broth."

"No one will help you? Not even the Communists, or the political prisoners?"

"No, to them I'm an abomination. And the beatings... they'll beat you whenever they can, the Kapos. They'll call you fairy or faggot or worse... but then, when no one's looking, they'll shove you into a privy and..." The tears welling up in his eyes began to spill over. "God, they're such fucking hypocrites."

Hildegard didn't know what to say. Franz continued to shake, stifling the sobs so the Kapos couldn't hear.

"Well… at least you can finally fit into that green sequin dress," Hildegard ventured. "No back rolls to be seen on you."

Franz stared at her incredulously, then broke into a quivering smile. "You bitch."

Hildegard grinned and pulled Franz into a quick hug. "I have to go. I'll see you. Don't let the bastards keep you down."

"I don't think you will be seeing me much longer." Franz got up shakily. "But when you get out of here, Miss Minni in Miniature, tell your mother I hope her ass is as big as a couch cushion."

"Hey, faggot!" a Kapo yelled, advancing over to Franz. "Get back to work!" He slammed a baton into Franz's stomach, causing him to double over, at which point his jaw collided with the Kapo's knee with a splintering *crack*. Hildegard hid behind a stack of tires and retreated out of sight.

Franz was right: Hildegard never saw him again. A few days later, Franz would be beaten within an inch of his life and sent to Auschwitz I, to the "clinic". The doctor on duty determined that he was suffering from internal hemorrhaging, and there was nothing to be done. They pulled four of his teeth, which had gold fillings. By then, he was comatose, so they didn't bother sending him to the gas chambers, just straight on to the crematoria, at which point The Empress took her exit in a slim black flourish of smoke.

1943.

Ernst had gone home for leave over Christmas, and Hildegard thanked God for that. She went to Kanada during those days, sat with Riziel at her work station, and didn't feel shame. No judging eyes of female prisoners, no special treatment: she was everyone's equal because she was equally mistreated, instead of uniquely miserable in equity.

"Maybe he'll get tired of me," she said to Riziel. "How many times can you sleep with someone who doesn't love you before you move on to someone new?"

"Ha! Ask my late husband," an older woman nearby said, dumping out a suitcase.

Riziel was silent.

"How's Moishe? I haven't seen him in a while." Hildegard sorted through men's shirts.

"They moved him to Auschwitz I," Riziel said, her shaven head collapsing into her thin, pallid hands.

"Oh, Riziel," Hildegard looked up at her. "Isn't there anything you can do? Can you get Bruna to talk to the Blockälteste?" She indicated with her eyes a pile of jewelry. *A bribe, perhaps?* she said with her mind.

"I tried," Riziel sniffled. "Bruna doesn't want to take the risk."

Hildegard stewed on this. "She's doing this to get back at me."

Riziel looked at her. "No, Hilde."

"Yes, she is. That bitch. It's because I threatened to tell Ernst about her."

"Not everything is about you!" Riziel burst out.

Hildegard recoiled.

Riziel looked as if she regretted saying it immediately. "Sorry."

"It's alright," Hildegard lied.

"Hilde," Riziel sighed, exhausted. "You're going through hell, and I'm sorry for you. But we're all going through hell. Literally, like Dante's Inferno. Different types of torture for different types of people."

Hildegard thought about this. "Maybe there's something I can do. Maybe Ernst could get Moishe transferred back."

Riziel shook her head. "It's not going to happen."

"Well what can I do?" Hildegard said. "I'm trying to help, but I don't know how. I don't know how to help."

Riziel sighed. "I don't know."

They sat in silence, sorting the evidence of lives once lived.

Ernst came back after Christmas. He brought a picture of his mother with him, as well as a picture of his father in his uniform from 1918.

How long has it been since I've seen a photograph? If any of us were allowed to keep photographs of our loved ones, would it make things better? Or would it make us want to kill ourselves even more? They wouldn't need so many gas chambers if we could be allowed to remember what's been stolen from us. She looked closely at the picture. Ernst looked like his father.

"Did your father die in the First World War?" Hildegard asked.

"No, I just like this picture of him," he smiled proudly.

"My father died in 1918," Hildegard said.

"I thought your father was hiding Jews?"

"That's actually my stepfather. Although both were in the Great War," Hildegard said. *Would they have liked each other? Were they both in heaven now, looking down on Hildegard with disdain?* "Do you have any brothers or sisters?"

"I had a sister, but she died as a baby. I'm my mother's pride and joy," Ernst said fondly.

Ah. So that explains it.

"Did you tell her about me?"

Ernst turned around. "Why would I do that?"

Good point. Mutti, you'll never guess! I have a whore in a concentration camp! Aren't you proud? At least she's a nice Aryan girl!

"Oh, don't be jealous," he chuckled, tipping her on the chin with the knuckle of his gloved hand. "Come, I have a belated Christmas present for you."

She followed him out of the officers' barracks, down the road, behind another barrack, into a room lined with tiles and shower spigots. Her heart dropped to the floor.

Tile rooms.

Showers.

She had heard the stories.

Every day, she heard the screams.

Now it was her turn.

She began shaking like a leaf.

"Get undressed," Ernst said softly.

Tears began forming in her eyes. This was it. He had come to his senses, or gotten bored as she predicted, and now he was tying up loose ends. He came back to kill her. He had taken her to a gas chamber to rid himself of her.

I'll be with my fathers and Miguel soon. And Esther. It's completely useless to think they could still be alive, and now I'm going to end up the same way as them. I just wish I didn't have to go through this part alone.

"Why are you crying?" he asked.

"Please don't kill me," Hildegard sobbed.

"What?" Ernst laughed. "You silly girl, I'm not going to kill you! I'm going to bathe you! Or rather, you're going to wash yourself." He produced soap and shampoo. "My dear, frankly, you stink. After we're together, I can't be walking around smelling like a brothel. I want you to wash yourself in the mornings. This should also take care of the lice. And," he produced a bottle of mouthwash from his pocket, "Merry Christmas!" He beamed.

Hildegard took the items. She was terrified. She couldn't control her shaking; she thought she was going to piss herself right there on the tile floor.

"Poor thing," he pulled an arm around her neck and kissed her lightly. "You haven't had a hot shower in years. Here," he turned on a spigot.

Hot water burst forth, steaming up the room. "You have ten minutes. Pamper yourself, my darling," he smiled, happy with his generosity, and walked out the door. "And we'll talk after," he winked, shutting the door behind him.

Hildegard walked into the hot water. She tried to pry open the shampoo bottle, but still feeling traumatized, her hands were shaking too badly. She used the bar of soap, but she dropped that too. Finally, her bladder let loose, and she watched urine spiral down into the drain. She began crying, hyperventilating. She crouched down over the drain and put her head between her knees, sitting there in the hot water, crying, until her ten minutes were up.

Hildegard walked back after Ernst was through with her. She turned her face to the side, only to find the picture of Mrs. Langstrom smiling down on her. That made it worse. She was already dry as a bone. She didn't have the courage to explain to Ernst that near-death experiences tended to not be particularly lubricating, so she let him be rough with her and tried to mask her winces.

She limped back to her barrack. They had agreed that the soap, shampoo, and mouthwash should be kept in Ernst's room because they would be stolen in a heartbeat in the barrack. And Hildegard would be ripped to shreds in the process.

The female prisoners watched her closely as she limped, saddle-sore, and took her place in line. An old woman made the number two sign with two fingers and spat on them. "Toi!"

Hildegard turned around. "What does that mean?"

"Shame on you," the old woman said, looking at her. Hildegard could see the judgment in her eyes.

"Shame on *me?*" Hildegard shot back, opening her arms wide and gesturing. "Old woman, look at where we are! Look at this factory of death! Shame on *me?*"

"Hilde, come away," Riziel took her by the shoulders. "Don't attract a Kapo." She looked over her shoulder at the old woman. "Mrs. Hoitl, you should be more careful. Solomon told us that those who guard their lips keep their lives."

"Is that a threat?" Mrs. Hoitl gasped.

"No, but if you get a wad of snot in your soup, don't come complaining to me." And with that, she turned on her heel like a little soldier and marched Hildegard away.

"It would at least improve the flavor," Riziel murmured.

There was another belated Christmas present for the prisoners: selection.

With more and more transports pushing into Auschwitz, the time had come to further thin the crops. Prisoners were ordered to strip: nakedness was one of the many ways the Nazis whittled down the Jews' senses of their own humanity to nothing. Then, a group of SS doctors ordered them to run; Doctor Mengele was also there with a clipboard. They were directed to show their tattoos as they ran. The object of the Nazis' game became clear: if you ran slow enough that the SS doctors could see the numbers on your arm, you wouldn't be here much longer.

The women pinched their cheeks to give themselves some color, some semblance of health. Hildegard and Riziel slapped each other... a red hand mark on both sides of their faces would look like a nice ruddy complexion when observed at a dead sprint.

There was, for some odd reason, an orchestra at Auschwitz. The orchestra's purpose was to play marching music to help the prisoners learn to march. Hildegard always thought it was strange... music? Here? Deprived of all earthly delights, except the greatest of them all: music? The orchestra began to play.

"On your mark, get set, go!" a female officer called.

Hildegard stared at her.

It was Else Knopff. The Hitler Youth camp recruiter from 1935.

"Hilde! Run!" Riziel called past her shoulder, already at a jog.

Hildegard snapped into runner's position and launched like a rocket. She held her breasts—what was left of them—to keep them from hurting as she channeled all the power into her legs. Hildegard passed Riziel, and Riziel caught up with her, pushing forward. As iron sharpens iron, so Hildegard and Riziel raced each other around the field.

The guards and doctors were laughing at them.

"Look at those Jews scurry!" Dr. Mengele laughed, pointing with his pencil.

They came to the end of the loop, huffing and holding their knees. The Nazi guards applauded, still laughing.

"10 points for the blonde!" Else guffawed.

"Nein, Else, Fraulein Long Nose came in first!" her companion chirped.

Hildegard realized Else didn't recognize her.

Good. Let me keep one scrap of pride for today, even if it's only a thread.

The slower prisoners finished the race, and then numbers were called. They were made to dress, then get on a Red Cross truck, which chugged in the direction of Birkenau.

Mrs. Hoitl was one of them.

Deep in her heart, like a thorned vine, Hildegard was glad.

14

1944: China Baby

In the early summer of 1944, Hildegard missed her period.

Many women did not have periods in Auschwitz. They claimed there was something in the coffee that was making them miss their monthlies. But really, when the female body is starving and malnourished, it goes into survival mode and decides that growing another human is off the menu, and the uterus closes up shop.

But Hildegard wasn't starving. Not compared to the others. She was getting double rations.

She looked forward to the one week out of the month when Ernst would leave her alone. She counted down the days. And in June, the days came and went. And they came and went in July, too.

Shit.

She knew it was certain when she couldn't keep the soup down. This was a passable enough excuse—most women who were new to the camp couldn't keep the soup down, because it was disgusting, worse than pig slop. But a veteran? A woman who had been there an unprecedented four years?

Riziel knew, too. When the second month passed and Hildegard still had not asked her to steal her a few sanitary napkins from Kanada,

Riziel knew the score. She looked at Hildegard, her eyes alert with terror.

"How could this happen?" Riziel whispered at night.

"You know how," Hildegard wiped away her tears, staring up at the ceiling. "It's the most natural thing in the world. Even in this unnatural death factory."

"He doesn't...?"

"He wouldn't," Hildegard said between gritted teeth. "He's the most selfish man I have ever met. His narcissism is on a sociopathic level."

"What do you expect? He's a Nazi."

That made Hildegard cry even harder. Knowing that Ernst Langstrom's bastard Nazi child was growing inside of her like a cancer made her even sicker than she already was.

How long could she hide it from him, from the guards? She knew what would happen; she had seen it happen to other girls the guards liked to play with. They would be sent to Dr. Gisella Perl, a Jewish gynecologist, and they would receive an abortion. (Performing hundreds of abortions would haunt Dr. Gisella Perl for years, but for these rape victims, it was the difference between life and death. After all, Auschwitz was a labor camp, not a maternity ward.) If she was unlucky enough to be sent to Dr. Mengele instead of Dr. Perl, the abortion would be botched (Dr. Mengele liked to play with all his victims, not just children), and the pregnant mother would die.

She thought about killing herself every day. She could just walk into the fence. She could reach for Ernst's gun and shoot herself. She could hang herself with her shirt in the middle of the night. She could just stop eating and let starvation do its work. But every time she decided to end her life, her body's instinct for survival—or maybe it was just cowardice—took over, and she couldn't do it, and she hated herself all the more.

Walking back from another session where Ernst failed to notice her delicate condition, she passed by a woman from another block. The woman bumped her shoulder as she passed.

"Watch it," Hildegard barked. Riziel approached slowly, sensing trouble.

"You've got some nerve," the woman who bumped her said coldly, spitting on the ground.

"Oh? And why's that?"

"The rest of us are being eaten alive by lice and rats, and you walk around the appelplatz smelling like a primrose," the woman raised her eyebrow. "All the fancy perfume in the world won't wash the stink of Nazi off you."

"I guess not," Hildegard said, acidic, shrugging. "But at least I smell better than you."

"Hilde," Riziel said warningly.

"How do you sleep at night, knowing you're a Nazi whore? Knowing you let a man inside of you who killed our mothers, killed our babies?"

"Well, my mother was a whore too, and she's still alive," Hildegard smiled bitterly. "I guess it's just survival of the fittest."

"*Hilde!*" Riziel gasped.

The woman slapped Hildegard, enough to make her lip bleed, but not enough to knock her down. Hildegard wiped the blood away with the back of her hand. "You're a fool, do you know that? Acting all high and mighty. Do you know what they're doing in Ravensbruck? They're taking women there and transferring them to Dachau, where they're being forced to whore themselves to prisoners. In exchange for rations."

The woman was silent. A crowd of women had gathered to watch the action.

"And you know they're doing this on purpose, right? To divide us. To make us hate each other instead of them. They're playing *you* like a fiddle."

"Pretty words from a pretty girl," the woman said, and she spat in Hildegard's face. At which point Hildegard gave up talking and lunged at her. She tackled her to the ground, put her knees on her upper arms, and began walloping her as hard as she could. She remembered what Karl had told her a long time ago in school: imagine you're punching through your target, not at it. She began punching and punching and imagining that this prisoner was Ernst, was Bruna, was Officer Engel, was Felix, was Herr Schulz, was everyone.

"Hilde, stop! Hilde, please, you're going to kill her!" Riziel shrieked, trying to pull her off.

"Halt! Enough!" a Kapo yelled, advancing toward them.

Hildegard wearily slumped off the woman, whose nose was twisted to the side and swollen, whose face and striped shirt were covered with blood. Hildegard wasn't even sure she was conscious.

"Before you come talking disrespect to me, remember I'm stronger than you, because whores get better food rations," she spat a bloody spew at her. "Bitch."

She pushed past the gathered prisoners and stalked off. A vision of her, smiling at camp in a photo, jumping off a cliff with a frightened girl who called her sister, flashed in her mind. Who was that girl?

Not me.

I'm prisoner A64390.

Hildegard watched airplanes painted with American flags circle the camp. There were a few muffled cheers, and she saw the eyes of prisoners around her filled with anticipation.

"Maybe the Americans will come and save us," a gaunt young girl whispered, daring to hope, allowing herself to smile. But the planes didn't return the next day.

The United States, having finally been roused to the cry of war two years ago after Axis-allied Japan attacked Pearl Harbor, had the benefit of being the last one standing. Thousands of fresh troops rushed to the aid of the battle-weary French and British. Propaganda posters encouraged men to help defeat the evil Adolf, and women to join the W.A.C.. Better late than never.

The pushing tide of German takeover now seemed to be receding, and Ernst knew it. It seemed inconceivable: could Germany actually lose this war? One evening, Ernst asked Hildegard to spend the night with him. He looked like he hadn't slept in days.

"No sex," he said to her. "Just... could you just hold me in your arms until I fall asleep?"

Hildegard lay there in her dirty clothes, listening to Ernst's steady breathing, listening deep down inside of her body to the second heartbeat, getting stronger and stronger. *When will he notice? When will it be too late? It's already too late. Will I ever have any control over my life, ever again?*

Ernst woke up from his slumber, feeling as though he had been asleep for twenty years, though he was only out for about an hour. He realized Hildegard wasn't in the bed with him. It was dark. Had she gone home already?

He opened his eyes and looked across the room at the other bed. Hildegard was sitting on it, trembling, tears streaming down her face. She had found his gun. She was holding it to her head.

"What are you doing?" he asked, though it seemed to be obvious.

"I'm pregnant," she sobbed.

Ernst sat up in bed, slowly pulling on his shirt. "Put the gun down," he said evenly.

"No," Hildegard said, pointing it at him.

"Hildegard."

"I hate this place," Hildegard said, shaking. "I hate it here. You've made me into a whore."

"You're not a whore to me," Ernst said, slowly putting up his hands. "You're the mother of my child."

"They're going to abort it!"

"No, they're not." He was looking deep into her eyes, willing her to calm down, like a snake charmer. "I won't let them. Now put the gun down."

He could hear the bullets rattling around in the chamber as she obeyed. He noticed she hadn't disabled the safety grip. She had probably never fired a pistol before in her life. He stood up and slowly walked across the room to the other bed.

Normally, there were two officers to a room, but for Hermann Langstrom's nephew, exceptions were made. There was technically a man assigned to this bed, but he had a wife and child in Oświęcim, and he only stayed here when he was in dutch. If his roommate had been here tonight, it would have been much safer for Ernst: no prisoner would be threatening an SS Officer with a Luger on his roommate's watch. His roommate would have killed her, and Hildegard would be nothing but a bloodstain on the ground. But then so would Ernst's unborn son.

"Listen to me," he said, taking her by the shoulders. "I told you I would take care of you. That's a promise. I'm not going to let anything happen to our child. Do you believe me?"

Hildegard looked pitifully up at him, and she collapsed into his arms, sobs racking her scant form.

On July 20th, 1944, Hitler's generals attempted to assassinate him in what they called Operation Valkyrie. Colonel Claus Schenk von Stauffenberg left a bomb in a briefcase at the Wolf's Lair, Hitler's secret meeting place in Poland. The mission was a failure, Hitler escaped, and the officers and politicians involved in the plot were rounded up and executed.

If it was any consolation, Hitler would be dead within less than a year. He would do the honor himself. So would Joseph Goebbels, the Goebbels family, Hitler's girlfriend-then-wife-within-an-hour Eva Braun, Hitler's German Shepherd Blondi, and Ernst's uncle Hermann.

The Germans saw the tide was beginning to turn. This troubled Ernst. Equally troubling was the beginning of the liquidation of Auschwitz in late July and early August, which would last the rest of the year. As the Allied Russian Army pushed closer and closer to Poland, and Allied America, France, Canada, and Britain gained a foothold in the west, Germany felt squeezed in and trapped: a taste of their own medicine.

The first camp to be liquidated was the Czechoslovakian block. Then, the SS selected only 1,408 prisoners from the Roma camp to be sent to Germany's central concentration camp in Buchenwald. The rest of the Roma were gassed and incinerated quickly.

Ernst came to Hildegard with a secret message:

"Listen to me. They're going to have a selection in the camp, and this one will be worse than any of the others. When you take off your clothes, they will see your pregnancy, and they will not hesitate to kill you. They might shoot you in the stomach right there. I want you to hide in the barracks. Hide in Block 16." (The barrack where he first raped her.) "I will tell the Kapo that you're performing a special task for me, so you won't be missed at roll call."

"Can I take Riziel?" she begged.

"I don't give a damn," Ernst said irritably. "But you cannot be seen. Understood?"

She nodded and kissed him. "Thank you," she said.

Hildegard and Riziel snuck out to Barrack 16, clutching each other, crying silently. Riziel put her hand on Hildegard's belly, and began to pray.

"Yisgadal, veyiskadash, shmey raba... oseh shalom bimromav hu ya-aseh shalom olaynu v'al kol Israel vimru amen."

"Amen," Hildegard echoed. "What are you praying? I've heard so many pray it here."

"The Kaddish. It's a prayer of mourning, a prayer for the dead. A prayer of exaltation. I'm asking for peace and justice for Israel."

"How can you exalt God's name, at a time like this?"

"Some Jews believe that saying the Kaddish over a loved one will help them... cross over. Like Job: despite mourning, we still praise Him." She took a shaky breath. "I'm saying it over the people who have been selected today."

Hildegard looked at her. "Can you teach me the words?"

The two women chanted silently under their breaths: *"Yisgadal, veyiskadash, shmey raba... oseh shalom bimromav hu ya-aseh shalom olaynu v'al kol Israel vimru amen."* They chanted over the terrified shrieks, the high smoky echo of pistol report, the hurried footfall of prisoners racing by. They chanted and chanted until Ernst came in and turned on the lights. Selection was over.

Still, more transports arrived. There was an urgency to the closings of the ghettos across Poland, Romania, and Hungary. Most of the world's most notable Holocaust survivors were transported to Auschwitz during this time. Their hellish nightmare was only beginning. But for Moishe Abramowicz, it was coming to an end.

Riziel ran up to Hildegard, eyes wide, in a cold sweat. "Moishe was selected!"

Hildegard's hands went to her face. "How could this happen?"

"He's so skinny already, now he's only skin and bones," Riziel cried, "they thought he was a Musselman." Musselmen were prisoners who had given up and were letting themselves waste away within the concentration camps. "He's so kind, I'm sure he was giving his rations away to others in his block…" She clenched her fists and held them to her forehead, squinching her eyes shut. "Damn him! *Damn him!*"

"Stop it, Riziel," Hildegard shook her by the shoulders. If Moishe truly was selected, it would be a curse on her if that was the last thing she said about her husband. "We'll think of something."

Riziel collapsed into tears, sobbing in the mud.

Hildegard washed herself thoroughly and pinched her cheeks, trying to look as alluring as possible. *If I have to whore myself, let it be for some good. Let me do one thing right.* She thought of Rahab, the prostitute double-agent who provided intel to the Israelites as they invaded Jericho. She thought of Esther, the Jewish girl who was forced to sully herself for King Xerxes, who pleaded with him to save her people from extermination. As the gallows awaited Esther's righteous cousin Mordecai, so too were there gallows in Auschwitz.

Esther Lange passed through her mind: the day she came in from her chores, her sad smile, unsure of who she could trust. Hildegard had thought about Esther often in the past years and realized she hadn't been a very good friend to Esther. It wasn't a house fire, all those years ago… Esther and her family were being terrorized by the Gestapo. And Hildegard was too blind, too lost in her own world, to help. *Not this time. Please, God, not this time.*

Hildegard asked Riziel to smuggle something for her to bribe Ernst. Riziel found a gold pocket watch with a sapphire set into the face.

Ernst was tense the night Hildegard approached him. "I have a present for you," she said, taking his hand.

"Oh?" Ernst said, partially interested.

"Yes, but I've been a bit naughty. It's not really mine to give," she said coyly, looking down.

"You have nothing to give," Ernst said wearily, plopping down on his bed. He ran his fingers through his blonde hair. He needed a haircut.

"You're a prisoner. That's the idea."

So far, this coercion was not going well. Hildegard situated herself between his legs, resting her arms on his knees. *Beg like a dog, Hilde. You're already lower than a dog, so go ahead and beg like one.* She produced the gold watch and flicked it open. "Look, the sapphire matches your eyes," she said cheerfully. *Whoever's watch this is, if you're already burnt up and looking down on me in anger, forgive me. I'm trying to save a life. What's a watch, in comparison to a human life?*

Ernst examined the watch in his hands. "You stole this."

Hildegard blanched. *This is not going well.*

"Do you know what the punishment for stealing is? I should have you hanged on the gallows tonight."

"It was stolen for *you*," she protested. "I can't give you anything," she added hastily, "except this child."

Ernst looked at her suspiciously.

Hildegard sighed. "I'm sorry. I shouldn't have stolen it. I can put it back," she opened her hand for the watch. *I'll find another way. Someone in this corrupt place will want a watch. Maybe I could bribe Commandant Hoess.*

"No, I'll keep it," Ernst said, looking at the watch again. "If it's that important to you, I'll keep this dead Jew's stolen pocket watch." He put it in his pocket. Hildegard's heart sank, but she decided to keep trying.

"What's on your mind?" she leaned her head on his knee, looking up at him innocently. "Something's troubling you."

Ernst leaned back against the wall, knocking his head against it softly, trying to clear it. "I shouldn't even be talking to you about this," he said. "You're a prisoner."

"After everything that we've been through together, am I still just a prisoner to you?" Hildegard asked. And, deep in her heart, she was a little hurt—just a drop, just a touch. *What am I to you? Why do you still keep me around after a year and a half? If I'm just your whore, why don't you grow bored and move on? If I'm more than someone to lie with, why won't you let me in?*

"You don't understand, you could never understand," Ernst said glumly. "You don't understand what it's like to be me. To have this weight on your shoulders. To know that, if everything goes to shit, it will all come down on you." He sighed and rubbed his face. The next line came in a whisper. "This war... what if we lose?"

Hildegard's sunken heart suddenly soared with hope. *Will we be saved? When will it end? Will it be soon?* She used the energy the hope gave her to make one last play. She stroked the inseam on his pants leg. "You're so good to me, Ernst. You're such a kind and generous soul, no wonder this troubles you. But have you ever considered... mercy?"

Ernst raised an eyebrow at her. "How do you mean?"

Here goes nothing. "You know my friend Riziel? Her husband Moishe has been selected for extermination. But he's such a good soul, like you... can't you do anything to save him?" She put on her winningest smile.

Ernst pushed her off his knees. "This has all been a bribe."

Panic. "No, Ernst, it's not like that—"

"You're just trying to bribe me. You don't actually care about me. You only care about soap and shampoo and perfume. You only want exceptions made for you."

Hildegard sputtered. She couldn't even begin to think of an argument.

"Are you that fucking stupid? Did you think you could get me to save a Jew? A *Jew?* Jews disgust me. Do you think your life is so precious to me that you could just walk out of this place like Moses, leading the Jews to freedom? Who do you think you are?" His voice rose in anger.

"Ernst..." Here came the tears.

"Don't bother crying to me. You make me sick. Get the hell out of here." He opened the door, and she ran out into the hot night, a cold sweat running down her face.

She went back to her barrack empty-handed. Not only did she fail in saving Moishe's life, but she may have also condemned her own.

It wouldn't have mattered anyway. By the time Hildegard gave Ernst the gold watch, Moishe was already dead.

Riziel got the news from another prisoner. "I'm sorry, Riziel," he whispered to her. "Moishe loved you. He loved you so much."

"Hey! A9918! Get back in line!" his Kapo barked.

"We're saying Kaddish for him today," the prisoner murmured over his shoulder. "The whole block. He was a righteous man, and he is in holy places now."

Riziel said nothing. Her face was a mask. She looked straight ahead.

Hildegard wept bitterly. "I'm sorry, Riziel, I'm so sorry. I tried, I really did." She squeezed her hand, she hugged Riziel tight. "Riziel please, look at me!"

Riziel looked at her, but it wasn't Riziel.

Hildegard wanted to pray the Kaddish for Moishe, but she didn't know the words. She asked Riziel to help her recite it. But Riziel only sat in her bed, curled up, staring at the wall.

"Let her be, child," an older woman said, taking Hildegard by the shoulders. "She is mourning. We will say Kaddish together."

Hildegard stood in a circle with nine other women, listening to the Hebrew words they chanted. She tried to conjure up a prayer herself, but her spirit would not fly farther than the ceiling. She had failed to save a good man's life.

Lunch time. Soup. She could barely stomach it. She could never stomach it, but today she wouldn't eat it even if it were a steaming side of beef and mashed potatoes. She didn't bother standing in line. She just sat with Riziel, who sat in the mud, staring at the trees beyond the fence. The trees swayed and whispered in the summer breeze. A bird soared by, and for one fleeting moment it blocked out the sun.

"A64390!"

"Here," Hildegard raised her hand.

The Kapo pointed to the edge of the yard. Ernst was leaning against the warehouse, one boot crossed in front of the other, as casual as a summer breeze. He had a daisy in his hand.

Hildegard squeezed Riziel's hand and stood up. She crossed the yard to him. He handed her the daisy.

"It's not nearly as beautiful as you," he said, putting on his best Prince Charming.

"I thought I made you sick," Hildegard said flatly.

"No, I said you make me crazy," Ernst smiled, tucking the daisy behind her ear. "We're two crazy lovers. Our son is going to be a lunatic," he chuckled.

Riziel stood up.

"'Our son' is going to be nothing," Hildegard retorted. "They're going to find out soon."

"Which is why you can't go doing anything stupid like stealing," Ernst explained paternally. *Don't do anything stupid.* It was a whisper. It was a distant memory. "What if you had been caught, Hilde? I can't protect you if you put yourself in danger," he stroked her face affectionately. His eyes flicked up over her head; they narrowed. "What's she doing?"

Hildegard turned around and saw Riziel was twenty feet away from the electric fence.

"RIZIEL!" she screamed and broke out in a run. *"Riziel, no!"*

God, please, let me catch her. Give me wings. She pushed the force into her legs, as she did a year ago, when she and Riziel raced each other in the selection. When they kept each other alive. If Riziel was gone, what was the point?

"Riziel! Riziel, don't!" she screeched, willing her legs to run faster. But she was carrying a child now, and her body could not do what it had so easily accomplished before. Riziel was ten steps away from the fence. She raised her hand, extending her fingers.

"Riziel, *NO!*" Hildegard screamed, but it was too late. Riziel collided with the electric fence, and there was a POP! and sizzle as Riziel was propelled backward. She lay there, the smell of burning flesh and hair emanating from her, staring blankly up into a cloudless blue sky.

Ernst dragged Hildegard, screaming and wailing, from the yard. She moaned in agony, her wails growing higher and higher into hyperventilation, until she passed out. The fact that she had not eaten anything in 24 hours and was growing a human inside of her also did not help. He had two prisoners carry her by the arms and legs to the clinic. She awoke and began screaming and crying, calling for Riziel and a host of other names, so she was given a tranquilizer shot. He paid the doctor on duty to let her sleep until he returned.

"Don't examine her. You understand? And if Mengele or that Jew bitch Perl shows up sniffing around, you make up an excuse. Say that she's been marked for extermination, if you want, but stall for time." He extended a few pricey Deutsche marks.

The doctor understood. It wasn't the first young girl a guard had brought in, though usually they were paying him off to take care of "the issue".

Ernst went out for a drink in Oświęcim. There were many other guards there, exhausted from a long day's work: processing thousands of new transports, shaving them, disinfecting them, rapidly selecting them, pushing them screaming and crying through gas chambers, burning them, working them... it was no better than shepherd's work, really. It wasn't the work of an army officer. He sipped his whiskey. The large cube of ice clinked around in his glass: noble, mammoth, but still trapped.

On the radio, Joseph Goebbels whipped up a crowd into a frenzy of cheers. He asked a series of ten rhetorical questions, demanding to know if they were truly patriotic, if they understood it was only Germany who could save the world from the chains of Bolshevism, if they were prepared to fight, if they were prepared to give up everything they had to ensure victory. "Yes! Yes! Yes!" the crowd cried, like a woman reaching climax. In the past, speeches like this aroused him for reasons he couldn't quite explain. He was the speaker and the spoken, he was the man and the woman, the lover and the ecstasy. Tonight, it chilled him to the bone. Goebbels was making himself perfectly clear: if Germany was going to lose the war, they would die fighting.

At midnight, Ernst Langstom left Oświęcim.

Hildegard opened her eyes in the dark.

She was in the cold, impeccably clean clinic. A doctor was on duty, but he was dozing under the yellow light of his desk lamp. There were no sounds except his gentle snoring and the death rattles of the emaciated and diseased prisoners lying in the hospital cots.

Most prisoners died of dysentery. The prisoners' only access to water was through the barrack sinks, which were connected to the sewage pipes. The intestines became infected. Stool became watery, then bloody. The dying person broke out in a fever, complaining deliriously of burning up. Water didn't help, because it was too contaminated to be of much use. Eventually, the prisoner keeled over and died a slow, painful death. Some were mercifully gassed before that point, but most were left to die on their own. Then the crematoria.

Hildegard wondered if this was finally the end. When would be the moment when she heard her own last breath? And then—no more Hildegard. No more Moishe, no more Riziel. No more Otto, no more Esther, no more Miguel. Every day she thought: *this is it, this is the end for me.* And every day it wasn't. And the next day was always a little bit worse.

She couldn't imagine herself in heaven with them. What would they think of her and how low she had sunk, how far she had crawled from the bright young woman she once was? She couldn't face God, she couldn't face any of them. So instead of looking forward to the end of her life, she looked backward. She imagined Otto and one of his rare smiles. She imagined her mother, standing under the stage lights, singing her heart out. She imagined Esther, exchanging grins with her in the darkness of the movie theater as they closed in on their childish matchmaking plot.

She imagined Miguel. He was walking toward her through a swaying golden field of grain, and the air was balmy and lovely. The sun was obscuring him from her, but he was smiling. He was grinning from ear to ear, a golden smile. He had just received his glass eye, and he was proud and whole, he felt like a man again. He wasn't a refugee, he was Miguel Benaroya, he was a man in love with her. She was so very lucky to receive a love as special as his. Whatever hell she was in now, however close to death she was now, at least she had that love once in her life, even if it was for a handful of months.

The baby, no bigger than a peach, fluttered in her stomach. Like a butterfly.

"Oh!" she murmured.

Are you in there, little one? You grow day by day.

This isn't fair. Not for me, not for you.

If you were mine, if you were really mine, the women in Himmelberg would have held a party for you. They would have showered you with gifts, and knit little hats for you, and embroidered things with your name. And I'm not sure you'll even have a name.

She sighed.

You didn't ask for this either, did you? You just grew, like a flower in a sidewalk. You grew right through the cracks, didn't you? You don't know any other way.

She imagined Otto holding the child in his arms. He was beaming with pride. He was a stoic man, but a proud grandpa. She would have loved to make him proud. *You* did *make him proud, Hilde. He loved you, he showed you a million times how he loved you. He took you in and loved you as his own.*

She pondered this, running a hand over her waxing belly, and closed her eyes.

If we get through this, little one, I'm going to keep you safe.

I promise.

A hand clamped over her mouth. She shrieked, and her eyes snapped open. Ernst was staring down at her, a finger over his lips.

"Get up. Go to the bathroom and put these on. *Hurry!*" he said.

Hildegard obeyed, carrying the bundle with her. She changed out of her clothes in the dark room, and as her eyes adjusted to the darkness, she saw the clothes she was putting on.

A Nazi female guard uniform.

Could she wear the clothes of the women who murdered their own? Could she wear the robes soaked in the blood of mothers, like her?

Her stomach fluttered again. *Alright, I'll do it for you.*

She tucked her short hair under the too-big cap. It was all too big for her; she only weighed eighty-nine pounds. She stuffed her prisoner's uniform in the tank of the toilet, and she thanked God there was no mirror in there so she wouldn't have to look herself in the eyes. Not that she would have recognized herself, anyway.

She quietly emerged from the water closet. Ernst was paying off the doctor, whispering in his ear. She crossed the room to him, quietly, like a church mouse. He grabbed her hand and led her out into the dark.

"Where are we going?" she whispered.

"You have to do exactly as I say, do you understand?" He looked back at her, dragging her on. "Your name is Ingmar Kovinski. You're a new recruit. But don't say anything unless you're explicitly asked. Go along with everything I say."

The searchlights swooped around. In the distance, dogs barked and howled as a new transport came in. This one was from Transylvania. Ernst walked as if he were doing a routine inspection, swinging his club, and Hildegard did the same. She tried to put herself back into her Hitler Youth days to draw inspiration, but she couldn't. She was a camp counselor then, not a mass murderer.

She passed by the rows of prisoners' barracks. 168 barracks for 750,000 prisoners. She passed by the four crematoria, one of which was burning up Riziel's charred form. One million bodies passed through the crematoria of Auschwitz. One million dead. One million ghosts followed her out.

In the confusion and chaos of another train arriving, Ernst and Hildegard passed through the gates of Birkenau. The train engine pulling the cattle cars chugged and hushed as the locomotive shut down. It shushed and whispered: *Hurry! Hurry! Hurry!*

Ernst held tight to Hildegard's hand. "Don't run, walk. Running will arouse suspicion. About a mile down the road, there's an old barn. Do you see it?"

Hildegard nodded.

"Go to the other side of the road. Take this flashlight. Pretend you're looking for prisoners with me. We're going to walk very slowly and very deliberately to that barn, and then we're going to go inside."

Hildegard obeyed. She swooped her flashlight from side to side, praying that she wouldn't actually see a prisoner hiding in the weeds, looking up at her out of the ditch with desperate eyes. But she never did see anyone. Because no one escaped Auschwitz. Not really.

They pretended to look in the barn, then they turned their flashlights off. There was a man in a pickup truck waiting for them.

"You have the money?"

Ernst handed him a wad of marks. The man counted it.

"Here are your clothes, and here are your passports," he instructed, handing them each a bundle. "Your names are Johannes and Ondine Petersen. You are Czech citizens," he looked at Ernst. "I can drive you as far as Krakow, but after that, you're getting out. And if they find you in the back of my truck, I don't know you, you hopped on when I wasn't looking. If you tell them what really happened, I'll shoot you both myself, starting with her," he nodded to Hildegard. "Got it?"

Ernst and Hildegard nodded.

"Get dressed and get on."

They changed into regular Polish clothes—how odd! She hadn't worn anything other than that old ratty work dress for four years, and to go from a prisoner's uniform to an SS uniform to a Polish disguise in only an hour!—and Hildegard put on a wig. The wig was scratchy, but it was blonde. It was Aryan. It wasn't the hair of a prisoner, although it was probably made from the hair of a prisoner. She silently thanked whoever donated their hair for her salvation.

Hildegard and Ernst climbed onto the back of the truck, and the man piled on boxes of nuts, bolts, and other factory parts from Buna over them. Ernst held her in his arms and she could feel his silent tears buried in her neck; he was clutching her hand and their fingers were interlaced. She was crying, too. She was praying and thanking God and silently mouthing *yisgadal, veyiskadash, shmey raba, yisgadal, veyiskadash, shmey raba...* until the stench of death in the air was long, long gone.

It wasn't until the next morning, when the man unloaded the truck in a forest near Krakow and booted them out, that Hildegard asked him where they were going.

"We're going to Czechoslovakia," he said, still holding her hand. "From there, we're going to get new passports. We'll pretend to be Czech citizens until we can afford to pretend to be Austrian citizens. And once we're Austrian citizens, we're going to become Swiss citizens. That transaction will be pricey. But, I think, your brilliant present will do the trick," he produced the stolen gold watch and shoved it back into his pocket. He kissed her hand. "Good work, china baby. I also procured a few other treasures for us along the way. I gave that girl Bruna a good wallop and confiscated all her pretty things from her. You're welcome," he winked impishly at her, giving her a roguish half-smile.

Hildegard, to her disbelief, felt sorry for Bruna. She was a real bitch, and she was an ogre, and she was oafishly greedy. But she was still a prisoner. She hadn't felt a warm shower or a man's touch or a good beer or a full stomach in years, just like Hildegard.

He stopped her in a clearing. It was a meadow, lined with a wooden fence. Cows lowed in a distant green field. The birds were chirping, and the sun streamed through the swaying trees. "This seems like just as good a spot as any," he smiled, nodding his approval. He produced Bruna's pearl necklace. "This is yours now," he said, coming behind her and looping it over her head. For a second, it was like he was strangling her with a garrote. Then he hooked the pearl strand into place and wrapped his arms around her, placing his hand on her belly.

"I'm going to make an honest woman out of you, Hildegard," he murmured in her ear, kissing her neck. "This child will not be a bastard, he will be a Langstrom."

The irony of exiting Auschwitz as the future Mrs. Langstrom when she entered it four years ago as the future Mrs. Benaroya hit Hildegard like a ton of bricks. It made her hair stand on end.

"Someone's hot to trot, eh?" Ernst squeezed his arms around her, stroking her breast with his thumb. "But not now. We have to wait until we're through Poland to celebrate."

They entered Krakow and went to the bus station. They bought a ticket for Zilina, Czechoslovakia. They sat on the bus and Hildegard was amazed at the wonders of a bus seat cushion. When was the last time she sat on a bus? Probably when she was 12 years old.

The bus ran parallel to the train tracks, and Hildegard watched cattle cars rumble by her. She knew what they were full of. She knew where it was going, and she said another little prayer. At the Czechoslovakian border, they had to show their passports.

"What is your purpose for entering Czechoslovakia?" an SS officer asked, eyeing the couple.

"My wife has an aunt living in Zilina," Ernst said. "We're going to tell her the happy news!" He rubbed Hildegard's stomach proudly. Her stomach turned. Or was it the baby? Did the baby know its father was near?

"Her name is Ingmar Kovinski, and her address is 34 Jedlikova Street, if we need to register our location," Hildegard piped up, making up an address off the top of her head to sound convincing. What were the odds this SS knew every street in Czechoslovakia?

"I don't give a damn who your aunt is, I just need to know why you're entering Czechoslovakia," the SS guard grunted, and he moved on.

When the SS left, Ernst put his arm around her and pulled her in to kiss her cheek. But he whispered into her ear: "I told you. Let me do the talking. Don't speak unless you're spoken to."

"I'm sorry," she whispered.

"I forgive you."

They got off the bus in Zilina, and there were hundreds of Jews being herded in lines and pushed onto cars. She wanted to scream: "Run! Run away into the woods! Don't get on that train! Better you be shot now than to see your babies suffocated in the gas chamber!" But she couldn't. So she didn't. She was glad to board another bus to Bratislava.

When they got to Bratislava, they found a hotel room and went down to dinner.

"Order anything you like, darling," Ernst smiled magnanimously at Hildegard. "I know you must be famished," he said pointedly.

Hildegard quietly asked for a bowl of goulash and spaetzle, and Ernst ordered for her in Slavic. His Slavic was not good for someone with a Czech passport, but he would only need to use it until he could procure an Austrian passport. Then it was back to speaking German all the way to Switzerland.

They went back to the hotel room, and before Ernst could drop his trousers, Hildegard ran into the bathroom to throw up. It wasn't pregnancy sickness; the food was too rich.

(Many liberated prisoners, after surviving starvation and overwork and death marches and freezing and prison beatings, would die during their first month of freedom. Their starved and beaten bodies had endured too much to ever recover. Nobel prize winner Elie Wiesel's father would die of dysentery. Miriam Mozes, a Mengele Twin, would die of kidney failure due to complications from Mengele's experiments. Anne Frank would die of typhus.)

It landed Hildegard in a hospital for three and a half weeks, where she would drift in and out of consciousness, being fed through a tube. She vaguely remembered Ernst was there. In the haze, she saw him: he was clutching her hand and crying, his blazing blue irises standing out against the redness of his eyes, as he pleaded, "Please, baby, don't leave me. Don't leave me alone. You're all I have left. Don't go where I can't follow."

It reminded her of something. Oh, yes: when Otto had a stroke and Wilhelmina had cried over his body, saying pretty much the same thing. Was this what it was like for Otto? Would Hildegard come out of this with half her body not working? Maybe Ernst would leave her alone, if she was half-invalid. What was it that Otto said to her mother?

"I'm not going anywhere."

Ernst hugged her to him, sobbing and thanking God. The nurses wiped tears away from their eyes, cooing at the lovely romantic scene.

Well, damn. Did I say that out loud? She turned her mind to the peach in her belly, growing now to the size of a grapefruit: *Well, kiddo, I'll hold on a little longer for you. I don't know if I'll make it through this whole pregnancy, but I'll take you as far as I can.* She was like the man in the truck. That made her laugh.

When she was released from the hospital, Ernst wanted to get married right away. "I almost lost you; I'm not losing you again."

She had nothing to wear but her Polish peasant clothes. He took her to a store and picked out a dress for her.

"I'm afraid we can't afford the wedding of your dreams," Ernst said patronizingly, as if she had asked him for a cathedral-length veil and a boy's choir singing "Canon in D", "but we'll have a lovely ceremony once we're safe in Switzerland."

The wedding of my dreams? I don't even have dreams any more. But it flashed through her mind anyway: Miguel was alive, he was smiling, he was walking to her through the golden grain, they were in a synagogue and there was stained glass and the light was streaming through the window, and he was singing, singing like he used to, singing that song that was like a bird in the wind...

They found a priest who would marry them without a Nazi-sanctioned marriage license. When the priest saw Hildegard's short hair, like a boy's, and her gaunt little body, and her protruding belly, he understood. He "found" a marriage license for them, and forged a government seal.

"What is your name, daughter?" he smiled at her, the pen ready.

"Ondine Petersen," Hildegard said, glancing for approval at Ernst.

"No," Ernst said. "Write down Hildegard Langstrom." He took her hands, and kissed them. "We're getting married before God. I don't want to lie in a church. I want this to be real."

You don't want to lie, you sick son of a bitch? You murdered God's children, you murdered the sons and daughters of God's covenant. This union would be legal, but it wouldn't be right. It would be evil. I'm promised to another, and you murdered him too.

"Why are you crying?" Ernst asked.

"I can't do this," she whimpered.

He pulled her aside. "Don't worry, Hilde. Plenty of women have been pregnant brides. I don't love you any less for it," he pulled her into a hug.

Pregnant brides? Is that what he thinks this is all about? She looked up at him. *He thinks I'm sad because I will somehow be letting him down. I'm just an extension of him. But I'm not his, I've never been his.*

She tried to push herself away. "This is wrong... I can't do it!"

He held her by the shoulders and looked sternly at her. "You'd be making a huge mistake. Think of everything I've done for you. Think of all I had to go through for you. If it weren't for me, you'd be dead with your friend. A victim of selection. You honestly think you would've survived if I hadn't made sure you had double rations? If I hadn't made sure you had a nice, cushy job? If I hadn't risked my own safety, my own *life*, sneaking you out so you could be free?"

"I'm grateful, I'm so grateful—"

"How long do you think you'll last without me?" Ernst continued, letting her go. "You don't have to marry me. You can walk away right now. Walk out that door, I won't follow you. But what kind of life do you think you'll have, a pregnant German girl in a foreign land? How long do you think you'll last before the Gestapo figure out who you are? Do you think the baby will survive? Do you think they'll let you keep him?"

Hildegard was silent.

Ernst gestured toward the door, eyebrows raised.

"I'm sorry," Hildegard said.

"Don't you ever forget what I've done for you to keep you safe," he said. He sighed, pinching the bridge of his nose. "Now you've gone and done it. You've ruined our wedding. I hope you're proud of yourself."

Hildegard felt two inches tall. She felt like a sliver of a trimmed fingernail, very small and very disposable. She took Ernst's hand numbly, staring at the carpet. What did it matter?

They walked down to the pulpit.

The priest pronounced them man and wife.

That was October 6th. Hildegard remembered, while Ernst was atop her, that she was twenty-six years old. She must have turned twenty-six while she was passed out in the hospital. She remembered her past birthdays. Twenty-five, twenty-four, twenty-three... these she had not celebrated, because she had given up counting the calendar around April of 1941. Twenty-two... her first month in Auschwitz: she had more pressing matters on her mind than her birthday. Twenty-one... she had gone out to Zum Hirschen with her friends. Or was it Zur Rentier? She smiled at the ridiculous memory of the competing innkeepers. This encouraged Ernst. Good. Now that she was married, it would be more work to convince him she liked this. Or less work? Maybe she could be one of those bland housewives, and her husband would get bored of her and take a mistress.

What else had she done on her twenty-first birthday? Oh, yes. The midnight screening of *The Wizard of Oz*. She thought of Dorothy singing "Somewhere Over the Rainbow"... wherever somewhere over the rainbow was, it sure as hell wasn't here. That thought made her sad, so she stopped thinking about the song. She thought of Miguel, and how she was crying, and how he was only her friend at that point, but he reached out and held her hand. Even then, he loved her. That made her happy. She replayed that moment in her mind until it was over.

The next day, across the border, women in Buna were smuggling small amounts of gunpowder to prisoners at Birkenau. The Sonderkommando of Crematorium 4 learned that they were going to be killed. They tried to blow up the crematoria and gas chambers of Birkenau, triggering a prisoner uprising. After all, there were hundreds of guards. There were thousands of prisoners. The uprising failed, the conspirators were sniffed out, an execution was staged. But hope was on the horizon. More specifically, the Red Army was on the horizon.

In the end, the crematoria were destroyed anyway. Blown to rubble by the Nazis under orders of SS chief Heinrich Himmler, in an attempt to destroy the evidence of mass genocide. (Can you wipe out the millions of blue tattoos, Himmler? Can you dig up all the bodies lying in mass graves? Can you blot out the memory of every German who watched *Der Erwig Jew?* Can you reverse the clock of a decade, of two thousand years of antisemitism?) This was in November, shortly before Ernst and Hildegard crossed the Austrian border.

In Hildegard's belly, the baby danced and kicked. *Let me out! Let me free!*

Not yet, little one. Not long now, she rubbed her stomach. *Be patient.*

She held Ernst's hand and guided it across her stomach as the baby rolled across her skin. She looked up at his amazed expression, and she couldn't help but smile.

In December, Ernst presented Hildegard with a Christmas present: a golden ring with an amber stone. They were living in Salzburg in an old apartment near Mozart's birthplace.

"How did you afford it? We've burnt through almost all the money!" Hildegard gasped.

"I've been working like a dog driving carriages," Ernst smiled proudly, examining the ring on her pale finger. This was how they had been making enough money for the final vault into Switzerland. "I told every tourist that I was saving up for a ring for my pregnant wife, and every one of them gave me double tips!" This was believable: Ernst was a charismatic charmer who made love to everyone with his conversation. Hildegard noticed that he got more and more outgoing the farther he got from Auschwitz.

"It's so beautiful," Hildegard smiled at him. "But we may need to sell it to afford Switzerland. It's expensive there, just mountains and cheese and banks."

"Don't," Ernst kissed her hand. "Don't sell it. Sell your necklace, sell your clothes, sell anything before you sell that one. That one's from me."

"It's all from you," Hildegard said. This was a good answer. This would keep him in good spirits, and her out of a spat. "But I feel horrible: I have nothing to give you! It's like 'The Gift of the Magi', except I don't have any hair left to sell!" Ernst laughed. "Maybe... maybe I could give you a Minni von Bismark."

"What's that?"

"It's... oh, it's not ladylike for me to say," Hildegard said coyly. "Anyway, it requires props, and I don't have any here."

"Oh, come on! Please!"

"No, you'll just have to wait for Switzerland. And for this one to pop out," she smiled, patting her stomach.

"Well, let's not wait. Let's go to Switzerland."

"Now?"

"In a few days. We can sneak in on foot. Sam, the carriage driver I swap shifts with, he told me there's a mountain pass."

"In the snow?"

"Sure! We're big, tough Aryans... it's just a little hike!"

On January 17th, as the Red Army rapidly approached, the Nazis moved 60,000 prisoners out of Auschwitz. There was no time to load them up into cattle cars; the Soviets were nearly knocking on the door. The SS drove along or jogged along and forced the teeming mass to run through the snow. Anyone who lagged behind was shot. Anyone who fell was trampled. They ran northwest to the nearest sub-camp. They ran without stopping for 30 miles. They ran more than a marathon overnight through the freezing snow on nothing but a mouthful of bread and a cup of rotten soup. 15,000 of those prisoners died from starvation or from freezing in the open snow, which was a welcome death once they collapsed, exhausted, to the ground. It was called the Death March.

The 7,000 sickly and dying, and the Mengele Twins, who were miraculously saved at the last minute from murder by virtue of time running out, were left at Auschwitz to starve, die, freeze... and were liberated by the Russian Army ten days later.

Hildegard marched through the snow, hugging her coat to her. She thanked God for her snow boots and pressed on. She was waddling in the snow, eight months pregnant. This had been a stupid idea. And worse, she was getting cramps in her stomach.

"Ernst, I need to stop," Hildegard groaned.

"We can't stop here," Ernst took her waist, guiding her along. "It's just a little further."

"There's something wrong," Hildegard said between gritted teeth. "The baby—"

She collapsed to the ground, crying out in pain. Ernst pulled out his Luger and fired a shot in the air.

Great. Bring down an avalanche on us too. Then we'll freeze to death before the Nazis shoot us.

It wasn't long before a border patrol truck rolled up. It had a red flag and a white cross. She thanked God for the white cross instead of a black swastika.

"What are you doing here?" A Swiss man in a uniform got out of his truck.

"We were hiking and we got lost—" Ernst lied.

"Bullshit. You're undocumented immigrants trying to sneak in," the Swiss officer put his hands on his hips. "Papers. Now."

Ernst produced their Austrian passports. Hildegard groaned and clutched her stomach.

"Please," Ernst begged. "My wife is pregnant. She needs a doctor."

"Why would you make a pregnant woman march through the snow, asshole?"

"It's not my fault!" Ernst protested. He produced the gold watch. "Please... help us."

Hildegard looked up at the Swiss guard. "I'm an escaped concentration camp prisoner. We've been on the run since August. Please, in God's name..." she wiped her nose, "I've been met with no pity and no mercy for four years. But there's a child now. It's coming. Please."

The Swiss guard looked at her. Perhaps he was thinking of his own wife, or his sister. He sighed and snatched the gold watch from Ernst's outstretched hand. "Get inside."

Whoever's watch this is, thank you. It saved a life. It saved three lives.

He plowed through the pass, flashing his lights as they pushed through the border. He drove them to a clinic, where a harried-looking doctor examined her. He noticed the blue tattoo on her left forearm. He saw her short hair, curling and shaggy like a lamb's.

"The baby is coming now," he said. "I will do my best, but you may lose it. We have very limited tools for a Cesarean section."

"I don't think I can do this," Hildegard cried, holding a nurse's arm as her legs were hoisted into stirrups.

"My dear, if you survived the camps, you can survive anything," the doctor said, not looking at her, pulling on gloves.

It was a quick but painful delivery. There was no epidural, but there was a little morphine at the end, when they had to pull the baby from her womb. The baby was silent and purple, a little raisin.

The doctor massaged the baby's back with deft, circular movements. His gloved hands were bloody and filmy.

Silence, except for the clock on the wall.

Each tick was slower and slower.

We've come so far... don't go now... stay with me.

The baby coughed, spluttered, cried to life. It was washed, wriggling in the nurse's arms.

"A girl," the doctor said, handing her to Hildegard.

"A girl?" Hildegard said, confused. "We thought it would be a boy."

"They always do," chuckled the nurse.

Ernst came in, and there were tears of joy in his eyes. *Don't let him be angry. Please, God, don't let him be angry because she's not a boy. Will he leave us, once and for all?*

"My little princess!" he said, clapping his hands together. "My tiny queen!"

Hildegard breathed a sigh of relief and handed her over to Ernst. He took her and smiled brilliantly with his daughter in his arms. It was bizarre, unsettling. He looked like a young, happy father. He didn't look like a rapist, like a murderer.

"Do you have a name?" the nurse asked.

Ernst looked at Hildegard hopefully. "Can we name her Margit, after my mother?"

"Whatever you like," Hildegard said tiredly. She was exhausted. She had lost blood. Would she die? Would she be one of those tragic stories where the mother dies in childbirth? She turned to the doctor, still dreamy from the morphine. "Am I going to die?"

He smiled and wiped her drenched hair from her brow. "You're going to be just fine. You just need rest. You," he pointed to Ernst. "Go home. Go prepare your house for the baby. Let her sleep."

One night alone, she smiled sleepily. *Where will we live? It doesn't matter. That's a problem for tomorrow. For now, I'm going to rest. For the first time in four years, I'm going to rest.*

She thought about dying. She thought she might enjoy sleeping so much, she would never wake up. But in the middle of the night, the baby started crying. She wearily trudged out of the hospital cot. She didn't need a nurse to show her what to do.

As the baby fed, she stared down at her. She was a wrinkly little loofah, a little sponge. She was knit together in hell on earth, but she was like a small angel. In fact, as Hildegard peered down at her, she noticed the baby looked just like her. Was this what Wilhelmina felt like, when Hildegard was born? Was this what Hildegard's grandmother felt like, when Wilhelmina was born? A line of women stretched back in Hildegard's imagination, all different forms of Hildegard from decades past, stretching back through eternity, all the way back to Eve. And, Hildegard thought with awe, someday this little Margit would feed a baby from her own breast. In the same exact skin that Hildegard was touching now. So soft, like an apricot.

Then, Margit looked up at Hildegard.

She smiled shyly, a little baby's smile of recognition.

For the second time in her life, Hildegard was in love.

15

1945: Leaving Home

They were living in Lucerne, in a little apartment by the Alpnachersee. The sparkling lake and pristine view of Mount Rigi made Hildegard homesick.

It was July. Margit was six months old. She had chubby cheeks and dark blue eyes, and her hair was a shining gold. She was a little cherub. She was irresistible to the people of Lucerne, who stopped on the street and cooed at her, and were rewarded with those shrieks and giggles of delightful, happy babies.

Hildegard would stare at her. How could such a happy baby be born from such terror and misery? She didn't know. God only knew.

Ernst worked odd jobs in Lucerne. He was hoping to charm his way into some kind of apprenticeship. He had no formal training in any job other than the military—he had joined the Hitler Youth, like Hildegard, and he had jumped right into a career in the SS before he graduated high school. He had never worked a plow, he had never planted a seed that wasn't his own, he had never grown anything. He had only knocked living things down. Now, at the end of the Second World War, what was there for him to do?

V-E Day, or Victory in Europe Day, was May 8th. There was a ticker tape parade in New York City. There was a reckoning in Germany. Already, SS were being hunted down and rounded up. Hitler was long dead, and so was Goebbels, and so was Mussolini, and Himmler. Top Nazis were on the run, especially from Jewish mercenaries looking for their bloody revenge.

Ernst had not told a single soul he was an SS officer at Auschwitz. He didn't talk about it with Hildegard. He didn't mention Auschwitz at all. It was as if it never happened for him. He expressed bitterness and resentment at not being able to return to Germany, but he never expressed remorse. People saw Hildegard's blue tattoo and treated her kindly, and they were charmed by her baby and her smooth-talking husband. So they never asked how the two of them met. They never gave a second glance to Ernst Langstrom, thinking *Is he...? Was he...? Is he still...?* Maybe they assumed he, too, was a prisoner. He wouldn't bother to correct them.

He was thinking about moving them to Argentina. "One last move," he said. "This one is for our own safety. Those bastards are hunting down people like us, and a lot of top officers are fleeing to South America." *Those bastards.* Where had she heard that before? Oh yes, in 1937.

"I don't want to move to South America," she said, nursing Margit. "I'm nursing a baby. I don't know if you recall, Ernst, but the last time we made a cross-country journey, the two of us nearly died."

Ernst took Margit from Hildegard. He kissed Margit on the head and put her in her crib. Then, in three steps across the room, he slapped Hildegard with the back of his hand, the force of which made her head snap back and tumble out of her chair. It reminded her of being tortured by the Nazis five years ago. Where were those Nazis now? Were they reduced to pulling fingernails off of their own wives' hands, like Ernst?

Ernst squatted down next to her and said in a low voice: "Don't you ever speak like that to me. I am your *husband.* I take care of you. I provide for you. I put food on your table and clothes on your child's back."

Margit began to cry.

Hildegard stared up at him. *I'm not going to apologize this time. I'm not going to do it.*

He walked out of the room, out of the apartment, down the stairs and towards town.

Hildegard picked up Margit and resumed nursing her. *He'll be back in a few hours, once he's out of his mercurial mood. He'll bring flowers, but no apology. Never an apology from Ernst Langstrom.*

Sure enough, there were flowers in front of his face when he strolled back in. Sunny white daisies, tied with a blue silk scarf. *How lovely, Ernst. Daisies, just like the one you brought me just before Riziel electrocuted herself and I was fool enough not to follow her example.*

"Thank you," Hildegard said. She went to get a vase.

"Come on, china baby. Don't be angry at me," he said, wrapping his arms around her.

"I'm not angry," Hildegard said.

"Good. I'm taking you out for dinner tonight. Put something ravishing on," he twirled her around. "And later we'll go dancing!"

"With a baby?" Hildegard smiled.

"Sure, with a baby. We have the rest of our lives to live out together! We can do whatever we want, go wherever we want!" *Like South America.*

How long could she keep up this fight? He would get what he wanted, one way or another. How long would it be before she found herself on a boat taking her away from everything she'd ever known? She tried to envision herself living in a dense, humid jungle. It would at least be completely different than the chilly, flat field of Birkenau, with its orderly brick barracks stretching to the horizon. But it would also be an ocean apart from her home, from the mountains of Himmelberg, from her mother. Was Wilhelmina even alive? It surely couldn't hurt to give her a phone call. The war was over, no more Gestapo listening in. The old telephone and its operator number floated up in Hildegard's memory.

They went to the Rathaus Brauerei. There was a covered bridge, bursting with flowers, and white swans glided underneath. Margit observed them with delighted curiosity, as a rocketeer would a creature from Mars. They sat by the lake, eating Swiss fondue and drinking good beer.

"You're not the scant little mouse I met in 1942 anymore," Ernst smiled. "In fact, you're positively chubby!" He laughed. Hildegard laughed too, out of politeness. "It looks good on you."

"Be careful," Hildegard said. "I wouldn't want you to eat your words. Women in my family get big. Big Aryan baby-makers." *Just like Hitler wanted. Here you are, mein Führer. One beautiful blonde Aryan maiden named Margit.*

"I like a woman with meat on her bones," Ernst smiled charmingly. He put his beer glass down. "In fact, big Aryan baby-making is what I want to talk to you about."

Hildegard gulped.

"I think we should have another one."

Hildegard put down her cheese-covered chunk of bread. She suddenly lost her appetite.

"I know, I know, we just had one six months ago. But I love Margit so much, I can't help but want another. I want a million of them!" He laughed. Margit laughed too, imitating her father.

"I don't know if it's a good idea to get pregnant while I'm still nursing," Hildegard said, trying to appear optimistic. *Please don't let this lead to a fight. Not here. Not in public.*

"Well, when will you be done nursing?"

Never.

"I'm not sure," Hildegard sighed. "There's so much of this mothering that I thought would come naturally to me, but I have so many questions on the right way to do things. I always thought my mother would be with me to help me figure it out," she smiled innocently.

Ernst sat back in his chair, sensing a chess game was about to begin. "You want to go back to Germany."

"I want to see my mother. I haven't seen her in five years. I haven't been able to write to her; she might be worried sick. She doesn't even know I'm alive—"

Ernst put up his hands good-naturedly. "Alright, alright. You've won me over. Go see your mother. Go talk about motherly things."

Hildegard clutched his knee affectionately. "Thank you, Ernst. Thank you! She'll be so happy to see her daughter is alive." She toodled at Margit's stomach. "And she'll be so happy to meet her new granddaughter!"

"No, Margit will stay here." Ernst bridged his fingers. And before Hildegard could reply: "It's not up for discussion."

He knows if I take Margit, I'll leave forever. But if Margit stays here, I have to come back.

Checkmate.

"That's fine with me," Hildegard said. "I'll bring her some pictures of Margit, and I'll pump some milk for her tonight. Plus we have plenty of formula and baby food. I shouldn't be gone longer than three days."

"Good," Ernst smiled.

He put her on the train to Munich. He didn't bother giving her a passport. No one needed passports to enter Germany these days. In fact, as a line was being drawn through the middle of Germany, dividing east from west, communist from capitalist, people stopped bothering to check them. Something new was on the horizon, and when it reared its ugly head, inevitably the people of Germany would yet again have to apply for new identification documentation.

She called Wilhelmina the day before. Wilhelmina would be waiting for her at the train station, the same one where they met the Fischers all those years before. How many others would be waiting for the children to come home in Himmelberg?

"You're sure you can handle Margit for three days?" Hildegard tilted her head, smiling.

"Sure. We'll be like peas and carrots," Ernst said, bouncing Margit in the crook of his arm, waving her little paw of a hand. "Say bye-bye to Mutti, little princess!"

Hildegard kissed Margit, inhaling her clean baby smell. She turned her face up and kissed Ernst, too.

"See you later," Ernst said. A command.

"I'll be back soon," Hildegard said. She patted her overnight bag. "I packed a picture of you for my mother. She's going to love you."

A delighted smile passed over his face. "I'll see you in three days, china baby."

Home. She was going home!

After five years, she could see it! Mount Siegfried!

She wanted to jump off the train, to break into a run, to burst from her fleshy cage like a bird and fly home with great blue wings. She saw Wilhelmina's matronly form, her body accepting the roundness of middle age, but still as beautiful as Marlene Dietrich. Wilhelmina's eyes met hers, and she began to weep.

She ran off the train, arms outstretched like when she was a child, crying "Mother! Mother!"

"I'm here, Hilde! I'm here!"

And they collapsed tearfully into each other's arms.

Wilhelmina walked her through Himmelberg. It was the same as her childhood, but not the same. It had fallen on hard times. The buildings were dirty and some were crumbling from the war, but the streets were still clean. This was, after all, still a German town.

They passed by the butcher shop, and Wilhelmina talked on and on about how they couldn't afford meat, and she had to butcher Valkyrie, and for a while they were just living off scraps. So much was donated to the war effort, there was nothing left.

They walked by the wall where Felix's mural once had been. It was whitewashed. "What happened to the mural?"

"Oh, we can't have that anymore," Wilhelmina said, waving it away as if she were talking about a dirty movie she once saw.

"Where is Felix?" Hildegard said. *I'd like to give him a piece of my mind. And then the end of my knife.*

"He disappeared right around the time you did," Wilhelmina shrugged. "We haven't seen him since. I heard he went to Munich or Berlin or something like that, but I haven't seen any artwork of his. He was awfully miserable when you left."

Hildegard stopped in the middle of the street. "I didn't *leave*, Mother. I was taken to a concentration camp. And Felix is the one who sold me out. I hope he's burning in hell, not 'somewhere in Munich.'"

"Shh!" Wilhelmina said, looking around hurriedly. "Don't talk about that out here."

She hurried her down the street and into her apartment. She sold the farm and all the Richter's property in 1943; she just couldn't afford to keep up with it anymore. "Anyway, Henri's father bought it. It's for the best; he can take better care of it than I can. And he's been so down in the dumps since Henri passed," she lowered her voice to a gossipy whisper, even though they were alone in her apartment. "Poor man. You know Henri was killed in France? But Karl is still alive. He's back now; he married Johanna two months ago. You should go see them!"

"I don't want to talk to another Nazi again in my life, if I can help it," Hildegard said.

"Oh, Hilde, don't be so dramatic," Wilhelmina rolled her eyes. This made Hildegard stand up abruptly.

"Don't be *so dramatic?*" she cried, her face reddening. Would she cry again this time? Or had all her tears dried up in Auschwitz? "Do you know what happened to me in Auschwitz? I was starved nearly to death. I was beaten. I was raped. I was raped *all the time.* And I had it easy. I was there when a million people choked to death in the gas chambers, when they were incinerated in giant ovens! I can't unsee it, Mother! I can't unsmell the stench of death! I wake up in the middle of the night, and I'm screaming because I think I'm back! *I'll never leave it!*" At this point, she was yelling. Was it right to vent all this out on her mother who loved her? Probably not. But she had no one to vent to for five years, no one except Riziel, and Riziel was dead. Maybe Riziel was venting too, maybe it was her voice coming through.

Wilhelmina's eyes filled with tears. "You... you were *raped?*" This came out in a whisper.

Hildegard sighed, worn out, and sat down. "Yes. And I wasn't the only one. I was just one who survived it." She pulled a picture of Margit out and gave it to her. "I have a daughter, Margit. You're a grandmother now. Frankly, she's the only reason I haven't hanged myself."

Wilhelmina wiped the tears from her eyes and she looked at the picture. She looked up at Hildegard. "Oh, Hilde... we didn't know it was *that* bad!"

Hildegard stared at her incredulously. "You didn't know?"

"No... none of this... none of it was in the papers, or the news... we had no way of knowing what was really going on!"

"But you *did* know," Hildegard countered. "You knew when you went to see *Der Erwig Jew.* You knew at the Olympics. You knew when Goebbels came to speak, and he was talking about annihilating the Jewish race…" She pointed an accusing finger. "I saw you! I saw you and Otto saluting!"

Wilhelmina looked at her helplessly.

"What did you think was going to happen, with all that 'Germany first, Germany forever' bullshit? Did you think Hitler was just going to let them walk away? Did you think it was going to be civil, democratic? It was always going to end in murder, in more stupid, meaningless bloodshed." She stood up and grabbed her bag. "You all were just too self-absorbed in your principles and political opinions to see it."

Hildegard walked out.

She walked down the road, out of the town square, towards the old farm. She didn't care if it wasn't Otto's anymore; she just wanted to see something that wasn't whitewashed, plainly and obviously hiding the disgusting, barbaric truth underneath. She wanted to be in nature. Nature died, and was reborn, and was the same, but was always somehow new. Nature had no memory, yet had an everlasting memory that stretched past beyond World War II, beyond the Spanish Civil War, beyond World War I, beyond Napoleon and Caesar and the Vikings, back to when the world was a dark, primordial ooze.

She saw the golden fields of wheat and thanked God they were still there, not lying fallow or burnt to a crisp. She ran to them, ran through them, stretching out her fingers and feeling their whiskery stalks tickle her palms. She breathed in the clean air and felt the sun on her face.

She couldn't believe she was standing in the memory where her imagination went to in all her dark moments. She was looking out at the same golden waves, the same warm sun. If she imagined hard enough, she could see Miguel coming down the road to meet her. He was walking through the wheat, he could see her, he was smiling. He wasn't smiling this time, he was staring. The sun blocked him from her view, so she could only see his dark silhouette, but as he got closer she could see him grinning with pride because he had a new glass eye, and he was whole. But he didn't have a glass eye this time; he had an eye patch.

"Hildegard?" he said.

And it wasn't a dream.

"Are you real?" she said, taken aback.

"Are *you?*" he replied.

They stood for a moment, comprehending, then broke into a run. *God, please, out of everything you've put me through, out of all the tests I've failed, let me not run through him and he's only a mirage, only a fever dream.*

But he wasn't a mirage. She collided with him and he toppled over, and she was kissing him and his strong arms were around her, and he was squeezing the life out of her, like if he let go she would slip away from him like water.

"I thought you were dead," she sobbed.

"I wasn't," he said, "I was in the camps."

"Me too," she said.

He rolled her over and kissed her lips, her cheeks, her forehead, her neck, her breasts, the tattoo on her left arm, her hand, and stopped.

"You're married?"

They were sitting at his kitchen table. He had a small house outside of town, a one bedroom with a small kitchen and sitting area. The decor was sparse, but the house was clean, typical of a bachelor's home. There was a pistol by the bedside table and a shotgun by the door.

"I like your decorations," Hildegard nodded to the shotgun. "You've really livened up the place."

"I'm still in a town of anti-Semites," Miguel shrugged, pouring her a glass of water.

"What are you doing here?" Hildegard asked. "I mean… what do you do here?"

"Still tenant farming," Miguel said, looking at her ring. "A lot of old farmers needed help after the war. After their sons didn't come home," *I told them so* was his unstated message, "they needed someone to do the heavy lifting. So I help where I can and take whatever payment they can give me. I've only been here a month."

"Are you doing well for yourself?"

He nodded and sipped his water. Then he put it down, as if to say: *Enough with this small talk.* "So…" he took a breath. "When did you get married?"

"When I got pregnant."

Miguel raised his eyebrows.

"By a Nazi."

Disgust flashed in his eyes. *How could you?* It was there, exactly as she had feared. Her worst nightmare of five years was coming true: having to face Miguel as a fallen woman.

"A Nazi guard," Hildegard said pointedly. *Don't make me say it, Miguel. Please.*

"Well," Miguel said, staring down at his water glass, "we all did what we needed to in order to survive."

"I wasn't *surviving,* Miguel," she said. *Ah, here come the tears. Right on cue. Great.* She wiped at her eyes angrily. "Don't you understand? I was in Auschwitz. In *Auschwitz.* I was a prisoner," she held up her tattooed arm, nearly knocking over her water glass, "and a guard got me pregnant. In 1944." She looked into his one eye, so full of hurt for betraying him. She lowered her voice to a whisper. "Do you understand?"

Recognition lit up in his eye. Guilt. There. He understood. He

325

reached for her left arm, and took her hand, in the same comforting way he had in 1939. "Hilde... Hilde. Hilde. I can't believe I'm saying your name. I can't believe I'm talking to you, to the *real* you." He breathed in through his nose. "I'm upset, obviously, that you've been taken by another. But I *do* understand." God, was he always this mature? Or had she just been spending so much time with Ernst, she just thought all men were emotionally stunted? But Miguel wasn't all men. Miguel was Miguel.

"When they sent me to Buchenwald," he continued, "I had to do horrible things. Unspeakable things. I passed selection because of my strength, yes, but because of that I was sent to work in the crematoria as a Sonderkommando. Hildegard," he took her other hand, and though he was looking desperately at her, he was back there too, he was still there, as she was, "I looked at the face of every murdered prisoner in that godforsaken camp. I burnt them up to ashes. This is forbidden, you understand. I committed a million sins, a million crimes—their blood is on my hands too, and that's what the Nazis wanted. That was their game. I see their sunken, leathery faces in my dreams." He took a shaky breath, coming out of it. "And I tried to say a prayer for them as I shoved their bodies in the fire, but after a while, the bodies grew too numerous, so I gave up trying.

"I decided to lose myself to my memories. The memory of you was all that kept me going. In my memories, I would bring my mother and my sister back, and my father was alive and we mended our fences, but mostly I thought of you. I would go over every little detail of your face, your body, willing myself not to lose you to the passage of time. It was the only way I could cope. You were the only thing that kept me from jumping upon the flames."

He was crying now, too. It was very beautiful.

"I thought of you too," she whispered. She cleared her throat, took a sip of water, and summoned her courage. *Talk about it with him.* "I thought you were dead... and after... after *he* did *that* to me, I would walk through the camp and go back to my bunk and just lie there... and I would think of you." She put her cheek in the palm of his hand, feeling its warmth. *He's alive. Thank you, God. Thank you for keeping him alive.* "I would think of you, and I prayed to God you would be in my dreams, so I could have one moment where I didn't want to die."

Miguel was up out of his seat in a heartbeat, pulling her up and kissing her deeply. She had her arms wrapped around his neck and her legs wrapped around his waist, and he carried her to his bed and undressed her, kissing her hungrily, kissing the scar on her stomach, and they were one again.

She cried after she climaxed. He was perched above her, and he cupped her face, running his thumb across her jawline, wiping away a tear.

"Did I hurt you?" he asked, concerned. "Is it... are you still healing?"

"No, it's not that," she smiled up at him. *It's that I haven't really made love in five years. I've just been repeatedly plunging myself into something toxic and evil, like chemical waste. It's the first time since 1940 that I haven't felt utter revulsion.* "You were wonderful," she said, curling up beside him. *I want to tell him everything, so he really understands. I don't want him to walk away thinking I put him up on a shelf, that I made a choice. As if I had any choice. But what do I tell him? If I tell him what Ernst did to me, the way he treats me now, Miguel will try to kill him.* Hildegard frowned. *And Ernst will win. He always wins, in the end.*

I can't lose him again.

He looked down at her. "What's wrong?"

She thought of a lie, then she settled on a truth. "I was just trying to muster up an apology for you. The Nazis took your mother's ring. I should have swallowed it; that's what an inmate suggested. But I didn't, and they stole it. I'm so sorry," she said, and she meant it.

Miguel looked at her strangely. "Why should you apologize for something the Nazis did to you?"

"Because that ring was special to you. It was special to me."

Miguel shrugged. "The Nazis took everything away from everyone. They took my Star of David, all my family's heirlooms that I buried. They took my glass eye," he indicated the eye patch. "They even took one of my molars for the silver filling."

"Well," she said, running her hand across his considerable body hair, "I personally like the eyepatch. It makes you look like a pirate, or some underground resistance leader... very dashing."

Though he was only thirty-three, Miguel looked as if he had aged ten years. There were silver spirals in the temples of his curls and deep ravines in his face. His eye was still strikingly brown, but exhausted. He looked like he had been through hell and back, which he had. Five years of shoveling coal and corpses into flaming ovens from sunup to sundown had done their work on him.

To make matters worse, he had developed a nasty cough. He sat up in bed, coughing and wheezing. Hildegard left the bed and got him his glass of water from the kitchen table. "Are you alright?" she asked, her brow furrowed.

"Fine," he said, spitting into a napkin by the bedside table and taking a gulp of water. "I got horribly sick after the Americans liberated us. The medic examined me and said I had black lung, that coal miner's disease. You know, from all the coal and ash." He took a deep breath and settled his coughing. "All the Sonderkommandos have it."

"The Americans?" Hildegard curled up, resting her arms on her knees. "What was it like to be liberated? I haven't heard anything; I've been running since 1944."

"The Nazis left in the middle of the night; no time to shoot us. The Americans came in and we were terrified of them and they were terrified of us. We looked like walking corpses, like striped ghosts. They were kind to us, but angry at the leftover Nazis. You could tell

they felt horrible, and they were masking it with anger and disgust."
He ran his fingers through his graying hair and scratched his beard.
"But it *was* disgusting. Piles of bodies everywhere. We couldn't even
burn them fast enough, the rate they were rushing in. Especially after
that giant group from Auschwitz—"

"Auschwitz?" Hildegard interrupted.

"Sure, Auschwitz. They ran them overnight to Gleiwitz, and the
ones who survived *that* were loaded up into a cattle car and shipped
here. I mean there... to Buchenwald."

Hildegard slowly lay back in Miguel's bed. It occurred to her that
this was the first time she and Miguel, who were once engaged and
had made love countless times, had ever made love in his bed. Or any
bed. It was always in secret, always out in the woods, in the bush. It
seemed lovely and romantic at the time, but now it was as if the whole
universe was conspiring to keep them apart. "You mean... you mean
if I had stayed... if I hadn't escaped Auschwitz with Ernst... he would
have left, and we wouldn't have married, and I would have met up
with you?"

Miguel looked down on her. His face was terribly sad.

Hildegard put her hands, balled up fists, into her eyes, and let out
an enraged scream. It was a scream of anger, of agony, of hurt, and
mourning. It was like Kaddish, but it was primal and full of white-hot
rage.

Miguel lay down with her and gathered her up in his arms. "You
wouldn't, Hildegard. You wouldn't have survived it. Hardly any
women survived it, much less pregnant women. Most of them were
shot or trampled or froze to death." He sighed. "It doesn't matter how
it happened... you're alive, and you're safe. For that, I give thanks to
God."

But I'm not safe, Miguel. I'm still in Hell; it's just I'm not surrounded by
barbed wire anymore.

She wrapped herself around him. She stroked his back and felt scars from lash marks. The memory of her had kept him alive, kept him living in Buchenwald, and she was bitterly disappointed she couldn't live up to the woman who had established so secure a foothold in his mind.

"Stay with me tonight," he breathed in her ear.

"I will."

They made love for most of the day, and in the evening he cooked for her, and he was his old self again: wily, intelligent, wicked, wonderful. She told him about Margit's wide-eyed wonder, and Riziel's cleverness and steadfastness, and Moishe's unbelievable kindness in the face of evil and adversity. They talked well into the evening, past midnight, and she didn't want to lose a minute of sleep to every moment she could spend with him. But eventually she fell asleep, and it was the best sleep of her life.

In the morning, he was making breakfast. Sunlight was streaming through the curtainless windows. The blue jays were singing their high call.

Hildegard shaded her eyes, squinting at him and smiling. "You ought to get a woman here to help you. To cook your meals, or at least put up some decent curtains."

"No," he said simply.

She had meant to be glib, but she instantly regretted saying it: it wasn't a playful jab, it was twisting the knife.

They ate and walked around Himmelberg. No one talked to them or remembered them. They were all of them—Hildegard, Miguel, the townspeople—unrecognizable: wizened, stooped, reserved. Hildegard thought she saw Gerda pass by, but it was a different woman. It seemed so much bigger when she was younger. Now she was amazed she could cross from one side to the other in a matter of blocks. That's what living in a 500-acre concentration camp will do: everything seems smaller, inconsequential. Yet the small, inconsequential things of this community that she previously swept under the rug added up and grew stronger over time, over ten, fifteen years, grew to be monstrous tigers, lurking in the dark.

Hildegard swallowed. "Will you stay here? In Himmelberg?"

"No," Miguel looked around contemptuously. "This place holds beautiful memories, but there is no longer any warmth for me here." He looked at her honestly. "I was just waiting around to see if you came back."

Hildegard bit her lip. *What was he saying? Was he leaving? Would they have to say goodbye again?* "Where will you go?"

"Morocco. I have a friend from Buchenwald; we were Sonderkommandos together. His family has a riad in the Jewish part of Marrakesh. He says it's like a ghetto, but Mohammad V, the Sultan of Morocco, protected the Jews during the Shoah." He laughed bitterly. "To think: I went north to escape genocide in Spain, when I could have gone south."

"And we would have never met," Hildegard said. *We would have never gone to the camps, we wouldn't be these weary, bitter shells of the firebrands we were... but we would have never even met.*

"Why don't you come with me? Right now," he took her hand and looked deeply into her eyes. "Let's run away right now."

Hildegard squeezed his hand. "Miguel... I... I'm not as I was. I'm a mother now. Margit needs me. What kind of a mother would I be, if I just abandoned her?"

He nodded. He was crestfallen, but he understood.

She took his hand and put it over her heart. "Miguel... you must know. I have only ever loved one man... and that's you."

He pulled her into a tight embrace. He inhaled the scent of her hair.

Could she bear to tear herself away from him, when she only just got him back? Could she muster the strength to do what she had to do?

"Here," he said, writing down a name and an address. "This is the name of my friend, Jabreel Elohim. This is his address in Morocco. This is where I'll be."

"Miguel..."

He smiled and shrugged. "I've waited for you this long."

She pulled him into a deep kiss. A kiss goodbye. "I love you," she murmured. She looked at him in his one eye, still like a hazelnut. "I will *always* love you."

He escorted her to the train station, and she tried to memorize the exact moment when he kissed her goodbye, when their clasping hands were cleaved apart by too much space and time.

"Remember," he said, smiling.

"I will," she said.

She watched his form, still so strong after all these years, get smaller and smaller as the train pulled away. She saw him put up his hand to her in farewell. She rolled down the window and extended her hand, her blonde hair blowing in the breeze.

She continued to watch Himmelberg shrink and shrink and shrink into the distance, behind the stretching green farmland, past the corn and the wheat, beyond the hills, behind the colossal Mount Siegfried, behind the Alps, until finally, finally, it was out of sight.

Epilogue

When she returned home, Ernst was feeding the baby out of a little jar of orange mush.

"You're home early!" he beamed up at her.

"I am," she smiled back at him, putting a brown paper bag down on the counter. "I talked with Mutti, and I walked around my hometown... and I got some perspective. It's time to move on with my life. I'm ready," she smiled radiantly, content with her decision. "I'm ready to try again."

Ernst clapped his hands together. Margit clapped her hands together, mimicking him.

"Did you see that? That was adorable!" He kissed Margit on the forehead. "Are you ready to become a big sister, Margit? Jealous girl, you'll have to share Daddy's love!"

"But first, I'm going to make you your favorite," she pulled glistening, plump bratwursts out of the bag. "And then," she added over her shoulder, "I'm going to give you a Minni Von Bismark."

"Why wait?" he grinned roguishly.

"Waiting's half the fun," she said, coy.

They dined on sausages and sauerkraut and seedy hot mustard. Hildegard purchased a bottle of champagne to celebrate, and Ernst unwrapped the cage and popped the cork.

"To building a family," Ernst said, raising his glass.

"And to true love," Hildegard agreed, clinking it against her own.

They put Margit to bed, who slept like an angel, as she always did.

"She takes after you," Ernst held her around the shoulders from behind. He kissed her neck. "An absolute heavenly body come down to earth. Not a drop of me in that one." His touch made her skin prickle; she could still feel where his lips had been.

Hildegard giggled and led him to the bedroom. "Let's see if we can't make an Ernst Junior for you."

Vam der Blegsam had really coined this trick, and Hildegard had overhead it in one of the many backstage gab sessions. It involved a few scarves, knotted to the bedposts, and a feather.

"I didn't realize I was married to a dominatrix," Ernst said, intrigued and already aroused.

"There's a lot about me you don't know," she smiled, dragging the feather lightly over his body.

"But I want to get to know you," Ernst said, looking at her with honesty. "I want to know who you *really* are. I want *that* one to love me."

She put aside the feather and straddled him.

"Are you ready?" she said, smiling sultrily.

"I'm ready," he grinned. He stopped and stared at her. "I love you."

She reached over and grabbed her pillow. Then she pressed down tight over his face.

She was going to make a speech, a long speech about how she would be damned if she ever willingly let him put his seed inside her again. She planned to pace in front of the bed, telling him how he had made her life a living hell for the past three years, and he was a devil, and he should beg God for forgiveness for all the people he had murdered and tortured, and she should be at the top of the list. But he never would beg for forgiveness, because it wasn't in his nature. Which is why he would be burning in hell in about five minutes.

But in the end, she didn't say any of it. She just pressed down, putting her full weight on the pillow on top of his face, using all the strength of her forearms, just as she had practiced every day kneading bread, ever since they were free from that godforsaken prison in Poland. He jerked and bucked and kicked, but the knotted scarves did their work. She remembered an especially tight knot from her Hitler Youth training; the blue scarf tightened and constricted, but it did not budge. He twitched and convulsed, and eventually he stopped moving at all. But he was a crafty one. He might be playing possum. She pressed down and pressed down, counting the seconds, counting to 300.

Then, carefully, so very carefully, she peeped under the pillow. He was dead. Finally, finally dead! She was free of him! But there wasn't much time.

She pulled on a pair of gloves and untied his wrists and ankles. She put the scarves in a bag, changed the pillowcase, and put the old pillowcase in a bag too. She would throw them in a fire later. But not here. She dragged Ernst's body over to the bathroom, pried a razor blade loose from his razor, and slit his wrists, begging the blood to come forth. As it flowed out over the bathroom tiles, she closed his eyes. He looked shocked, like he had been murdered. He needed to look at peace. She stepped carefully, avoiding the blood flow.

She produced a letter from her bag. She had been learning his handwriting for weeks, analyzing the swoops and strikes of his j's and h's and t's. The letter read:

Dear Hilde:

By now, you will have found my body. I pray that you and Margit can forgive me. I pray God can forgive me. When I close my eyes, I see the burning faces of Jews and Gentiles I condemned to the gas chambers of Auschwitz. I can no longer live with myself. I can no longer live with the guilt of knowing I participated in genocide.

I will always love you.

Ernst.

Would it work? Would they believe this narcissistic sociopath killed himself out of guilt? Over killing Jews? Probably not. Probably, the policemen who found this letter would be guilty of killing a few Jews themselves.

But it wouldn't matter: by that point, she would be long gone.

She grabbed the fake passports they used to get into Switzerland out of the safe, and stuffed them in with her own German passport, the one she got from Wilhelmina. Ernst wouldn't tell her the safe's combination, but she had been watching. She didn't even need to watch him to learn it. It was his birthday.

She crept down the hall and grabbed Margit and two days' worth of items. She had told all the neighbors she was taking Margit to see her grandmother in Germany for the weekend, which would buy her two more days. And it wouldn't matter, really: Marrakesh was only 28 hours away. She would drive and drive and drive, and they could buy whatever they needed when they reached Morocco.

She took the keys and carefully opened the garage, closing it behind her, quietly backing their new car into the driveway and out down the lane. She smiled at Margit, stroking her hair as her child slept peacefully. When she reached the end of the road, she pulled out onto the highway, heading south towards Geneva. Then onto Montpelier, and then down the coast of Spain, and finally across the Straits of Gibraltar.

She let the scarf slip through her fingers, relishing in the moment as it fluttered away, the last piece of him, to sink into the waters of the Mediterranean, down and down. She was free of him. She was free of everything.

"I'm coming, Miguel," she whispered. "I'm coming."

Afterword

Holocaust survivor and Nobel Peace Prize winner Elie Wiesel once said, "For the survivor who chooses to testify, it is clear: his duty is to bear witness for the dead and for the living. He has no right to deprive future generations of a past that belongs to our collective memory. To forget would be not only dangerous but offensive; to forget the dead would be akin to killing them a second time."

Two-thirds of the world's Jewish population were annihilated in the decade of Hitler's reign, but 10 million Jews survived to bear witness to the atrocities of the Holocaust. Almost 80 years have passed, and there are fewer than 350 thousand Holocaust survivors left on the planet. Most survivors are nonagenarians. Some are over 100.

We don't have much time left to listen.

Now, more than ever, we must learn as much as we can from the eyewitness accounts of the worst crime in modern history... and that includes the perpetrators. After teaching and researching the Holocaust for nearly ten years, I became interested in reading the accounts of "everyday Germans." Most of these people will tell you it all began with minor prejudice and apathy. It was easier to mind your own business than to speak up, and it turned into letting someone with a louder voice do the speaking for you. These were a cultured, educated people who were fed a steady diet of nationalism and, in the end, chose warped political opinions over their own moral compass.

Soon, it will be our turn to tell the story. Or it will most assuredly happen again. Maybe it's already started.

Thank you to Laurie, my editor, who helped me transform my manuscript from a history textbook to the story of one woman's struggle between survival and integrity.

Thank you to Richard, my cover designer, who brought the girl from a propaganda poster to life.

Thank you to Josh for the better title. A+

Thank you to Paris, Brady, Cori, Tracy, Annabeth, Kelcey, Courtnie, Taylor, and Savanna. You gave me the confidence I needed to move forward.

And finally, thank you to Alex, my greatest supporter, my first reader. I love you.

Printed in Great Britain
by Amazon